Pb 02/20

2013

PETERBOROUGH LIBRARIES

24 Hour renewal line 08458 505606

This book is to be returned on or before the latest date shown above, but may be renewed up to three times if the book is not in demand. Ask at your local library for details

Please note that charges

D1421445

60000 0000 70658

Also by Charlaine Harris from Gollancz:

SOOKIE STACKHOUSE

Dead Until Dark
Living Dead in Dallas
Club Dead
Dead to the World
Dead as a Doornail
Definitely Dead
All Together Dead
From Dead to Worse
Dead and Gone
Dead in the Family
Dead Reckoning
Deadlocked
A Touch of Dead
The Sookie Stackhouse
  Companion

The Sookie Stackhouse
novels are also available in
three omnibus editions

HARPER CONNELLY

Grave Sight
Grave Surprise
An Ice Cold Grave
Grave Secret

LILY BARD

Shakespeare's Landlord
Shakespeare's Champion
Shakespeare's Christmas
Shakespeare's Trollop
Shakespeare's Counselor

The Lily Bard novels are also
available in an omnibus edition

AURORA TEAGARDEN

Real Murders
A Bone to Pick
Three Bedrooms, One Corpse
The Julius House
Dead Over Heels
A Fool and His Honey
Last Scene Alive
Poppy Done to Death

The Aurora Teagarden novels
are also available in two
omnibus editions

Wolfsbane and Mistletoe
  (*co-edited with Toni L.P. Kelner*)
Many Bloody Returns
  (*co-edited with Toni L.P. Kelner*)
Crimes by Moonlight
Death's Excellent Vacation
  (*co-edited with Toni L.P. Kelner*)

MYSTERY WRITERS OF AMERICA PRESENTS:

CRIMES BY MOONLIGHT

Edited by Charlaine Harris

Collection copyright © Mystery Writers of America, Inc. 2010
The Edgar® name is a registered service mark of the Mystery Writers
of America, Inc.
'Introduction' copyright © Charlaine Harris, Inc. 2010
'Dahlia Underground' copyright © Charlaine Harris, Inc. 2010
'Hixton' copyright © William Kent Krueger 2010
'Small Change' copyright © Margaret Maron 2010
'The Trespassers' copyright © Brendan DuBois 2010
'Madeeda' copyright © Harley Jane Kozak 2010
'House of Horrors' copyright © S. W. Hubbard 2010
'Sift, Almost Invisible, Through' copyright © Jeffrey Somers 2010
'The Bedroom Door' copyright © Elaine Viets 2010
'The Conqueror Worm' copyright © Barbara D'Amato 2010
'In Memory of the *Sibylline*' copyright © Lou Kemp 2010
'The Bloodflower' copyright © Martin Meyers 2010
'The Awareness' copyright © Terrie Farley Moran 2010
'Tadesville' copyright © Jack Fredrickson 2010
'Limbo' copyright © Steve Brewer 2010
'The Insider' copyright © Mike Wiecek 2010
'Swing Shift' copyright © Dana Cameron 2010
'Riding High' copyright © Carolyn Hart 2010
'Grave Matter' copyright © Mickey Spillane Publishing, L.L.C.
'Death of a Vampire' copyright © Parnell Hall 2010
'Taking the Long View' copyright © Toni L. P. Kelner 2010
All rights reserved

The right of Charlaine Harris to be identified as the editor of this work
has been asserted by her in accordance with the
Copyright, Designs and Patents Act 1988.

First published in Great Britain in 2011 by Gollancz
An imprint of the Orion Publishing Group
Orion House, 5 Upper St Martin's Lane, London WC2H 9EA
An Hachette UK Company

This edition published in 2012 by Gollancz

A CIP catalogue record for this book is available
from the British Library

ISBN 978 0 575 09803 9

Typeset at The Spartan Press Ltd,
Lymington, Hants

Printed in Great Britain by Clays Ltd, St Ives plc

The Orion Publishing Group's policy is to use papers that are natural,
renewable and recyclable products and made from wood grown in
sustainable forests. The logging and manufacturing processes are expected
to conform to the environmental regulations of the country of origin.

www.orionbooks.co.uk

**Peterborough
City Council**

60000 0000 70658	
Askews & Holts	Jul-2012
SHO	£7.99

Contents

Introduction by Charlaine Harris   vii

Dahlia Underground by Charlaine Harris   1

Hixton by William Kent Krueger   25

Small Change by Margaret Maron   36

The Trespassers by Brendan DuBois   55

Madeeda by Harley Jane Kozak   74

House of Horrors by S. W. Hubbard   97

Sift, Almost Invisible, Through by Jeffrey Somers   115

The Bedroom Door by Elaine Viets   132

The Conqueror Worm by Barbara D'Amato   149

In Memory of the Sibylline by Lou Kemp   160

The Bloodflower by Martin Meyers   186

The Awareness by Terrie Farley Moran   207

Tadesville by Jack Fredrickson   227

Limbo by Steve Brewer   249

The Insider by Mike Wiecek   262

Swing Shift by Dana Cameron   277

Riding High by Carolyn Hart   299

Grave Matter
   by Max Allan Collins and Mickey Spillane   316

Death of a Vampire by Parnell Hall   336

Taking the Long View by Toni L. P. Kelner   359

Introduction

After years of belonging to the mystery community, I'm used to being regarded as nonthreatening, good-natured . . . sometimes even (shudder) 'sweet'. All that changed when I was asked to edit the MWA anthology that had been designated *supernatural*.

I sent out an e-mail to some of my favorite writers, all MWA members, to let them know the good news: I was offering them a slot in *Crimes by Moonlight*.

You would think I had offered to ship them a rattlesnake.

Instead of greeting this golden opportunity with cries of glee, I got a batch of awkward e-mails that began, 'Gee, I don't know . . . I've never written woo-woo.' (That's a highly technical industry term.) 'I don't know about trying to do a supernatural,' they moaned. I had to practically poke some of my fellow writers with a sharp stick to get them in line.

I must admit there were a few who did react as I'd expected. Some mystery writers were simply waiting for the chance to cross over to the dark side. I'm keeping my eye on them.

In the end, my call for stories got some amazing responses.

This volume consists of entries by writers you've read and loved for years, and writers who aren't well-known yet. What all these writers have in common is their membership in MWA and their willingness to tackle an offbeat story element.

Half the stories were ones I requested. The rest of the stories were submitted without any identifiers to a stellar panel of volunteer judges: noted writers Daniel J. Hale,

Dana Cameron, Doug Allyn, Jane Cleland, and Heather Graham. The number of blind submissions came to more than three hundred, so my hat is off to these stalwarts, who may never volunteer for anything again in their lives. Barry Zeman oversaw the whole process from start to finish and was a great help, and John Helfers at Tekno Books was willing to let me wail in his ear when the process got to be overwhelming.

After all the work of writing, editing, selecting, reediting, and literally hundreds of e-mails, here's the final result. Our work is done. Now all that remains is for readers to enjoy the result.

We're counting on it.

– Charlaine Harris

DAHLIA UNDERGROUND

Charlaine Harris

Dahlia Lynley-Chivers woke up as soon as the sun went down. But this awakening was like none she'd experienced in her long second life: on her back, pinned down, and injured.

Badly injured.

Dahlia cursed in a language that had not been spoken for centuries. She'd lost a lot of blood. Though the air was filled with smoke and dust, she could smell a body close to her. The blood of the dead person was repellent, but it would help.

She carefully extended her right arm to discover it was free and unbroken, unlike her left. Her left leg was immovable, though her right leg wasn't, because the beam trapping her lay at a slant.

While she was evaluating her situation, Dahlia wondered what the hell had happened when she was in her day sleep. She heard distant screams and sirens, while around and above her lay destruction. A huge pane of glass, intact, had landed upright on a vampire, shearing him in half. Though he was beginning to flake away, he looked familiar.

Her memory began filling in the blanks.

The Pyramid. She'd suddenly decided to spend the day at the Pyramid, the vampire hotel in Rhodes. The disintegrating vampire had been a handsome male in the service of the

Queen of Indiana, and she'd accepted an invitation to dally with him rather than return to her room in the mansion of the Sheriff of Rhodes.

Though the night had been notable, the day must have been more so.

High above her, Dahlia could see a bit of night sky lit by flashes of artificial light. Every now and then there was an ominous creak or groan from the heap of twisted metal, shattered glass, and concrete. Dahlia wondered how long it would be before it shifted. She might yet end up in the same condition as her bedmate. Dahlia had not been afraid in a long time, but she was almost afraid now. She wasn't so afraid she was going to yell for human help, though.

A smaller beam was lying crossways on the one that pinned her, very close to her right hand. Dahlia figured if she could grip the smaller beam, she'd get enough purchase to drag herself out. Then she could work her way over to the dead human, feed, and begin the perilous climb upward.

She had a plan.

Dahlia's right hand gripped the crossbeam, and she pulled. But she realized instantly that her left leg would rip off unless the heavier beam was lifted at least another inch.

'Well,' said Dahlia. 'Crap.'

Dahlia was extremely strong, but extricating herself cost another hour. By the time her leg slid free, she was close to exhaustion. As she rested, she looked down at herself. Ugh! She was naked and streaked with dirt, soot, blood, and pale, powdery dust. She held up a strand of her long, wavy hair, normally coal black. In the dim light, it looked white. She'd been there awhile. How much time before dawn? She made herself move.

The corpse was that of a uniformed hotel maid. Her neck had been broken in the explosion. Since she hadn't bled much, Dahlia was able to tank up. The blood of the dead was even worse than the bottled blood substitute that had enabled vampires to become legal citizens of the United

States. The vampires could truthfully say they no longer needed to feed from live humans. Of course, they still enjoyed it *much* more.

Dahlia lay across the maid's body, gathering strength for the climb up through the rubble. For a black moment, her normal confidence wavered, and she wasn't sure she could manage it.

'Hello!' called a hoarse voice from above. 'This is Captain Ted Fortescue, Rhodes Fire Department! Anyone alive down there?'

She thought about remaining silent. Then she bit her lip. Dahlia was very proud, but she was also a survivor of no mean skill. 'I'm here,' Dahlia called up out of the darkness.

'Human or vamp?'

'Vampire,' she said defiantly, even though she feared he'd leave her where she was when he found out she wasn't a breather.

'Ma'am, how hungry are you?'

He'd been coached. Good. 'I've had the blood of a corpse. I will not attack you.'

' 'Cause we can have Red Stuff O Positive ready when we raise you . . .'

'Not necessary.'

'There's a corpse?'

'Two, Ted Fortescue. A vampire, though he's mostly gone. A human woman dead before I found her.'

'We gotta take her word for it,' said a lighter voice.

'Can you grip a rope if we send it down?' Fortescue called.

'Yes,' Dahlia said. 'If I try to climb, the ruins will shift.' Humans were going to save her. Humans. Though Dahlia hadn't wanted to build her character, after all these hundreds of years it was apparently going to be built.

'Okay, here comes the rope.'

The lifeline uncoiled about a yard from Dahlia. She pulled herself to it with her right arm. Gripping the pieces of wreckage that looked most firmly lodged, Dahlia pushed herself erect. Luckily, she was a very small woman. She seized the rope with her right hand. Gritting her teeth, she wrapped her right leg around the rope and called, 'Pull!'

After a swaying, painful ascent, Dahlia Lynley-Chivers emerged into a nighttime landscape of horror.

One glance at Dahlia had Ted Fortescue bellowing for a blanket. The captain looked almost as battered as she did. His brown face was as dirty as hers, his close-shaved hair white from the powdery dust. Above his mask, his wide brown eyes were shocked.

Dahlia found his smell enticing. She needed some blood very soon. But her need was drowned by the humiliation of having to stand with the man's support until her blanket was passed up. When he'd wrapped her in it with impersonal hands, Fortescue handed Dahlia down to the next human in line until she reached the base of the mountain of debris. The last person in the chain directed Dahlia to a line of humans waiting on the nearest clear sidewalk. She said, 'Those are people willing to give you a drink, ma'am. Please try not to go overboard.'

'They volunteered?' Dahlia tried not to sound disbelieving.

'Yes, ma'am. A lot of people are upset that the Fellowship of the Sun took such an extreme action against your people.'

'The Fellowship is taking responsibility?'

'Yes. I guess they figured a vampire conference would be a prime target. Some of their own people hired onto the hotel staff. But they didn't feel the necessity to tell their fellow humans to get out before it blew. In fact, their news release says it served the staff right for serving vampires. Not too many people are happy with the Fellowship.'

'My home is here in Rhodes. Is there a way I can get a ride to my house?'

'Get your drink, if you want it, and then head over to that other line over there. They'll help you out.'

'Thank you for your courtesy,' Dahlia said stiffly. 'Can you help me over to the donors? My arm and leg are broken.'

Captain Ted Fortescue had descended from the mountain of rubble by that time, and he overheard Dahlia's words.

'Jesus Christ, why didn't you tell me?' Ted Fortescue took Dahlia in his arms and carried her to the donor line on the sidewalk.

'Thanks so much,' Dahlia said through clenched teeth. 'Where do you serve?'

'We're the Thirty-four Company from the station at the corner of Almond and Lincoln. You gonna be okay, now?'

She assured him she could stand on one leg while she fed. He needed to get back to his work, so he left her there. Dahlia watched him walk away.

For a short time, she'd loved a werewolf. He hadn't been exactly human, of course, though close enough to cause her qualms. Dahlia had always felt the same kind of contempt for humans that most humans feel for Brussels sprouts. They were good for her health, but she didn't like their proximity.

The donor was a short woman with long white hair. Her name was Sue, she told Dahlia, and Sue held Dahlia's hand during the feeding. If Dahlia had been herself, she would have been put off by the woman's prattle about 'we're all one family.' She didn't like her food to talk. But tonight was different.

Having fed, Dahlia was able to hobble to the impromptu cab rank, where a free voucher got her a ride to her home. The vampires who lived in Cedric's mansion, already beside themselves with grief and rage, were glad to see a survivor come through the door. All Dahlia wanted to do was shower and crawl into her own bed in her own room in the windowless basement.

The next night, all the Rhodes vampires met in the mansion's common room. At least fifty vampires from the central United States had died in the bombing, the newspapers said. Their deaths were not the worst part of the attack, to this assemblage. The worst part was the loss of face. Their city had been targeted, and the attack obviously had been planned well in advance – but they had not detected it or forestalled it, though the plan had been devised and carried out by *humans*.

'We have been dishonored,' Cedric, Sheriff of Rhodes, said. Every vampire in the city had been present at the meeting, from those who had their own homes to those who lived in the nest. Even Dahlia's friend Taffy, married to a werewolf, had been present.

Cedric turned his large blue eyes on Dahlia. Pink tears glistened in their corners. 'Our sister Dahlia nearly met her final death and had to be rescued by humans.'

'I accepted human help because it cut short the time I was trapped,' Dahlia said, her back absolutely straight and her face utterly composed, though it was an effort.

'We must meet this challenge directly,' said Cedric, 'This is our city. Now we are at war.'

The vamps of Rhodes had not been at war since Prohibition, when some bloodsuckers from Chicago, frightened away by the aggression of Al Capone's henchmen, had tried to move into the tunnels below Rhodes. They'd survived one night.

'Tell us what to do,' Taffy said. Taffy was tall and buxom, her physique emphasized by the slut-biker outfit her husband, Don, favored.

'Taffy, you and Dahlia must visit the headquarters of the Fellowship. Get in by whatever means necessary. Look for membership lists. We want to know their leaders.'

'This will have been done by the police,' Taffy said.

'And will the police share with us what they found?' Cedric had a point.

'I'll do whatever I can to bring the whoresons to justice,' Dahlia said carefully, 'but the lists will be on computers, and Taffy and I are not conversant with these machines.'

'One of the Arkansas vampires is adept with computers, but he was burned so badly he'll take time to heal,' Cedric said. 'Wait! I know someone.' He whipped out his cell phone again. It was the one piece of modern technology that thoroughly entranced the sheriff. 'His name is Melponeus, he's a half demon, and his services do not come cheap.' Cedric, who was cheapness personified except when it came to maintaining his pride, grasped the financial nettle firmly.

The half demon was at the mansion within thirty minutes. He was a short man with reddish skin, a head of thickly curling chestnut hair, and pale eyes the color of snowmelt. When Dahlia greeted him at the door, those pale eyes showed instant admiration. Dahlia, though used to this, was nevertheless pleased. She was glad she'd worn her pink three-piece suit with the pencil skirt.

'I hope you're as good with modern technology as your reputation has it,' she said tartly and beckoned him to follow her to the common room.

'I love a good, strong vampire woman,' Melponeus said. 'Such a woman, if she is willing, can take a lot of . . . energetic activity.'

'I am several hundred years old,' Dahlia said. 'I assure you, I can take anything you could imagine handing out.' She didn't turn to look at the half demon, but her lips curled in a little smile.

'You're older than Cedric,' Melponeus observed. 'But you're not the sheriff.'

'I don't want to be,' Dahlia said. 'And some think I'm not diplomatic enough.'

'I remember your name, now. It was you who broke the newscaster's arm?'

'She wouldn't stop asking me questions, after I'd warned her,' Dahlia said reasonably. 'I told her I would break her arm if she didn't leave me alone.'

'Foolish woman,' Melponeus said.

'Deserved what she got,' Dahlia agreed. She was thinking that after the honor of the nest had been restored, she might find out what it felt like to kiss lips as full and hot as the half demon's. Since hers were always cold, the sensation might be interesting.

Cedric greeted Melponeus with appropriate dignity, mentioned a price, and Melponeus agreed to accompany Dahlia and Taffy. When the three were setting out, Dahlia realized no one knew the location of the Fellowship's organizational offices. Taffy had to look it up in the phone book. 'This is the kind of thing detective novels don't cover,' Taffy complained.

'You haven't read a detective novel since Agatha Christie quit writing,' Dahlia said. 'Don't whine.'

'She's quit writing?' Taffy was really put out. 'When did that happen?'

'She died. Probably fifty years ago.'

'And why should I know that?'

'There have been plenty of novels since then. You should read some of them,' said Dahlia, who seldom read herself. 'We've got the address. Let's pay them a visit.' In Taffy's Trans Am, they drove west into the old part of Rhodes.

They left the Trans Am on Trask, which ran a block south of Field Street, the location of the modest storefront housing the Fellowship headquarters. The small businesses in the area had already closed for the night. The occasional pedestrian hurried along, since the evening was chilly. The three approached Field through a filthy alley two blocks west of their goal. Since they could all remember times when filth and debris were the norm, this didn't bother

8

them. The two vampires and the half demon hung in the shadows of a trash bin while they evaluated the Fellowship headquarters.

'Cameras,' Melponeus murmured.

'I see them,' Dahlia said. There were cameras all around the building. After a low-voiced discussion, Dalia returned to Trask Street and ran silently east until she was pretty sure she was in line with the Fellowship building. She slid into the next alleyway and headed north. About halfway down the alley, Dahlia found a nice dark patch she didn't believe human eyes could penetrate. She crouched and gathered herself. She launched herself upward, landing neatly on the roof. Dahlia was confident that even the Fellowship wouldn't think of pointing a camera upward. She was right.

After a quick smile of self-congratulation, she took off her designer heels and made a great leap, landing across the street on the roof of the two-storey building housing the Fellowship. She swung her legs over. Her fingers and toes clamped into the little spaces between the lines of brick, and she worked her way to the first camera. With a quick twist, she removed it from its mounting. She pitched the camera onto the roof, then did the same with all the others. Then she put on her shoes again.

She waved at Taffy and Melponeus, who began trotting toward the Fellowship. Dahlia leaped down from the roof to join them, landing on the sidewalk as lightly as a feather, though she was wearing three-inch heels.

'Good job,' said Taffy, and Dahlia inclined her head.

'I'm impressed,' Melponeus said, looking at Dahlia's legs. 'Taffy, let's see who's minding the store.'

Taffy knocked on the door, which bore the distinctive Fellowship symbol – a sun, represented by a circle with wavy rays leading outward. Within the circle was a pyramid.

'What does the pyramid mean?' Taffy asked.

'Earth for Humans, Eradication of Vampires, Eternal

Victory,' Melponeus said. 'Kind of ironic that the hotel was the same shape. Maybe that sparked the plan.'

A young man came to the door. Through the thick glass (bulletproof?) the three could see he was a reedy Asian guy in his twenties with a soul patch.

Taffy gave him her best smile and said, 'Young man, I want to come in.'

If she hadn't called him 'young man,' he might have unlocked the door, because Taffy had a great no-fangs smile, and her tight leather pants added a powerful incentive. But the 'young' roused his suspicion, since Taffy looked (at most) twenty-five. He began punching numbers on a cell phone.

'Look at me,' Dahlia said in a voice that managed to compel, even through the glass. And he did, no matter what he'd been taught.

'Open the door,' she said. And her voice was so reasonable that the young man did just that.

Melponeus immediately set to work looking at the Fellowship computers. Dahlia sat opposite Asian Soul Patch at a table covered with coffee stains and notepads.

She said, 'What is your name?'

'Jeffrey Tan.'

'You're Fellowship?'

'I hate vampires. I killed one myself.'

'Did you really?'

'Yes, I did.'

While Taffy searched the office building and Melponeus began copying files onto a disc, Dahlia asked a few more questions. Jeffrey Tan had been dating a vampire, a girl he'd known before she went over. They'd been going at it hot and heavy one night, and she'd bitten him. Terrified, he'd stabbed her with a handy wooden chopstick. (Unfortunately for the young vampire, Jeffrey's mother had brought him a traditional meal that day.)

In a flash, Jeffrey's lover had been shriveling and flaking on his bed.

He had to live with himself, and the easiest way to do that was to find other people who thought he'd been perfectly justified.

Dahlia, who'd heard this sort of story many times before, had a fleeting moment of sympathy for Jeffrey, since she'd become reacquainted with panic the night before. But she squelched the moment ruthlessly. She asked, 'Did you help bomb the Pyramid?'

'No, but I applaud the courage and determination of our soldiers,' he said unconvincingly.

'Yes, slaughtering people who are asleep is brave. Do you know who planned and executed this action?'

'They're hiding, getting ready,' he said, his eyelids flickering furiously. 'The vamp lovers in the police department and the fire department who rescued vampires, they'll die next.'

'Where are these heroes hiding?' Dahlia asked.

Melponeus, who'd been looking at the screen of one of the office computers, said, 'I think I may have the membership list,' at nearly the same moment as Taffy pulled a large file out of the filing cabinet.

'Here's a list of the properties they lease or own,' Taffy said, as Melponeus began downloading the list. 'Oh, I checked out the basement. No one there.'

A phone began ringing. Jeffrey Tan reached for it, but Dahlia stayed his hand. 'What does the phone call mean?' she asked.

'I told them the cameras went out. They're calling to check on me,' he said, and he seemed to be coming out of his trance. His gaze began flickering from Taffy to Dahlia to Melponeus.

'You said the Fellowship was going after firefighters?' Dahlia had a sudden misgiving.

'We have pictures of every traitor who worked the rescue at the Pyramid.'

Melponeus said, 'We'd better hustle.'

'Shall I kill him?' Taffy asked.

'No, that would be too much of a red flag,' Dahlia said. 'Though I'd enjoy it very much. Look at me, Jeffrey!'

He couldn't disobey, but he was struggling.

'We were here to check for your leaders,' Dahlia said, gripping his chin to force his attention on her. 'They weren't here, so we left full of frustration.'

'Yes,' he said, his face slack again.

The three left the building as quickly and quietly as they'd entered. In silent accord, Dahlia and Taffy flanked Melponeus and held him, leaping to the top of the building. The three made their getaway across the roofs. By the time they'd gone two blocks, cars were parking in front of the Fellowship office.

'That was almost too easy,' Dahlia said, on their return to the mansion. She and Taffy were drinking Red Stuff, and Melponeus was sipping coffee, very strong and very black. Cedric had come to the common room to listen to their report. 'They left one human, and such a puppy, to guard the office? When they'd have to figure we'd be looking?'

'Humans do underestimate us,' Taffy said. 'Their thinking's limited.'

'And we underestimate them,' Dahlia snapped. 'Look who wiped out over fifty vampires at once. Even that puppy killed his girlfriend with a chopstick.'

'I'm half-human,' Melponeus said, 'Some of us are honorable.'

Though Taffy and Cedric looked in another direction, embarrassed, Dahlia met his snowmelt eyes and inclined her head regally.

Cedric said, 'What do you suggest we do, Dahlia?'

'This list of properties has to be checked out, as does the membership list,' Dahlia said. 'We'll be spread very thin, but I think we can do it. After all . . .' She didn't have to emphasize their responsibility.

'You're in charge, Dahlia,' Cedric said. 'Melponeus, if you will come with me, Lakeisha will write a cheque.'

'How will we do this?' Taffy asked when they had left.

'Divide into teams. Give each team a short list of properties to search,' Dahlia said. 'Each place must be searched very thoroughly but very discreetly. One special team has to kidnap a Fellowship officer, a person without family. This team can't be averse to forceful persuasion. We need to know if there's some place not on this list, perhaps a place belonging to one member, that's large enough to hide ten to fifteen people. The newspaper said that's roughly how many Fellowship fanatics are missing. We'll check the people we can find against the list to get a better count.'

Cedric returned in time to hear. He nodded. 'This seems sound,' he said. 'Especially the torture part.' He smiled.

'Thank you, Sheriff.' Dahlia braced herself. 'Someone must be detailed to warn the humans involved in the rescue. They saved lives that night; not just human lives.'

'Some of them were not pleased to rescue vampires,' Cedric said. 'I read that in the newspapers, too.'

'However they felt, they did it. We can't abandon those who've done us a service.'

'Are you telling me my duty, Dahlia?'

'Sorry, Sheriff.' Dahlia looked away to compose her face.

'This is very unlike you.'

'I've never been hauled out of a pit before.'

'The half demon – the half human – would take no money for his service,' Cedric said. 'He told me we were on the same side.' Dahlia tried not to look self-conscious. She mostly succeeded.

Cedric nodded to Dahlia. 'All right, go.'

That was how Dahlia came to be walking into the firehouse of the Thirty-four Company at the corner of Almond and

Lincoln. Though the night was chilly, the door to the firehouse was open. The men and women inside were washing the fire trucks under floodlights. None of them whistled when Dahlia approached, though she was the center of attention in her black belted coat and black high heels.

'A cold one,' said the biggest firefighter of all, a burly guy over six feet tall. 'Whatcha want, vampie?'

To rip your impudent throat out, Dahlia thought. But she recognized his high voice; he had helped the captain haul her up out of hell. 'I need to speak to Captain Fortescue,' she said.

That brought a chorus of whistles and comments about Ted's wife and her reaction to his extracurricular pastimes.

If Dahlia had been a breather, she'd have sighed.

Ted Fortescue came out, wiping his hands on a towel. His men and women fell silent when the captain looked around to meet their eyes. He recognized Dahlia immediately, somewhat to her surprise. 'Evening. Have you recovered from your broken leg?'

'I have,' Dahlia replied. Her back was stiff as a poker. 'I have come to warn you. The people of the Fellowship of the Sun have said they'll take vengeance on those who rescued vampires.'

'They're going to target first responders?' Fortescue was appalled.

'Yes,' Dahlia said.

'They'll lose all public sympathy for their cause,' he said slowly, 'aside from the obvious point, they believe in *killing* vampires and *recruiting* humans.'

'I don't pretend to make sense of what humans do,' she said. 'You saved my life. Now I am doing my best to save yours.'

'Well . . . thanks,' he said. The firefighters looked from the captain to the vampire, obviously thinking he should say something else. 'You were human, once,' Fortescue said.

Dahlia was taken aback. She fumbled for a response. 'I

was a human for eighteen years. I have been a vampire for . . .' She shook her head. 'Nine hundred years, perhaps.'

There was a little moment of total silence.

'Good luck to you, Ted Fortescue, and to all of you who helped us,' Dahlia said. She looked at each face around her. She would remember each one. 'I'll dispose of them all if I can,' she promised the firefighters, and then she walked away.

'Commando Barbie,' one of the women muttered, but Dahlia heard her. In fact, she smiled a little, all to herself.

Worry was not a familiar pastime for Dahlia, who was more of a direct action person. During the bit of dark remaining, Dahlia and Taffy visited two Fellowship locations, a 'church' on the south side and a 'meeting hall' on the east. Both buildings were easy to break into, and the two vampires searched both very thoroughly. They were straightforward modern constructions: no hidden passages, secret rooms, or false floors.

The next night similar results were reported by the other search teams.

The Rhodes vampires felt the pressure. By the time they had to retreat to day sleep lairs, they'd only learned where the Fellowship plotters weren't. Their shame was mounting.

Even the abduction-and-torture team reported failure. True, they managed to find a family-free Fellowship official, and true, they managed to snatch her unobserved, but to their immense irritation, the woman had a weak heart. She died too early in the proceedings to offer any useful information. In fact, the team simply restored her body to her house, and no one was the wiser.

Taffy arrived at the mansion the next night radiating excitement. She made a beeline for the common room. Dahlia was sitting at the table, lost in unhappy thought. 'Don says we should look in the tunnels!' Taffy said, seizing her friend.

Dahlia said, 'If you shake me again, I'll break both your arms.'

Taffy let her go with alacrity. 'Sorry! I'm just so excited!'

'That's a very good idea,' Dahlia said. 'We should have thought of the tunnels earlier.'

The tunnel system lying below the original city center of Rhodes was extensive, and it had once connected all the major buildings in the area. The tunnels had seen much use in the years before and during Prohibition. In the decades since, some passages had been blocked up as part of new construction. Vampires seldom used the tunnels anymore . . . but they had in years past, along with all kinds of other creatures, including regular humans.

'Do the tunnels run under Field Street?' Dahlia asked Taffy.

'Don's faxing us a map.'

Don, Taffy's werewolf husband, had a friend who was a historian at Rhodes's City University. Don's friend faxed the map to the little office where Lakeisha took care of Cedric's correspondence. Lakeisha had been an executive assistant in life, and Cedric had brought her over expressly to be his executive assistant in death. Lakeisha knew her office machinery and had a thorough grounding in modern communications, skills most of the older vampires found baffling.

Lakeisha had had the advantage of knowing she was going to be brought over, so she'd had her hair washed, cut, and styled before her death. She was perpetually cute. 'I don't think you've ever gotten a fax before, Dahlia,' Lakeisha said.

'I hope I never get another one.'

'Grumpy, grumpy!' Lakeisha chided. Dahlia snarled at her.

'Did we get up on the wrong side of the coffin tonight?' Lakeisha said.

'It's annoying that you're not frightened of me, and it's a mistake.'

'You don't want to make Cedric mad,' the young vampire said calmly.

Dahlia snatched up the tunnel map, and she and Taffy retreated to the common room to study it.

'Yes! We gotcha, assholes!' Taffy said, after the two had found Field Street and examined it.

'I'll give Don something nice,' Dahlia said.

'Not a groomer's brush, like you sent last time? That shit gets old,' Taffy said.

'No, something really nice.'

'Not another bag of doggie treats!'

'I'm serious; it'll be very appropriate. Lakeisha, we need you,' Dahlia called. Normally, Lakeisha would have insisted the request come through Cedric, but circumstances were hardly ordinary.

Lakeisha used the copying machine and then the intercom. When everyone had assembled in the common room, she passed out copies of the map.

Dahlia stood up on the hearth, so they could all see her. She was wearing her black leather jumpsuit and was happily aware she was being admired. Melponeus was there; she could see his curls and reddish face in the corner. Good.

'Thanks to Taffy, we've gotten a map of the tunnels,' Dahlia said when the silence was complete. 'They run under the Fellowship headquarters, and if the leaders entered the tunnels after their attack against us, they may still be there. Has anyone here been down below the city in the last twenty years?'

'I have,' said Melponeus. 'I was in the tunnels five years ago, chasing an imp because . . . well, it's not relevant. There are more dead ends in the tunnels now than your map shows. The Fullmore Street tunnel is blocked with rubble at the intersection with Gill.' Pens moved over paper. 'The Banner Street tunnel is divided in the middle.

Someone built a bank aboveground, and in the process they made the tunnel impassable – though I've heard someone's cut a hole in that wall.' Melponeus went on to list two more closed or abbreviated tunnels.

'Thanks, Melponeus,' Dahlia said. 'We owe you.'

'Oh, I'll collect,' he said, a gleam in his eye.

It was a measure of Dahlia's reputation that no one sniggered.

Cedric strolled through, carrying a pipe and wearing a smoking jacket. Taffy rolled her eyes at Dahlia.

'Do you have a plan of action, then?' he said.

'Yes, my sheriff.'

'Good luck. Oh, by the way.'

Every vampire froze.

'You *must* bring them back alive,' Cedric said. 'I know you want to have fun with them. In fact, I'd planned to ask you to bring me one to play with. But I've gotten a phone call from the chief of police, who said . . . and I think this is interesting . . . that some of his officers told him they'd been running across vampires in unexpected places, asking un-expected questions, and he certainly hoped we weren't taking any vigilante action of our own, since the whole Rhodes police department is anxious to bring the Fellow-ship terrorists to justice.'

None of the vampires cast guilty looks at each other – they were all much too seasoned for that.

'Of course we were planning to kill them,' Dahlia said. 'What else?'

'I'm afraid you must alter your plan,' Cedric told her, using his 'sympathetic but firm' voice that carried so well. 'Think of how wonderful it will look, a picture of you hand-ing over the culprits to the police. Think of how people will say that we've honored our commitment to refrain from taking human blood – even the blood of our enemies.'

Dahlia looked mutinous. 'Cedric, we'd anticipated . . .'

'Having a good old-fashioned party,' he said. 'I regret

that, too. But when you find these murderers, they go to police headquarters. Undrained and intact.'

And, in turn, every head nodded.

Five teams of two vamps each had been dispatched to the five tunnel accesses closest to Fellowship headquarters. Dahlia thought it possible the bombers had blasted or cut through some of the more recent walls. She would have done so if *she'd* been planning on using the tunnels as a refuge.

These teams were armed with shotguns. None of them were happy about it. Most vampires (especially the older ones) thought carrying a gun implied a certain lack of confidence in one's own lethality.

Dahlia divided the rest of the Rhodes vamps into two parties. Each would enter the tunnels about a mile away from Fellowship headquarters, one from the east and one from the west. That way, the hunting party could descend without alerting their prey. A couple of cars took Dahlia's party (Taffy headed the other one) to the east entrance she'd selected. This access happened to lie below a restaurant that had opened before World War I.

The Cappelini's Ristorante staff was used to parties trailing through on the 'Old Rhodes' tour, but they were taken aback when the eight o'clock tour party consisted wholly of bloodsuckers. Dahlia hung back. Though she was tiny and pretty, she was also unmistakably menacing. Lakeisha beamed her perky smile, tipped heavily, and the atmosphere relaxed.

The party, which consisted of Dahlia, Lakeisha, and three male vamps (Roscoe, Parnell, and Jonathan) all passed through a door the teenage tour guide had unlocked. They descended the stairs into the Cappelini basement. The very nervous young woman pointed out how various things were stored, talked about when the building had been erected, and revealed how many pounds of pasta the restaurant had served since it had opened its doors. Though the vampires gave her polite attention, she was visibly nervous as she prepared to enter the old tunnels.

She unlocked yet another door, this one a very old wooden slab. Greeted by a rush of cool air, the party descended a very narrow flight of stairs, then a steep and twisting ramp, and came to yet another door, much lower than modern doors and heavily locked. Their guide unlocked the last door, keeping up her patter the whole time, though with an effort. She flipped a light switch, and the tunnel appeared, running straight for about ten yards before turning to veer right.

Lakeisha said, 'Let me ask you a question.' Relieved, the girl looked at the cute dark-skinned vampire inquiringly. Lakeisha said, 'See how big my eyes are?' The next minute, the girl was under. 'Sit on the floor here and wait until we come back,' Lakeisha said, and the girl smiled and nodded agreeably.

The vampires were all used to enclosed spaces, and they all had excellent vision. Dahlia barely seemed to touch the ground as she began to move forward. At first, two of them could walk abreast. After the jog to the right, the old tunnel narrowed.

The walls were brick, plastered here and there. Every now and then the narrow space widened into a storeroom, littered with old signs, broken chairs, all sorts of debris discarded from the businesses above. From time to time a ghostly door, sometimes with glass panels still intact, offered access to an underground saloon or whorehouse that hadn't seen a customer in seventy years.

'This is great,' Roscoe said. Though Dahlia didn't reply, she agreed completely.

They didn't meet any other tours, because Cedric had booked them all. For two hours, the vampires owned the tunnels below old Rhodes.

Dahlia brought the party to a halt when she figured they were two blocks away from Field Street. She whispered:

'You heard Cedric. No killing. If they resist, you can break a bone.' Despite the embargo, they were all tense with anticipation. It had been a long time since a worthy battle had come their way. This was a good moment to be a vampire. With a sharp nod, Dahlia turned and raced down the last section of tunnel.

In the end, the conquering of the Fellowship bombers was almost anticlimactic. There were only seven conspirators below the Fellowship headquarters. Of those, two had been too close to their own handiwork and had been injured by flying debris from the Pyramid. Only three men resisted with any determination, and Taffy, who got to the group seconds before Dahlia, had subdued the largest of these with no trouble at all by kicking him in the ribs. Jonathan and Roscoe took care of the others.

Rather than herd their hostages back to Cappelini's, Dahlia decided to surface at the closest access point. Lakeisha used her cell phone to call the two vampires guarding that spot, their signal to alert the police that there were prisoners to deliver.

Instead of feeling triumphant, Dahlia found herself doubtful. Surely there should have been more Fellowship people in hiding?

'Wait!' she called at the first flight of stairs. She turned. Taffy, right behind her, was carrying the man whose ribs she'd broken. He was groaning, the noise irritating her. To make sure a rib didn't puncture the human's lung, Taffy was carrying the man in front of her. Dahlia looked into his unshaven face.

'What's your name?' she asked, and the man began to recite some membership number the Fellowship had allotted him.

'That's even more irritating than the pain noises,' she said. 'Shut up, asshole.'

He cut himself off in mid-number.

The practical Lakeisha extracted a wallet from his pants. 'This particular asshole is named Nick DeLeo.'

'Ever talked to a vampire before, Nick?'

'I don't deal with hell spawn,' the man said.

'I was not spawned by hell. I met with something much older than myself in Crete, more years ago than you can imagine. I will still be here when your children are dust, if anyone deigns to breed with you.' That seemed doubtful to Dahlia. 'Where are the others?'

'I'm not supposed to tell you that,' he said. It was hard for him to look formidable when a woman was carrying him, and he gave up the attempt when Dahlia came even closer. He flinched.

'Yes,' Dahlia said with some satisfaction. 'I'm truly frightening. You can hardly imagine the pain I'll cause you, if you don't tell me what I want to know.'

'Don't tell him, Ni – aaargh!' A scream effectively ended another hostage's exhortation.

'Oh, Roscoe, is he hurt?' Dahlia asked with patently false concern.

'Hard to lend his buddy moral support with a broken jaw,' Roscoe said. 'Oops.'

Dahlia smiled down at Nick. 'I have ripped people apart with my bare hands. And I enjoyed it, too.'

Nick believed Dahlia. 'The others have gone to get the firefighters who fished the vamps out of the Pyramid,' he said. 'It's easier to get the firefighters; they're not armed. Three of us are going to each station around here that responded. They're going to shoot until their weapons are empty except for one bullet, and then they'll kill themselves. Holy martyrs to the cause.'

'That's a *terrible* plan,' Lakeisha said. 'You think this will discourage people from helping vampires? Make them want to join your stupid Fellowship? The slaughter of public servants?'

'We have a new goal,' Dahlia said. 'We deposit these

losers with the police. We go to the places they're going to attack. They have a head start on us, so let's be quick.'

Up the stairs they swarmed, to be met by media galore. The police knew a good photo op, too. As soon as possible, Dahlia and her nest mates faded away into the shadows. The others had their own assignments, but Dahlia herself ran full tilt toward the corner of Almond and Lincoln.

Four of the Pyramid conspirators were converging on the Thirty-four Company.

At least the big doors were shut. The firefighters inside were cooking, sleeping, playing video games – until the first rifle shot whistled through the upstairs window, missing one of their drivers by a hair. Then shots were pouring into the station from all directions. There was screaming and cursing and panic.

Until, one by one, the rifles stopped firing.

The newspaper photographers would have liked to take a picture of the four Fellowship members piled in a heap on the concrete in front of the station with Dahlia standing on top of them. But Dahlia was too clever for that. Instead, the next day's paper had a wonderful picture of tiny Dahlia in her black leather jumpsuit in the center of a huddle of firefighters, hoisted up on the shoulder of Captain Ted Fortescue.

Any tendency the fire company might have to rhapsodize sentimentally over Dahlia's one-woman antiterrorist action was dampened when they got a good look at the broken bones and bloody injuries the five foot nothing vampire had inflicted – though all four gunmen were alive, at least for a while.

The newspapers were happy with their pictures, the firefighters were happy to be alive and mostly uninjured, the Fellowship fanatics were secretly glad to be out of the tunnels and to anticipate reiterating their inane credo at their trials, Cedric was happy that his vampires had obeyed his direction, and the vampires felt they had at least made a beginning on their revenge for the Pyramid bombing.

Happiest of all was Melponeus the half demon, because he and Dahlia celebrated the victory until Melponeus had to crawl back to his demon brethren with weak knees and a silly grin.

As for Dahlia, she developed a strange new habit. She felt she had established a relationship with the men and women of Company Number Thirty-four.

She began to drop in from time to time. By her third visit, the humans were matter-of-fact about her presence. Ted Fortescue absentmindedly offered her some chili instead of the Red Stuff they'd started keeping at the back of the refrigerator.

When the city council of Rhodes voted to give Dahlia a special commendation for her defense of the firehouse, everyone from the Thirty-four Company attended.

'I feel like they're my pets,' Dahlia confided to Taffy.

Taffy wisely hid her smile.

And when one of the shooters was released on a technicality, and every firefighter in the Thirty-four sounded off about it while Dahlia was there learning how to play Grand Theft Auto, none of the firefighters were surprised when the shooter vanished twenty-four hours later.

'Dahlia's like, our mascot,' said one firefighter to Ted Fortescue.

'Shell be around a lot longer than we are,' Ted Fortescue said. 'Especially if you ever say anything like that where she can hear you.'

But no one was foolish enough for that.

HIXTON

William Kent Krueger

A couple of miles outside the little town of Citadel, Wisconsin, the gravel road dropped into a tree-shaded hollow, and beyond that lay marshland. As soon as he cleared the trees, D'Angelo saw the cabin. It sat back from the road a full quarter mile. The turnoff was marked by a wood-burned sign that read 'Hams. Smoked and Honey Cured.' He drove his new '53 Studebaker Starliner down a narrow dirt causeway between sinister-looking pools of dark water full of cattails gone brown. The high ground where the cabin stood also held a sturdy barn, an animal pen, and a large garden plot littered with stubble from a recent harvest. In the backyard, a young woman paused in hanging the wash and watched him come. The sheets on the line hung heavy in the still air, white against the gray of the overcast sky and the brown of the marsh reeds and the black of the water. An old man sat in a rocker on the front porch. When D'Angelo got out of the Stude-baker, he saw that the old man's lap was crossed by the barrel of a shotgun.

'Far enough,' the old man said before D'Angelo had even taken a step.

'Greet all your customers this way?'

'Until I'm sure they're customers.'

'A wonder you sell anything.'

'No wonder once you taste the product. You a customer?'

'What do I look like?'

'A man who answers a question with a question.'

D'Angelo smiled. 'Heard in town that you make the best hams this side of the Mississippi.'

'Any side of the Mississippi, mister.'

'You smoke the hams yourself?'

The old man gave a brief wave toward a smokehouse in a far corner of the yard. 'Right over there. What's your pleasure? Hickory smoked or honey cured?'

'Hickory smoked'll do.'

The old man nodded but didn't move. He studied D'Angelo carefully. 'Wherebouts you from? Cuz you're not from around here.'

'You neither,' D'Angelo said.

'We're talking about you right now.' The old man's grip tightened on the shotgun.

'Nebraska,' D'Angelo said. 'Place called Hixton.'

'Hixton?' The old man leaned forward. 'Son, it's not ham you came for. What do you want?'

'Just to talk.'

'About what?

'Five missing boys in Hixton.'

'Hixton was a long time ago and far away from here.'

'Then there's no harm in talking.'

'What's your name?'

'Martin.'

'That a last name?'

'Last name's D'Angelo. And you're Albert Gorman.'

'Why you want to know about Hixton?'

'I'm a newspaper reporter, Mr Gorman. I'm working on a story.'

'No one cares about Hixton. Too long ago.' He was more than seventy, with a face parched by the sun. The squint of his eyes may also have been due to the sun, but D'Angelo thought not. 'Ah, what the hell,' Gorman finally said, and beckoned his visitor forward.

There was another chair on the porch. D'Angelo took it, wondering if it was where the young woman sat with the old man.

'How'd you find me?' Gorman asked.

'It's what I do. Find people. Find things. Find the truth.'

'The truth?' Gorman laughed, a sound as parched as his face. 'People don't want the truth. If they looked straight at the truth, it'd scorch their eyeballs right off their skulls.'

Several swine trotted out from a small structure inside the pen D'Angelo had seen on his approach. The animals came to the fence and stuck their pink snouts between the rails. Beyond the pen lay the marsh, which stretched away in all directions under the dismal sky.

D'Angelo said, 'It would be difficult for someone to come at you without being seen.'

'Damn near impossible,' Gorman agreed.

'Twenty years ago, you left Hixton in a great hurry. What were you afraid of, Mr Gorman? And what are you afraid of still?'

Through that squint of his eyes, the old man studied the marsh. He finally said, 'What do you know about Hixton?'

This is what D'Angelo knew and what he told Gorman.

In the fall of 1933, a teenage boy named Lester Bennett attended a dance held in the gymnasium at Hixton Senior High School. He'd gone without a date. A shy boy, he hadn't danced with anyone. He'd left alone and had never made it home.

Two months later another boy, Skip Grogan, age sixteen, went out at 4:00 a.m. to do his morning newspaper route. He was a quiet but conscientious kid. No friends to speak of. An only child, and his mother doted on him. He delivered half the papers that morning, from State Street to Main, but delivered nothing after that. Like Lester Bennett, he simply vanished.

In February a kid named Jason Weller went for a hayride sponsored by the Kiwanis Club. He was an awkward kid who reluctantly accompanied his cousin, a girl in need of a date. They nestled in the hay of the wagon with lots of other teenagers. Afterward, they drank hot chocolate and ate sugar donuts around a bonfire. Then he walked his cousin home under a full moon, said good night, and was never seen again. The people of Hixton were understandably upset. They raised a hue and cry and demanded to know why the authorities didn't have a clue about the missing boys. The local police asked for the help of a state investigator. Albert Gorman was sent in answer.

'Sorry sons of bitches, those local cops,' Gorman said. 'I took one look at their case notes and knew the only way they'd get their man was if he walked into the office, confessed, took the key, and locked himself in a cell.'

'Did you think you'd have better luck?' D'Angelo asked.

'Luck? Wasn't any luck to it. Solving a crime is simply the steady elimination of possibilities.'

'What were the possibilities?'

Gorman rocked back in his chair. He lifted the shotgun from his lap and leaned it against the cabin wall, still within easy reach. He folded his hands over his belly, which had probably once been hard and flat but with time had grown doughy. He wore a white shirt open at the collar, the thinner white of an undershirt visible beneath. His khakis were spotless and pressed to a sharp crease. His boots were black and shined. D'Angelo wondered if it was the young woman in the backyard who took such good care of him.

'First I looked at the commonalities,' Gorman said. 'All teenage boys, all attending high school, all socially inept and isolated, all caught alone in the dark. This suggested to me that the victims weren't chosen at random. They'd been carefully selected by someone who knew them and knew their activities and their schedules. So I asked myself who would have that kind of knowledge of all these boys? My answer was someone at the high school. A teacher, maybe, or counselor or administrator.

'It probably wouldn't be someone who'd been there for a while, or the disappearances would have begun earlier. So I looked at those who were new to the school that year. There were only two. An English teacher, Miss Evelyn Hargrove. And the baseball coach, Hank Abernathy. Miss Hargrove was a wisp of a thing from Alabama, fresh out of college, all fluttery and feathery and smelling of exotic scents, and the boys in school were gaga over her. She lived in a rooming house with three other single women, and they all did everything together and knew each other's habits intimately and played canasta every night that they didn't have dates, which was the case more often than not. Turned out on two of the three nights that a boy went missing Hargrove was playing canasta.

'So I turned my full attention to Abernathy. Now there was an odd duck.'

The cabin door opened, and the young woman D'Angelo had seen hanging the wash stepped outside. She was pretty, with fair, soft skin, eyes dark blue as a sky sliding into nightfall, long black hair, and she smelled of fresh laundry. She wore a plain white dress that reached to her ankles, and the collar ran just below the fragile hollow of her throat. When she appeared, the swine in the pen began an uproar of grunting. To D'Angelo, who knew nothing about pigs, it appeared that they might be hoping she had slop for them, or whatever it was that they were fed.

'Excuse me for interrupting,' she said with a pleasant smile. 'I just wondered if you gentlemen might care for a refreshment.'

Gorman said, 'Mr D'Angelo, this is my daughter. Sweetie, this is Martin D'Angelo.'

She said, 'Would lemonade and cookies appeal to anyone?'

'Fine with me,' Gorman said.

'I'd like that,' D'Angelo replied, and he watched the tilt of the young woman's hips as she turned and the undulating slope of her ass as she walked away.

'Mr D'Angelo?' the old man said.

D'Angelo returned his attention to his host. 'You said Abernathy was an odd duck.'

'Talented athlete. Could have played in the majors, but what did he do? He coached in a little town in the middle of nowhere. I asked myself why a man would do that. What he was running from, hiding from?'

'Was he married?'

'Nope, and that was another unusual thing. Good-looking as they came, but he had no wife, no sweetheart.'

Through an open window drifted the sound of Gorman's daughter softly singing. Listening to the haunting lilt, D'Angelo almost lost the thread of his thoughts. With an effort, he pulled himself back and said, 'What did that suggest to you?'

'I figured maybe he was the kind of man who had no interest in women. And if that was true, it might point toward an explanation for the missing boys. But I had no evidence, no proof, and it would have been stupid to tip my hand. So I put men to watching him.'

'And then the fourth boy disappeared,' D'Angelo said.

'Yep. Early spring, two months after the last kid.'

'Edward Greeley,' D'Angelo said. 'A young man with ambition, a desire for Broadway or the movies. He had the lead in the senior class play, *The Boyfriend*. After the final performance, he went to a cast party at the home of Gwendolyn Murdoch, the drama teacher who'd directed the play. She caught him spiking the punch with rum from a silver flask he'd brought, which she confiscated. She gave it to the police during their investigation.'

'You've done your homework,' Gorman said.

'What about your surveillance of the baseball coach?'

'According to the man I assigned to him that night,

Abernathy went to the movies and then to a diner for a late meal. He was sitting on a stool, eating, when Edward Greeley left the party and vanished.'

'Which effectively eliminated him as a suspect?'

'Pretty much. From what I understand, he eventually married a librarian in a neighboring town, so maybe he was just going through a period of adjustment in Hixton. Who knows?'

'Where did that leave you?'

'Looking for other possibilities.'

Gorman's daughter shoved the screen door open with her hip and stepped onto the porch, holding a plate of cookies in one hand and a pitcher of iced lemonade in the other. D'Angelo stood up quickly. 'Let me help you.'

The pigs near the marsh set up a rage of grunting again, but the young woman ignored them.

'Thank you,' she said sweetly. She handed D'Angelo the cookies and set the pitcher on the wide flat of the porch rail. 'I'll be right back with glasses.'

D'Angelo was tempted to follow her into the dark of the cabin, but Gorman's voice held him back. 'Sit down. We haven't finished talking.'

D'Angelo placed the cookies next to the pitcher and returned to his seat. The swine had fallen silent again but continued to stare at the cabin.

'Other possibilities?' he said.

Gorman nodded. 'I figured there was some other common thread to the boys that I wasn't seeing. I racked my brain trying to think what it could be. The pressure from the local police and from the populace was tremendous, I can tell you. I lost a lot of sleep thinking it through.'

Gorman's daughter returned with two glasses and poured lemonade for both men. She asked, 'Have you tried one of my cookies, Mr D'Angelo? They're just sugar cookies, but I do a pretty good job with them, if I do say so myself.'

D'Angelo took one, bit into it, and thought he'd never

tasted a cookie quite so delicious, and he told her so. She smiled, a blush rising in her cheeks, and D'Angelo decided he'd never seen a young woman so beautiful.

'Finish your cookie, Mr D'Angelo,' Gorman said. 'We still have talking to do. Leave us, Sweetie.'

She left them. D'Angelo finished his cookie, sat down, and felt an immense emptiness in the wake of the young woman's departure. A deep longing for her rose in his chest.

'Like I said,' Gorman went on, 'I lost a lot of sleep thinking it over, I looked at their friends, but they didn't have many and none in common, I looked at people in the town they might all have had contact with, a minister, maybe, or a postman. Nothing there. Early on I'd looked at the routes they'd all taken on the night of their disappearance and didn't see anything of interest. But I revisited that possibility and, without the blinders of a particular suspect narrowing my vision, I saw something.'

The young woman's voice came through the window again, and her song was like a soft rope wrapping itself around D'Angelo's heart and pulling it to her.

'What did you see?' he asked absently.

'That their paths all crossed at the Sweet Shoppe, a little confectionary in Hixton. It was a relatively new establishment, run by a woman named Circe Cane. I talked to the parents of the missing boys, and they told me their sons liked to frequent the shop, dropping in after school or on Saturdays. They talked with great affection about Miss Cane and about the wonderful sweets she served. So I began to investigate this Cane woman, trying to discover her background before she'd come to Hixton. And you know what, Mr D'Angelo? I hit nothing but dead ends. Which in itself told me a whole lot. I began watching the Sweet Shoppe and Miss Cane myself.'

'And then the last boy went missing,' D'Angelo managed to say above the swirl of fog that seemed to be filling his head.

'That's right.'

'He was a boy who'd graduated and was preparing to go into the army,' D'Angelo said. He spoke slowly, deliberately, as if he were a drunk trying to make sense.

'Yes,' Gorman said. 'One night he took his little brother to a movie, and when it was over, they went to the Sweet Shoppe. Afterward he delivered his brother home safely, then returned alone to the Sweet Shoppe. It was late, almost midnight. Main Street was deserted. He stood on the sidewalk in front of the confectionary, where earlier he'd had lemonade and a sugar cookie. And he listened to the song Circe Cane sang to him through the upstairs window. He reached for the door and found it unlocked, and he went inside and never came out. And no one saw him do these things.'

'No one except you,' D'Angelo said.

Gorman nodded. 'Except me.'

'Why?' D'Angelo stood up, struggling to keep his thinking straight, to fight against the current of the song inside his head that was drawing him further into the fog. 'Why didn't you do anything to stop him?'

'Oh, I tried,' Gorman said. 'I slipped in after him and followed him upstairs, where Circe Cane lived. I listened at the door, and what I heard I couldn't believe.'

'What?' D'Angelo asked, desperately trying to stay with the old man's words. 'What did you hear?'

'Circe Cane talking low and sweet to that boy, and I heard the boy answering. At first, it was in his own voice, but slowly that changed until what came from him was the sound of an animal.'

'What animal?'

'A pig, Mr D'Angelo,' the young woman said in a lilting voice as she stepped from the cabin door. 'I find them such wonderful little creatures. Sweet and loyal and, in the end, quite delicious.'

D'Angelo turned to Gorman as the world around him tilted and reeled. 'Why didn't you . . . why didn't you . . .'

'Why didn't I tell someone? Because, Mr D'Angelo, who would believe such a story? No, I left my job and left Nebraska and came with Circe to this place, where I've done my best all these years to protect her secret and keep her safe. Here, as you so correctly pointed out, I can see all that approaches. We have enough of those pesky traveling salesmen drop by that Circe's little pen over there is never empty. And this marshland around us, it swallows a car without a trace, believe me.' Gorman looked at Circe with deep contentment. 'In return she's fed me. There's nothing she can't coax from the earth. She's a marvelous house-keeper, cook, and companion.' He reached out and ran a wrinkled hand over the soft, fair skin of her forearm. 'She has other charms as well, which I'm sure you can easily imagine.'

D'Angelo felt his legs grow weak, and he collapsed into the chair.

'D'Angelo,' Gorman said. 'I know that name. The last boy in Hixton, his name was D'Angelo, too. And his little brother would be about your age now, if I remember correctly. A newspaper reporter, Mr D'Angelo? I think not. I think you came looking for an answer.'

'D'Angelo? Oh yes, I remember that one,' Circe said with genuine delight. 'Such a sweet thing, and he fattened up so nicely, too.'

She reached out and touched D'Angelo's leg in a way that made him feel like livestock appraised for auction. And then the fog enveloped him completely, and he fell into a place as dark as the marsh water.

He woke in a bed that carried the fresh smell of clean sheets dried on a clothesline. There was another scent as well, something exotic and deeply intoxicating. And there was the unmistakable softness of a woman's bare breast pressed against his shoulder. He turned his head on the

34

pillow and found her gazing into his eyes, her own eyes the deep blue of desire. Without a thought he made love to her. It was glorious and like nothing he'd ever known.

Later he woke again, and the cabin was full of the wonderful aroma of a meal cooking. He found her in the kitchen, wearing a long, flowered apron over her simple white dress.

'Sit down,' she said cheerfully. 'Dinner's ready.'

He sat at the table, still a little benumbed. 'Where's Gorman?'

'Albert served his purpose for many years,' she said, 'but it was time for someone new. I like you. You found me, not an easy thing. You suspected the danger, but you came anyway. And you did it because of your brother. Intelligence, courage, and loyalty, traits I've always greatly admired. Ulysses was much the same.' She came to his side, set a plate of food in front of him, bent, and gently kissed his shoulder. 'You know,' she said, 'you even look a little like him.'

D'Angelo stared at her adoringly and murmured, 'I'd forgotten you. But you look the same as you did all those years ago in the Sweet Shoppe.' He glanced down at his plate, which Circe had filled with herbed potatoes and green peas and applesauce. At the center was a steaming slice of pork loin cooked to perfection.

'The meat might be a little tough,' she said, sitting across from him and taking up her napkin. 'The swine it came from was much older than I prefer, but I have always hated to waste a good pig.'

D'Angelo hesitated only a moment and then dug in.

SMALL CHANGE

Margaret Maron

I'm lying on the backward-facing seat of an SUV that is being driven much too fast, and I am rigid with apprehension. One good swerve and I could roll off the seat and bang against the rear window and then what? Would I break something crucial? Be maimed for life?

When I laid a trap to catch the thief that was ripping off my dad's antique store, I never dreamed I'd get trapped, too.

At least we aren't headed out of town. Not yet anyhow. I catch glimpses of passing street signs, but the names are unfamiliar. The van makes a final turn and coasts to a stop, then I hear a squeal of hinges. We pass through a set of steel gates and move slowly down what looks like an alley lined in garage doors.

Of course! A self-storage facility. Where else to stash stolen antiques?

Moments later, the SUV backs up to one of the units and comes to a full stop. I hear the doors open and shut, and a woman rolls up the door on the storage unit and starts unloading. To my intense disappointment, I don't recognize her before she drapes a padded blanket over me.

'Careful!' a low voice warns from behind me. Man? Woman? I can't tell.

At least I'm being handled gently. They ease me down

onto the concrete floor. I can't see through the blanket, and I'm starting to feel claustrophobic. What would they do if I suddenly screamed? I'm too scared to find out.

In no time at all, I hear the door roll down, and the van drives away.

I immediately concentrate all my will to fight my way out of that blanket. It's pitch-black here and cold, cold. I feel along the edges of the door. If there's a way to release the lock from inside, I can't find it. I'm thirteen years old. Way too old to start bawling like a baby, even if I am freezing. Nothing for it but to burrow back into that padded blanket and remember how I wound up in this fix . . .

I probably wouldn't be here if my mother hadn't been struck by lightning when I was three. It was a bolt out of the blue. Literally. No chance to take cover or escape.

Dad's mom came to live with us, but when she died five years later, Dad decided I was old enough to do without a babysitter. Every morning since then he pours us each a bowl of cereal and drops me off at school with lunch money. After school, I walk the eight blocks to his antique store where I do my homework, then read or help out.

Supper is usually a bowl of canned soup or the evening special at a nearby restaurant. Back at the house, Dad reads one of the many auction catalogs he gets in the mail, or we watch *Antiques Roadshow* and the History Channel. We're both in our beds by nine o'clock. At least he is. Lately, I've been sneaking back downstairs and out into the backyard to test the limits of what I can do.

He's a rather absentminded father, a kindly man more interested in the past than the present. He doesn't care about my As in math or science as long as I make at least a C in history and know that a Chippendale is a desirable piece of furniture and not a desirable male stripper.

Friends? Hey, I've got friends.

Lots of friends.

Okay, okay, maybe not close friends. My classmates like me well enough though. I get asked to all the birthday parties, despite being something of a loner. I'm pretty good with a computer, but I don't do Facebook. I don't text or Twitter either, so no one's ever claimed me as her best friend. I don't mind. Honest. When I was a little kid, the shop was more fun than any playdate, and as long as I was careful and put everything back where it belonged, Dad used to let me amuse myself with the antique toys or the cases of estate jewelry.

In short, I was as normal – or what passes for normal – as any other little girl until the hormones kicked in last spring and I suddenly 'became a woman,' as our gym teacher put it. It was not as huge a trauma for me as for some of my older classmates who had to endure sniggers and crude remarks from gorky boys whose voices were cracking like peanut brittle. Mrs Kim had thoroughly explained what was going to happen to us and I had watched most of the girls in my class become women before it happened to me, so I was prepared. I had begun to wear a small bra, and I had a package of sanitary pads stashed in the back of the linen closet.

Unfortunately, my first period began during the last period of school one warm spring day. Even more unfortunately, I was wearing white clam diggers. As soon as I walked out of the classroom and headed down the sidewalk toward the store, it was as if there were a gang of feral dogs on my trail – three pimply faced boys who jeered and called, 'Hey, Laurel! What'd you do? Sit down in ketchup?' and 'Oooh, Laurel! Hurt yourself? Want us to call a doctor?'

One of them pulled out his cell phone to take pictures of my backside.

Embarrassed and humiliated, I began to run, which of course only encouraged them. The store seemed miles away, and as I darted around a corner, the only hiding place in sight was a thick hedge of azalea bushes in full bloom. Even as I dived into them and buried myself among the leafy branches, I knew it was a mistake. With nowhere else to look, they would surely zero in on the head-high azaleas.

'Hey! Where'd she go?' I heard one of the panting boys ask when he turned the corner and saw the empty sidewalk ahead.

'There's her book bag,' said another. 'She must be in the bushes.'

I froze as they pushed aside the flowering twigs. One acne-inflamed face was so close to mine, I could have spit on it, yet he didn't seem to see me.

'What do you boys think you're doing?' a woman suddenly screeched from her doorway. 'Is that you, Thomas Bertram? You break any of my bushes, and I'm calling your mother.'

Tommy's mother is built like a Humvee, and it's rumored that she keeps a leather strap hanging in her kitchen. The speed with which Tommy took off down the sidewalk behind his friends makes me believe the rumors.

When the woman walked out into her yard, I wanted to run, too, but every instinct told me to stay still, don't move. To my surprise, the woman didn't seem to see me either. Muttering to herself about destructive kids today, she pushed aside the twigs and azalea flowers to look for damage. Her frown deepened. 'That's odd,' she said. 'I don't remember a white azalea here.'

I winced as she put out her hand to me and plucked a flower. It felt as if she had pulled out some of my hair, but I managed not to yelp.

When she walked away, I tried to leave, but I couldn't move. To my horror, I was no longer flesh and blood. My fingers were leafy twigs. My curly hair, ruffled white flowers. I tried to scream, but I had no voice. No mouth. No larynx.

Eventually, panic gave way to despair. The legend of Daphne and Apollo was familiar to me because of my

39

name: Daphne had turned into a laurel tree to escape being raped by a horny god whereas I, Laurel Hudson, had changed into an azalea to escape that bunch of adolescent jackals. But Daphne had wanted to become a tree while I—?

I suddenly realized that yeah, okay, when I dived into this clump of bushes, I did want to merge with them and disappear. There was nothing in the legend to suggest that Daphne ever regretted becoming a laurel tree and wanted to be human again, but if I wanted it as desperately as I'd wanted to hide—?

'*I want to be a girl again. I want to be a girl again*,' I chanted mutely.

Nothing.

I was still an azalea.

'It's pretty, Jean,' said a voice above me, 'but I don't recognize this variety. You really need to water it, though. It's starting to wilt.'

'I watered this whole bed last night,' said the woman who had chased away my tormentors. Evidently she had brought a gardening friend out to see me. 'Maybe it needs more water than usual. Tomorrow I'll dig it up, prune it back, and move it around to the patio where I can keep an eye on it.'

Dig me up? Prune me back?

As soon as they went back into the house, I concentrated on skin, hair, teeth, toenails – summoning up all the pictures of blood veins and nervous systems in my health and science textbook. To my total relief, my twigs abruptly became fingers again, my flowers were hair, my branches arms and legs. I scrambled out of the bushes, grabbed my book bag, and ran to the shop. Dad was too busy with a customer to notice that I was almost an hour late.

I was stunned by what had happened to me, but I was still a kid, and over the next three days, I almost convinced myself that I had imagined it all.

Then it happened again.

I was polishing a Victorian armchair that Dad had recently acquired. As I ran my oiled cloth over the carved filigrees, working the cloth into every dusty cranny, I suddenly heard the voice of doom from the front of the store.

Aunt Verna. Dad's older sister. Twice a year she passes through town on her way to and from her summer house in Maine, and she always stops by the store so that we can take her to lunch where she spends the whole meal telling me to sit up straight, not to talk with my mouth full, and to 'speak up, child. I asked you a question.' She finds fault with everything I do or say or wear, and to make matters worse, the last time she was here, she saw that I had taken to wearing a bra and she leaned over the table to ask in an arch whisper if I'd had a visit from my 'little friend down south' yet.

I pretended I didn't know what she meant, and when she noticed Dad's puzzled look, she let it drop. 'Just remember though, Laurel. I'm your only female relative, and if you have any questions, you can always come to me.'

As if.

I so wanted to avoid another lunch with Aunt Verna, that before I knew it, I had changed into a duplicate of the chair I had been polishing.

'That wasn't very kind of you to disappear like that and leave me to face your aunt alone,' Dad told me later.

'Sorry,' I said and tried to look contrite.

I spent the whole weekend experimenting with my strange new talent, and it didn't take me long to figure out how to get even with Tommy Bertram. He and his two pals usually stopped at Elm and Madison every afternoon before splitting off to their own houses. They would lean against a lamppost or on the sturdy blue and red steel mailbox that stood on that corner and snicker about which girls had the biggest 'racks' or how studying was for nerds. So juvenile.

So stupid. They never noticed when a second blue and red steel mailbox appeared beside the first one.

Next day, I slipped notes into the lockers of a couple of eighth-grade boys whose girlfriends I'd heard them trashing, and guess what? After school, those three got their butts kicked big time.

Oh, and guess what else? Ten minutes into the unit test, our history teacher found the cheat notes Tommy had taped to his arm, so it was a real bad day for him all around.

While my new talent was useful for avoiding unpleasant aunts and getting back at obnoxious boys, I didn't see any real benefits until this winter when things started to go missing from the store. Dad owns the store, but he rents space to several other dealers and takes the money for them when they're not there.

As the economy got worse, more and more people came into the shop offering quality heirlooms, but fewer and fewer of the walk-ins were buying. Without our Internet website, Dad might have had to close the store. As it was, three of our dealers had to pack it in, and for a while their rental spaces stood empty.

Just when trade dropped off to its slowest after Christmas, someone came in to ask if we would sell some things she had recently inherited. 'It's stuff my mother's great-grandfather acquired when he was in the China trade back in the 1890s.'

Dad tried to explain that he knew very little about Chinese antiques, but the woman wouldn't take no for an answer. Next day, she arrived with a pile of cartons, some odd pieces of furniture, and a document that authorized him to sell everything for a generous percentage of the net.

'You're sure about this?' Dad asked dubiously as the movers stacked the boxes in a room near the front counter that serves as both a workroom and temporary storage.

'I'm positive. I need the money.'

'But what about an inventory?' Dad said. 'Do you even know what's here or what the pieces are worth?'

'I'm not worried,' the woman told him. 'You sold some things for a friend of mine, and she says you're the most honest man she ever met.'

As soon as she left, we opened a couple of cartons at random. Inside were amazing porcelains, bronzes, and stone animals. Tucked in among the boxes were several lacquered chests and screens. Everything was meticulously documented in an old ledger book, which also held the original bills of sale.

While Dad gave himself a crash course on Chinese antiques, I took pictures and uploaded them to our eBay account. We put a dozen decorative items up for auction right away; and at the end of two weeks, we were both astonished to see the prices they brought, mostly from people with Chinese names.

'They've got the money now,' said Mr Fong, one of our new dealers, as he watched me pack up a small stone Fu dog to ship to the West Coast. He shook his head enviously. 'A few years ago, it was the Japanese. Now it's the Chinese who want to buy their history back.'

Could Mr Fong have been the second person in the SUV? Was he the one who cautioned the woman to be careful with me? Our shoplifter?

Dad may not deal in museum-quality antiques, but he does have high standards, and he requires that our dealers meet those standards by frequently refreshing their displays. Some of them rent space in three or four different stores, which means that they're constantly moving things in and out and that they're not always clear about what's where. When we take a customer's money, we save the tag that was on the item because it has the dealer's ID number and the asking price. That goes into the till with the customer's payment, whether cash, check, or plastic, and that's when a dealer will delete it from his inventory list.

It was Martha Cook, a dealer who's been with Dad for years, who first noticed that she was missing a small occasional table. Mass-produced, mid-twentieth century, but made of solid mahogany and in beautiful condition. Good value for the $75 Martha was asking.

Then Jimmy Weston reported that a pair of bronze book-ends had vanished from his space. 'Who the heck steals twenty-dollar book-ends?' he asked indignantly.

'A klepto?' wondered Jane Armstead, the part-time clerk who covers for Dad when he's on a buying trip and I'm in school. 'There's no other logic to what's being taken.'

Jane's a divorced freelance artist who's put on a few pounds over the years. Her long hair is streaked with gray now, and she just coils it around and secures it to the top of her head with hairpins and a couple of ivory chopsticks. Her clothes used to be shabby chic; now they're just shabby because her commissions have fallen off. Even though she's worked here off and on since I was in kindergarten, Jane is a little ditzy and no expert in antiques, but she was right about the illogic of the thefts. The only thing Jimmy Weston's bronze bookends had in common with a trio of 1930s lead soldiers, a chipped Art Deco vase, and a pair of Kendall Loring's silver-plated candlesticks was their portability. Nor were they worth much. Except for Martha's table, nothing was priced at over fifty dollars.

'They took your candlesticks and left the sterling toast rack that was sitting right beside it?' said Jane. 'Weird.'

'Indeed,' Ms Loring said crisply. 'Especially since the toast rack is Georgian and worth five times the candlesticks.'

Dad started listing the Chinese things on eBay in the middle of January, three new dealers joined the store in February, and the shoplifting began soon after that.

*

It has to be one of those three, I think as my eyes adjust to the darkness. Is it coincidence, or did they suddenly show up because they saw those Chinese things on eBay and thought they could come clean us out? I see a paper-thin line of light where the door doesn't fit the sill completely. No real help. There's nothing I can change into that would let me move through such a narrow opening. As the March chill penetrates my prison, I move farther away from the cold metal roll-up door and fumble around till I find a second padded blanket to insulate me from the concrete floor while I think about those new dealers.

Thomas Fong is from San Francisco. Late forties. Married, though we've never seen his wife. With that name, you'd expect someone small, dark, and inscrutable. You'd be wrong. He's tall, blue-eyed, and four generations removed from the mainland, but his Chinese roots led him to an appreciation of classical Chinese antiques, and he specializes in decorative pieces of Asian origin. 'Unfortunately, they're mostly things that were made for export and not very old,' he told me. 'Post-1945.' Very nosy. Forever trying to get a look inside the storage room. Even though he's not there every day, he always seems to be around when I photograph a new batch of items.

Next comes Kendall Loring from Detroit. Mid-thirties. Still single. Skinny. Brown hair that's curlier than mine, and she's even nosier than Mr Fong. First day in the door, she's asking questions about school and who my friends are and what my mom was like and if I think Dad will ever get married again. Sort of cute, but way too young for Dad. If I were on Facebook, she'd probably be banging at the electronic door begging to be my friend. Says she doesn't like Chinese arts and deals only in estate jewelry and silver. Could she have been the second person in the van? Maybe her candlesticks weren't really stolen. Maybe that was to keep us from suspecting her when other things disappeared.

Last is a youngish widow from New York City. Neva

45

Earle. Forty and fighting it. Friendly enough, but more reserved than either Fong or Loring. Her space is an eclectic mix of porcelain and ceramics, everything from Staffordshire dogs to beautiful Dresden plates. Would she – *Omigod, what's that noise?*

It sounds almost like someone's touching a sheet of bubble wrap. Mice? Rats? I squint through the gloom, but it's too dark to see anything distinctly. I flounce my blanket to flush whatever creature it is and to get a fix on its location, but all is silent again. 'Nerves,' I mutter to myself. Eventually I relax and go back to analyzing the situation.

Despite all our care in watching our customers like a hawk, occasional small items continued to walk off. Jane started asking customers to leave their tote bags at the front counter when she was covering the store for Dad, but he couldn't bring himself to do it.

'It'll look like we don't trust them,' he said.

'We don't,' Jane and I chorused.

Things finally came to a head last week. My fault. We keep the storeroom locked, of course, but once an item's been listed online, I'm not as careful as I should be about putting it back under lock and key. When Dad went to crate up a lacquered chest that had sold for well over its $2000 reserve, it was gone. I had covered it with an old patchwork quilt and left it on the floor beside the table I use as a staging platform for my camera. Instead of the Chinese chest, the patchwork quilt covered a plain oak chest of our own that was worth only a fraction of the other.

The police came and poked around, but what could they do? No door had been forced, and taking fingerprints in such a public place would have been useless. 'We'll file an incident report so you can put in an insurance claim,' they told Dad, 'but you might want to change your locks. Looks like an inside job by someone with a key.'

'Well, that's stupid,' I told Dad when they were gone.

'You and Jane have the only keys, and Jane hasn't been in since I left the chest out.'

'Of course, it wasn't Jane,' said Dad. 'I hate to say it, but I'm afraid it must be one of the new people. All three of them restocked their booths this week, so they were back and forth with dollies. If you could remember when you last saw the chest—?'

But I couldn't. This was Thursday. I knew it was there last Saturday morning because a customer had been interested in the quilt until she realized that one end of it had been damaged in a fire, but the chest could have been taken twenty minutes later, and who would notice?

Dad was due to be out of town all weekend for an antique fair. I had finally convinced him that I was old enough to stay home alone, but as soon as he left Friday morning, I ditched school and headed for the shop.

Jane was behind the counter and surprised to see me. 'No school?'

'Teacher workday,' I said glibly. 'I'm going to take pictures of another box of stuff in the storeroom.'

No sooner had I unlocked the door and switched on the light inside than Mr Fong was right there at my elbow. He insisted on helping me carry things out to my tabletop photography studio. This time, I didn't discourage him. He wasn't particularly interested in a tall ceramic statue of a goddess – 'Early twentieth century, made for export and a dime a dozen,' he said dismissively – but a Ming dynasty vase with a scaly blue dragon prancing around the flared bowl really made him salivate.

'Lovely,' said Neva Earle on her way in with a heavy box of English stoneware strapped to her dolly. She held a Blue Willow platter next to the vase and said ruefully, 'You can certainly see the difference in quality, can't you?'

'I don't know,' said Martha Cook. 'I have a weakness for Blue Willow. You ought to let me display that platter for you on one of my sideboards.'

They walked away together, and a customer called Mr Fong back to his booth to discuss a Korean screen.

I finished photographing the Ming vase and moved on to the ceramic goddess. She might not be valuable, but her serene face, half the size of my own, appealed to me, and I took several pictures of her from all angles.

'You have a nice touch with the camera,' said Kendall Loring, who had suddenly appeared from nowhere. 'I checked out your website. Good crisp pictures.'

'Thanks,' I muttered.

'I guess you got your eye for form from your dad,' she said. 'What about your mom? Was she a photographer, too?'

I shrugged. 'Dad never said, Ms Loring.'

'Please. Call me Kendall. You don't look much like him, so I guess you must take after her.'

'I wouldn't know,' I said. 'She didn't like to have her picture taken.'

'No pictures at all?'

'Just a snapshot he took when she wasn't expecting it,' I said grudgingly.

'Was she as pretty as you?'

Oh please, I thought to myself.

'Does it still hurt for him to talk about her?'

God, she was nosy! But her questions made me realize how little I knew about my mother. Could she have been a shape-shifter, too? Even though he never brought her up, Dad certainly answered every question I'd ever thought to ask. They had met in college. The only child of two only children, her father died when she was in college and her mother three years later. As the only grandchild on both sides of her family, she had inherited a ton of beautiful old pieces, which is how she and Dad started the store. No other family that he'd ever heard about. But where she was born? Her maiden name? Her favorite songs and movies? I'd never thought to ask. And there was no way I could say,

'Hey, Dad, Mom ever change into a rocking chair when you weren't looking?'

Not that I was going to tell Ms Call-Me-Kendall Loring any of this. I made a big show of being absorbed in my work, and she eventually took the hint and went on back to her booth.

Leaving the Ming vase on the table, I shoved the ceramic goddess back into the storeroom and locked the door.

Behind the counter, Jane was absorbed in pulling up type fonts on the computer. As a freelance artist, she mixed aesthetic commissions with commercial ones and was always looking for ideas. She told me she hadn't sold a thing since Christmas except for a Valentine poster, so money was tight for her. I saw that she was totally oblivious to me, and no one else was around. Two seconds later, I was a copy of the ceramic goddess.

Talk about boring. I watched all day, but the only time it got halfway interesting was when Mr Fong paused to admire the vase again and asked Jane if I'd meant to leave it out like that. 'Isn't Laurel afraid someone will walk off with it?'

Jane had missed our earlier comments about the worth of the vase and gave an indifferent shrug. 'She'll probably come back and put it away.'

Shortly before closing time, I shifted back into my own shape.

'Oh, there you are,' said Jane. She closed her sketchbook, logged off the computer, and began totaling up the day's meager receipts. 'I thought you were going to help me out on the counter.'

'Sorry,' I said, making a dash for the restroom. Although I could somehow see and hear in my changed state, I didn't feel hunger, thirst, or any other bodily needs. The instant I changed back, though, my bladder felt like it was going to pop and I was ravenously hungry.

Kendall Loring was on her way out as I helped Jane lock up. I hadn't realized she was still in the store.

As she pulled on her gloves and tightened a blue wool scarf around her neck, she gave me a hopeful smile and said, 'Could I buy you supper?'

'Why thanks, I'd love that,' said Jane. She was busy setting the burglar alarm and didn't realize the invitation was meant for me alone.

A blast of icy March wind stung my cheeks when we stepped outside and waited for Jane to turn the key in the lock. I managed a fake smile of regret. 'That's awfully nice of you, Ms Loring, but I have to read a book for a school report. Thanks anyhow. You and Jane have fun.'

Sitting here in my dark, icy prison, the memory of her sour look gives me my first smile since I'd been locked in.

'You missed a good meal, Laurel,' Jane said when I got to the store this morning. 'Best steak I've had in ages. And Kendall's so interesting to talk to. We must have rattled on for two hours.'

Didn't take a genius to know who did the rattling. By the time their dinner was over, Kendall Loring had probably heard everything Jane knows about Dad and me.

Once I'd finished my usual Saturday morning chores, I put the Ming vase back on my photography table and fiddled with the camera some more. When I was sure that all the dealers in the store knew the vase was there, I draped an old tablecloth over it to look as if I was trying to disguise it. Because Saturday is our busiest day, it was almost noon before I found a safe time to shift into the shape of that ceramic goddess. At least it was more interesting than yesterday. More people in and out. Martha Cook sold a nice Sheraton-style china cabinet, and Jimmy Weston finally unloaded a large gilt-framed mirror that he'd been switching from store to store for several months.

Thomas Fong came by to lift the cloth on the vase and run his hand over it enviously.

'Careful you don't rub the scales off that dragon,' Neva Earle teased as she passed him on her way out of the store.

At one point, I thought I had spotted a shoplifter when a woman took a needlepoint cushion from a nearby stand while Jane was away from the counter and brazenly walked out of the store with it. She brought it right back, though, and I realized that she had a swatch of upholstery in her other hand and had merely wanted to see if the two colors matched in natural light.

I was so busy watching her that I didn't realize that someone had approached from the other side until a heavy cloth was thrown over me. A moment later I was wheeled out to the sidewalk on a dolly and shoved into the back of the van. The cloth slipped enough for me to see a pair of female hands cushion the Ming vase in a cardboard box beside me, and that was it, until those same hands unloaded me at the storage facility and locked me inside.

I must have slept because that thin line of light beneath the door is even thinner now. Sunset, and I still haven't come up with a way out of this predicament.

'I could turn into water,' I mutter aloud to myself. 'Run under the sill and onto the pavement.'

Like a whispered thought came a soft 'No!'

My own subconscious telling me what I want to hear? I've been afraid to try liquids. Too amorphous. What if I couldn't hold it together and soaked into the ground? What if there's a storm drain right outside this door, and I'm swept down to lose my identity in dirty water before all of me seeps past the sill?

A moment later, I hear a vehicle stop outside and voices. A key turns in the lock. Before the door rolls up, I drop my blankets, push my way deeper into the locker, and shift into the shape of a cardboard box tall enough to see over the other boxes.

As light floods in, I see for the first time, an upright, five-foot-tall wooden bear identical to one in the store. They must have stolen it when they took me. I focus my attention on the two women. They're silhouetted against the sunset, and I can't immediately make out their faces.

'Where's the goddess?' one of them says, taking a step closer.

'I left it right there,' says the other one.

'You idiot! You brought that stupid bear.'

The other starts to protest when suddenly the bear gives a tremendous roar. To their horror, it lurches forward and swipes its claws at the woman in front.

Terrified, both women bolt screaming down the alley-way.

The bear drops to all fours, growls menacingly, then stops and turns toward me. I concentrate on being cardboard. I think cardboard thoughts and try to give off a cardboard smell.

The bear laughs and says. 'It's okay, Laurel. You can come out now.'

A shimmer of fur, and there's Kendall Loring.

I stare at her, stupefied, and slowly shift into my own shape.

'I see you didn't think to wear a coat either,' she says. 'Come on. Let's see if they left a cell phone in the car.'

I'm too stunned to argue and just follow her meekly out to the car, where we find a purse and a cell phone. When the women get up the nerve to return, we're locked inside the SUV with the heater going, and Kendall's called the police. They bang on the windows and threaten us with seven kinds of hurt until a police cruiser pulls up outside the gate and an agile young patrol officer climbs over the gate and demands to know what's going on.

Neva Earle tries to bluster her way out of it, but she and

her accomplice sound crazy when they start raving about a bear, and besides, I've identified the lacquered chest that she stole from the store last week.

The police take us down to the station to sort it all out. Kendall tells a convincing story of how we saw them take the Ming dynasty vase from the store and followed them. They don't think to ask where Kendall's car is or how we got past the locked gate. The vase and the chest are enough for them to charge Neva Earle and her partner, and the nice young patrol officer drives us both to Kendall's apartment.

That's where I learn that she's my cousin. My grandmother actually had two daughters, not one as I've been told.

'My mom was a shape-shifter, too,' Kendall says, 'only our grandparents were horrified and so scared of her that she ran away from home when she was sixteen. Your mom was only four at the time, and maybe they never told her she had an older sister. When I finally got Mother to tell me her real name, her parents were dead, and no one knew what happened to your mom. One of the neighbors thought she'd married a man named Hudson. Do you know how many Hudsons there are?'

I shake my head.

'Thousands,' she says grimly. 'From Alaska to Florida. Two years ago, though, Mother was on eBay looking at jewelry for our store in Detroit, and she spotted this.'

She hands me an oval cameo brooch, set in gold and rimmed with garnets. White on pink, it's carved with the profiles of three women. Nothing I'd ever wear, I had assured my dad when I asked if I could put it on eBay along with some other pieces of antique jewelry. I think it fetched around $300.

'It was my grandmother's,' I say.

'I know. My mom recognized it.'

'You came here because of a brooch?'

'Mother's gone,' she says simply. 'I suppose you could say

53

she drowned. She was dying of cancer, and last summer she just merged into Lake Michigan. I have no other family.'

She won't beg. I can see that.

'Okay,' I say at last. 'But you have to teach me how to do animals. I can't keep myself from wilting when I'm a plant, so I've been afraid to try a living form.'

She laughs and shifts into the shape of a large golden retriever and almost licks me to death before I can make her stop.

Oh, and the shoplifter? The next time Jane covered for Dad, I said, 'I'm sorry you're having a rough time right now, Jane, but you can't steal any more money, okay?'

See, the stolen items were portable, but they were also so cheap that most customers wouldn't bother with a credit card. On Saturday morning, I watched a woman pay cash for a Blue Willow cup and saucer from Neva Earle's booth. Jane pointed out a tiny chip on the underside of the saucer and told her it was being sold 'as is,' meaning it could not be returned. Then she simply pocketed the cash.

I suppose I should have had her fired or arrested, but she's been around since I was a baby. Besides, business is starting to pick up again, so Dad has her working more hours, and she's gradually paying back what she stole.

Dad's as absentminded as ever, but he's noticed that Kendall and I are friends.

I'm still not totally convinced that Kendall's interested only in me and not Dad, too, and I'm not sure how I feel about that. A cousin's one thing. A shape-shifting step-mom's quite another.

Oh, and last week? I changed into a tiger and scared Tommy Bertram so bad he wet his pants.

Wait'll he sees my dragon.

THE TRESPASSERS

Brendan Dubois

I was dreaming that something was chewing on my ankles when the phone thankfully rang, and I fumbled at the side of the bed and grabbed the cordless phone, and murmured something intelligible into the receiver. I looked at the bloodred numerals of the clock radio and saw that it was 2:34 a.m. A hellish time for about anything, especially a phone ringing in the dark.

The female voice on the other end said, 'Sorry to wake you, Chief, but you've got a situation.'

I yawned, scratched at an intimate place or two, and swung around and put my feet on the carpet. Behind me my wife, Tracy, kept on slumbering. Sweet girl, she could sleep through most everything, including a Cat Five hurricane hammering at the windows.

'Go ahead. What's going on?' I asked.

The voice – which I now recognized as one of the duty dispatchers for the county – said, 'You've got an untimely death.'

Damn, I thought. It was Saturday morning. This meant that I probably had to kiss the weekend good-bye, even though I had earlier promised Tracy a nice drive south to visit her parents in Concord . . . but with an untimely death in town, that was all done.

'Go on. Where?'

'Fourteen Mast Road. Officer Harris is there, securing the scene.'

'Fourteen? Did you say Fourteen Mast Road?'

'That's right, Chief.'

Damn. The Logan place. Tracy shifted on the other side of the bed and then started gently snoring.

I yawned, scratched myself in another, somewhat less intimate place, and said, 'All right. Tell Harris I'm rolling, should be there in about fifteen minutes. All right?'

'Absolutely,' the dispatcher said. 'You want me to contact the state police?'

I hesitated. Protocol demanded that the state police be called in for something like this, especially in a small town like Salem Falls, New Hampshire, which had a three-man police department, one-third of which was on vacation, one-third of which was on the job, and one-third of which was sitting in a pair of pajama bottoms, talking to a young lady who probably wasn't more than twenty-one years of age.

'No, that's all right,' I said. 'I'll take care of it when I get to the scene.

I sensed the uneasiness coming through the phone line, but she was a professional and said, 'As you say, Chief.'

I hung up the phone and managed to get dressed and out the door without waking my wife or our two girls – ages eight and five – which I thought was a major accomplishment.

In my cruiser the engine started on the third try, and I backed out to Rutland Road, where I live with my family. I flipped on the heater as I drove down Rutland, the headlights picking up the dead leaves scattered across the cracked asphalt. It was the middle of October, just a couple of weeks left before Halloween, but I didn't see any trick-or-treaters about, just quiet homes with one or two displaying a flickering blue light in the window that either meant an insomniac or someone who had fallen asleep while watching *The Tonight Show*. There were also a couple of lighted displays of pumpkins or witches from those who really enjoyed celebrating this time of year, and I'm sure they were new arrivals to our fair town.

And speaking of lights, I didn't bother switching on the overhead light bar. I knew Fourteen Mast Road quite well, knew I'd be there in less than ten minutes, and so what was the point of switching on the strobes and getting all gung ho? But I did switch on the Motorola police radio, slung underneath the dash, and contacted the same polite woman I had talked to earlier.

'County, this is Salem Falls Unit One, responding to Fourteen Mast Road.'

And her brisk voice replied, 'Salem Falls Unit One, ten-four.'

And I resumed driving, shivering in the coldness of the cruiser's interior, wondering what in hell I was about to step into, and also wondering if the fine townspeople of Salem Falls would finally purchase me a new police cruiser at the next town meeting.

Fourteen Mast Road was on the left side of a narrow country road, at the top of a hill that offered great views of the Montcalm Valley and the Green Mountains of Vermont, over on the other side of the border. The house was an old Victorian, three storeys tall, painted yellow with white and black trim. It had a nicely trimmed lawn and a wraparound porch, and I saw a Salem Falls police cruiser parked in the driveway behind a white Ford van, which, in turn, was parked behind a light blue Volvo. It looked like most of the lights were on inside, and I was happy to see that the cruiser – operated by Officer Melanie Harris – had its strobe lights off. Nothing like flashing lights to get attention, and even in a small town like Salem Falls, it would take just under an hour for most of the adult population to know something was amiss at the Logan place.

I pulled over on the side of the road – the driveway being full – and called off one more time to dispatch, 'Salem Falls Unit One, off at the scene,' heard a quick reply, and then switched off the engine. I got out and walked up a flagstone path to the porch and checked out the Ford van. It had Massachusetts plates – which got my attention – and on the side of the van was one of those magnetic signs that said N.E.G.H. with a 1-800 phone number underneath, and some odd logo with a broomstick and sheet.

I went up the porch steps, past a couple more Halloween decorations, the door opened up, and Officer Melanie Harris came out, shaking her head, a slight smile on her chubby face. 'Chief, you're really not going to believe this one—'

'Tell me what you got,' I interrupted, 'Let's start with that. County dispatch said untimely death. The fire department been called out?'

'I called them right after I had dispatch call you. They should be here in a few minutes.'

'Okay, go on.'

It was chilly out on the porch, and I looked through some transparent white lace curtains. I saw what looked to be three people, sitting in a living room. I rubbed my hands, and Harris looked through her notepad and said, 'What we have here is Ralph Toland and his wife, Carrie. They've lived here just under a year. Ralph runs some sort of online financial service company, and his wife helps with the books and billing.'

'Where they originally from?'

'Vermont.'

'Oh,' I said and saw the twinkle in Melanie's eyes with the way I pronounced the word. Years ago, during my grandparents' time, Vermont was a state not unlike New Hampshire: solid Republican, flinty Yankee, self-sufficient, low taxes, that sort of thing. But now Vermont was just a suburb for rich New Yorkers, just like the southern part of our state was a suburb for rich Massachusetts types.

'Right, oh,' she said, referring back to her notes.

'And who's the other guy in there with them?'

She flipped a page in the notebook. 'This is where it gets . . . interesting, Chief. The other fellow in the living room, that's Josh Lincoln. He was one half of a team from the NEGH.'

'The NE what?'

She cocked her head. 'You don't watch much cable TV, do you, Chief?'

I said, 'Mostly it's Nickelodeon or the Food Network. Look, don't keep me guessing.'

'Sorry,' she said. 'NEGH. New England Ghost Hunters. Josh and his buddy Peter Grolin, they belong to this outfit that hunts ghosts, spirits, paranormal phenomena, that sort of thing. They go to haunted houses or other buildings, stake them out for the night, film their results, and it gets shown on one of those weird cable channels in the high numbers. They were spending the night here, and something happened, and Peter . . . well, Peter, he's dead.'

'Oh, Christ,' I said. 'Ghost hunters. Here. Did you find out whose bright idea that was?'

'The male half of the Vermont immigrants,' Melanie said. 'I guess . . . well, he claims that he and his wife, ever since they moved into the place, there's been, quote, events, unquote. And the wife, she's thinking of turning the place into a bed-and-breakfast—'

'Like this county needs another Victorian bed-and-breakfast.'

Another smile from my young officer, who's the daughter of the selectmen chairman, and who works twice as hard to prove she doesn't get any favors. She said, 'But that's the deal, Chief. This one, they could say it was haunted. That, plus the view of Vermont and the buttered scones for breakfast, I guess they thought that was a selling point.'

I tried to peer through the window, just saw the three shapes, sitting there silently. 'What happened to Peter?'

Melanie's smile faded a bit. 'You can see for yourself. Kinda gross. Looks like he took a fall from the third floor stairs, went down to the second floor landing, and . . . well, the railing for the landing. There was this lovely sculpted ear of corn or something on the railing, very kitschy and decorative, but it had a sharp point and went right through his throat. Bled right out, up there on the landing.'

I took my uniform hat off, rubbed at my head. 'All right. You got statements from all three of them?'

'Yep,' she said.

'You got pictures and preliminary measurements?'

'Yep, again.'

'What's your gut telling you?'

She looked at me with a calm, clear expression, and said, 'Untimely death. That's all. Nothing suspicious.'

I stared right back at her. 'Okay. Not bad . . . but you screwed one thing up.'

'Oh?'

I motioned to the living room. 'You left the three of them alone in there, while you were out talking with me. Those are all witnesses. They should be separated so they don't get a chance to chat and compare stories, and come up with a nice little narrative.'

Melanie said, 'Good point, Chief, Won't do it again. But still . . . guy took a tumble.'

'Sure,' I said, going to the door. 'But if we find out later that somebody in here pushed him, the attorney general will be all over our ass. Look, stay out here and keep the eager beavers from the fire department from coming in. You've done well.'

She smiled. 'Thanks, Chief.'

And so I opened the door and entered what was

technically a crime scene, but which I thought was something else as well.

If I was concerned about a crime being committed, I suppose I should have checked out the body of the recently deceased, but I was more interested in talking to the witnesses, aka residents, who were in the house at the time the young man died. Sitting on a couch that looked overstuffed and upholstered, like it belonged to some Manhattan designer's idea of what constituted Victorian style, were Ralph and Carrie Toland. Ralph had on a pair of gray sweatpants and a T-shirt that said *COLBY*, while his wife had a light blue terry cloth robe on, her white-knuckled hands tight about the top. Her blonde hair was mussed and her eyes were red-rimmed, like she had been silently crying for the past hour. Ralph was about ten years my junior, black hair cut nice and short, but his face was just a bit flabby and shocked, like he could not believe that his entire life had led up to this, a pleasant home in a pleasant town with a dead body on the next floor.

Slumped in an easy chair that was an uneasy match to the couch was Josh Lincoln, who looked to be about the same age as our county dispatcher. He had on black sneakers, blue jeans, and a black long-sleeved T-shirt that had the same logo displayed on the van outside. There were tattoos on the back of his hands, and he had earrings in both ears. His dark hair was in a ponytail, and he was just staring at his feet.

'Mr Toland? Sir?'

Ralph looked up, like he just recognized that someone else was in the room, and said, 'Yes?'

'Sir, I'm Chief Hoyt Graham, Salem Falls Police. Is there a place where we could talk, just for a few minutes? Just the two of us?'

'Um, sure,' he said, getting up from the couch, squeezing his wife's free hand. 'Sure, come with me,' and then Carrie looked up at him, her face pinched, and whispered, 'Your fault, damn you, your fault.'

He sighed and ran a hand across the top of his head, and I followed him as he walked into a kitchen, flicking on a light. I took in all the stainless steel gear and thought my wife would drool at seeing such a display. He took a stool and so did I, and I said, 'I know you've talked to Officer Harris, but I just want to hear it from you, what happened.'

He shook his head and sighed and said, 'Damn . . . I mean, it seemed like a hoot at the time, you know? I was watching some TV last month, saw this program on the paranormal, and saw a bit on an outfit called the New England Ghost Hunters. And Carrie and I thought it would be great to have someone come here and investigate our house.'

Sure, I thought. *Your idea and your wife's idea*. I wasn't buying it, but I went on and said, 'And what would be the purpose of this . . . investigation?'

He shrugged. 'Some publicity. We're thinking of converting this place into a bed-and-breakfast, and we thought a television program about what's been going on here would be wonderful in getting our name out to the public.'

'Has the planning board approved your proposal?'

'Not yet, but our lawyer's confident it will get approval.'

I flipped over a page in the notebook and thought, *Then your lawyer doesn't know Salem Falls that well*, but poor Ralph was already having a terrible night, so I didn't want to add to his misery. Aloud I said, 'So tell me, sir, what's been going on that you thought about bringing in ghost hunters?'

Ralph looked embarrassed and said, 'Oh, stuff.'

'What stuff?'

'Well . . . ever since we moved in, there's been . . . incidents.'

I tried to keep the impatience out of my voice. 'Like what? I don't like games, Mr Toland, so tell me what's been going on here, what's occurred so that you felt compelled to bring in two strangers from Massachusetts to spend the night here, one of whom is now dead in your house.'

That certainly got his attention, and he stared at a point about a foot above my left shoulder and said, 'Little stuff at first. Carrie's always on me for leaving the toilet seat up, and I swear, I always put the seat down . . . and she'd always find it up. And doors would open and shut by themselves . . . and you'd be walking down the stairs and man, you'd just get a blast of cold air . . . and at night . . . well, sometimes it got worse at night.'

I didn't say a word. Just waited, and he added, 'Just as you'd be drifting off to sleep, there'd be whispers out there, whispers that you could barely hear . . . and when you'd sit up, they'd go away. Or if you went around, thinking maybe the TV or a radio was left on, there'd be nothing. But back into bed . . . more whispers. And . . . shadows on the wall . . . odd lights that would just flicker at the corner of your eye . . .'

I sighed. 'Mr Toland . . . this house is more than a century old. Odd things happen to the foundation. The house can settle and either close or open doors, make creaking noises, or let in drafts that'll freeze your fingers. Old pipes can rattle or gurgle water . . . make it sound like whispers. And lights . . . the eye can play tricks at night, especially . . . well, especially when you're predisposed to think something's going on.'

He stopped staring over my shoulder, now looked at my face. He said, 'Two weeks ago, my wife woke up screaming, saying something cold had grabbed onto her foot. And before you ask, no, it wasn't me. So don't tell me it's just an old house, all right?'

I went to my notebook. 'All right, we'll leave that be. Now, tell me about these two ghost hunters.'

Another shrug. 'At the time . . . like I said, it was just a

63

hoot. I called their one-eight-hundred number, they came up here, asked if they could spend the night, and we said, sure. They have all this gear, you know, cameras that can take pictures in the night, stuff that measures variations in temperature and electromagnetic radiation. I was going to stay up with them, but they said, no, they got better results with the homeowners not being present. So Carrie and I went to bed, and just before two a.m . . . I woke up, heard some screaming, and then a thumping sound, and then more yelling. That's when I got out of bed.'

'Where did you go?'

'Up to where I heard Josh yelling, yelling about his bud Peter. His friend . . . it was awful. Blood everywhere. And that's when I had Carrie call nine-one-one.'

'And what was Josh yelling about his friend Peter?'

'Upset talk . . . that's all . . . that he had fallen, was bleeding hard, what was he going to tell his parents, stuff like that.'

'All right,' I said. 'Is there anything else you can tell me that might help with our investigation?'

He shook his head. 'To think something like this would happen in our house . . .'

And I don't know, maybe I was feeling grumpy or something for being woken up and having my weekend ruined, but I said, 'Oh, one thing, Mr Toland. Just so you know.'

'What's that?'

'Earlier you said this was your house. Not entirely accurate. This is the Logan house, named after the man who built it, back in 1882. It may be your house for a while, but it will always be the Logan house. Funny thing, I know, but that's one of the funny things about small towns. Now, if you don't mind, I'd like to talk to your wife for a few minutes.'

I don't think Mr Toland liked being corrected like that, and truth be told, I didn't particularly care.

*

Next I spoke to Carrie Toland in her fine kitchen, which was mostly a waste of time. She was at times weepy and other times angry, and she mostly repeated what her husband had said, with one notable exception, that the visit of the alleged paranormal experts was entirely her husband's idea, and not hers.

And when Peter had died a couple of hours ago, she was fast asleep and heard a thump, and yelling, and that's all she knew. She got up from bed with her husband, went upstairs to the second-floor landing, and when she saw the blood on the stairs and the crumpled form of Peter, she retreated back downstairs to the living room and called 911.

'All right,' I said, looking at my notebook. 'But tell me this. Your husband claims that ever since you moved into the house, that there's been . . . incidents. True?'

She tried to draw her bathrobe even closer about her neck. 'I . . . I don't know.'

'Could you be a bit more precise, Mrs Toland?'

'Ralph . . . he's really the one who thinks something's been going on here. At first, it was a little joke, you know? That there was somebody else living here, somebody sharing our house. We even talked about charging rent or something . . . just a little joke.'

'Were you waking up a couple of weeks ago, screaming that something had grabbed your leg, was that a little joke?'

Her eyes were sharp, and I could just imagine what she'd be saying to her husband at the first opportunity, about telling family secrets, and she said, 'No. That was just a nightmare. Nothing else.'

'Your husband believed otherwise.'

'Maybe so, but I never really believed. I just thought it was Ralph and his imagination . . .'

And then her mood and voice changed. 'His damn imagination. And look what it's brought us. A dead boy in the house. A dead boy.'

She shivered and said bitterly, 'But maybe Ralph will be

happy now. A real dead body in our house. Maybe that poor boy's spirit will haunt us now . . .' Then the sniffling started, and I patted her on the shoulder and said we were done for now.

Josh Lincoln, the surviving 50 percent of the New England Ghost Hunters field team, seemed kind of shaky, so we sat at a dining room table in the rear, adjacent to the kitchen. I took notes as we talked, and after getting his age, hometown, and that usual stuff, I said, 'So. How long have you been doing this kind of work?'

'Just over a year,' he said glumly, looking down at his tattooed hands.

'What else do you do?'

'Huh?'

I said gently, 'Oh, come on, Josh. This can't be a paying gig, can it? What else do you do?'

He looked a bit embarrassed. 'Tend bar. In Newburyport, Massachusetts.'

'And your buddy Josh?'

'Dishwasher. Same place as me.'

'So how did you end up doing this?'

Josh shrugged. 'We love Goth stuff, the supernatural, that sort of thing. King, Poe, Lovecraft . . . and Newburyport's got a lot of haunted history. We read up on ghosts and ghost-hunting on the Web, seemed like fun, you know? Do stuff firsthand. Got some gear, made a connection with a cable station, and there you go . . .'

'And probably get to boast some to the young ladies, right?'

Just the hint of a smile. 'Maybe.'

'And how did you end up here, in Salem Falls?'

'The guy that owns the house, he gave us a ring. And once we looked into the history of this house, man, of what happened here—'

I held up a hand. 'I know. The Logan place. I'm a native. I know all about it.'

'Oh,' he said.

'So how many times have you done investigations like this?'

'About ten, fifteen times,' he said.

'Any ghosts? Spirits? Things that go bump in the night?'

Josh rubbed his hands together. 'Indications . . . increased levels of electromagnetic radiation, some whispers caught on audiotape, flashes of light . . . stuff like that.'

'But no pirate ghosts, waving a sword, that sort of thing?'

He wiped at his eyes. 'Look, maybe you're having fun with this, you know? But my buddy's dead out there.'

I felt properly chastened. 'My apologies. You're right. Look, Josh, what happened when Peter came down the stairs? Where were you?'

He took a breath. 'I was in the living room. There was some indication in the far corner . . . just a sudden dip in the temperature. Peter was upstairs, on the third floor. Then I heard him moving fast, and a yell . . . and then he fell. I ran upstairs and just saw him there . . . bleeding . . . and . . . it was so quick, you know? It didn't take long. The woman . . . Christ, I forget her name, she called nine-one-one and then that woman cop showed up. And that's about that.'

'All right,' I said, making my last notes. 'You said he yelled . . . did you hear him saying anything in particular?'

He wiped at his eyes again. 'I . . . I don't know. He said something.'

'And what was that? What did he say?'

Josh suddenly looked about thirty years older. 'He said . . . he said . . . "It's coming after me. It's coming after me."'

Out in the living room, I saw the reflection of red strobe lights, bouncing off the wallpapered walls, and on the porch, there were a handful of Salem Falls volunteer fire-fighters, eager to do their job. I went out on the porch and nodded to my officer, and spotted Skip Durban, the chief of the volunteer fire department. He weighs about three hundred pounds and needs to have a specially tailored fire coat, but he's been the chief for nearly a decade, and while his department may be volunteer, it is very professional.

'Looks like an untimely death, Skip, but you know the drill. Can't move the body until the county medical examiner says he's dead.'

Skip, being a good sort, just nodded and said, 'State police coming?'

I said to Melanie, 'Would you take care of that, then? Contact the State Police Major Crimes Unit and the medical examiner. Sort of slipped my mind.'

Melanie looked coolly at me and said, 'Not a problem, Chief.'

Skip said, 'Mind if I get a look?'

I said, 'Give me a couple of minutes first, all right, Skip? I haven't seen the poor bastard yet . . . just want to get first impressions by myself.'

Skip said, 'Sure.'

And I was going to ask him to have his guys switch off the red strobe lights, but he was being so agreeable, I let it pass.

Back in the house, I ignored my three interviewees and decided it was finally time to see the death scene for myself, I went up the first floor steps – nice wide oak steps – and then to the landing, where I detected the odor of blood and other bodily fluids. The poor guy was dead, all right. He was crumpled up on his side, facing the living room, and his throat was a bloody mess. Blood had sprayed out onto the banister and the wall, no doubt from a severed artery. I stepped a bit closer. Peter looked to be about the same age as his friend downstairs, had on jeans and black sneakers, and he had on the same kind of T-shirt, save his was short-sleeved, showing off tattoos on both bare arms. His eyes, thankfully, were closed. I looked up the stairs going up to the third floor, looked at the banister, an old, carved, ornate piece of work, matching the adjacent railings.

And my officer had been right. The railing here on the landing was low, much lower than any present-day building inspector would allow, and on either end of the railing, there were carved, decorative pieces that in fact looked like narrow corncobs. The one at the end facing the stairs going down was nice and plain. The one at the end facing the stairs going up was bloody, and it looked like the top three or so inches had been broken off.

I stepped around Peter and his pool of blood, looked upstairs to the third floor. This set of stairs was narrow and steeper, and the wood was highly polished. Easy to see what must have happened. The young guy was up on the third floor, got spooked, and tried to come downstairs quickly. Slipped on the steps, fell, and impaled his throat on that nice hundred-year-old bit of decorative railing work.

Untimely death. My officer had called it, I had confirmed it, and I was sure the medical examiner and whatever state police detective on duty tonight would sign off on it as well.

Still . . . one more thing to look at. I felt a hint of cold air on the back of my neck, a draft from somewhere, no doubt.

I looked down at Peter, saw a cassette recorder at his side, and about two feet away from his left hand, one of those miniature camcorders. I picked up the cassette recorder, reversed the tape a bit, and held it close to my ear, so I could hear what was on there. I listened for a minute, and then stopped the tape, and then played with the tape controls for a moment.

I put the cassette recorder down, picked up the camcorder, and repeated the process, looking through the narrow viewfinder, seeing what had been recorded. When I was done with that, I worked the controls one more time and then put everything back down on the floor, and then I felt that cold breeze upon the back of my neck again.

I stood up. Upstairs a door suddenly slammed shut, like the same errant breeze against my neck had caused it to close. And after that, I went downstairs, through the living room, and outside to the porch.

I smiled at the patient Skip. 'Go take a look before the circus starts.'

And the circus came and stayed for a few more hours, as the medical examiner looked at the body and confirmed that yes, indeed, the poor boy was dead, which allowed the patient volunteer firefighters of Salem Falls to remove the body and take it to the Pearson Funeral Home, next town over in Montcalm, but not before two polite and large state police detectives took their own photos, performed their own measurements, and interviewed the three witnesses. Eventually the Tolands were left in the living room with my officer Harris while Josh sat on the porch.

Then the two detectives and I huddled in the kitchen – as the morning sun started streaming through the windows – and we eventually came to the logical and only conclusion, that one Peter Grolin of Newburyport, Massachusetts, had in fact died accidentally, with no indication of foul play, and that the cassette recording and the camcorder recording showed no evidence that anything untoward had happened to the unfortunate young man.

With that we all wished that someone knew how to work the fancy coffee machine in the corner, because a hot cup of joe would sure taste good right about now, and then the taller of the two detectives said, 'So, this is the Logan place. Funny, always heard about it, but never thought I'd be inside of it . . . especially looking at a dead body. Ironic, huh?'

His partner, who was trying to decipher the controls on

the coffee machine, looked up and said, 'What about the Logan house?'

The other detective said, 'Read more than *Sports Illustrated*, maybe you'll learn something. Chief, you're a townie. Want to let my buddy here know about the Logan house?'

I smiled and said, 'Breck Logan built this place back in 1882. Was the wealthiest man in the county. Built mills along the Connecticut River and got even wealthier. Never married, never had any close relatives . . . and died in 1903.'

The detective by the coffee machine said, 'And that's it?'

The other detective laughed. 'Hell, no. The chief isn't telling you the good stuff, the gory stuff. Right?'

I nodded. 'Yeah, right. Story was . . . though never printed anywhere, that the good Mr Logan was a devil worshipper. That he led a coven of devil worshippers. That his devil worship and the worship of the others allowed both him and the town to thrive . . . and that over the years, some French-Canadian girls who came down to work in his mills disappeared. That some of their fathers came down in 1903 . . . to confront Mr Logan about it . . . and before they could get any information out of him, he went upstairs to the attic of this house and blew his head off with a shotgun. And that some of the fathers from Quebec started digging on the property . . . and found bones and skulls. End of story.'

'Right,' the detective at the table said. 'End of story, but not of lesson.'

'What lesson?' the other detective asked.

'That these nice little villages and towns, they can have the darkest and bloodiest secrets imaginable. Even a pretty little town like Salem Falls, with a fancy-schmancy downtown, nice little computer firms in the old mill buildings, still doing fine. Right, Chief?'

I smiled. 'Right.'

There came a moment, then, when the Logan house was empty, and I went back upstairs, past the blood-stained floor, and then upstairs again. I opened up the door and felt a blast of cold air on my face, and then took a set of very narrow and creaking steps up to the attic. There were boxes up there, piles of junk, and even though it was now daylight, it was still dark, with very little light streaming in from slats at either side of the attic. I rubbed my hands and looked into the darkness, and then let my eyes adjust to the lack of light. There was something off to the right. I ignored it. Kept staring into the darkness, thinking about the night, thinking about what had happened, thinking of what I had learned.

Thought about the cassette recorder, and what I had heard, the shaky and frightened voice of Peter Grolin: 'Something's going on up here, I don't know, I'm freezing Josh, I'm freezing, and oh Christ, something's coming down the stairs . . . it's coming near me . . . it's coming after me . . . it's coming after me!'

Then the sound of something falling, something gurgling, and then the whisper of static.

And what I had seen on the camcorder viewing screen, filmed in night vision: the same narrow steps leading up to the attic, the door opening, and an illuminated shape, oozing down, coming closer, closer . . .

An illuminated shape.

Like the one I could see from the corner of my eye, in the attic with me.

I took a breath. 'You didn't have to do that. I know you were provoked. But you didn't have to do that.'

The shape flickered, moved. I took another breath. 'I promise you, things won't change. They won't get a permit for the bed-and-breakfast. And there won't be any more ghost hunters. No more trespassers. I promise. Okay?'

The shape flickered one more time and then disappeared,

but not before I saw what was there, the slightly out-of-focus image of a man wearing a turn-of-the-last-century frock coat and pants, with a head that looked like a bloody, shattered pumpkin.

As I went back out to the porch, I had a warm thought, that maybe the weekend could be salvaged after all. My wife and girls would be pleased. Outside, Josh was slowly loading some gear into his white van, the Toland couple was having a heated discussion at one end of the porch, and the two state police detectives were conferring over their notebooks. I came down the stairs, yawning, and then the younger state detective – the one who had finally got the coffee machine up and running – came over to me and shook my hand.

'Nice to have met you, Chief,' he said. 'And I'm sure you hope you don't see us again, any time soon.'

I gave his hand a firm shake, smiling, since he was right, since you only saw state police detectives in my line of work for serious matters. 'If you don't take offense, yeah, you're absolutely right.'

He grinned and looked around at the Logan house, at its neighboring homes, and said, 'First time I've ever been in Salem Falls. Nice little town. Hell, a great little town. I've been to a lot of towns in this part of the state that are barely hanging on by their fingernails . . . but you guys have been lucky.'

'That we have,' I said.

Then the younger detective gave a forced little laugh, like he was trying to make a joke and knew he wasn't succeeding. 'You know, somebody might say that those old devil worshippers, they're still around, making sure the town still stays prosperous.'

I looked at him, kept my expression slightly amused, and finally said, 'You're right. Some might say.'

MADEEDA

Harley Jane Kozak

The August air was hot and heavy with the scent of jasmine the morning my children toddled downstairs and told me a lady was sleeping in my bed.

It was 9:30 a.m. I remember that prosaic detail because I was telling myself it wasn't an hour for the heebie-jeebies. Nor the season for cold dread. Even in a remote California canyon with no neighbors within screaming distance, no humans but the twins tugging at my hands and the baby in my belly. And there were chickens outside, left by the previous owner, hardly the trappings of a haunted house. It was a faux-rustic house, 1970s casual chic. Very unscary. *Chickens. Don't be one*, I told myself and let the children pull me toward the staircase. Our overfed dog, Tooth, lumbered behind.

If someone were in the house, I'd have heard. That's the beauty of old, ratty, creaky, in-need-of-renovation, soft pine floors. And an old, ratty, paranoid spaniel. I climbed thirteen steps from the landing to the second floor, each one a warning system, the boys ahead of me, Tooth's toe-nails clattering alongside me.

The bed was in disarray. The comforter, all bunched up on my husband's side of the bed, could hide a couple of bodies. I moved closer, telling Tooth to stop whining. The twins were there already, standing on tiptoe to look under the covers.

'She's not here,' Charlie said, at the same moment Paco said, 'Where did she go?'

'She went back to twelvey twenty-one-y,' Charlie added.

One down pillow still bore the imprint of a head. I tossed it aside and yanked the sheet toward the wrought-iron headboard, smoothing it down and tucking it in. A faint scent – Shalimar? – seemed to waft upward, but that had to be my imagination. Pregnant nose. 'What did the lady look like?' I asked, adopting a cheery, sitcom-mom voice.

'She has purple hair,' Charlie said. 'Curly.'

'All of her is purple,' added Paco.

The boys' consonants, like their numbers, were still works in progress, so the words came out 'coolly' and 'people.' I found the description reassuring.

'Part of her is green,' Charlie said. 'She has a fancy dress. A blue dress.'

'A ugly dress,' Paco said. 'She's a mean lady.'

Charlie nodded. 'A mean witch.'

That night, when I told Richard, my husband, that the boys had seen a green and purple witch in our bed, he did not express concern. He did not, in fact, look up from the Dow Jones Industrials. 'Hm. What'd you do?'

'I made the bed.'

I did not mention to him that I'd already made the bed earlier that morning.

Not that the boys couldn't drag a chair across the room in order to climb onto the bed and undo the sheets. This is what I told myself the next afternoon at the farmers' market, two freeway stops away. Except the chair had been in its usual place by the closet, and the boys, at age two plus, were not in the habit of covering their tracks. It wasn't age-appropriate behavior. Even now Paco, in the double stroller, was brazenly throwing grapes at a sparrow while telling me he wasn't throwing grapes at a sparrow. But I couldn't think of another explanation, except for pregnant brain. Could I swear that I had made the bed? Not absolutely, but beyond a reasonable doubt. *You made your bed and now you have to lie in it*, my grandma would say, but in fact, I made my bed every morning precisely so I wouldn't be tempted to lie in it, minutes later, for a quick two-hour nap. Sleep was a siren song these days, my drug, my crack cocaine. Sleep was more seductive than sex, food, or True Love. The only thing stronger was the biological imperative to answer the cry of 'Mommy!'

'Mommy, Charlie see Madeeda,' Paco said.

'Who's Madeeda?' I glanced down at my son's upturned face. Charlie was slumped next to him, asleep, mouth open.

'The bad witch.'

'The one who was sleeping in Mommy and Daddy's bed?'

Paco nodded. A stand of irises distracted me, sending an odor my way. And something else – vanilla? Jasmine? 'Where did you see her?' I asked.

'Not me. Charlie.'

'Where did Charlie see her?'

'Here.'

I stopped instantly, looking around. Another shopper bumped into me from behind. He apologized. I counter-apologized. He maneuvered past me. I moved the stroller over to a grassy area and squatted. 'Paco. When did Charlie see the lady? Back near the car?'

'Right now,' Paco said. 'In the clouds. Twelvey twenty-one-y.' And before I could stop him, he was rousing his brother by squeezing his hair.

Charlie woke up hot and cranky, and it took several ounces of apple juice and some string cheese to restore equilibrium. He had, as it turned out, seen the witch fly across the sky. And 'twelvey twenty-one-y' did indeed figure into it; Charlie was very clear about that, but whether it

76

described a particular cloud, time, or latitude was hard to say.

That night when I told Richard that the boys could apparently eavesdrop on each other's dreams, he was so engrossed in the Somdahl & Associates prospectus he was reading, he could only manage a 'Huh.' I decided it wasn't the time to announce we had a recurring witch in our midst.

Over the next few days Madeeda's presence in our conversation was pervasive, and I found myself ascribing to her a voice, deep and foreign-accented, whispering numbers in my ear. Which was odd. I, unlike the men in my life, found numbers uninteresting. I formed a picture of Madeeda, too, a lithe creature with a concave belly. Of course, most people seemed lithe to me, as the baby in my belly grew heavier and my pregnancy shorts grew tighter. It was too hot for clothes, and I let the boys run around wearing only Pull-Ups, but my own choices were limited. I wasn't Californian enough to be less than fully dressed, given my figure. I cranked up the AC in the house, but it produced more noise than cold air, the creaks and thuds emanating from the vents like captives in a dungeon. I needed to stay out of the sun and off my feet, Dr Iqbal had said. So I plopped the boys at the kitchen table, pointed a desk fan at them, and brought out crayons. 'Draw Madeeda for me,' I said.

My attention was drawn to the bay window, where the afternoon light streamed through, showing the dirt on the outside, the dust inside, and a crack up in one corner. I needed a professional window washer, but even a walk through the Yellow Pages sounded exhausting, and they'd probably be prohibitively expensive, like everything else in LA. Richard had loved the look of this imitation farmhouse, snapped up in a short sale, but we'd been unprepared for how expensive quaint can be. Maintenance had not been high on the previous owner's agenda in his steady march toward bankruptcy.

As I watched, the crack in the window seemed to grow. Which was impossible, of course, but—

'Mommy. Look.' Charlie tugged at my sleeve to show me his Madeeda, a stick figure without arms, which is to say, an inverted V. Paco's was a close-up, a large, torsoless head with vacant eyes.

'Very nice, guys,' I said, and turned back to the window. The crack was halfway down now. Surely that wasn't normal window behavior. A windshield hit with a flying pebble might do that, but could a regular window just fracture for no reason? I was scaring myself. I forced my attention back to the table and picked up a crayon. I would sketch. I liked sketching.

'That's Madeeda,' Charlie said, after a moment.

'This?' I'd drawn a gaunt woman with a green face and long purple hair flowing in cascades around her head. She had a flat chest and ballerina-skinny arms. Because I can't do credible feet, hers appeared to be *en pointe*, a few inches above the ground, giving her a floaty, untethered quality. 'This is what Madeeda looks like?' I asked.

Charlie nodded. Paco nodded.

'Twelvy twenty-one-y,' Charlie said. 'Madeeda.'

'And Madeeda says if we don't listen we are going to hell,' Paco added.

That night while chopping vegetables, I phoned Karen, my cousin in Denver. 'Is it normal for twins to share an imaginary playmate?'

Karen snorted. 'I can't even get my twins to share breakfast cereal. I need two of every thing, on separate shelves. It's like keeping kosher. What's that noise?'

'I'm chopping carrots.'

'You're cooking at – what, ten p.m.?'

'Only nine here. It's for tomorrow. Crock-Pot beef bourguignon. I'm doing a lot of night cooking now. It's the weirdest thing; I can't sleep. I can always sleep.' I glanced at the window, illuminated by the back porch light. It now sported two full-length vertical cracks.

'How's Richard's new job?'

'Like his old job, but without the friends. Long hours. Lots of stress.'

'So what's going on?'

'The boys are seeing a witch.'

There was a pause. The *chop chop* of my carrots sounded preter-naturally loud. Would it be more shocking, or less, if I'd said, 'the boys are seeing a psychiatrist'?

'A nice witch?' Karen asked finally.

'Well, they say she's a mean witch. But I'm a mean mommy half the time, so take that with a grain of salt. I don't get a bad feeling from her so much as a sad one.'

'So, wait. You see her, too?'

'No, not at all. Ouch.' The serrated knife edge sliced across my finger, leaving in its wake drops of blood. They dripped onto the carrot rounds.

'Aunt Pauline saw ghosts, you know,' Karen said.

'Madeeda's a witch, not a ghost.'

'The witch has a name?'

'Mmm.' I found a SpongeBob Band-Aid in the junk drawer and ripped it open with my teeth. 'What kind of ghosts did Aunt Pauline see?'

'Apparently Grandpa stopped by the night he died. Stood at the foot of her bed in his uniform, told her to take care of Grandma. She saw a few other people on their way out, too. It was sort of her specialty.'

'I didn't know it worked like that. What about the tunnel and the white light and all the relatives waiting on the other side?' Tooth, crabby about something, started to whine. I pointed with my toe to his dog food bowl, indicating un-touched kibble.

'Some people,' Karen said, 'apparently need to make a pit stop before hitting the road.'

*

79

The plants were dying. I noticed this the next afternoon as the sun reached the picture window in the living room. My African violets, survivors of a five-day cross-country move, were all failing at the same rate, velvety leaves turning dry and brittle, pink and purple blossoms curling inward at the edges, like the stocking feet of the Wicked Witch of the East. I touched the rock-hard soil. It wasn't possible. I'd watered them yesterday. I had. I knew I had. And they'd been okay. My mother had given them to me, for luck. 'Bloom where you're planted,' she'd said. I leaned over and whispered encouragement and apology to each of them in turn, my voice cracking. It seemed to me that a faint scent of Shalimar arose from them.

'Mommy's crying,' Paco told Charlie.

'Mommy's flowers are sick,' I said, wiping my eyes. 'Maybe they don't like it here. Maybe they want to go back to Pennsylvania.'

Tooth ambled over to me. I expected him to lick my tears but instead, he threw up at my feet.

'Oh, poor doggie—' I held his shoulders, as his body heaved convulsively. When he was still again, I told the boys to stay back, then went to the kitchen for a towel.

'Tooth throw up,' Paco pointed out, as I made my awkward way to my knees to wipe up the viscous substance. The old floorboards were cracked, and I imagined the vomit seeping into it and settling, like rot.

'Madeeda make Tooth throw up,' Charlie added. 'Madeeda sick.'

'Madeeda make everything sick.'

I sat back on my heels and looked at my sons. They nodded in unison.

I called the vet, and then I called Richard. The vet got back to me right away.

'You're not making sense.' It was close to midnight when Richard came through the front door and collapsed into the recliner, still holding his briefcase. 'First you tell me Tooth was poisoned, then you say he ate a plastic bag. What'd the vet say?'

I moved aside a toy cell phone and perched on the sofa opposite him. 'He barfed up the plastic bag in the car on the way to the vet. So the vet said it was probably the plastic bag, and I could leave him overnight, but I didn't. I brought him home.' And saved us a couple hundred dollars, I thought, but didn't say, because Richard would find that irritating, would respond with 'Money's no object,' as if saying it would make it so. And anyway, it hadn't been about money; Tooth would hate to be away from us.

'He looks okay now.' Richard snapped his fingers, and Tooth shuffled over to him, heavy tail doing a slow wag. 'Is there anything to eat, by the way?'

'Beef bourguignon. And yeah, he's okay at the moment, but . . .' I looked across the room. The African violets were doing better, too. No, not just better. They looked completely fine. Thriving, in fact. Robust.

'So why are you going on about him being poisoned?'

'I'm not,' I said, unnerved now, staring at the African violets. 'The boys are. And they didn't use the word *poison*.'

Richard loosened his tie. 'What word did they use?'

' "The witch make Toof fwowe up." '

He half smiled. 'What witch?'

'Madeeda.'

The smile died. 'What?'

I blinked. 'Madeeda, That's her name. What's wrong?'

'Nothing.' He bent over to untie his shoes. The hair on top of his head was thinning; how had I never seen this before? 'Where'd they come up with that?'

'The name? I have no idea. I've asked the neighbors if it sounds like anyone who lives around here, and I've Googled her, using different spellings. Among other things, I found a South African soccer player and a dessert recipe from Sudan.'

Richard eased off his shoes. 'Why?'

'Why what?'

'Why are you Googling her?'

'Because . . . I think, you know . . . she's haunting us.'

Richard rubbed his eyes, then opened his briefcase. 'I think your next call should be to Dr Iqbal.'

'Why? I feel fine. The baby feels fine.'

He brought out a folder of papers and closed his briefcase. 'Sweetheart, you think a soccer player is poisoning the dog and the plants. You call me at work, expecting me to do something about it. I want Dr Iqbal to say it's some hormonal thing. I'd feel better.'

And I hadn't even told him about the cracked kitchen window. 'You can't be that worried,' I said. 'You never returned my call.'

'It was a bad day. Big meetings. If you'd said it was an emergency, Jillian would've put you through.'

'The meetings just now finished, at eleven p.m.?' I hated the edge in my voice.

'I'm sorry, I should've called.' He leaned back in his chair and closed his eyes, briefcase and papers still on his lap. 'We're on a triage system at the office. Life-and-death matters get handled. Everything else waits, and . . .' There was a pause. Was he asleep?

'Wake up!' I screamed. '*This* is a life-and-death matter.'

Richard's eyes flew open, and he looked as shocked as I felt. This wasn't me. I wasn't a screamer. I was a happy camper, a team player. And why was I screaming, anyway? Tooth was better. My African violets were positively hearty. I made my voice calm. 'Do you want dinner?'

'Uh—' He was at a loss now, not knowing which comment to respond to.

I sighed. 'Okay, never mind all that. What's with work? Why was it a bad day?'

He closed his eyes again. 'I don't want to talk about it.'

'I don't care if you want to talk about it. I want to know.'

'I don't want to worry you.'

'Well, there's a wrong answer. Now you *have* to tell me.'

He shook his head.

'Richard,' I said. 'Don't make me come over there and sit on you. I've been tiptoeing around this for days, around *you*, and I'm not in the mood anymore.'

With an agonized squeak, the recliner flattened out, moving my husband backward until his feet dangled off the floor. He looked like he was waiting for a root canal. Just as I was about to yell again, his eyes opened and contemplated the water-stained ceiling. 'A few weeks ago I was working on an account. I had a question about the California tax code, so I looked at the books of another account, just as a reference. A big client. Somdahl's biggest.'

'Who?' I asked.

'Clarien Industries. Pharmaceuticals. Anyhow, I looked through the Clarien profit and loss statements and compared it to their tax returns and came across . . . irregularities.'

' "Irregularities." Like, math errors?'

'That would be one interpretation.' Tooth's tail thumped on the wood floor. We both looked at him. Fast asleep. Dog dreaming. 'I brought it to Werner's attention.'

'And?'

'He said he'd look into it. Mention it to Somdahl.'

'And?'

'I didn't hear anything, so I brought it up again. With Werner. Then Somdahl himself summons me into his office. Offers me coffee, tea, fucking cappuccino, like I'm his best friend, like a prospective client. Then he blames the whole Clarien thing on Fenwick. The guy I replaced. Says Fenwick had a substance abuse problem and was unreliable, and that's why he was let go. But now Somdahl is stuck with this Clarien problem, and what are we going to do about it? If we come clean, we're talking millions in penalties, for them, maybe for us. We don't just lose the client, we get sued for malpractice, other clients think "sinking ship", and they jump. The firm wouldn't survive it. We're already down 46 percent from last year. Layoffs up another 7 percent last month. I'm doing the work of four people. We all are. Probably what drove Fenwick to drugs.'

My body was shaking. How had Richard kept this to himself? The clues had been lying around for weeks, like dust bunnies under the furniture, too troublesome for me to seek out. Somdahl & Associates, the job we'd left the East Coast for, the dream partnership, the hot corporation, the write-up in *Fortune* magazine, the big break. The opportunity of a lifetime, the one that, when it knocks, you throw open the door so fast the glass shatters. Richard hadn't needed to think twice. That was my job, the second-guessing, but I'd packed up our life, sold our house, walked away from family, friends, history, a neighborhood filled with other kids. Other moms.

'Richard.'

'What?'

'You can't be part of a cover-up.'

He was silent for a moment. Then, 'I don't have to. I just forget I saw it. Then Somdahl's secretary misfiles Clarien.'

'That's the definition of a cover-up. You don't have to be running the paper shredder to be part of it.'

'Who do I tell? The SEC? And what if they don't respond? Nothing comes of it. But there goes my career.'

'Somdahl seems to think they'll respond—'

'Somdahl can't take the chance.' Richard rubbed his face. 'And what if it happens like he says? The firm goes under. Everyone you met last month at the picnic, all those people unemployed. Stocks worthless, pensions gone. Because of me.'

'Not because of you, because of stuff that happened before you got there. Don't let them guilt you into a conspiracy—'

'Nobody likes a whistle-blower—'

'I like you, I'll—'

'There's no profit in it, no percentage—'

'Goddamn it, Richie, you're sounding like them.' I felt the edges of hysteria closing in on me. 'And isn't it illegal, by the way? What they're hiding? What you're hiding now? Because the thought of you behind bars is frankly scarier than who likes you or doesn't like you at fucking Somdahl & Associates.'

Richard was staring at me now openly. I hadn't used the *F* word since the birth of the boys. 'I don't need you coming unglued,' he said. 'That's not helping. And I'm not making any decisions tonight.'

Yes, you are, I wanted to scream. But I saw myself reflected behind him, in the mirror over the fireplace mantel. Big-bellied and wild-eyed. *Paranoid. Hormonal. Hysterical. Sees witches.*

I took a deep breath, as deep as the baby pushing against my diaphragm would allow. Enforced calm. 'Want some beef bourguignon?'

Richard shook his head, still staring at me. 'I'm not hungry anymore.'

I went into the kitchen, Tooth trailing me. I unplugged the Crock-Pot, dumped its contents into a colander, turned the faucet on it full blast, picked out the beef, and threw the rest in the compost bin. I fed the meat to Tooth, a piece at a time. He rewarded me by licking my fingers clean and not throwing up.

I felt ill. I wanted to rewind the clock, go back an hour to when my biggest problem was witches. I wanted to know less, or I needed to know more. I needed sleep. I looked at the bay window, and all thoughts of sleep fled.

The window was perfect. Uncracked.

I walked, shaking, back to the living room. Richard was snoring now. I bent to put an afghan over him, then read, through his splayed fingers, the cover page of the report on his lap. 'Somdahl & Associates Internal Memo – do not photocopy or distribute.' I began to ease it out of his hands, but he stirred, so I let it go. I covered him with the afghan and climbed the creaking stairs.

I lay a long time with Tooth up against my belly in the king-sized bed. I didn't think I could sleep, but suddenly I was dreaming, haunted by a series of numbers that I struggled to focus on. They were important numbers, I knew, like the gestational age of a baby, or a dosage of medicine, so I tried to memorize them. But there were ten of them, much harder to keep track of than twelvey twenty-one-y. I realized I'd been dreaming of the numbers each night, over and over, like the fairy tale of the Twelve Dancing Princesses, and that each morning the numbers were gone.

And by morning they were gone.

I woke to the sound of a door closing. Richard going for a run, maybe. It was just after five, still dark outside. My mind felt fuzzy, like bits of brain had been left behind in my dreams. I lay there drowsy, heartsick, anxious. I tried to focus on what we'd do if – when? – Richard lost his job, how we'd live, but instead my mind came up with an alternate spelling of Madeeda: *Matita*. Paco and Charlie didn't distinguish between *Ds* and *Ts*. I sat up, determined to Google this. It was a pointless impulse, as relevant as Madame Defarge knitting by the guillotine, but I couldn't help myself.

On the kitchen table was a note: 'Gone in to work early. I'll call. Don't worry.' Early? It was practically the middle of the night. And was there ever a command as unenforceable as 'Don't worry'?

I woke the computer and typed in 'matita' and clicked on the first of a few hundred thousand hyperlinks.

Matita Pereira, an elusive bird known for its melancholic song. The bird is one form taken by the Saci, a one-legged mulatto child,

86

legendary character in Brazilian folklore, who wears a magical red cap that makes him disappear and reappear, and requires him to grant wishes to anyone who steals it.

What was I to make of this? Brazilian folklore was no more meaningful than South African soccer players and Sudanese desserts. Although I did have a red baseball cap, left in the trunk of my car by someone from Richard's office. Not stolen, of course, but not mine either, I kept forgetting to return it, and it often came in handy when I got caught bare-headed in the merciless California sun.

I slumped in the desk chair. What did it matter? My Madeeda obsession was a distraction from the real problem, Richard's ethical dilemma, now my dilemma. Could we, as Richard proposed, forget it? Was doing nothing the wisest course, financially? Almost certainly. Morally? No. But was this my decision to make? What about everyone else at Somdahl & Associates? What about our own three children? Didn't we owe them a roof over their heads?

Tooth came into the room and stretched, wanting to be let outside. 'I wish,' I said to him, 'that I knew what to do.'

Something shifted inside me, something palpable, physical, and I realized I was sitting in something wet. As though my bladder had gone out of control, or my water had broken. But it wasn't amniotic fluid or urine. The brown leather chair was darkening rapidly, and when I touched it, my fingers came away red with blood.

'Bleeding in early pregnancy can often be insignificant.' Dr Iqbal sat on a swivel stool at the foot of the exam table. The wand in his hand made little circular motions on my bare stomach, now wet with gel. His eyes were on the black-and-white TV screen, which showed a grainy image of my unborn daughter. 'However—'

'However—?' I looked at his face, trying to find reassurance. The hospital lighting did not become him, 'She's okay, though?' I persisted. 'You can tell, right? You'd know, right?'

'There's movement, her heart rate's normal, cord's not wrapped around her.'

'But—?'

'But bleeding in the last trimester's never good.' He glanced at me. 'This one's a head-scratcher. It could be placenta previa, but it's not. It's not placental abruption. And it's not labor. Also, you're not bleeding now. You're sure it was actual bleeding? Not just spotting?'

'It was flowing. Gushing. All over the chair I was sitting in.' Which was leather, at least. I'd cleaned it as well as I could, waiting for the ambulance. Cleaned myself, too, although traces of blood remained on my inner thighs.

'And the color? True red? Or brownish? Pinkish?'

'Red. Ketchup red.' It was a relief to say it, with no equivocation. A relief to be here in the hospital, all anti-septic and stainless steel and charm-free linoleum. No creaky floors. No personality. No rustic appeal.

Dr Iqbal switched off the monitor, then grabbed a paper towel and wiped the gel from his wand and from my stomach. 'Richard still here?'

'He just left. Went home to take care of the kids. A friend's been watching them since five thirty a.m., but she has to get to work.' She wasn't really a friend; she was a woman I'd met exactly twice at a Mommy and Me class. But I had her phone number, and she'd come over at once, without hesitation. She was a friend now, I realized.

'Well, let's take a wait-and-see attitude. The baby's thirty-six weeks, so if she had to come out now, she could. But she's better off staying in, and without a clear reason to induce . . . I'll keep you here a day or two for observation.'

I nodded, suddenly dead tired. If the baby was safe, that was all that mattered. Somdahl & Associates seemed very far away at the moment, and as I lapsed into a half sleep, I thought how absurd it was, in this overlit hospital room, to believe in witches.

And once more I dreamed of numbers.

'Don't squish your mommy,' Richard said.

'They're okay,' I said. Charlie and Paco were in the hospital bed with me, Charlie holding the TV remote and Paco pressing the buttons that raised and lowered the mattress. I'd missed them. I was never away from them.

'I'm gonna use the bathroom, and then we'll go. The sitter's coming at noon.' Richard had called a babysitting agency so he could go back to work. This was a good thing; I'd need backup help when I went into labor.

'Is that your bathroom?' Paco asked, pointing to the door that Richard closed behind him. I nodded.

'Madeeda has a bathroom, too,' Charlie said. 'And Madeeda has a curtain in her room.' He pointed to the curtain separating me from the empty bed across the room. 'Madeeda has a TV on the ceiling.'

'Just like Mommy.' I smiled, playing along. 'So Madeeda lives in a hospital now?'

Charlie nodded. 'In this hospital.'

My smile faltered. 'Really?'

'Upstairs,' Paco said.

I felt cold suddenly. 'Do you know where upstairs?'

'Uh-huh.'

'You could take me there?' I asked.

Paco shook his head. 'Paco and Charlie can't go there. Only Mommy.'

'Why?'

'Madeeda told us.'

'How would I find it, though? Her room?'

Charlie said, 'The numbers!' Paco laughed and bounced on the bed. 'Twelvey twenty-one-y.'

I waited until Richard and the boys left, then got out of bed. A nurse had just checked my vital signs and done foetal

89

monitoring, so I was unhooked from everything and free to move around. I didn't hesitate. I wrapped a second hospital gown over the first, backward, so that the gap in the back was covered, then padded out to the elevator banks in my socks and loafers. Once inside, I pressed the button marked 12.

It was quiet on the twelfth floor. Compared to Admissions and the bustle of Labor & Delivery, it was a graveyard. I followed the signs for the east corridor. E.

The nurses' station was empty. I walked past it, down a hallway with a flickering fluorescent light. This was an old section of the hospital, unrenovated. I found myself shivering as I walked.

Some of the doors with the 12E prefix were closed, some of the rooms unoccupied, and the few patients I saw through open doorways were asleep. It seemed like a place people came to die.

I was whispering as I walked. '. . . twelve E nineteen, twelve E twenty. Twelvie twenty-one.' I paused before the open door. There were nameplates for the two patients, e and w. The bed on the west side of the room was empty. It was the patient in 12E21e that I'd come to see. M. Quadros, according to the nameplate.

Even in her sleep I recognized her. She was younger than me, but not much. Long, curly hair, a reddish purple that could only come out of a bottle. Memorable hair, even if you've only seen it once, even though it now had an inch of black roots showing at the scalp. Her face was pale and showed the remnants of bruises. Her long, lovely arms were bruised, too, purple and green around the sites where blood had been drawn or tubes inserted. She was skinny, the sad little blue gown and blanket not thick enough to hide the bones jutting through. She no longer smelled like Shalimar.

'Hello,' I said to her, but she didn't respond. I touched her face, very gently, but she didn't respond to that either.

I wondered how long she'd lain there. I'd seen her only a month before.

We'd met at the Somdahl & Associates Fourth of July barbecue. Even with the hair she wouldn't have stood out among the crowd of strangers, and I, as a company spouse, wouldn't have made an impression on her either, but for a clumsy gesture. A drunken partner had spilled a pitcher of beer on her T-shirt, and instead of apologizing made lewd remarks about how good some women look wet. Another man tried to intervene, no doubt thinking 'sexual harassment lawsuit' but the drunk wouldn't give way gracefully. While the two men worked it out, I'd walked over to the beer-soaked woman and touched her shoulder. I had an extra shirt in my car, I told her. When she hesitated, I put an arm around her, and she let me lead her away.

'Thanks,' she said. 'Asshole. All week I work for him. Now I must eat and drink with him.' She had an accent that I couldn't identify. Some Romance language.

'Who is he?' I asked.

She'd looked at me with a raised eyebrow. 'Albert Werner. The CFO. You must be new.'

'My husband is,' I'd said. 'I'm just the spouse. Jane England.'

'You're married to—'

'Richard England.'

Her eyelashes fluttered, a butterfly's gesture. 'Your husband is Richard England.'

'Yes, do you know him?'

There was a pause. 'Yes.'

We were at the car now and she was waiting, so I opened the trunk and she added, 'You are the Good Samaritan.'

'No problem.' I pulled a pink T-shirt out of the emergency diaper bag. Clipped to the bag was a plastic-framed photo of Paco and Charlie with Tooth. 'I have twin toddlers, so someone's always spilling something on me, or my breasts used to leak, when I was nursing. I'm just in the habit of carrying around a change of clothes.'

'I didn't realize Richard England had children,' she said, touching the photo. Staring at it.

It was one of those remarks – actually, it was the third remark in two minutes – that sent a shiver of sexual jealousy down my spine. But she looked at me then, intently, and said, 'Your husband. He's tall, yes? Large nose.'

I nodded.

'Yes,' she said. 'Last week, I carried heavy boxes into the conference room, for the meeting. Eight men around the table, and only your husband, he jumps up to hold the door and then he takes all the boxes from me, to help me. All the boxes.'

I didn't know what to say to that, but she turned her back to me and pulled off her beer-soaked shirt. I looked at her flawless skin, her narrow ribs, her spine, her lacy little bra straps, and I was relieved that I didn't need to feel jealousy.

She turned around, dressed once more. 'Jane, Thank you. It really is kind of you to give me the shirt off your back. I can't think of many people at this picnic who would do this. I won't forget it.'

I reached out to pluck from her wild hair a tiny piece of paper caught there. A Band-Aid wrapper, escaped from the diaper bag.

'And you have twins,' she said, smiling for the first time. 'This is very lucky. A blessing. Boys, yes? And a dog.'

'Yes.' I smiled back at her. 'I'm sorry, I don't know your name.'

'Matilda,' she said. At least, that's the name I guessed at, but it was hard to know, because it came out quickly, except for the middle syllable, drawn out so musically. *Mateelda* . . .

Later I noticed that she'd left her red baseball cap in the trunk of my car.

*

The nurse's shoes were silent, and I only saw her when I turned. I gasped. She jumped.

'Jesus!' she said, a hand to her heart. 'Wasn't expecting anyone.' She wore turquoise scrubs and Nike running shoes.

'Is it not visiting hours?' I asked.

'No, it's just you're her first visitor. On my shift, anyway.' The nurse checked her watch and made a note on the chart held in a binder.

'I just now found out she was in the hospital,' I said. The nurse was reading the chart and didn't reply. 'How long has she been here?'

'This floor? Five days.'

'And how long in the hospital?'

She flipped a page. 'Admitted ten days ago to the ER, then surgery, then intensive care, and then up here.'

'What is "up here", exactly?'

The nurse looked up at me, glanced down at my stomach, and turned back to the chart. *Patient confidentiality rules*, I imagined her thinking. 'This is a hospice room. She's a DNR. Do Not Resuscitate.'

Madeeda was dying. I took a deep breath. 'What happened to her?'

She looked up again, and her eyes narrowed. 'You okay to be up and walking around?'

I nodded. 'I'm fine. I'm just . . . Sorry, she was a friend, but I only just now heard about her.'

'Why don't you sit down?'

'Okay.' I perched on the leatherette chair next to the bed. Thinking, *We're dressed alike, Madeeda and I. Sharing clothes again*. 'What happened to her? Can you tell me?'

'Assaulted,' she said. 'And left for dead. It was in the paper.'

'Oh, God.' My chest heaved at the thought. 'Do they know who did it?'

She checked a catheter and made a note on the chart. 'All

I know is they had cops outside ICU. But once her brain functioning stopped, they pulled the security.'

Since she was no use to the cops anymore. And no danger to anyone else. 'But no one's visited her?' I looked at the elaborate tropical arrangement on the bedside table, not quite fresh. A Somdahl & Associates business card peeked out from among the calla lilies. 'No one from her office?'

The nurse wrapped a blood pressure cuff around Madeeda's bruised arm. Her movements were gentle but efficient. 'Where'd she work? We figured she was with the government.'

My throat went dry. 'Why would you think that?'

'Her ICU nurse. She said the people in the waiting room looked like they were gathered for a tax audit. Short hair, sensible shoes, no flowers.'

'No, she was a secretary,' I said. 'Somdahl & Associates. No one there wears sensible shoes.' How could you work in a place and not have coworkers come visit? Even in a coma, I'd like to think someone might keep me company. 'Can I ask you,' I said, 'what will happen when she dies? I mean, will you call people and notify them?'

'People in general? No.' She looked again at the chart, and flipped a page. Her eyebrows lifted, a spark of surprise, quickly masked.

A buzzer sounded, and a disembodied voice asked for a Nurse Shayne to please come to room 12E13w stat. 'Excuse me,' she said and left quickly, taking the chart with her.

I had to follow her. Taciturn as she was, I had to make her tell me more, tell me something, anything. I stood shakily, clumsy with the weight of the baby, gave a last look to Madeeda, then left the room.

The nurse was already moving around the corner, out of sight. But there, next to the door, in a tiny alcove, was a cart on wheels. In the cart were binders. Patients' charts. A dozen or more. Clearly labeled. I grabbed 'M. Quadros. 12E21e.'

I read the binder tabs and flipped to 'patient information'. I was terrified to be caught by the nurse, and half afraid, too, that Labor & Delivery would have sent out a search party by now. But there it was. Under 'notes' was an arrow, pointing to a business card stuck in the tab page's plastic sleeve.

On the card was a number. Familiar, like something I'd seen in a dream.

Important, like the gestational age of a baby or a dosage of medicine, but more common: a phone number. It belonged to someone named Bruce Schoenbrod, who worked in the office of the United States Attorney.

You could argue that telling the truth once you're pretty sure the jig is up is less virtuous than telling the truth because it's the right thing to do. I didn't really care about virtue that day. I just wanted to keep Richard out of federal prison.

I talked to Richard from the phone next to my bed in Labor & Delivery. I gave him the number and told him to call it and tell Bruce Schoenbrod everything. I told him that if he didn't make the call, I would. There wasn't any doubt in my mind; Madeeda had already given information to the US Attorney. The US Attorney had listened. Somdahl & Associates was going down, with or without my husband's statement, but unless he came clean before the feds moved in, he'd go down, too.

I don't know why I understood these things with such clarity. I don't know why Richard listened to me. I don't know why Bruce Schoenbrod had picked the week after to seek indictments, and not the week before.

I don't know why a woman who'd known me for half an hour chose to save my husband, when six of Richard's colleagues ended up on trial. Five, after Albert Werner put a bullet through his brain while out on bail. I could only guess.

Somdahl & Associates crashed, along with Clarien, the pharmaceutical company, and two others whose files turned up 'irregularities'. A lot of people suffered financial loss, unemployment, near-devastation as a result. Including us. But through all of it I felt lucky. Blessed. And able to sleep nights, sleep deeply, from the moment Richard made that phone call. But only for three weeks.

Madeeda died the day after I saw her in the hospital. Twenty-one days later my daughter was born. We named her Grace.

HOUSE OF HORRORS

S. W. Hubbard

'That'll be fifty-eight seventy-five with tax,' the greasy guy at the ticket window said. John winced as the clerk drew the credit card out of his reluctant fingers.

'You're buying a happy family memory,' his wife murmured in his ear.

Happy my ass. Day one of the Harrigan family-togetherness weekend at the Jersey Shore: blistering sunburns for all.

Day two: jellyfish attack.

Day three: riptide warning.

So Miriam declared a boardwalk excursion. No problem. Give the kids fifty bucks and let them have at it. He and Miriam could walk on the beach and watch the pounding surf. But no, this was *togetherness* weekend. So each person had to choose one activity, and everyone else had to go along cheerfully, John swore if his wife didn't stop reading these damn parenting advice books he was going to cut up her library card.

Christopher had chosen the bumper cars, Grace the spinning teacups, Miriam the Ferris wheel. But for a jaded teenager like Gordon, only one thing would do.

The House of Horrors.

Blood oozed from the house's masonry. Hideous shrieks blared from its cracked windows. A vulture hovered over the spiked door. Before the clerk brought the credit card slip to be signed, John made one last bid to dodge the cheesy tourist trap. Crouching down so he could look their skinny little girl in the eye, he asked, 'Grace, do you want to go into this haunted house? It's just pretend scary, but if you're afraid, I could take you somewhere else.'

'Dad!' Gordon protested. 'That's not fair! I did Grace's lame teacups. She has to do this.'

John opened his mouth to scold, then closed it again at Miriam's warning look. This beach weekend was their first significant outing since they'd gotten Grace. They were supposed to be celebrating the expansion of their family, not squabbling and sulking.

John studied the nine-year-old. There was a transparent quality to her, she was so slight. Could something scary possibly be good for her after all she'd been through? Her pale green-gold eyes stared at him unblinkingly as the wind whipped her fine hair into a staticky halo around her head. She conveyed neither anxiety nor eagerness, just a steady trust in him as a father.

A trust he'd done nothing, as yet, to earn.

Miriam had connected with the child from the moment she'd seen her picture on the website of foster children awaiting permanent homes. For John, the paternal attachment hadn't formed quite so readily. He worried it never would.

Not that Grace was a difficult child. In fact, she was almost absurdly easy to take care of. She ate what she was served, went to bed without complaint, and did her homework with painstaking attention to detail. John found her compliance unnerving. On top of that, she was so damn quiet! She'd slip into a room so silently he never knew she was there. He'd look up to find her watching him. Last week he'd nearly sawed off his thumb when she appeared out of nowhere in his basement workshop.

'She does it because she craves your attention and doesn't

know how to get it,' Miriam explained. Insert knife and twist. He wanted to do right by this little girl, he really did. But he wasn't sure he'd ever feel for her the visceral bond he felt for his two sons. 'Don't worry,' Miriam had assured him. 'You'll grow to love her. Give it time.'

The clerk slapped down the credit card slip and slid a pen across the ticket counter. John watched as Grace carefully studied each person in her new family. She would see annoyance on Gordons face, concern on Miriam's, and finally, fear on Christopher's. Only a year older than Grace, Christopher was a sensitive soul, upset by life's smallest tragedies – signs for lost pets, roadkill, a stranger's passing funeral procession. The haunted house had him looking decidedly queasy.

Grace turned back to John. 'I want to go. If it gets too scary, I'll grab on to Christopher. He'll protect me.'

John and Miriam exchanged a smile. Grace had succeeded in bolstering Christopher and appeasing Gordon in one move. She'd learned quite a bit about managing brothers in just three weeks.

PURCHASE YOUR SOUVENIR PHOTO AS YOU EXIT. YOU'LL KNOW WHAT YOU LOOK LIKE WHEN YOU'VE SEEN A GHOST! The signs hung over a bank of computer monitors in the entranceway to the House of Horrors, each screen showing a different group of gullible tourists, their eyes opened wide, their mouths perfect Os of shock. John hustled the younger kids along, and they joined a line of teenagers waiting to pass through Purgatory's Portal.

Rowdy and eager to call attention to themselves, the older kids swarmed around a lean boy with droopy jeans and a mop of blond hair that he repeatedly flicked out of his eyes. The biggest fish in this little school of minnows, he let his hand rest suggestively on one girl's hip, while shoving the other boys around and insulting their manhood.

'Hey,' he called out to the ticket taker, 'what should we do if my friend shits his pants in there?'

Miriam shot them a ferocious look, and the boy made a show of apologizing.

'Oh, pardon me, ma'am. I didn't mean to use profanity in the presence of women and children.'

The gang of friends howled with laughter, as Gordon tried to disappear into the woodwork. Meanwhile, Christopher was busy reading the signs posted all around them. IF YOU'RE PARALYZED WITH FEAR, STAND STILL AND SCREAM. SOMETHING WILL COME AND GET YOU! BE ALERT FOR FLYING KNIVES. DON'T WORRY – THE BATS DON'T BITE.

'Dad.' Christopher tugged on his father's sleeve. 'Maybe we shouldn't go in there. Bats can spread rabies.'

'Ooo, maybe we shouldn't go in,' the blond kid said, imitating Christopher's earnest, high-pitched voice. 'Ya hear that?' He shoved one of his crew. 'You might get rabies and start foaming at the mouth.'

Christopher flushed bright red, as Gordon tried to pretend he didn't know his family. But Grace stared the teenager down, her pointy chin thrust forward, sixty pounds of defiance. While John weighed whether saying something to the teens would make matters better or worse, a green light flashed and a recorded voice intoned, 'Next group – prepare to meet your doom!' The gang of kids stepped into the House of Horrors, their screams echoing back into the waiting area.

'Dad? Dad? Where are you?'

They'd only taken about twenty steps into the House of Horrors, and already Christopher sounded like he was heading for a meltdown.

'I'm right behind you, buddy. Don't worry – you can't get lost.' The 'tour', John belatedly understood, took place entirely in the dark. It was so completely black they couldn't see one another, although John knew Gordon was in the lead, guided by tiny pinpricks of red light. Miriam followed, then Grace and Christopher. John brought up the rear, keeping a reassuring hand on his son's shoulder.

'Augh! Something grabbed me!' Gordon screamed.

Christopher clutched his father's hand. 'Help him, Dad!'

'He's okay. There are people behind curtains who reach out and touch you, that's all.'

Indeed, Gordon was now laughing. 'This is insane. Wait'll you guys get to this next part.'

A bright light flashed, revealing a noir tableau: a man in a grave, covered by writhing snakes.

This time John choked back a scream. He hated snakes, even fake ones. His heart rate ratcheted up; beads of cold sweat broke out on his neck. 'How are you doing up there, Grace?' he asked when his blood stopped pounding in his ears.

'I'm fine.' Her reedy voice sounded steadier than anyone else's.

Next the solid floor gave way to something squishy that sucked at their shoes.

Christopher reared back. 'What's that?'

John nudged him forward. 'Soft plastic. You're imagining something worse. That's what makes it scary.' John congratulated himself on sounding so calm. Truth was, he hated not knowing what would happen next, hated feeling out of control. Whoever designed the House of Horrors knew what they were doing. He was afraid.

Bang! Another brilliant flash revealed a leering face and a smoking gun.

'Aieee!'

Miriam, screeching like a banshee. John wondered how close they were to the end. He listened for sounds of the teenagers ahead of them, but heard nothing. Maybe it was almost over.

More grasping hands, more slimy surfaces. They felt their

way across a rocking bridge, squeezed though a passageway where growling animals exhaled on them, and finally turned a corner into the light.

'We made it!' Christopher shouted as he stepped into the lobby.

'Awesome! That rocked!' Gordon said.

'Yeah, it was really cool.' The daylight restored Christopher's bravado. 'What was your favorite part? I bet yours was the snakes, Dad.'

'Oh, definitely the snakes.' John put his hand on Grace's shoulder. 'How about you, honey? Are you mad at the boys for taking you into that awful place?'

She looked up at him soberly. 'I'm not mad. None of it was real.'

'Let's see our picture,' Christopher shouted, running over to the computer monitors.

John followed his wife and children, passing the group of now-quiet teenagers waiting restlessly near the exit. The blond boy wasn't with them. The prettiest of the girls complained to the others. 'Oh my God, can we just *go*? Shane's stunts are getting so *old*.'

'There we are. Number seven.' Gordon pointed out their group.

They studied the monitors, laughing and pointing out their ridiculous expressions.

John stood silent. There was something off about that picture. Then it clicked.

Grace wasn't in it.

Mirim and Grace napped in the back of the minivan; Christopher played with his Game Boy; Gordon rode shotgun with John, controlling the radio as they drove home.

John still stewed over Grace's absence from the House of Horrors photo. 'Why does it bother you so much?' Miriam had asked as they packed to leave. 'We weren't going to buy the picture anyway.'

'I just don't understand how she could have gotten cut out. She was right in the middle of the group.'

'She must've slipped ahead of Gordon at one point.' Miriam's voice held no concern. 'It was so dark, and things kept brushing up against me. I wouldn't have noticed.'

John wanted to accept the logical explanation, yet remained troubled. Of the five of them, why did it have to be Grace who was omitted from the family photo? It was as if the House of Horrors knew she was a foster child, not a real Harrigan. She didn't act like it bothered her, but who knew? She held her emotions close. No drama queen, Grace.

Is that why he had trouble warming up to her? Because she was so unlike his image of what a little girl – a daughter – should be? Where were the giggles and hugs and silly songs? The tears and pouts and stomped feet? Maybe that's the daughter he would have gotten if he had let Miriam go through another pregnancy as she pushed forty. But John was a student of statistics, and he simply couldn't accept the risk. Down syndrome . . . prematurity . . . respiratory failure . . . cerebral palsy – the 'Advanced Maternal Age' chapter in the pregnancy handbook offered twenty pages of nightmare scenarios.

They had argued for months about having a third child. And Grace had been the compromise. Perfectly healthy, obviously bright, in need of a home after enduring some hard knocks. A chance to save a life instead of create a new one that might go horribly awry.

John remembered how she looked when they first brought her home: hair that seemed to have been cut by a blind man with a dull penknife, pathetically skinny ankles sprouting from outgrown jeans, her only toy a mournful one-eyed stuffed dog. Of course he felt compassion for her – anyone would. But love? Even after Miriam spruced the child up and made her look, outwardly, like every other little girl in the neighborhood, there was something off-putting about Grace. Something that kept John at bay.

'Hey, Dad, listen to this,' Gordon's excited voice brought John out of his funk. His son cranked up the radio, and a newscaster's voice filled the minivan.

'New Jersey State Police are investigating the disappearance of sixteen-year-old Shane Malone. The teenager was last seen at a popular tourist attraction, the House of Horrors, in Seaside Heights. According to authorities, Malone apparently entered the dark, mazelike haunted house and never emerged. A search of the building revealed no signs of foul play. Pretty strange stuff, folks. Please keep an eye out for Shane. He's five ten, one hundred fifty pounds, blond hair, blue eyes. And now, here's the Red Hot Chili Peppers . . .'

'Did you see how much Grace ate for breakfast this morning?' John said as he helped load the dishwasher the following Saturday morning. 'Three big pancakes and four strips of bacon, and she's still as thin as a rail.'

'It must be a holdover from her babyhood. Do you think she remembers being hungry?' It wasn't the first time Miriam had asked this. She was plagued by what she knew of her foster daughter's past. The five days Grace had spent as a toddler alone in her apartment with Mittens the cat, sharing dry kibble from a bag Mittens had resourcefully clawed open. CAT SAVES ABANDONED TYKE – John and Miriam remembered reading the headlines six years ago, never suspecting at the time that the traumatized child in the story would one day live with them.

If Grace remembered, she never spoke of it. She acted as if her life began when she walked through their door.

'Just keep pumping her full of food, honey,' John told his wife. 'Buy her a hot dog at the game today.'

'I don't like baseball,' a light voice piped.

John spun around to find Grace standing the in kitchen doorway. 'Can I please stay home?' she asked.

'Not all alone.' John grabbed the Windex and started spraying the counters.

Miriam and Grace both stared at him quizzically. 'She wouldn't be alone,' Miriam said. 'You said at breakfast you were staying home to do some yard work.'

'Oh. Yeah, right.' John scrubbed at a sticky spot. 'I just meant she wouldn't have anyone to play with, since I'll be working.'

'I don't want to play. I'll help you work.'

'Isn't that nice! Daddy's little helper!' Miriam beamed.

'Great,' John said.

'There you are.' Christopher charged into the kitchen and grabbed Grace by the arm. 'Let's go out to our clubhouse until it's time for me to go to my game.'

'Grace is so good for Christopher,' Miriam said, watching the kids run out to the patch of woods behind the house. 'She gives him a chance to be the leader, instead of following Gordon around like a lost lamb.'

'Do you think they should be out there alone?' John asked. 'Is it safe?'

The police had called earlier in the week looking for any information the Harrigans could provide about the House of Horrors and the group of teenagers with Shane Malone. John had answered all their questions, even put Gordon on the line since he had been the first person to follow Shane's group. The detective had seemed disappointed in what little they had to offer.

Miriam gave him a quick hug. 'I know. I've been feeling overprotective lately, too. I keep thinking it could have been one of our kids, snatched away in the dark while we were right there beside them.'

John stared through the kitchen window. 'You're right. It could just as easily have been Gordon or Christopher.'

'Or Grace,' Miriam said. She shivered. 'I can't imagine how horrible it would be not knowing where your child is.'

John put his arm around Miriam's shoulders. 'You're right. Nothing is worse than not knowing.'

John got so absorbed in trimming the ivy in the side yard he didn't notice when the boys and Miriam left for the baseball game, and he forgot about Grace's offer to help him. Then he ripped up a particularly ornery vine, staggered backward, and there she was, staring at him expectantly from the edge of the lawn.

'Do you want to load the ivy clippings into the garden cart?' was all he could think to offer.

She didn't answer, didn't even smile, but ran off to get the cart at lightning speed. They spent the next hour working as partners. He showed her how to use the garden shears; she stopped him from chopping down an azalea. Grace's keen eyes missed nothing – she pointed out a bird's nest in the rain gutter and a praying mantis eating aphids off Miriam's roses. And as skinny as she was, she was strong, wheeling cartloads of clippings to the curb.

While Grace was off with the last load, John admired the manicured border. Some ivy leaves trembled, and a garter snake came slithering out. It crossed inches away from his sneaker and curled on the flagstone path to soak up some sun. As John stared at it, the tiny snake lifted its head and shot its forked tongue out at him. John felt a revulsion so deep the trees and lawn seemed to melt away. The whole world was the snake. He wanted to scream, but he couldn't force a sound from his constricted throat.

Then a fragile hand slipped into his. 'Don't be afraid,' Grace said.

John smiled down at their clasped hands. When he glanced back at the walk, the snake was gone. He scanned the ivy. No movement there.

'Where did it go?' he asked Grace.

The doors of the minivan slammed, and running feet pounded down the driveway.

Grace's pale green-gold eyes met his without hesitation, and she smiled. Then she pivoted and scampered off to meet Christopher, shouting the answer over her shoulder.

'Away.'

John rolled through the channels after the kids went to bed, while Miriam stretched out beside him reading a book. The Mets were busy blowing a lead. He'd seen this episode of *Friends* so many times he could practically recite the dialogue. Despite Miriam's dirty look, he kept clicking until a sound bite brought him up short.

'. . . missing teen, Shane Malone. Authorities are calling this a true locked-room mystery,' the voice-over said as the camera zoomed in on the House of Horrors. 'There are only three doors in the building, and all three were manned on the day of the disappearance. No one saw Shane leave, and the honor student and high school quarterback remains missing even as police work round the clock to find him.'

The screen flashed to a yearbook photo of Shane in a shirt and tie, hair neatly trimmed, smiling confidently at the camera.

'Kid was kind of a jerk, wasn't he?' John asked as he stared at the TV. 'He made fun of his friends and mocked Christopher, a kid he didn't even know.'

'He was rude, that's all,' Miriam said. 'No worse than Gordon can be.'

No worse than Gordon, except Gordon was here, and Shane had disappeared.

John studied his wife. Her hands, still so slender and delicate, were never still, even when she was reading. Absently, she looped a strand of honey-colored hair behind her ear. The summer sun had brightened it, but some of the highlights were silver, not gold. Her brow furrowed as she concentrated on her book. How much Christopher looked like her! How similar was Gordon's nervous energy! Suddenly John felt crushed by the love he felt for Miriam and for his sons. No harm could ever be allowed to come to them. Never.

John flung back the covers.

'Where are you going?' Miriam asked.

'To check on the boys. And Grace.'

Gordon slept flat on his back with his hands at his sides, a carving on a royal tomb. He was as tall as his mother; his feet were as big as his father's, but to John, Gordon looked as innocent as he had the day they'd first laid him in his crib. Christopher sprawled diagonally across his bed, one foot dangling, one arm hugging the pillow. John rearranged the blankets and listened to the sweet harmonic breathing of his sons. Reassured, he backed out of their room and opened the door across the hall.

Miriam had gone off the deep end with the princess motif. Bubblegum-pink walls, frothy white curtains, pink shag rug, and, in the center of the floor, a canopy bed. He squinted, trying to make out Grace's tiny form in the midst of all those pink covers. Finally he spied her curled on the far edge of the bed, as if she were sharing it with a sumo wrestler, so insubstantial she barely dented the pillow.

As John watched, Grace rolled over and slowly sat up. Her eyes were wide open, and although she faced him, John could tell that she didn't see him. When Christopher had episodes of sleepwalking, this was what he looked like – awake and asleep at the same time.

Grace stretched out one arm, palm flat like a crossing guard stopping traffic. 'You can't come back,' she said distinctly. She was quiet for a moment, as if listening. John felt an irrepressible urge to look over his shoulder. Then Grace spoke again. 'He's not like you, that's why.'

Who? Who was different? Who was she talking to?

'Grace!'

The sharpness of John's voice jolted the little girl. She

blinked, and her eyes came into focus. She yawned. 'Is it time for school?'

'No, it's the middle of the night. You were talking in your sleep, so I came to check on you.'

'What did I say?' she murmured as she sank back into her pillows.

John shifted his weight. His bare feet felt terribly cold, even standing on the fluffy rug. 'You were saying someone couldn't come back.'

'That boy.' Grace burrowed into the covers. 'He's been asking, but I won't try.'

John lowered himself onto the foot of the bed and rubbed his sweaty palms on the quilt. 'Try what?'

Grace rolled onto her side and drew her legs up. She was wearing pajamas printed with a pattern of cats and mice having a tea party. Her voice was soft and groggy. 'To bring him back.'

John leaned closer to hear. A sweet smell of shampoo and fabric softener and sleep enveloped Grace. 'Back from where?'

A hand touched John's shoulder. He leapt off the bed, wild-eyed.

'I didn't mean to startle you, honey.' Miriam patted his arm. 'What's going on?'

'Grace was dreaming,' John said, trying to steady his breathing. 'She's going back to sleep now.'

'Good news!' Eyes shining, Miriam flung her arms around John the minute he walked in from work. He danced around with her, enjoying her happiness without knowing its source.

'I just got the call from Social Services,' she said. 'Grace has been cleared for adoption!'

John froze.

'Honey? Isn't that great?'

He slipped out of Miriam's embrace. 'Uh, yeah. I didn't

think it would be so soon. I thought they needed to get her biological parents to sign something.'

'The police weren't able to track them down. Why even try? They were drug addicts – the social worker says their parental rights have been terminated.'

'What about the aunt who Grace lived with for a while?' John asked.

'She's not claiming Grace, either. She's so stressed out by her financial problems since her husband abandoned her and her kids, she can't cope with another child.'

'Doesn't he pay child support?' John asked.

Miriam shrugged. 'If the government doesn't know where you are, they can't make you pay.'

John was silent, staring at a spot somewhere to the left of the refrigerator. All he could see was the brown and green garter snake.

There, and not there.

The sinking sun cast long shadows over the backyard. John sat in the family room nursing a beer. A cool breeze blew through the sliding doors, carrying voices into the room.

'I shouldn't have done it. I made a bad mistake.'

John cocked his head to listen. That was Grace.

'It's not your fault. You didn't know.'

Christopher was reassuring her about something. What wasn't her fault? What didn't she know?

'Well, I know *now*,' Grace said impatiently. 'It's not the same as when I sent my parents away. I have to try to fix it. Otherwise it's just not fair.'

'Don't worry,' Christopher said as he slid the screen door open. 'I'll help you.'

'Don't worry about what?' John's newspaper trembled in his hands.

Christopher and Grace stood side by side. 'Nothing,' they chorused, and ran off.

Watching their sneakered feet pumping in unison, John felt a strangling vine of dread twist around his heart.

He went into the kitchen. *All Things Considered* played on the radio. Five yellow plaid placemats waited on the table. Miriam stood at the counter chopping vegetables.

Where to begin?

'Honey? I'm . . . I'm a little worried about Grace.'

Miriam stopped chopping.

'She seems to think . . . I mean, I just overheard her tell Chris that she . . . she sent away—'

'Oh, that.' Miriam waved a carrot. 'Lately she's been telling me all about how she sent away her parents.'

'You *know* about this?'

'She was abandoned by the two people who were supposed to love her more than anyone else in the world. This fantasy is her way of coping, gaining control,' Miriam's voice took on a tone John associated with his fifth-grade social studies teacher. 'It's called magical thinking, and it's actually very normal for a child in her circumstances.'

John squinted at his wife. 'Normal? I call that weird, Miriam.'

'If she can believe that she sent her parents away because they hurt her cat – that's what she says, that she sent them away to protect Mittens – then she doesn't have to accept the reality that they abandoned her.'

'Does she think she can send other people away, too?' John's mouth tasted sour. Had Grace told Miriam what she'd done to Shane Malone? Would Miriam have some kind of child psychology mumbo jumbo to explain that away?

'Yes, she says she had to send her uncle away to protect her aunt and cousins. He was abusive, you know.' Miriam's hand pumped the knife up and down, reducing the carrot to an orange mound. 'That's how she rationalized the fact that her aunt couldn't afford to keep her when the uncle abandoned the family.'

'Anyone else?'

Miriam eyed him. 'Of course not.'

'So, when she tells you these things, what do you say?' John asked. 'Do you try to reason with her?'

Miriam smiled and shook her head. 'What good would it do? The books all say that once she feels safe and secure, she'll gradually let go of her magical thinking.'

John rubbed his temples. 'What if she doesn't let it go? Maybe there's . . .' He took a deep breath and chose his words carefully. 'Maybe her problems are too big for us to handle, Miriam. Maybe we're not the right family for Grace, It wouldn't be fair to the boys—'

Miriam's eyes widened, and she stopped chopping. 'You get one thing through your head, John.' She wagged the knife to emphasize each word. 'We are *not* abandoning that child. Grace has found her forever home, and it's right here with us.'

John slipped out to the back deck with the laptop and Googled magical thinking. What he read seemed to confirm Miriam's theory. Small consolation – if the kid wasn't dangerous, she was crazy. Something in the computer's browser history caught his eye: garter snakes. He clicked on it and a picture of a green and brown snake filled the screen.

Recoiling, he rushed to close the window. Before he could, a skinny arm reached around him, and a short finger tapped the screen. 'They're not dangerous at all,' Grace said. She pursed her lips disapprovingly. 'You were silly to be scared. Because of you, I did something unfair.'

John's hands clenched the arms of his chair.

'Unfair?'

'I sent the little snake away because he scared you. But he wouldn't have hurt you. I've been trying to bring him back, but I can't.' Grace's head drooped, and she scuffed her sneaker across the deck. 'That makes me sad.'

John forced himself to relax his grip on the deck chair. Miriam said to humor her. He spoke softly. 'Can you send anyone away, Grace?'

She looked at him through her wispy bangs as if he'd asked if she could fly. 'Of course not. It only works if I need to protect someone.'

Like Christopher.

John looked into her fierce, righteous face, and he knew fear. Would he wake up one day and find Gordon gone because he called his little bother a twerp or trounced him in a video game?

'Grace, Shane Malone was just a rude teenager. He didn't hurt Christopher.'

She regarded him with that special look children use when they're astounded by the stupidity of the adults who control their lives. 'I wasn't protecting Christopher. I was helping the girl with Shane. When the bright light flashed, I saw Shane hurting her, trying to do what my uncle used to do to my cousin, Lori, when he sneaked into her room at night. The girl screamed, but no one came to help, because everyone screams in that place. So I sent Shane away.'

'There you are,' Miriam appeared at the sliding glass door with the phone in her hand. 'It's the detective working on the Shane Malone disappearance.'

John accepted the receiver. The mild summer air felt as treacherous as a riptide.

'Sorry to bother you again, Mr Harrigan,' the detective said. 'I happened to notice a discrepancy. The credit card records indicate you paid for five admissions, but your family photo shows only four people. Who's missing?'

John's hand tightened on the phone. 'Uh . . . Grace. She's nine. She was hiding behind me because she was scared. When the flash went off, she must've jumped back and got cut out of the picture.'

How quickly the lie had formed in his mind. How glibly it flowed from his lips. John realized he was holding his breath, waiting to hear if the detective accepted this explanation.

'That's what I figured, but I had to check.'

John could hear the disappointment in the detective's voice.

'Just for the record, Grace is your daughter?'

John looked across the deck. Grace stood by the railing, her fair hair illuminated by the rising moon. She'd caught a firefly in her hand and was studying its rhythmic flashing. Then she shook her hand and smiled as it flew into the night.

'Yes,' John said. 'Grace is my daughter.'

SIFT, ALMOST
INVISIBLE, THROUGH

Jeffrey Somers

I

'What am I looking at?'

The little man, Richard Harrows, pushed his thin wire glasses up the bridge of his nose and leaned forward a little. Philip K. Marks looked up at him and kept his face blank.

'A photo, Mr Marks.'

'Did you take it?'

'No. This was last year, on vacation. I'd asked someone to take my picture.'

Marks hoped the little man wouldn't launch into a description of the trip. 'Okay, Why am I looking at it?'

'Because of him.'

Harrows reached over the desk to point a nail-bitten, shaking finger at the photo. Marks followed it to where a thin man had been caught by the camera, leaning against a railing. Marks glanced up.

'So?'

Richard Harrows was a balding, short man with a precise and nervous air. Marks had seen plenty of people in his time, and his professional opinion of Richard Harrows was that the man was the sort of honest-by-default person you could trust but never rely on.

'Look closer, Mr Marks.'

Marks sighed and returned his attention to the photograph. The man was tall, and wearing a dark suit and white shirt. He was off to the left side of the framed area, behind Harrows' shoulder, leaning casually against the railing, one hand in a pocket. Marks studied his blurry form and blinked, looking up at Harrows.

'You know this guy?'

Harrows laughed nervously. 'I've never seen him. Not in the flesh.'

'Because I would swear he's looking at you. Or at the camera.' Marks shook his head. It was an odd impression, the more so because the focus of the camera was obviously nowhere near the man.

'Ah, yes,' Harrows said with another little laugh, 'you see, Mr Marks, that was the beginning of the problem. He wasn't there. He's never actually been anywhere, but he's showing up in pictures of me, as if he *were*.'

Marks glanced up sharply. 'Excuse me?'

'Look.' Harrows produced a small stack of photos. 'Here are samples from the past year. The one you have is the first, and it is from almost a year ago exactly. Here are others.'

Marks took the stack and examined them in turn. In each photo of Harrows, obviously taken at different times, during different seasons, in different places, the thin man appeared, in the same dark suit, looking directly at the camera, always just off from the actual focus of the picture.

'You're sure you've never met him? That you don't know him?'

Harrows shook his head. 'Mr Marks, I would swear that he was never *there*. I would have a photo taken of me somewhere, anywhere – I like to travel, you see – and be sure he wasn't there. This is more recently, when I became aware of him, you see. Then, I'd develop the film, and there he'd be.'

Marks shook his head. 'It is odd how he seems to be

following you, and how he seems to know you're posing for photos, but I still don't see—'

'Mr Marks, I came to you because of your reputation—'

'For being someone who believes every line of bullshit that comes through my office,' Marks finished. 'I'm well aware of my reputation, Mr Harrows. I'd like to think I also have a reputation for getting *paid* to look into things.'

'Mr Marks,' Harrows said slowly, 'I think you will be interested in my story, because if you look at the photos again – they are arranged in chronological order – you will note that he appears to be getting closer.'

Marks looked through the photos again and felt a chill go through him. He could see, over the course of the fifteen or twenty photos, that the thin man *was* slightly closer to the camera each time.

Marks looked up. 'All right, Mr Harrows—'

Harrows held up a hand. 'Finally, Mr Marks, there is this.' He pulled another photo from his inside jacket pocket and handed it to the reporter. 'Taken just two days ago, at my father's house. Family reunion, of sorts.'

Marks looked at the photo. He picked out Harrows, two men who appeared to be his brothers or close cousins, and an older man unmistakably his father, mixed in with about ten or fifteen men and women. They stood in an attractive and comfortable-looking living room, sporting two large bay windows. Marks almost jumped when he noticed the thin man standing, partially obscured by a drape, outside one of the windows. He appeared to be bending down slightly to see around the fabric.

'Damn near shit myself,' Harrows said.

'I'll bet.' Marks considered. 'May I keep these?'

Harrows smiled. 'You'll look into it?'

Marks smiled and raised his eyebrows. 'You'll pay me?'

II

Phillip K. Marks was a man in his late thirties, a slight dusting of beard on his face, and a sloppy suit of brown clothes on his broad, tall frame. He smoked cigarettes in a never-ending chain and had a half-full bottle of cheap bourbon in one desk drawer that would be empty within a month. He made a small living doing whatever people wanted to pay him for, relying on word of mouth for advertising. A man lacking any remarkable skills at all, he was proud of himself for having found a niche, even one whose only requirement was a tolerance for pain, humiliation, and dogged relentlessness.

After Harrows had left his small, rented office, Marks pulled out the bottle and poured himself two fingers of liquor, lit a new cigarette off the coal of the old one, and sat back in his chair contemplating the photographs for some time. Without taking his eyes from the newest one, he reached for the phone, dialed by feel, and waited a moment.

'Ralph Tomlin, please.'

He turned the family reunion upside down thoughtfully.

'Hey, Ralph, Phil Marks. Yeah. Sure. Yeah. Listen, you think you could squeeze in a favor? Sure, it's right up your alley. Some photos. Well, I just want to see if they've been faked or altered in some way. Ah, peace of mind, you know. You're handed something and told, hey look at this, you want to be sure you know what you're looking at. A bunch of photographs – maybe fifteen. You got time?'

He sat up and fished an envelope from his desk. 'Great – thanks. I'll stop by, then. You're a gem, Ralph. And I don't forget that I owe you a few drinks – we could meet for dinner tonight, you hand over your findings, I'll buy, what do you say? Okay, see you then.'

He hung up the phone, slid the photos into the envelope, and stood up.

'Christ,' he muttered, 'if I'd known, I would have stayed in school, become an engineer.'

'They're real, Phil.'

Marks took the crumpled envelope and squinted at it. 'You're sure?'

Ralph Tomlin nodded, eating dried noodles one at a time from his hand. 'As far as I can tell, Phil. I did the standard tests – searched for standard stock overlays, pixel differentials, inverted shadings. That's not 100 percent definitive, but you only gave me a few hours. Give me a week, I'll take it apart dot by dot. But based on what I did today, it would require serious expertise to have faked those. So they're either real or absolutely amazing, one-of-a-kind fakes.'

Marks nodded. 'Okay. I doubt I need to look that hard at these.' He glanced up at Tomlin, who was a round man, jowly, red-faced, cheerful-seeming. 'What did you think of them?'

Tomlin chewed and shrugged, swallowed. 'Look like vacation shots to me. Amateur, not particularly inspired – the kind of pictures you get when you hand a cheap camera to random strangers and ask them to take your picture. Sentimental value only, I'd imagine.' He cleared his throat. 'Although since you gave them to me, I can only imagine that there's something not obvious about them.'

Marks held up one at random. 'Did you notice the man in the dark suit?'

Ralph squinted. 'Okay, I see him now.'

'He's in every one.'

Ralph nodded. 'Okay.'

Marks took the photo back. 'No one knows who he is or why he's showing up every time this guy poses for a picture. That's the story. So far, at least.'

'Sounds pretty boring, Phil.'

Marks shrugged. 'Most stories are. You check out nine to

find one that gets interesting. Now, you order anything you want, baby.'

Ralph snorted. 'Thanks. You're a big spender, big boy. So what now with this?'

Marks stuffed the envelope into his jacket. 'I'll talk to the fellow who gave them to me, put a little pressure on him, see what comes out.' He shrugged. 'It's a necessary step. You'd be amazed how many real crazy people approach me, feed me bullshit. Sometimes they come up with some pretty complex bullshit, too.'

Ralph shook his head, holding up a menu. 'No, Phil, I wouldn't.'

III

'Mr Harrows,' Marks huffed, 'thanks for coming.'

Harrows took the offered hand quickly and sat down. Marks wheezed around to the other side of the desk and collapsed into his own chair.

'You have some findings?' Harrows asked.

Marks shook his head. 'Not yet, Mr Harrows. I've asked you here to ask a few more questions and to perform an experiment. I spent the last two days doing some basic fact-checking.'

Harrows seemed unhappy. 'Checking up on me?'

'You didn't think I wouldn't, did you?'

Harrows shrugged and looked down at the floor for a moment. 'Well? What do you need from me?'

Marks settled himself into the cracked leather of his chair. He placed a large paper bag on the desk and reached into it. 'First, I'd like to ask you if you've ever experienced anything that could be described as "paranormal".'

Harrows shook his head. 'I didn't even realize that *this* would be considered such until I began noticing . . . him. In the earlier photos I showed you, he was distant – part of the background, really, and easy to miss. By the time I started to see him, he was . . . closer.'

Marks nodded. 'Okay. Let me ask you this, then, and please be perfectly honest. Do you recognize the man?'

'I've wracked my brain, Mr Marks. Nothing about him stirs any memory at all.' Harrows laughed a little. 'Believe me, I was convinced at first that this . . . ghost, or whatever, was haunting me, so therefore, there must be a connection. I've thought about it and thought about it, and have come up with nothing more than pure imagination.'

Marks began pulling cameras from the paper bag. 'Have you gone through older photographs, perhaps?'

Harrows nodded. 'Sure, sure. Went through fifty years' worth of family photos, looking for someone who resembled the man. Nothing.'

Marks placed six cameras on his desk, including an expensive digital camera with a wireless instant printer and a small video camera. 'Mr Harrows, in the samples you showed me, you were in all of the photos – most were vacation shots, where you had asked someone to take your picture, correct? Have you ever noticed our friend in photos you yourself took?'

'No. I've checked. When I am behind the camera, he is nowhere to be seen.'

Marks nodded. 'Hmmph. Well.' He sat up in his seat. 'Well, let's experiment, gain all the data possible. I've got here some random cameras. Certainly not a scientific experiment, but it will at least show us some possible guidelines. I propose to take photos of you – lots of them – using different cameras and see if our friend shows up in them, I'm beginning to have a rudimentary theory – not about *what* or *who*, but merely concerning some of the rules of the phenomenon's behavior. Let's get started, shall we?'

Harrows looked at his hands for a moment, then nodded. 'Fine.'

Marks had Harrows stand against one of the walls of the

small office. He took three or four photos with each camera, from different angles and different distances. 'I noticed,' he said as he snapped them, 'that in all the photos you showed me, you never had your back to a wall. I wonder if that will have any impact.'

Harrows looked startled. 'I hadn't thought of that.'

Marks continued to snap photos. 'May not mean anything – but that's the point; we need data. Now, when I film you, just act natural. Move about a bit. I want to see if your movement has any impact.'

Marks lifted the video camera to his eye and pointed it at Harrows.

'See anything?'

Marks didn't stop filming. 'Calm down, Mr Harrows. If I see any ghosts, I'll let you know. Everything looks normal. But then I assume you did not see this man when you actually posed for the photos?'

Harrows nodded, shifting awkwardly.

'Okay,' Marks continued, 'let's just get enough video to have something to work with, a minute or so, and then we'll get this film developed and see what can be seen.'

'Okay,' Harrows said with little enthusiasm.

A few minutes later, Marks examined the photographs one by one, passing them across the desk to Harrows, who stared at them with decreasing happiness.

'Well,' Marks said when the last of them had been glanced over. 'We've managed to ascertain only one more fact of the case.'

'Hmmmn?' Harrows gurgled from his depressed spot in the chair. 'What's that?'

Marks gestured at the photos, each showing the tall, thin man in the dark suit, apparently creeping up behind Harrows. 'Well, he's still getting closer.'

In each of the photos, the thin man seemed to have just entered Marks's office, and was seen, shadowy and indistinct, striding purposefully toward Mr Harrows. Almost directly behind Harrows, he was obscured from the camera and appeared only as shoulders, feet, arms, the shape of a head. It was impossible to detect any true details. The figure was a collection of brights and shadows, which coalesced into a human form only when viewed from a distance.

After Harrows had left, Marks sat at his desk and studied the photos one after another. In each, the thin man appeared to be closer to Harrows by a half step, a few inches. In the last one, he was still only halfway between the doorway and Harrows.

'Who are you, then?' Marks murmured, sipping bourbon in the pale pool of yellow light generated by his desk lamp. 'Why are you haunting our Mr Harrows? *Are* you haunting Mr Harrows? Are you getting closer to him, or is he getting closer to you?'

The photos remained mute. Marks tossed them onto the desk and sat for a moment, staring off into the shadows of his office. He reached over and picked up the instant camera, turned it so the lens was facing him, and leaned back in his chair.

'You around?' he murmured. 'You want to chat?'

A twitch of his finger, and the flash exploded, filling the room with a second's worth of blue light. Blinking in the aftermath, Marks plucked the emerging photo from the tiny printer and shook it back and forth, letting it develop. He turned it over and squinted down at it, a strange, languid grin spreading across his face. 'Well, hello there,' he said quietly.

The photo was of an out-of-focus and off-center shot of Marks, his nose seemingly too large, his eyes shut against the flash, unattractive and distorted. Over his left shoulder, seeming to lean directly over Marks's shoulder, was the thin man, clearer than before but still grainy, more a collection of dots than a solid figure. In one hand, held oddly toward the bottom of the frame, he held a white square, indistinct.

Marks squinted at it, held the photo alternatively near his eyes and far away, finally setting it down on the desk, unsatisfied.

He whirled and put the phone to his ear.

'Ralph? I know it's late. Sorry. Listen, I have another favor to ask you.'

IV

'Phil, I damn near shit myself.'

Ralph Tomlin led Phillip K. Marks through gray, unmarked corridors. Marks paid no attention to the fake cubicle walls, didn't acknowledge anyone they passed. With his oversized raincoat and unshaven demeanor, he stood out. People stared.

'Well? What is it?'

Tomlin shook his head. 'Sit down at my desk here. Take a look. You have to see it yourself.'

Marks sat down at the small desk, which was dominated by a huge computer monitor, bigger than any Marks had ever seen. On it was displayed a clear scan of the Polaroid: Marks, blurry, crushed against the camera lens, the Thin Man, dark and skeletal, grinning over his shoulder, holding something awkwardly in his hand.

'Okay.' Marks said testily.

'Now, here's a blowup and clarification of the lower right-hand corner of the photo, where that guy's "hand" is. I use the air quotes because that really isn't a man, Phil.'

'I knew that, considering that he wasn't in the room when I took the photo.'

'No, I mean *nothing* was there, Phil. The figure we see there is an optical illusion, a collection of dots: white and black. He's a black-and-white halftone, is what he is. But here's the disturbing part: the blowup. He's holding a card, Phil. For want of a better term, I'd say it was a business card.'

Ralph clicked a key and stepped back as the picture on the screen changed to a detail of the photo: a rectangular, white space, surrounded by the blurred and indistinct lines of the Thin Man's hand. The card, at this magnification, and with the aid of clarifying software, had words printed on it:

I AM DEATH

Marks leaned back in the chair, let out an explosive burst of breath. 'Oh, shit.'

Tomlin nodded, staring raptly at the fuzzy image. 'Oh shit is right.' He grinned. 'Phil, ever since you started down this weirdo path of yours, you've shown me some really odd things from time to time. This one gave me chills. So, what do you think?'

Marks shook his head dazedly, his eyes locked on the fuzzy words on the screen. 'About what?'

Tomlin snorted and glanced down at Marks. 'Is he coming for your subject,' he asked, 'or you?'

Marks finally tore his eyes from the screen. 'Is that supposed to be helpful in some way?'

Tomlin shrugged happily. 'I'd just get your subject into an emergency room, if I was you, buddy. If Death's following him around like that, there's got to be a reason.'

Marks's smile was barren. 'Unless he's after me now, right?'

V

Marks walked the dark streets after hours, smoking ill-advised cigarettes and pondering his new concern. As the sun disappeared and the shadowed streets stopped looking cheerily familiar, he wondered unhappily if he was being stalked by a specter, if a photo taken by a helpful stranger might reveal a companion. They were not cheering thoughts. He stopped in a favorite bar, the Full Moon, and ordered a double bourbon on ice, sat in the back by himself, and sipped it slowly, staring at the wall.

'What's the story, Phil?'

Marks glanced up, surprised, and found Jerry, the jowly owner. 'Sorry, Jer, I was woolgathering.'

'Can see that, Philly. Everything okay?'

'Sure.' Marks paused, studying his drink, then looked up again. 'Jer, what if you had to tell someone something bad. Something . . . sad. Something that maybe they didn't need to know, but you felt duty-bound to tell them.'

Jerry laughed, his belly bouncing within its tight shirt. 'I do, every night, Phil, round closing time.'

Marks smiled faintly. 'What if you had to tell someone they were going to die?'

Jerry looked away. 'Jeez, Phil—'

Marks shook his head, leaned back in his chair. 'Shit, I'm sorry, Jer. Just got a lot of stuff on my mind. Don't pay any attention to me.'

'Easy enough.' Jerry turned away and then hesitated, looking back over his shoulder. 'You weren't going to tell *me* that, were you, Phil?'

Marks shook his head. 'No, no, Jerry. Not you. Just someone I've been working with.' He paused, and just as Jerry was about to turn back, Marks continued. 'Hey, Jer, you got a camera around here?'

Jerry started walking back to the bar. 'Yeah, actually. Keep an old Polaroid on hand for when we get trouble-makers and have ta ban 'em. I got quite a wall of shame in my office.' He glanced back as he walked away. 'Why, Philly?'

Marks gulped the last of his drink. 'Take my picture, okay?'

Jerry retrieved the camera from behind the bar and hefted his bulk back toward Marks's table. 'Sure, sure. Why not?'

Marks nodded absently, pushing his hands through each of his pockets until he'd recovered a small pad of paper and a black-ink pen. He wrote quickly and tore a sheet off, holding it up under his chin as Jerry approached.

'Ready?'

Marks nodded. The flash went off, and Jerry lowered the camera as the picture was spit out. 'Who's this for? With the note and all?'

Marks crumpled the piece of paper up and tossed it on the table. 'I'll know in a moment, Jer. Let me see the print.'

Jerry tore it from the camera and handed it gingerly to him. Marks took it between two fingers and shook it carefully, drying it in the air, then held it up and studied it, silently, for a few seconds.

'You see something strange?' Jerry asked. 'I'm prepared for anything, after the last few times you brought your work in here.'

Marks laughed, a grim bark that made Jerry frown. 'Jer, sometimes I guess I ought to just leave everything alone, you know?' He stood up and tossed a bill on the table. 'I gotta go track down my subject.'

Jerry let Marks push past him and watched him walk out of the bar purposefully, head down. Then he turned back to the table and plucked the photo from it. Looking down at it, squinting in the bad light, he gasped. Sitting at the same table as Marks was a tall, thin man in a dark suit . . . or at least that's what it looked like to Jerry. The man was shadowed and indistinct.

Jerry's eyes flicked to the table and then back to the photo. In his bar, the table was gouged by a million nervous hands and a few serious vandals. In the photo, words had been carved onto the table:

I LIKE YOU BETTER

VI

It was an innocuous-enough apartment door, but Marks gave in to instinct and looked the whole hallway over before stepping forward and knocking firmly. After a moment, there was a shuffling from inside and then:

'Who's there?'

'Mr Harrows, it's Phillip K. Marks.'

The metallic sounds of locks being undone, and then the door cracked open slightly. Marks waved sardonically at the eye that appeared to look him over. The door shut again and reopened quickly.

'Mr Marks. I'm sorry, I've been a little on edge since we had our discussion. I apologize.'

'No need.' Marks said smoothly. 'I think I'm beginning to understand.'

Harrows nodded pleasantly, then looked around the hallway. 'Mr Marks – why are you here?'

Marks looked around. 'I don't mean to be rude, Mr Harrows, but I have to ask you for two favors.'

'Favors?'

'First, and most importantly, do you have anything to drink?'

Harrows studied Marks for a moment, and then nodded. 'Yes, Mr Marks, I think I have a bottle of Old Smuggler in the kitchen. It'll give you one hell of a headache in the morning.'

Marks nodded. 'Thank you. I'll take a double.'

Harrows shrugged his eyebrows and turned to enter the kitchen. 'You said you had two favors to ask of me, Mr Marks?'

'I'd like to take your picture one more time.'

Harrows paused and then continued into the kitchen. 'May I ask why?' he called back.

Marks glanced around the room. 'Let's just say I need to confirm an unfortunate suspicion. The good news is, I'll probably be able to set your mind at ease about the whole situation in a few minutes.'

Harrows returned with Marks's drink. 'Jelly glass, sorry.'

Marks shrugged and took the drink eagerly. 'Christ, that's terrible.' He drained it with a grunt and a grimace, and handed it back, pulling a small camera from his pocket. 'Smile!'

Harrows blinked in surprise at the flash.

Marks tore the photo from the camera and began shaking it in the air. He smiled a thin, sickly smile at Harrows. 'Well, we'll know in a moment.'

They stood facing each other as Marks fanned the print. When he stopped and turned it over, they both glanced down. Harrows blinked again.

'He's gone.'

Marks nodded glumly. 'So he is.'

'Why, that's good.' Harrows said in a muted tone. 'I think that's good. Do I have you to thank for this?'

Marks nodded again. 'I am afraid so. Thank you, Mr Harrows. I don't think I'll have to trouble you again.'

He squinted at Marks, who just stood there carelessly, numb. 'Mr Marks, what's wrong?'

Marks shook himself. 'Nothing, Mr Harrows. I'll bid you good night. I would tell you to keep my number and call me if you need anything else, but I somehow doubt I'll be around much longer. Keep the camera.'

'Mr Marks?'

Marks turned and let himself out. Harrows called after him one last time but did not follow.

Marks headed toward the nearest bar he knew, feeling rusty inside. Half a block away, he noted a convenience store and turned for it impulsively. Inside he bought a pint bottle of bourbon and another thing of film, which he unwrapped while standing there before the bemused, dark-skinned man behind the register. He loaded the film and held the camera up to his eye, stretching a grin across his face.

'Smile!' he hissed. Startled, the dark-skinned man flashed a brief grin. Marks captured it with a bright flash. A motor whirred. A gummy print erupted from the front of the camera. Marks flapped it in the air and then studied it eagerly. His skeletal grin faded.

'Thanks,' he muttered, handing the print to the puzzled man. 'I'll need more film. As many packs as you have.'

Marks made his way up and down the streets, a stiff, permanent smile fixed to his face. He stopped everyone he saw and repeated the same pitch to them:

'Excuse me, let me take your picture? It's a public service, and it's free. A few seconds, and you can keep it if you like it.'

Most of the people he approached allowed him to photograph them and posed awkwardly, cheerfully. Marks would snap the photo with a minimum of fuss, would shake the photo out recklessly, would glance at it, and would hand it to his subject wordlessly, his smile more brittle each time, and would move on wordlessly.

He did this hundreds of times, wandering the streets randomly, moving rapidly from person to person. After several hours of this, his voice was rough and cracked, his gait was shuffling, but he persisted, often bullying people into allowing him to photograph them.

At four in the morning there weren't many people left on the quieted streets, and Marks finally allowed himself to lean against a parked car, slumping in exhaustion.

'Who knows? Could be anything,' he muttered to himself. 'No rhyme or reason. None that we would understand.'

He shook his head, trying to clear it. He worked his stiff hands, clawed from clutching the camera.

'Who knows why? Bad luck. Been doing this stuff for too long.'

'Move it on, buddy.'

Marks glanced up sharply and found a uniformed police-man standing across from him, pointing his club at Marks's chest.

'What?'

The cop waved the club up the sidewalk. 'Move it on home, pal. Had a good time, and now you can go sleep it off.'

Marks stared at the cop as if he didn't understand.

'Now, pal.'

From somewhere, Marks produced a smile, palsied and faint. He held the camera up to his eye and squinted. The cop's stern face resolved in the lens.

'Just a photo before I go, please.'

The cop frowned sourly when Marks pressed the button and the flash went off tiredly. Marks held up a placating hand as he plucked the print from the camera and began waving it in the air.

'I'll go. I swear, Officer. And I'll give you the photo. It's just a hobby.'

Eagerly, he peered down at the picture. Stood still for a moment, and then slumped back against the car, his eyes closed.

The policeman took a hesitant half step forward. 'You okay, buddy?'

Marks opened his eyes and smiled an easy, happy, glint-ingly predatory grin. The cop blinked in the face of its hard, bright cheeriness.

'I'm fine now, Officer. You have a good night.' Marks pushed away from the car and paused to study the cop for a moment. 'Enjoy it.'

Whistling, he turned and walked away.

THE BEDROOM DOOR

Elaine Viets

'I saw your partner Angela in my bedroom door,' Grandma said.

'Angela, my interior design partner?' I asked. 'That Angela?'

'The skinny one with the red hair,' Grandma said.

'Damn. She's a good partner,' I said. 'I'll hate to lose her. She's going to be dead in three days.'

A shrill scream split the air, and I jumped. Then I realized it was the teakettle boiling on Grandma's Magic Chef stove. She dropped two tea bags in a blue pot, poured in boiling water, and cut me a slab of homemade apple pie.

That gave me time to recover. I'd blurted something horribly selfish. Angela was going to die, and my first thought was how it would inconvenience me.

'I wanted to warn you in case something happened,' Grandma said.

Something bad.

My grandmother had the 'second sight', but it wasn't a gift anyone would want. She couldn't say, 'Sell your stock this afternoon. The market's going to tank.' Grandma saw only misery with her second sight.

The doorway to Grandma's bedroom was a portal to the other side. For ten years, people had appeared in Grandma's bedroom doorway three days before they died. Some were friends, some were family, but all had a connection to Grandma.

The soon to be dead showed themselves at night bathed in warm light, while Grandma shook and shivered under her chenille spread. They never appeared when she took an afternoon nap or had a sick headache. They never said anything. They were just there, and then they weren't.

I asked the crucial question. 'What was Angela wearing?'

The dead in the doorway always wore whatever they had on when they passed to the other side.

'Not a stitch,' Grandma said, disapproval in her voice. 'And let me tell you, she's not a natural redhead.'

'She's not a natural anything, Grandma. Angela puts on heels and a suit to take out the trash. This is good pie.'

'Thanks,' Grandma said. 'I put up the apples last fall.'

'If you saw Angela naked, maybe she had a heart attack in the shower,' I said.

'I don't think so,' Grandma said. 'I saw your aunt Tillie when she had her stroke in the bathtub. Her hair was wet, and she clutched a bar of Palmolive soap. Tillie was my own sister, but that woman had serious cellulite. Angela was perfectly dry and looked like she'd just gotten out of bed. Her hair was mussed and her lipstick was smeared.'

'Maybe I should say something to her,' I said, taking another bite of pie.

'No!' Grandma said. 'You can't! Remember Bill.'

Her favorite brother had shown up in Grandma's doorway wearing a green hospital gown. Grandma was so upset, she called Bill at two in the morning about her deadly vision and scared the stuffing out of the man. When Bill had chest pains three days later, he refused to go to the hospital. By the time he collapsed and was taken to St Mary's by ambulance, it was too late. Bill died in the ER wearing a hospital gown.

Grandma swore she'd never say anything to anyone again. She kept silent when my father showed up in her doorway minus his head and his wedding ring. Grandma never liked Dad. She knew he cheated on her daughter. Heck, the whole neighborhood knew. Mom always forgave my father and took him back. Grandma thought her daughter would be better off without him. Three days later, when Dad was supposed to be at work, an irate husband blew away my father's head with a shotgun as he slipped out of a hot-sheet motel. The errant wife locked herself in the bathroom and survived.

Somehow, Mom found out that Grandma knew about Dad's death in advance. She never forgave Grandma – or spoke to her again. Two years later, Mom appeared in Grandma's bedroom doorway in a hospital gown. She was dying of cancer. Grandma rushed to St John's Mercy and begged her daughter to forgive her. Mom went to her grave in stone-hard silence.

My cousin Jimmy wore jungle fatigues in Grandma's doorway. Grandma wept when she saw her favorite grandson with a seeping chest wound. Then she called the Red Cross and said she needed to get in touch with Jimmy – it was an emergency.

'Does this concern a death in the family?' the Red Cross contact said.

'Not yet,' Grandma said.

The Red Cross dismissed her as a harmless nutcase. Three days later Cousin Jimmy was shot in Vietnam, but we didn't know about his death for two weeks.

Grandma mourned Jimmy and blamed herself. 'I should have lied,' she said. 'I should have said his mother had died, and then they would have let my grandbaby come home.' But she was unable to lie about what she saw. It was part of her unwanted gift.

Here's the weird thing about my grandmother: She looked like a picture-book Grandma. She had a comfortable flour-sack figure and permed gray hair. She put up grape jelly, made apple butter in a big kettle, baked pies with flaky crusts, canned her own tomatoes – and saw dead people in her bedroom doorway.

My grandfather did not stop by Grandma's door before his heart attack. Grandma believed that was her punishment for her silence when my father was murdered. She found her husband of fifty years dead at the kitchen table, a deck of cards spread out on the Formica top. He'd been cheating at solitaire.

Why did Grandma see the dead three days before they passed over – when they were still alive? Grandma said time didn't run in a straight line, the way we saw it in schoolbooks. 'Time is all around us,' she said. 'It's happening all at once.' That was a pretty fair explanation of quantum physics from a woman who'd never finished grade school.

Much of what Grandma saw didn't make sense until after it happened. Aunt Leila appeared in the doorway wearing a raincoat and fluffy pink bedroom slippers. Grandma thought that outfit was so ridiculous, she blamed the pickled herring she'd had for dinner. After three Turns, she decided to warn Leila. Grandma's younger sister lived in a snooty suburb of St Louis called Ladue. Leila thought Grandma's town, Mehlville, was low-rent.

'I was wearing a raincoat and slippers? What have you been drinking, Emma?' Leila asked. 'I wouldn't be caught dead in that getup.'

But she was. Three days later, Leila overslept, and her daughter, Annie, missed the school bus. Annie could lose her perfect attendance award. Aunt Leila threw her raincoat over her nightgown, grabbed her purse, and drove Annie to school. Aunt Leila was killed driving home when a woman ran a stop sign on McKnight Road. Leila was wearing fluffy pink slippers and a raincoat.

'I should have tried harder,' Grandma wept. 'She wouldn't believe me. Now I'm warning you.'

'What was I wearing in your doorway?' I asked. I couldn't keep the fear out of my voice. I had a fifteen-year-old daughter. I wanted to see my Sarah go to her senior prom. I wanted to be there when she graduated from college, and at her wedding. I wanted to hold my grandchild in my arms.

'Oh, I didn't see you,' Grandma said. 'I just had a feeling.'

I took a deep breath and relaxed. Grandma's 'feelings' were right maybe half the time. I had a 50 percent chance of escape.

In 2006, Grandma 'had a feeling' the St Louis Cardinals would win the World Series and talked me into getting season tickets with her. She was triumphant when they won. Of course, she also thought the Cards would win in 2008. They had a miserable season. The Philadelphia Phillies won the World Series against the Tampa Bay Rays.

I took Grandma to the race track twice because she 'had a feeling.' The first time, she won twenty-seven dollars. The second time, she lost fifty bucks on broken-down nags in what I called the Dog Food Trifecta – all three of her horses came in last.

Still, Grandma might be right this time. I fortified myself with more pie and asked, 'Well, if I didn't stop in your doorway, what's going to happen?'

'I'm not sure,' Grandma said. 'But it involves you and Angela and a crime.'

'Angela in a crime? No one is more honest than Angela. She keeps our books and insists on an independent audit every year. Besides, our design business doesn't make enough money for her to steal.'

'I didn't say she was stealing,' Grandma said. 'Your Jack is working late a lot lately, isn't he?'

'Jack's architectural firm won the renovation project for the old NorCo shoe company building. They're turning it into loft apartments. His proposal is due in two weeks.'

Why the sudden shift from my business partner to my husband? Oh, no. Jack wouldn't. She wouldn't. Angela was no angel, but she wouldn't have an affair with my husband. Would she?

I put down my pie fork. 'Grandma, Jack is working late. And he doesn't like Angela. She's not interested in him, either.'

'That's what your father used to say, until—' Grandma said.

'He was shot,' I interrupted. 'Jack is nothing like my father. That's why I married him.'

'But what about Angela? She's a good-looking woman.'

'Much better looking than me,' I said.

'Francine! I would never say that,' Grandma said.

'No, but you think it, like everyone else. Angela has a boyfriend. Actually, he's a friend with benefits.'

'What's that?' Grandma said.

'It means she likes him, and she sleeps with him sometimes when she feels like it.'

'In my day, we called that a husband,' Grandma said.

'I'd better go,' I said. 'It's getting late, and I need to get home before Sarah.'

'You worry too much,' Grandma said. 'She's not a little girl anymore.'

'She's a teenager, which is even more dangerous.'

'Sarah's not using drugs, is she?' Grandma asked.

'No, she's just surly. I can't do anything right.'

'She'll grow out of it,' Grandma said. 'Take her some apple pie. Do you think it's boy trouble?'

'She says boys are gross,' I said. 'I'm happy she believes that for now.'

'So many young girls get in trouble,' Grandma said, as she put half a pie in a Tupperware container. 'I'm thankful Sarah's still a child.' Grandma handed the pie to me.

I kissed her forehead. 'I guess I'm overprotective,' I said. 'But Sarah is a young fifteen.'

'She doesn't dress like a young girl,' Grandma said. 'At Thanksgiving, she was wearing an outfit that made her look like—'

'A slut,' I finished.

Grandma's lips tightened into a thin, angry line. 'I would never say that about my great-grandbaby. But that short skirt and belly-baring top did make her look older than her years.'

'That's how girls dress now, Grandma,' I said. 'It looks slutty by our standards, but I didn't want her to be what I was in high school.'

'What? An A student?' Grandma said.

'A nerd,' I said. 'Thanks for the pie. I'm sure she'll love it.'

Grandma followed me to her front door. 'Francine, if you need money for anything, you can always come to me. I only have a couple hundred in the bank, but I own this house. It's not worth much, but the land is valuable. Some developer wants to build another subdivision on this road. He's made an offer for that lot across the street and my five acres.'

'Thanks, Grandma, but where would you live? You keep your house and your independence.'

'Okay, but the money is yours when you need it. Lawyers are expensive.'

'I don't need a lawyer,' I said. 'Where did that come from?'

'Just a feeling,' Grandma said.

Grandma had bought the green three-room rambler when Mehlville was still the middle of nowhere. New highways had made the suburb more accessible and the land more valuable.

I worried all the way to my next stop, my Maplewood design office. I tried to remember what I knew about Angela's 'friend with benefits'. His name was Allan, he was a CPA, and Angela had redecorated his office in what we privately called 'clubby classic'. Allan wanted leather wing chairs, forest green walls, and hunting prints. Not terribly innovative, but most people didn't want an innovative accountant. I gathered Allan wasn't much more exciting outside the office. Angela had said he was a presentable escort and 'okay in the sack, but he won't set the world on fire. Besides, I like them young, you know what I mean? Allans my age. He's too old for me.' She'd laughed.

Lately, Angela had been uncommonly cheerful. Her pale complexion had the glow of a well-loved woman. Maybe she did have a new boyfriend. Good for her.

I knew Angela didn't have time for an affair with my husband. She was too busy mentoring Megan, the new intern from the university's design school. Thanks to Angela, we got the school's best young talent working for us. Interns were good at tracking down online resources and running out for paint samples, material swatches, and coffee. They were low-paid errand girls, but they got terrific recommendation letters and experience. Our firm, Smart Women, was a good name to put on their resumes.

I didn't like dealing with the college students. The girls showed up late, hungover, or not at all. They needed constant attention. They whined that their parents didn't give them enough money. I'd worked my way through college and thought most were spoiled brats. Angela said working with young talent was invigorating. She could have them.

Even my own daughter, who wanted to be an interior designer, would rather work with Angela. Sarah said all I did was criticize her. I only suggested a few small improvements. I was happy my daughter wanted to follow in my footsteps. Sarah's rejection hurt, but maybe we needed a buffer for now. We'd just had a fight over the October cell phone bill. Sarah had text-messaged another two hundred dollars onto it.

Sarah must have cried on Angela's shoulder. Angela told me many parents had monster texting bills from their kids. She e-mailed me some family phone plans with unlimited text messaging. 'Sarah needs to stay in touch with her friends,' Angela said. 'It's harmless. All the kids do it.'

Exactly what Sarah had said. I didn't want to reward my

daughter for running up bills, but maybe I should look into those plans. I'd spent hours talking on the phone to my best friend, Sue, when I was in high school. I couldn't remember a word we'd said, but those calls were vital to me at Sarah's age. My daughter was a good kid. Heaven knows what I'd put my mother through when I was fifteen.

Smart Women, our interior design office, was close to my home. Ten years ago, Angela and I had bought an old two-story brick building on Manchester Road for a good price. We'd created an amazing office with lots of natural light, open space, and hardwood floors. Smart Women was close to three major highways and the rich areas that used our services. Maplewood, an older suburb, had become trendy, and our property value skyrocketed.

It was dark when I parked my Lexus in back of the building and slipped quietly through the side door. I could see my daughter and my design partner standing over a drawing board. I knew they were working on the McDaniels vacation condo at the Lake of the Ozarks. The overhead lights turned Angela's red hair into fire. My daughter's long blonde hair was spun gold. Sarah seemed older in the dim light, and I could see the young woman she would soon become. Both women were dressed in black sweaters and pants. I watched the scene without making a sound.

'We could use a beachy theme in the great room, which has the best view of the lake,' Angela said. 'What about a conversation group of wicker chairs and a white couch facing those big windows? We could use the blue accent pillows.'

Ordinary, I thought. The McDaniels would want something more stylish. That's why they hired Smart Women.

'What happens when one of the McDaniels' boys visits?' my daughter said. 'The condo only has one bedroom. That couch won't stay white if the boys crash on it. I go to school with the youngest, Judson. He's a slob. I've seen him eat spaghetti out of the can. Maybe we should think about a pullout sofa to give the room flexibility.'

'Good idea,' Angela said. 'What do you think of coral for the sofa?'

'It's spaghetti-colored,' my daughter said, then paused. 'I meant that as a joke, Angela. I love the color, and we can keep your blue accent pillows, too. You've made the room vibrant.'

I was so proud of my daughter. Sarah was smart, talented – and tactful. I could see my daughter's name on our letterhead in a few years.

In the meantime, I was hungry. I tiptoed out and carefully shut the door so I wouldn't disturb them. Then I called my husband. It was only five thirty, and Jack was still at work. I asked him if he'd like to meet me for dinner at Acero, his favorite Maplewood restaurant.

'I was just finishing up,' Jack said. 'I should have this project done before the deadline. Probably tomorrow night.'

'Good,' I said. 'Maybe you'll get a bonus.'

'Only if the clients like it. Are you serious about Acero?'

'My treat,' I said.

'Could I order the mushroom ravioli with black truffles?'

'You can have whatever your heart desires,' I said. 'Including me.'

'You're dessert,' he said. 'Black truffles first.'

Acero wasn't a spaghetti-and-meatballs Italian restaurant. I ordered the grilled skate wing in browned butter. The meat looked like a large, plump wing. It was hard to believe it came from such a prehistoric-looking creature as the ray-like skate.

'This is heavenly,' I told Jack.

'Maybe it's an angel wing,' he teased.

We finished dinner and drove by Smart Women on the way home. The lights were still on. 'Our daughter is working with Angela tonight,' I said. 'That means we have the house to ourselves.'

'Are you propositioning me?' Jack asked.

'Absolutely. I'm a smart woman, remember?' We hurried home.

Sarah walked in the door at eight o'clock. Jack and I were watching a movie in the media room, holding hands. We'd had an hour to make love.

'Hi, honey, how was your day?' Jack joked.

Sarah smiled at her father and said, 'Good. I worked with Angela on the McDaniels' beach house, and we came up with this cool idea for the great room.'

Our daughter talked a mile a minute, the way she did when she was happy. Then she kissed her father good night, ignored me, and went upstairs.

She's going to be upset when Angela dies, I thought meanly. *But maybe I'll get my daughter back. Sarah will have to work with me.*

I slept badly that night. In my dreams, a ghostly Angela pleaded with me not to let her die. I woke up drenched with sweat and went to the kitchen to fix a calming cup of tea. I couldn't save Angela, and she wouldn't believe me if I told her she'd soon be dead.

I was trapped, and she was doomed. I wished Grandma had never told me about Angela. I knew her supernatural knowledge was a dark burden, but I didn't want it, either. I didn't sleep the rest of that night.

The next day, I was tired and preoccupied. At work I botched an order for upholstery fabric, gave the wrong number for my trade discount to a wholesale house, and spilled a mug of coffee all over my desk.

'What's wrong?' Angela asked. 'You look pale.'

So did Angela. Maybe it was her new light pink lipstick. It was a shade I hadn't seen since the 1960s. It must be back in style, or Angela wouldn't wear it.

'I'm probably coming down with the flu,' I said.

'Why don't you go home?' Angela said, 'I can finish up here.'

I was glad to leave. I couldn't meet her eyes, knowing she had one more day to live. Trouble was coming, and all I could do was avoid it. But I was worried about my daughter. What if Sarah was with Angela when my partner died? What if Sarah was hurt, too? Or caught up somehow in Grandma's mysterious crime? I had to keep my daughter safe tomorrow.

When school was out, I called Sarah on her cell phone. 'Hi,' she said, her voice sullen.

'Sarah, your father should be finishing his big project tomorrow. I thought we could take him out to dinner to celebrate.'

'Can't, Mom,' she said. 'I'm rehearsing for the school musical, remember?'

'Right,' I said. 'I forgot.'

What musical? When did she tell me that? 'You never talk about your part,' I said.

'I'm in the chorus and a crowd scene. Big whoop.'

There it was again, that surly teenage voice. I tamped down my anger. If Sarah was at school, she wouldn't be around Angela on a dangerous day. I called my husband at work to invite him to dinner tomorrow night.

'I just hope I get everything finished, after I bragged to you about how well it was going,' he said. 'I've hit a snag. I'll be working late tonight and maybe tomorrow. Don't wait for dinner, promise?'

'Sure.'

Sarah came home about six and went straight to her room without greeting me.

'Do you want dinner, honey?' I asked.

'Not hungry,' she said. The two words were dropped on me like flat stones. I spent the night brooding on the couch, aimlessly channel surfing. When would Sarah return to her cheerful self? Why was her father working late? Jack wouldn't lie to me, would he? Not after the way he'd loved me last night. Of course, my father had lied to my mother. Easily.

Jack came home after midnight and woke me up. I'd fallen asleep on the couch, 'Come on, sweetheart,' he whispered. 'You'll be more comfortable in our bed. I want to hold you.'

I followed him upstairs, trying to drown out the voices that said he was betraying me. Jack took off his tie and rumpled suit jacket. 'I have a lipstick stain on my collar,' he said. 'Do we have any stain remover?'

'How did you get lipstick on your collar?' I asked, trying to sound light and unconcerned.

'Sandy, the office manager, is moving to Seattle with her new husband. You remember her. The pretty one with the brown eyes and dark hair. We had a party at the office, and she gave me a good-bye kiss.'

That sounded like the kind of excuse my father used, I thought. My father the cheater.

'Just drop it in the laundry basket,' I said. 'I'll treat the stain in the morning.'

The lipstick on the collar nagged at me. I spent another restless night, then got up to kiss Jack good-bye and see my daughter off to school. She was wearing a tiny skirt and a scoop-neck top.

'Sarah, is that outfit appropriate for school?' I asked.

'Mom,' she said. 'Everybody dresses like this. Anyway, I'm going to be late for the bus.'

'At least put on a jacket over it.' I handed her the cropped jacket we'd bought as part of her back-to-school wardrobe.

'Gotta run,' she said and was out the door before I could tell if she'd put it on or stuffed it in her backpack. I sighed. At least she hadn't dropped the jacket on a chair.

I examined the lipstick stain on my husband's shirt. The lipstick was a pale pink. Would a brunette wear that color?

Didn't Sandy wear darker colors? But Angela was wearing something similar. It must be back in style.

Angela. What if that wasn't Sandy's lipstick on my husband's shirt collar? What if it was Angela's?

'*Your Jack is working late a lot lately, isn't he?*' my grandmother had asked. I'd defended him. He didn't get in until midnight last night. He was working late tonight, too. On his project – or on Angela?

I had to know. I wasn't going to be a fool like my mother. I drove over to Jack's office in downtown Kirkwood. His car was parked in the company lot in his reserved space. I parked across the street and waited. At twelve fifteen, he left the building and went to Spencer's Grill. I got out, pulled my winter hat low, and walked past the old-fashioned diner. Jack was sitting at the counter, reading a magazine and munching a grilled cheese sandwich.

I watched him walk back to his office while I stood in a store across the street. Jack had a corner office, and I could see him at his desk. The lights were on in the gray winter afternoon, and the building was too busy for a dalliance. I went home until five thirty and called him.

'Still have to work late, honey?' I asked.

'Afraid so,' he said. 'I'm sorry to leave you home alone again, but you can spend the time thinking about what you can do with the extra money. Maybe we can take a February vacation to someplace warm.'

'I'd love to go to the Caribbean. What about St Bart's? Or St John's?'

'Any saint you want,' he said.

He hung up, and I started brooding again. My husband had sounded suspiciously cheery – the way my father did when he was cheating on my mother. Mom took it, year after year. Well, I wasn't going to be Jack's doormat. If he was cheating, I wanted to know. Then I'd get the best divorce lawyer.

I waited until seven o'clock, when I knew Jack would be

getting hungry, and drove to a Maplewood brew pub, the Schlafly Bottleworks. I ordered a bison burger. I'd surprise him with his favorite sandwich if he was at the office working. If not, well, he'd get a different surprise.

I saw Jack's light was on and his blinds were drawn. I barged right into his office.

'Surprise!' I yelled.

Jack was surprised. He was sitting at his drawing board, with paper spread everywhere.

I felt foolish, standing there with a bison burger. 'I brought you a present.' I handed him the bag.

Jack's face lit up when he unwrapped his burger. 'You didn't have to,' he said. 'But you've saved me from eating pretzels from the snack machine.'

'That's free-range bison,' I said. 'I wonder where in the US the buffalo roam.'

'Like me, not far from home,' he said, kissing me on the nose. 'Now I really do have to get back to work.'

'I have to get home,' I said. 'Sarah's rehearsing for the school musical. She should be back any moment.'

It was so cold my car didn't warm up on the short drive home. I passed Smart Women and saw the lights were off. I hoped Angela was enjoying her last night on earth. She only had four hours left, if Grandma was right. Of course, Grandma had been wrong about my husband, Jack. Maybe she was wrong about Angela, too. Maybe she was turning as strange as her brother Oswald, who lived in the state mental institution and talked to imaginary people.

Our house was dark when I parked in front of it. I killed the lights and went in the front door. Sarah wasn't home yet, unless she'd fallen asleep.

I heard a noise upstairs. 'Hello?' I called. No answer. I armed myself with the fireplace poker. I took out my cell phone and pressed 911, but didn't hit the call button. I slipped it in my pocket and tiptoed upstairs.

More noise, thumping and moaning. The sounds were

coming from our bedroom. A burglar was hurting Sarah. I raced down the hall, flipped on the bedroom light, and saw Angela in my bed. Naked.

With my daughter.

Their clothes were scattered all over the floor.

'You slut,' I shrieked. 'That's my innocent daughter!'

I struck out with the poker and hit Angela on the head, I heard Sarah scream, 'No, Mom, you don't understand!' She tried to grab my arm, but I shook her away.

I kept hitting Angela until I realized that brilliant red was not her hair, but her blood. By then Angela was dead, and my sobbing daughter had called the police.

When my husband got home at midnight, I was being led away in handcuffs.

My daughter still won't speak to me. Sarah told the police and the reporters that she loved Angela and they were planning to marry someplace where it was legal. Sarah said she didn't tell me about their romance because she was afraid I'd overreact, and Angela's murder proved she was right. I didn't want my daughter to be known as a nerd, and she isn't. The tabloids call her the Lesbian Lolita.

Will I be convicted of murder?

My lawyer says it depends on the jury. The law is tricky in Missouri. Seventeen is the age of consent, but if Angela believed Sarah was older and my daughter had given her consent, then Angela would not have been guilty of sex with a minor.

But Angela knew Sarah was only fifteen. She went to our daughter's birthday dinner with us. My husband can't find the photos to prove that. I wonder if my daughter destroyed them. She's testifying for the prosecution. They're saying my little Sarah was sexually emancipated. A TV talk show shrink said when Sarah brought her lover into her parents' bedroom she was declaring herself a sexual being. He didn't mention that the bed was a lot bigger than hers.

Jack sold our house to help pay for the best criminal

lawyer in the city. He and Sarah rent a small apartment near his office. Grandma sleeps on a pullout sofa in the living room. She's moved in with them. She sold her house to pay for my legal bills. My grandmother wants to testify on my behalf. My lawyer says she'll help prove a family history of mental illness.

The last time Grandma visited me in jail, I asked if she saw my future. Grandma said she saw nothing. The dead no longer visit her in the new apartment. She's glad her so-called gift is gone.

Her tiny house has been leveled, and an upscale subdivision is being built on the site. These grand houses will have two baths, marble fireplaces, three bedrooms, and walk-in closets.

I wonder if one will have a walk-in bedroom doorway.

THE CONQUEROR WORM

Barbara D'Amato

Neal Hofstra had been home from work just three minutes – time enough to throw his coat on the sofa, stop in the bathroom, get a bottle of water from the fridge, and sit down at his computer and click up his e-mail. Although he complained about e-mail to his girlfriend, Sandy, claiming that because of it he never got away from his job, in fact he loved it. Neal was aware he wasn't the most assertive man on the planet. Telephone conversations made him uneasy. He never quite knew how to end one and was left saying, 'Well, okay—' or 'Um, that'll be fine, then,' and hoping the person on the other end would firmly say 'Good-bye.' But with e-mail he could get the wording exactly right. Plus he could send off a note to a friend or even an order to a supplier – his job was supply manager for a chain of office supply stores – at any time of the day or night and not have to worry about disturbing the addressee. When he was forced to actually telephone somebody, he was sure he was interrupting. After all, if the person was at work, she was busy and shouldn't be bothered. And if she was at home, she was resting and shouldn't be bothered.

He sat down in his swivel chair and opened nkHofstra. He clicked on in-box. Three new messages in the in-box. It was like opening surprise packages.

From subject received

Sandy Hossler dinner tonight? 11/5/2008 2:44 PM

JDPutnam Brant erasable pens order 11/5/2008 5:01 PM

Earl Think reminder 11/5/2008 5:17 PM

The one from his girlfriend Sandy was a nice thing. He'd like to do dinner tonight, but he deleted it and would get back to her in a couple of minutes. The one from his boss with the pen order wasn't such a nice thing. The 5:01 time made it irritatingly clear that Mr Putnam knew he had left work on the stroke of five.

Well, screw him. Neal would get the stupid pens order in tonight. Brant's took orders 24/7.

The mystery e-mailer was interesting. No attachment, so he opened it.

The message read:

Hello, Inky.

Neal shoved himself away from the desk so hard his chair caught its wheels on an electric cable, and he tipped over onto the floor. Grabbing the chair by the back, he slammed it down in front of the desk and dropped into it.

The rest of the message read '*Just asking how you are after all this time.*' It was signed '*I. Amoco.*'

Neal hit reply and typed '*Who are you?*' Then he hit send. He got up and walked around the room a couple of times until he realized he was holding his breath. The message was a joke. A stupid joke. He ought to be angry. No, he *was* angry. He sat back down and, furious, he deleted the original message with a hard thumb on the delete key.

But now there was an incoming message. This one from Moca Hooy, which had to be something different. Neal opened it.

You know who I am. Your old friend Berko.

Although Neal was trembling now, he managed to type a reply.

But you're dead.

A ten-second pause and another message. This one from acc most.

Nope. Can't get out of it that way, Inky.

Neal punched Delete. Went to the second message and deleted it. Then, thinking he was going to vomit, he ran to the bathroom. But as soon as he got there, the anger took over instead. He washed his hot face with cold water. Then washed it again.

All right. He was furious with whoever it was. But this was not the time to get crazy. Who else knew him by the name Inky? Berko had invented the nickname from his initials, N. K. Hofstra. He was always making up mildly insulting nicknames, like calling Henry Caringella Zorro because he got a zero on his first differential equations test. It wasn't quite insulting, because it wasn't Zero. Berko never used these names except in one-on-one conversations, as if it were some sort of intimate endearment. Neal had only heard about the Zorro name because Henry told him. Neal had certainly not told anybody about the Inky name.

Time to trace this thing. He wished he were a computer genius. Sitting back down again, he checked his in-box. Gone, of course. He had deleted the messages. But they would be in the delete file.

He clicked on the delete file. Oddly, the messages weren't there. Could he have emptied the file? Well, he certainly didn't remember doing so, and there was the deleted message from Sandy. And besides, he would have had to answer 'Yes' when the program asked whether he was sure he wanted to permanently delete the messages, and then he would have had to return to his in-box, because that had been up on the screen when he got back from the bathroom.

And he certainly had not done all that and been unaware of it. There had been no mental blackout. He was angry, not insane.

What was the name the first message had come in under? Something about an oil company? He couldn't remember.

Of course! He was so rattled he wasn't thinking. Look in *sent items!* The first message would be there, attached to his response.

But it wasn't. It and his response were gone.

The phone rang. He was trembling so much he could hardly answer.

'Hi, hon. Get my e-mail? Let's do dinner.'

'Sandy, I don't think I'm up for dinner tonight.'

'What's wrong?'

'I'm not feeling very well.'

'You sound funny. I'll come over and take care of you.'

'No, honey. I think I'd better just hunker down. I'll call if I need you.'

She was ringing his doorbell twenty minutes later.

He had loved Sandy when he first heard her speak. Her voice summed her up so well – gentle, willing to listen but willing to speak her mind, too. There was a trace of sadness in Sandy, which he thought was the result of her divorce. She had the air of a person who had made a mistake and grown as a result.

The first time she visited his apartment, he'd cooked for her. She'd had a hard day at her job as a paralegal. The lawyers had kept her working through lunch. Without thinking much about it, he'd taken a carton of eggs from the refrigerator. He cracked six into a bowl, whisked them with a fork, and poured them gently into a pan where butter was bubbling on low heat. While they were scrambling, he took lox and a red onion out of the refrigerator. He sliced two bagels and lowered them into the toaster.

Sandy said, 'Now I know you're not a computer nerd.'

'What?'

'You cook.'

'Oh, yeah. You mean I don't send out for pizza and have empty pizza boxes and Mountain Dew cans all over the floor.'

'Exactly.'

Tonight, she had not only hurried over, she had brought a large shopping bag that emitted the odors of Thai curry beef and coconut milk soup.

'Now I'll go to the kitchen and dish out, and then we'll eat, and you'll tell me what's wrong.'

While she was in the kitchen – a very tiny space with one work counter and room for a two-foot-diameter round table and two chairs, Neal edged cautiously to his computer. He touched the keyboard gingerly and looked at the monitor.

Another message. '*Ah, much of sadness, more of sin, Inky. I'm going to get even.*'

'Sandy! Come here quick! I'll show you.'

'What?'

'Look at this!'

She peered over his shoulder. 'What, Neal? A message from your boss?'

Sandy said, 'You'd better call Beetlejuice.'

He explained what was happening, the vanishing messages, but not the underlying reason. And certainly not the horrible thing he had done that caused all this. He knew he had to tell her eventually, but he had to work up to it. What would she think of him, once she knew? He didn't want to lose her.

Beetlejuice Thomas said he'd come right over.

The man had been named by a mother with an antic imagination. But he thought his name was pretty funny. 'Nobody forgets who I am,' he said.

When he burst in the door, he shouted, 'You lucky folk, it's me!'

But seeing Neal's face, he sobered up.

Neal explained, just as he had to Sandy, what was happening, but not the story behind it.

Beetlejuice sat at Neal's desk, flexed his fingers dramatically, and said, 'Got any Jolt?'

'No. Sorry.'

'Mountain Dew?'

'I think so.'

Beetlejuice clicked keys for several minutes and began to look annoyed.

Neal said, 'No luck?'

'Not yet. Why don't you go get a soda for yourself and let me work?'

'Have you ever seen a problem like this before?'

Hearing Neal's tacit criticism, he said, 'Yes, actually, I have.'

'Did you fix it?'

'I'm researching it.'

'So when was this?'

'A couple of weeks ago.'

'Did you find the problem?'

'I haven't yet.'

'How is the person who has the problem dealing with it?'

'I haven't heard from him recently. I'll have to check.'

Neal paced back and forth. Sandy brought him a glass of grape drink, but he just held it. He felt queasy. He peered over Beetlejuice's shoulder. Which wasn't appreciated.

'Go away! Just let me work. I'm restoring the backup of your e-mail data.'

Suddenly, Neal was hit by a thought. 'Um – Beetle? When you get the e-mail, do you see it?'

'What?'

'Will you see the actual e-mail?'

'Yeah. Duh. You're saying if I just find the messages, I shouldn't open them?'

'Uh, yes.'

Beetlejuice and Sandy exchanged glances.

After a few minutes, Beetlejuice pushed the chair back and worked his shoulders.

'Got it?' Neal said.

'Well, no.'

'Now what?'

'Will you just let me do this? Now I'm going to run a data-recovery utility.'

Sandy sat on the sofa with her hands folded and her back stiff. Neal paced. A couple of times he thought he caught Sandy looking at him speculatively.

Finally Beetlejuice said, 'It just doesn't find them.'

'You mean we can't tell whether the e-mails were ever sent?'

'Dude, I don't think they ever came in.'

'But they did. I saw them!'

'Come on, Neal, man. Everybody gets times when they're over-stressed.'

'I did *not* imagine this!'

'Maybe that crappy boss is getting on your nerves.'

'No,' Neal said. He was not going to get mad at Beetle. After all, the man had come over here to help. Or at least he wasn't going to show that he was mad. 'Yeah – well,' he said.

'You know, Hofstra, there's no such thing as a ghost in a machine.'

When Beetle left, Neal knew it was time to be honest.

'Sandy – listen.'

'What?'

'The e-mails are talking about something I did. Four years ago, I was out at a bar with a friend. His name was Berko. We came out later – maybe midnight – and we were half-way down the block when these four guys jumped us.'

'Oh, my God!'

'They said they wanted money, and we gave them our

155

wallets, but they started beating us anyway with crowbars, or tire irons, I don't know. I pulled out my cell phone, but they stomped on it, and I ran.'

'And you survived.'

'Yes. But Berko didn't. If I'd stayed there and fought back, he might have.'

'Why wouldn't you have been killed, too?'

'Uh – I might have been.'

'Honey, it was their fault, their evil, not yours.'

'What I did was my fault—'

'Everybody has something like that in their lives. Guilt is a terrible thing to go on feeling.'

'But I *am* guilty.'

'These things eat away at you. I know.'

He didn't answer.

'I've had personal experience with this, Neal.'

'Well, you told me about your divorce. But I don't think that's the same, no matter how much you may blame yourself.'

'I didn't tell you all of it. I didn't tell you the reason for our divorce.'

'People are allowed to have differences—'

'No! Neal, we had a daughter.'

Neal shifted uncomfortably.

'She was four years old. Patricia. We called her Tishy.'

'If it hurts you too much, don't tell me.'

She went on anyway. 'Tishy and I always went to the store together. She loved to pick out things for dinner. She had – we had the proper child safety seat in the car for her, properly installed in the backseat. She always used it. She was such a good girl. She had gotten to the age where she was very proud of fastening the seat belt herself. She'd get in and say, "Buckle up." When she was younger, she called it "uckle up".'

Neal shifted again but didn't say anything.

'So this Tuesday, we got in to drive to the store. She

climbed into her seat and buckled up. I heard the buckle click. I heard it! But she must have pushed it and let it go. We drove down Elk Road. There's a stop sign going the other way. A driver – a young woman with three fraternity buddies in her car – ran the sign and broadsided us. Tisha was thrown sideways into the left rear door. She died. I only had a bump on my forehead.'

Sandy had not cried until she told how little she had been injured.

'The seat belt was defective,' Neal said.

'No. She hadn't latched it. I heard a click, but I didn't check. *I didn't check!*'

Sandy left. Neal had said he needed to be alone. He had tried to comfort her, but all the while, he was thinking, *You made a careless mistake. I didn't make a mistake.*

I didn't make a mistake. I made a decision to be cowardly. What I didn't tell Sandy was – I could have run down the street and found a store open and called 911. But I was afraid they'd follow me. So I ducked into an alley and hid behind a bunch of trash cans until I heard them leave.

Until I heard them leave. Oh, God. Berko was dying by then. He was surely beyond help by the time I found an open liquor store and called the cops.

I am slime.

A new message appeared. It was from Earl Think. It said, *You killed me.*

Quickly, Neal grabbed up his iPhone and took a picture of the monitor screen. He looked at the phone screen. Nothing.

But it had been there. Really, it had. It wasn't his imagination or the effect of a guilty conscience.

Except – what difference did it make? He was guilty whether the messages were real or the product of his self-loathing. He had done something terribly wrong and cowardly, and he had killed his friend.

And he realized he could never tell Sandy the whole truth, that he had not only run away into the alley and hidden behind those trash cans. He had waited. He could have run down the street and found a phone, but he ran and hid and waited until he heard the muggers leave. It had taken another three or four minutes for them to finish stomping Berko. If he hadn't wanted to hide so fast, if he hadn't been afraid they'd follow him, if he had run down the street, Berko might have lived.

Neal was crying now. He was a coward and a worthless human being.

He went into the kitchen and rummaged in a bottom cabinet until he found the vodka, which he practically never drank. Carrying the bottle by the neck, he went into the bathroom and found aspirin. Then he returned to the computer and sat in his swivel chair and took a long drink from the bottle. He started to choke, but he kept calm. After a couple of minutes, he chewed two of the aspirin, then decided to wash them down with more vodka. He waited several minutes to make sure he wasn't going to choke again. Then he repeated the process.

In the flash of a fading brain, Neal realized, anagrams! The *thing* was playing with him. Coma hooy = yahoo.com. Earl think earth-link. L. Amoco = aol.com. But it all didn't matter.

Sandy had reached her home troubled. Neal had been devastated, whatever was happening. When she had left, his eyes were wide and his cheeks looked hollow. He was having some sort of stress-induced hallucinations.

She gave herself a couple of minutes, to see whether her nerves would quiet down. Maybe she was overreacting.

But half an hour later, she was only more worried.

All right. She picked up the phone. He hadn't said not to call, after all.

But there was no answer. She let it ring a dozen times.

Well, no answer didn't necessarily mean he was in trouble. He quite often didn't answer the phone if he was entering orders for work. And he sometimes turned off the phone if he was going to bed. He'd had a stressful evening, that was for sure. Maybe he figured a good night's sleep would straighten him out.

At Neal's apartment, he heard the phone very distantly. He made no attempt to answer it. In fact, he couldn't quite remember where he had left it, and it sounded funny, echoey and hollow. He drank some more vodka, took another two aspirin, and put his head down on the desk.

Sandy knew she wasn't going to relax until she was certain Neal was all right. She picked up her keys to drive back to his place, then hesitated. Maybe that was going too far too fast. He could be working, and he might be annoyed if she just burst in. What she'd do first is e-mail him. If he was working, he'd get a ding that there was an incoming message. He'd be alert for one, if he was awake, because he was waiting for the phantom e-mailer. If he didn't answer her e-mail in, say, half an hour, she'd drive over.

She went to her desk and opened her e-mail.

Hmm, there was a message for her. She'd just take a minute to check it.

She opened the e-mail. The message said,

Hi, Mommy.

IN MEMORY OF THE *SIBYLLINE*

Lou Kemp

The many men so beautiful
And they all dead did lie!
And a million million slimy things
Liv'd on – and so did I.
The Rime of the Ancient Mariner – *Coleridge*

Like a shower of fairy dust on fire, the embers from Townsend's pipe blew across the railing and into the night, lost long before they fell into the waves.

He cupped his pipe to protect the remaining embers and to keep his hands warm. It seemed like only hours ago when the *Christianna* had sailed out of Cascais under a warm Portuguese sun.

A pregnant moon hung low over the sea. The waves reflected moonlight on iridescent crests that rolled by the *Christianna* as frothy and lacy as underskirts. Townsend gazed upward. The conflagration of stars seemed endless. Somewhere beyond them lay places the sailors of the future would travel. He'd be content to reach Alexandria and with a wee bit of luck it would be more temperate than his last visit in 1812. He nearly froze before he reached Cairo.

Although he did not hear footsteps, Townsend became aware of another presence at the rail. Townsend looked closer and saw that it was an older academic he'd met as he boarded the ship. A deep and pervading sadness seemed to weigh upon the man's shoulders.

'Good evening, Mr Perideaux,' Townsend said.

'A beautiful night, no?' Perideaux's cigarette flickered in the darkness, revealing a faint sheen of perspiration decorating his brow.

Although his words seemed calm enough, it appeared that Perideaux needed to be reassured in some manner, perhaps only to hear another voice in the vastness of the night. Townsend could sympathize with that thought. The undercurrent of fear existed most tangibly when a lone ship rode the waves in the dead of night. It was long after eleven bells, and the crewmen in the rigging above were only a suggestion of movement. Or life.

'Yes, a beautiful night,' Townsend agreed.

Perideaux made no response. The man's attention seemed transfixed some distance off the port bow as his gaze swept the sea from side to side, as if searching for something.

Under their feet, the *Christianna* creaked and groaned as she climbed a wave. Townsend relit his pipe. The damned thing could never stay lit for more than a few minutes. He wondered if Perideaux expected to see another ship cross their wake.

If Townsend hadn't been watching his companion closely, he wouldn't have seen the delicate shudder that traveled down the man. Perideaux said, 'Felicity, oh, Felicity,' and he grabbed hold of the railing.

At first Townsend could perceive nothing except the inky night and the roiling waves. Then he saw the outline of a ship. Within seconds, the vessel seemed to glow and solidify. Three masts pointed to the sky, and brass rails glimmered underneath canvases that billowed, tickled by the wind. Shadows walked the deck. She floated nearly a league in the distance, without lights, without substance.

A gurgling sound came from Perideaux's throat, and he whispered, 'The *Dutchman*.'

Townsend heard him, but couldn't stop watching the phantom ship that appeared to fade away until the moonlight pierced through her, and then she became distinct once again.

From a porthole I watched as Madagascar slipped away into the distance. Already, a hot sun reflected off the sea, obscuring the city with so much brightness that the smoke-shrouded shacks and fishing boats blended to gray, leaving just a suggestion of civilization behind the foam-capped waves.

My cabin was on the leeward deck, only a few paces from the captain's quarters and those of the passengers. Through the portholes blew a fragrant breeze, bringing the suggestion of frying sausages and the calls of the sailors as they worked high above in the rigging and swung from spar to spar. The *LeHanna* was a barkentine and considered to be of good size.

I'd determined that my cabin door would not open. Presumably because it was locked. However, I had no trouble hearing footsteps on the wooden deck approach and stop just outside.

Through the porthole, I could see most of my guard in profile. The newcomer confronting him was a tall man, nearly my height, scholarly and pale.

'We're pleased to have you aboard, Dr Perideaux,' said the guard.

The trick to observing someone without staring and causing them to turn and stare back is to look a bit off to the side. In this instance, I watched the sky just beyond Dr Perideaux's large ears. There was no mistaking the steel in his voice.

'Are you? Is that why you feel it necessary to brandish a musket around my family?'

The guard replied, 'I'm sorry you feel that way, sir. But I have my orders.'

'What orders? What do you have to guard? I just sent Felicity back to the cabin for her safety.'

'I'm sure your daughter will find something to do there,' the guard said.

Dr Perideaux pointed at the cabin door. 'I demand to know what is in there.'

'No one is to enter this cabin. And no one will.'

With a clatter of boots, Captain Hume arrived wearing a wide smile and insincere eyes. Perhaps Dr Perideaux noted the captain's eyes, for his tone did not change.

'Captain, what is in there?'

Although a short man, the captain did not shrink from the doctor's aggressive stance, nor did he raise his voice.

'Please calm yourself. I'm sure you do not want to upset your wife.' The ship's bell rang thirteen times for the hour, drowning out his next words. '. . . simple matter. We have charge of a prisoner. He is to be dropped off at Victoria Island tomorrow.'

'Why is he up here with the passengers?' Dr Perideaux demanded. 'Why is he not kept below with the crew?'

I enjoyed Captain Hume's slight hesitation. How would he put it? Would he tell the truth or prevaricate?

'Doctor, I have specific orders that the prisoner is not to have contact with a living soul. He has to be separated from the crew.'

The doctor stared at the captain. 'Why?'

'I cannot tell you.' Captain Hume placed a hand on Perideaux's shoulder. 'Please. Keep your family away from this area. Entertain them. I believe your wife is not well?'

Dr Perideaux rubbed his chin and frowned. 'No, she is not. The baby is due shortly.'

'All the more reason for you to join her. Perhaps with a cup of tea?'

*

163

A rain shower visited the ship with the lightest touch. The *LeHanna* climbed the waves rhythmically, descending and rising as lovers do, hesitating to savor the moment slowly.

The last few days had marked the end of summer in Madagascar, and I'd grown tired of the food and lack of good lager. On balance, the muggy nights were warm with scents made more pungent with the heat and promise of whatever I could find in the bohemian quarters. When we reached Seville, it would be autumn, and the bougainvilleas would still bloom in veils of brilliant color. I had no intention of being dumped on Victoria Island like a rancid bag of potatoes.

The penal colony on Victoria Island offered little besides hard labor and the most notorious criminals for company. The sharks that circled the island did so knowing that there would always be another convict swimming toward the sun, tiring . . . and then succumbing. I shuddered delicately and resumed my reading.

The dulcet sound of snoring filtered through my cabin door. I arose and moved to the porthole to watch my guard as he slept. The full sun, a satisfied belly, and the repetitive motion of the waves had lulled him to sleep against the wall of the cabin. Or it could have been something else? Perhaps dropped into his plate of stew?

A young girl approached from the stern. She wore her red curls tied in a ribbon that matched her dress of robin's egg blue. She was probably eight years of age, but checked over her shoulder with the furtiveness of a well-seasoned Singapore pickpocket. If I interpreted her smile correctly, she seemed content with what she saw.

As she passed by, I said, 'Hello, poppet.'

Innocent eyes widened, searching for my voice.

'Up here, my dear.' I unlocked the door. It would be a simple matter to lock it again if the guard awoke and became curious.

She stood under the porthole and squinted. 'I can't see you. Who are you?'

Such a sweet little lamb. Where was her nanny or her father or whoever keeps the unsuspecting from characters like me?

'My name is Celwyn. Would you like to come inside?'

The child hesitated but a moment before stepping over the legs of the sleeping guard.

By the time she'd opened the door, I'd moved to the far corner of the stateroom and sat behind the petite drop table common to all sea cabins. It had been a while since I'd been around a tiny person, but she would most likely be less intimidated if I was closer to her level. The child poked her head inside the door, noting my traveling trunk with its mysterious contents visible to a curious eye and finally myself. I must have passed a childlike test, for she came inside, leaving the door ajar. Perhaps she felt more afraid of her parents finding her than she was of me.

If you wonder why I did not venture forth from my unlocked cabin, it wasn't time yet to do so. Crafting a perfect situation from raw elements is so much more entertaining than being tossed about by random acts of fate. Or shot at by pistols.

'Please sit down,' I said to my new friend.

She took several steps and then flounced into the chair across from me. Up close, I could see some of her father in the intelligent eyes, but her beauty would come from her mother.

'Who are you? Why are you alone in here?' she asked.

'May I call you Felicity?'

A miniature jaw dropped open. 'How did you know my name?'

I gestured toward the deck outside. 'Your father mentioned you.' How many other children named Felicity would there be on a cargo ship on its way to the Cape?

'Oh.' She studied me for a moment like her mother would peruse a menu. 'I suppose that would be all right.'

Rather verbose for a little one. She eyed me with the inquisitiveness of a young cat. To her, I would appear similar to any other gentleman she would encounter: strong of face, whiskered, and dressed in a linen suit and brocade waistcoat. Not as many men would wear a ruby on his finger such as I wore, nor savor the aroma of a particularly obscure and fine tobacco that I'd stashed in my trunk. Very few men were as feared as I, which was a pity; I am misunderstood most of the time.

'Would you like something to drink? Milk?'

Felicity nodded assent, and then frowned. 'I don't see any milk.'

'Look around. I'm sure you will,' I said.

Her eyes traveled the rather small room, and when they returned to the table, a glass of milk sat before her. Her mouth opened, but no sound came out.

'Help yourself,' I said.

Felicity touched the glass with a fingertip and then drew it closer until she could sniff the contents. With a lingering look of doubt upon me, she drank. Half of the milk remained when she licked her lips and asked, 'Where did you get this?' She looked under the table. When she sat up, the glass was full again.

The girl blinked rapidly, and then her eyes darted from object to object in confusion. She asked, 'How did you do that?'

I smiled. 'Do you always believe only what you can see? Or do you believe in things you cannot see?'

Her eyebrows nearly touched as she thought. 'Only what I can see is real,' she answered.

I pointed to the glass. 'Is the milk real?'

'Of course it is, silly.' To prove it, she drank more milk, all the while keeping her eyes on me. My, my, such suspicion. When she replaced the glass on the table, it was once more full to the brim.

For several moments she stared at the glass before daring to look at me. 'How did you do that?'

I shrugged and asked, 'What is in that pouch?'

She had placed a velvet pouch on the table when she joined me. At the mention of it, she didn't hesitate to open the strings that closed it and dump the contents on the table between us.

'These are my jacks. This is the ball you play jacks with,' Felicity said.

She tossed the ball, which was about the size and color of an apricot, into the air, and caught it again. On the second toss, she deftly picked up several of the tiny metal stars scattered on the table. 'Do you know how to play?' she asked and without waiting for a reply added, 'Of course, you have to pick up all the stars and not lose the ball.'

With that admonition, Felicity threw the ball into the air again. It hung, suspended between us, above her head. Her eyes grew as wide as her little face. Before she could cry, the ball descended again. Slowly.

Her hand automatically reached for the metal stars. Felicity squeaked and stood up. The stars had become tiny frogs made of the finest crystal. Even in the muted daylight, they reflected light delightfully.

'Oh, my!' the child exclaimed and gathered them into her hands. The ball bounced off the table and into my trunk.

I ushered Felicity to the door. The pouch of crystal frogs was clutched in both of her hands. As I reached for the door handle, she asked, 'May I come visit you again?'

'Certainly. But only if the guard is asleep. This is our secret.' I placed a finger to my lips. By the time we reached Seville, I might even have a young apprentice to teach some less sinister magic tricks to.

Felicity put a finger to her lips and then slipped out the door with a giggle.

The ship's bell had sounded the next hour when boots thundered on the wooden deck. Voices raised the alarm. Above the commotion, Captain Hume's oaths could be heard outside my door: 'Damnation! Wiggins is dead! Get that doctor out here.'

'What for?' It sounded like a sailor located in the rigging above me. He apparently had an excellent view of my newly departed guard. 'His throat has been cut open like a pig's.'

Sounds of more of the curious arriving, then the extreme annoyance of Dr Perideaux when he saw the body.

'Captain!' Dr Perideaux bellowed.

'Yes, Doctor.'

'This man is not sick. He has been murdered.' The doctor's voice shook, and his words were measured. 'You are responsible for every act upon this ship!'

'I am aware of that,' Captain Hume replied with just as much control.

'Did your prisoner do it?' Dr Perideaux inquired.

I noted a significant hesitation before the captain answered, 'That would be impossible.'

Someone tried the handle on my door. It remained locked.

'How do you know your prisoner is in there?' Dr Perideaux demanded.

'Because I am sure he is,' Captain Hume said. 'Here . . . is the key to the door. As you can see, it was still in the guard's pocket. However, I will humor you.'

I yawned and waited.

As the door opened, the dying sun streamed into my cabin, bringing warmth against the approaching evening. The captain filled the doorway. From over his shoulder, the doctor peered inside.

I put down my book and stood. 'Come in. I'm afraid I cannot offer you any refreshment but my company.'

Dr Perideaux's curiosity won out. He pushed by Captain Hume and into the room. I had been correct. We were of the same height, well over six foot. Our builds were similar too;

I could have traded waistcoats with him. Mine, however, would have been finer than the rather dated one the doctor wore.

I bowed. 'May I introduce myself? Jonas Celwyn, lately of Singapore and Madagascar.'

Captain Hume kicked the door shut and advanced to stand between us. He removed his hat, revealing a glistening sheen on his balding dome. A bead of perspiration trickled onto his ear.

'Doctor, this is not wise. As you can see, the prisoner is still here. He is in a locked room from which he could not have murdered the guard. Come along, please.'

'What were you charged with, sir?' Dr Perideaux ignored the tug on his sleeve as he addressed me.

I shrugged. 'If I were to list all of the nefarious crimes I'd been charged with, we would still be here long after the dinner bell.' A few minutes ago I'd caught the scent of roasting beef. Hopefully there would be a nice salad to go with the meal, and possibly a fine bottle of wine.

'I repeat, what were you convicted of?' Dr Perideaux's tone sounded much colder than a Bavarian street in winter.

Captain Hume gave up tugging on his sleeve and yanked open the cabin door. He gestured to one of his officers. 'Johnson. Come in here. Escort Dr Perideaux back to his cabin. Now.'

The doctor didn't budge. He stood so close I could see the flecks of gold in his irises. The stubborn line of his lips indicated the crew would have to carry him out before he'd accede to the captain's order.

'Get him out of here,' Captain Hume growled.

Officer Johnson reached for Perideaux. The officer started to speak, but his words turned to a strangled gasp as his hand passed through the doctor's forearm, not once, but twice.

As Dr Perideaux watched his sleeve in fascinated horror, I replied, 'Something so ridiculous. Witchcraft.'

A supremely talented and creative magician would have been a more accurate portrayal.

My assessment of the good doctor had been correct. He was a persistent cuss. It couldn't have been another hour before I became aware of the doctor in whispered conversation with my newest guard. I didn't even have to lean against the door to hear them.

'. . . have items you'd like to buy when we reach port,' Dr Perideaux said.

The guard grunted. 'Course I do.'

'Perhaps this would prove useful to you?'

'Aye, it would. It sure would. For this much you can sniff around this bastard's door for more than a moment.' The guard laughed. 'I have to go to the head, and I'm sure I'll be gone awhile.'

In a moment I heard a slight scratching sound outside the door. From the porthole I could make out the lower half of the doctor as he crouched beside my door. It appeared he was examining the door hinges.

By the next morning, the day brought stronger wind and vigorous waves. The *LeHanna* climbed them easily, bottoming out, and climbing again. On the western horizon purplish, opalescent clouds seemed to be gathering in a thickening haze. Interesting; I hoped we were not sailing into a storm.

We passed Tila dunmati a little after noon, and within the hour the fate of the ship changed. It began with a warning call from the crow's nest. Another ship approached, sailing directly toward us.

The general excitement aboard the *LeHanna* increased with the terse orders shouted from the bridge, bringing the ship to. The lad in the crow's nest called down, 'Dutch flag, sir. Fully armed.'

Most provocative information; I wondered what they wanted with the *LeHanna!*

Nearly a half hour later, our ship slowed until she floated in the waves in an exaggerated rocking motion. If this kept up, I surely would be seasick.

The other ship adjusted their course. They no longer rode the wind but drifted off our leeward side about five hundred feet away, edging closer with each swell of the waves.

Our crew grew silent. It seemed like our ship held its breath, waiting. At last, Captain Hume barked an order. But it was only to the crew to man their positions and await his orders. From my porthole, I could see him standing mid-ships, near the railing. He said something to First Officer Greer at his side. Officer Greer saluted and in seconds had marched to my cabin and accosted my guard.

'Open the door,' Greer ordered him.

The guard held the door open with one hand and trained his pistol on me with the other. After the murderous incident with my last warder, the procedure for guarding me had changed. Now, they brandished a pistol, not a musket.

Greer entered my cabin and glanced around before saying, 'Gather your things, Celwyn. You're leaving.'

'Where am I going?' I asked.

'No questions. Either pack your things, or you'll leave without them.'

When I emerged on deck, two more guards gripped my arms, and another lugged my trunk. As I walked, I reveled in the sun and drank the fresh air like a newborn calf.

During the time it took to pack my belongings, a boat had been launched from the other ship. It contained six crew-men and a man who was obviously their captain. He sat at the rear of the boat, examining the *LeHanna* with an air of ownership. Between the bulkheads and in the rigging of the other ship, dozens of muskets were trained on the deck of our ship. Why hadn't the crew of our ship reacted? The crew numbered less than thirty, and they were lined up at attention, not at battle stations.

With his officers flanking him, Captain Hume stood in front of the bridge, arms folded, feet apart. His officers maintained a stern stance, but their eyes bounced everywhere. The tension in Hume's officers increased as the other crewmen left the rowboat and scampered up the rope ladder. They attained the deck and walked toward Captain Hume, ignoring the rest of the *LeHanna's* crew. I strode over to the bridge and joined them.

'No restraints? I no longer frighten you?' I held up my naked wrists to Captain Hume.

He didn't quite look at me, but said, 'Be quiet, you ruffian. If necessary, Greer will knock you out to insure your silence.'

I had a good idea of what Captain Hume was up to. And an even better idea of what he deserved.

As the crewmen swaggered toward us, I studied their captain. Perhaps forty years of age, with strict bearing and well-tended whiskers, he was a barrel of a man. Solid muscles and apelike arms swung at his sides. He shoved one of the *LeHanna* crewmen out of his way, and the rest parted without chancing contact with him.

Up close, the most innocent blue eyes swept over Captain Hume and his officers. Taking his time assessing the ship, the man noted each doorway, the bulkheads, the shining brass fixtures, and other evidence of care in the ship's maintenance. He'd assume the ship had a good larder, and even more profitable machinery stored below. Finally, he addressed us in a baritone with the faintest of Dutch accents.

'I am Captain Falkenburg of the *Sibylline*.'

A simple statement, but out of the corner of my eye, I spied Captain Hume wetting his lips. A bead of sweat trickled from under his hat and ran down his collar. If it hadn't occurred to the rest of the crew, it should have: this appeared to be a pirate ship flying under the innocence of a legitimate flag.

Captain Falkenburg turned on his counterpart. 'What are you carrying?'

Sweat began pouring down Captain Hume's pudgy cheeks. Beyond him, the deck of the *Sibylline* swarmed with dozens of pirates who had not been visible before. They watched the *LeHanna* silently, evidence of strict discipline. Captain Hume flicked a quick glance at them and then addressed the pirate captain.

'Spices and sugarcane. Nothing more.'

'Nothing, Hume?' The pirate smiled broadly, and I could see he'd been opening wine bottles with his teeth. More of interest: I wondered who else noted that we'd had a chance encounter with a buccaneer who happened to know Captain Hume's name.

Several of the *LeHanna's* officers shot swift and speculative looks at their captain. He didn't return them but swallowed several times without speaking.

Captain Falkenburg laughed, and the sound seemed to chill the crew of the *LeHanna*. Wide-eyed, every one of them stared at their captain. With Hume's next words, some jaws dropped, too.

'Our agreement is still good. I have what you want,' Captain Hume blurted. He looked at me, nearly in the eye, and added, 'I also have another token of good faith. A prize of sorts.'

'Eh?' The pirate captain picked his teeth with the sharp point of a blade, spat, and then regarded Captain Hume with his brows up.

Undeterred, Captain Hume explained, 'Mr Celwyn here is the cousin of the British ambassador to Portugal. Surely, you can ransom him. He was to have stopped off for a short time on Victoria to assess conditions there. They won't miss him for several extra days. Perhaps weeks.'

I turned on the bastard. He wouldn't look at me. Ah.

Plainly dear Captain Hume was letting me know that I could have my freedom if I went with the *Sibylline* or be dumped on the penal colony on schedule – if the *LeHanna*, survived this meeting.

Captain Falkenburg didn't seem impressed. His glance rested on the cabins below the bridge. 'This can't be all you have, Hume.'

Most anxious to please, Captain Hume nearly curtseyed like a matron in front of a queen. He assured the pirate, 'Oh, no! You will receive what I promised you. One moment, please.'

He turned to his first officer. I caught parts of his whispered instructions, enough to know that the crew of the *LeHanna* would trade Dr Perideaux's family in exchange for their lives. Apparently, the doctor had something the pirates wanted.

First Officer Greer wasted no time gathering a contingent of crewmen and marching over to Dr Perideaux's cabin. It was then that I decided to allow myself to be transported aboard the other ship; I must protect my new apprentice, after all.

More than an hour later, the doctor, his family, and I were removed to the *Sibylline*. I did my best to reassure Felicity and carried her aboard the pirate ship while the doctor helped his wife. In a billowing pale blue dress, Mrs Perideaux appeared angelic and as fragile as a porcelain figurine. She maintained a white-knuckled grip on her husband's shoulders as he steadied her on deck.

We huddled together and watched as the pirates used ropes to bring our trunks up to the deck. With hungry eyes divided between the woman and the trunks before them, the pirates hovered close by. Their stench competed with the foulness of the ship. Mrs Perideaux clung to her husband, and the child buried herself in her mother's skirts and whimpered.

I squatted beside her and tapped Felicity on the shoulder. 'Poppet, we must be brave. And quiet.'

One tearstained blue eye chanced looking at me, and then she buried her face in her mother's skirts again.

I said, 'Remember the crystal frogs?' Without turning around, Felicity nodded. I placed a hand on her shoulder, and her whimpers subsided. 'Just wait,' I added softly before standing once more.

As the last of our trunks were brought aboard the pirate ship, the *LeHanna* made sail, looking to gain yards swiftly in the growing wind. We watched her for a moment before Captain Falkenburg turned his attention to his captives.

Standing at Captain Falkenburg's elbow, and surveying the rest of the pirates with distain, stood a scarecrow of a man as pale and cold as death. When I saw his eyes, I inserted myself between his line of vision and the family.

'Well,' Captain Falkenburg said as he circled the trunks at his feet. As the wind whipped around us, seeming to grow stronger by the moment, the pirates straddled the yardarms and unfurled sails. The boom swung to the left, creaking with the weight of the masts.

The scarecrow murmured something in Falkenburg's ear. The captain smiled with approval. 'Excellent, Borodin, Blast her.' Borodin crossed to the pirates by the cannons, gave orders, and in a moment returned to join our party.

Captain Falkenburg's expression caused the doctor to step back. 'Tell me. Where is it, Doctor? Save time, save your family, and just tell me.'

Dr Perideaux grew paler, and the stubborn set of his jaw weakened, but he didn't speak.

Beyond the pirate captain, along the port side, the pirates lit fuses on the cannons as they jabbered and hopped around like colorful crickets. In the near distance, the other ship climbed waves, guilt-driven and anxious to get away.

We watched, knowing what would befall the ship as soon

as the pirate ship had a clear shot. The *LeHanna* ascended another wave and disappeared down the other side. As the tops of her masts sank lower, and still lower, the wave rose higher. Much higher than the sea conditions would suggest. Slowly, the wave crested and descended. The chattering of the pirates increased as they realized what had happened; the sea had swallowed the *LeHanna*; sails, crewmen, deceit, and all. As if she had never existed.

Curses in dozens of languages colored the deck as the pirates ran from bow to stern, looking for the other ship. Some scrambled up the masts and across the spars trying to see more. Captain Falkenburg grabbed a spyglass from Borodin and didn't say a word as he scanned the area. Even without a glass, it appeared that not even a sliver of wood remained of the *LeHanna*.

Such a pity. Or not.

Captain Falkenburg lowered the glass and with deliberation gazed at us, one by one. Finally his eyes rested on me. I shrugged. It would be illogical to think anything but the sea claimed the *LeHanna*, would it not? The sea is mysterious; at best, it is a beautiful abyss capable of capricious treachery. Drowning is not the only thing that awaits the unwary.

The pirate captain turned toward his crew, who still squawked and chattered nervously. '*Enough.*' Without raising his voice, he restored order. 'Silvestri, recalculate our course to the south. Get us moving, Borodin.' Then Captain Falkenburg returned his attention to Dr Perideaux.

'Again, and for the last time, Doctor, where is it?' There was no mistaking the menace in his words; each one seemed to be a blow to the doctor, and he winced as the pirate took a step toward him.

A wave slammed the pirate ship broadside, heaving the doctor and pirate captain into the bulkhead. I held Mrs Perideaux and Felicity steady. In seconds, the sun had disappeared as armies of clouds rolled over our heads, and the sea became a mass of whitecaps climbing as high as the deck. The wind whistled around the pirates, circled the salon and cabins, and whirled upward into the masts.

The rain began like a celestial sword had slit open the sky. With an eye on the growing squall, Borodin pulled Captain Falkenburg aside. They watched another wave as it rose level with the deck, and if they didn't like that wave, hundreds more ascended upon each other as far as the eye could see. Only hours from rounding the Cape, and it seemed we had entered an exceedingly stormy sea. Someone with a more suspicious mind would remember that it had been so calm an hour ago.

Captain Falkenburg barked orders and then glanced back at us. 'Put them into the salon. Hurry up, you bastards!'

As if we'd rehearsed it a thousand times, the doctor and I surrounded his family so that the pirates wouldn't. When the woman and child had entered the salon, I hooked a finger at Perideaux, and he followed me back on deck. Through the heavy rain, we beheld a curious sight.

Half a dozen pirates stood around our trunks, cursing. One of them, a particularly hairy and primitive specimen, screamed and held his blackened hand in front of the others. The pirate nearest to my trunk reached for it and then bawled in pain. I patted a yawn: they seemed to be slow to learn from what they saw.

The other pirates hovered around the distressed pirate and conferred, as best they could, while casting worried glances at the bridge, where Captain Falkenburg paced and swilled wine. Another few moments and the largest pirate approached the doctor's trunk. His hand flamed and the flesh melted away as his scream carried much farther than the bridge, riding the waves into the lowering darkness.

That should be enough of a demonstration. Perideaux followed me to the center of the deck to our trunks. The remaining pirates gave us a large berth. I grabbed my trunk by the handle and rested it against my hip. The doctor, with the barest hesitation, did the same with one of his trunks.

I bowed. 'After you, Doctor.' We wasted no time carting the luggage back to the salon. After our last trip back to the salon, we stepped inside and the door slammed behind us, and I heard the sound of several hammers nailing wood across the opening.

As we dragged the trunks into the center of the salon, Felicity and Mrs Perideaux observed us with the kind of fascination that indicated they'd seen and heard the pirates' attempts to touch the trunks. Felicity's eyes held the same wonder as when she couldn't believe her milk glass had magically been refilled. This time, she included her father in the assessment, certain he'd also been responsible for the pirates' reaction.

Mrs Perideaux's gaze stayed on me, and she held her daughter close. She wet her lips.

'What just happened?' she pulled Felicity closer.

The wind howled around the ship like mythical demons chasing each other, bouncing against the walls, crashing into the spars overhead. The rain slashed at the portholes, first on one side, then the other side of the salon.

Our new quarters did not appear to be as much of a pigsty as I had expected. I deduced only the pirate captain used the salon, and he believed in displaying his treasures. Racks of wine, oil paintings, lace curtains, and a mahogany table surrounded us. Red velvet settees faced each other at the lee side of the room, and a polished oak bar took up the entire fore side.

I explored the bar, and magically, the pirate captain happened to have a jug of ice-cold milk and a carafe of sparkling water awaiting his guests. By the time I'd placed them on the table between the settees and poured, Felicity had broken free of her mother's embrace and joined me on the facing settee.

'Felicity—' her mother exclaimed and pulled her back to the other side.

Dr Perideaux remained by the bar, deep in thought, regarding me with a furrowed brow. 'Would you be so kind as to bring more glasses, sir?' I asked him. The sound of my voice startled him, but he seemed glad of an opportunity to do something and not ponder too seriously our predicament. Or perhaps what had caused the pirates to abandon their attempts to touch our luggage weighed on his mind.

The pirate ship fell deeply into a trough. He waited for the ship to climb again before he retrieved the glasses and joined his wife on the sofa. Perideaux took his time pouring the water before looking up.

'I believe we have sailed into a hurricane, Doctor,' I said.

As if to confirm my observation, the wind shrilled, startling our little party. Felicity whimpered a response. The portholes rattled, and we held on to our refreshments as the pirate ship creaked loudly in protest. The *Sibylline* picked up speed. She shuddered from bow to stern, scattered the glasses on the bar, and then sailed faster yet.

Perideaux glanced left and then right, his anxious glance straight at me confirmed that something he deemed unexplainable had just happened. The speed of the ship could not be accounted for under the stormy circumstances. No longer did the vessel appear to be under the control of the pirates. Wind drove the ship, out of control, first one direction, and then much faster than man could change course, another direction. She raced ahead, bounded up the sides of the waves, and bottomed out again before climbing laboriously upward once more.

It was then that Dr Perideaux noticed his wife's pallor, as I had a few moments earlier. She was heavy with child, had been abducted by pirates, and was in the company of a man she feared. Perideaux put his arm around her and bowed his head.

The doctor's wife paled again, dangerously so in my opinion. She had not yet lost the fear in her eyes when she glanced at me.

Perideaux said, 'My dear, this is Mr Celwyn. Mr Celwyn, this is my wife, Mrs Helen Perideaux.' He nodded toward me like he wasn't sure of what I'd done, but he knew it had helped. 'We are in your debt, sir.'

'Nonsense.' I winked at Felicity, and she did her best to wink back. 'We will weather this storm.'

Mrs Perideaux gripped her husband's hand and studied me. I returned the regard. Her chin quivered, and her eyes were hard. In a moment she said, 'I still need to know what we're going to do.' She left me to stare at her husband. 'Our safety, Jonathan. Those men . . .'

Dr Perideaux held her, and before things got out of hand, I said, 'I promise you, madame, they will not harm you. Or your family.'

She raised her head from her husband's embrace and looked at him, then at me. 'But what will we do?' she wailed. As she spoke, a spasm of pain crossed her face, and she paled. Instantly, Dr Perideaux's expression changed, and there was no one in the world more important than his wife.

'Is it the baby?' he asked her.

'No, no.' Mrs Perideaux replied and patted his hand as she uttered the lie.

Felicity left her mother's side and approached the trunks.

Dr Perideaux said, 'Felicity—'

'It is all right. I assure you, sir,' I said.

Felicity peered at the myriad stickers that decorated my trunk like a garish Christmas present. 'What is Mary Katch?' she asked.

'Marrakech,' her father corrected.

Night was falling. I arose and lit a lamp and then traveled the room discovering candles to light. In the cupboards I found some biscuits and then beckoned to the doctor. He made sure his wife was comfortable against a mound of pillows before joining me behind the bar.

I kept my voice low. 'If it becomes necessary, there are clean blankets here. And a quantity of water.' There hadn't been, but I'm a helpful soul.

'I sincerely hope we will not need them tonight,' he said with a glance at his wife. He looked at me, and his gaze didn't waver. 'Don't you think it is time for a moment of candor? I mean, sir, we may be fighting for our lives at any moment.' He lowered his voice. 'Or we may succumb to the storm. I'd like to know who is fighting with me. Or dying with us.' From outside the salon the heavy steps of the pirates tromped by.

'Well put,' I said. I placed both hands on the bar and then removed them. A plate of cheeses and savory meats sat before us. 'Perhaps your wife or daughter is hungry.' I handed him the plate. It fell through his fingers and clattered to the bar surface. 'Please take it to them.' I offered it to him again. 'Eat. You will feel better.'

After another look at me, he dutifully delivered the plate to the settee. Perideaux nibbled a bit of cheese before presenting the plate to his wife. His expression indicated he approved. I do have excellent taste.

When his family was sufficiently distracted, he returned to stand behind the bar with me. 'That was a most welcome and deliberate diversion, Mr Celwyn.' He pointed to the plate as Felicity selected a sliver of ham. 'Explain it.'

I yawned. This would require something stronger than water. It appeared that although the pirate captain seemed fond of wine, he also had stored a single bottle of malt below the bar.

'There's so much to say and yet so little.' I poured two shots, and then poured one for the doctor. 'What do you know of the black arts? Of magic?'

As I spoke, the *Sibylline* lurched to starboard. She slid down a wave on her side in a most sickening manner before gradually righting herself. The wind howled and screamed, competing with the pirates shouting from the deck. By now the sails would be shredded, and they'd try to steer by the rudder, if they tried at all.

When the doctor could speak again, he said, 'Parlor tricks; that is all magic is. There is no basis of fact,' His attention rested upon his wife, but I could see him thinking as he tried to find an explanation for what he'd seen with the trunks and what his wife enjoyed nibbling only a few feet away from us. He probably did not consider the storm anything more than bad luck.

'Not exactly,' I said.

Perideaux seemed to have come to a deduction or perhaps a belated question he had wanted to ask. 'Why did Captain Hume insist you be separated from his crew? Why were you locked up?' He licked his lips and glanced at his wife. 'I'd prefer that Helen not know anything of this.'

I shrugged. 'As you wish.' I poured more malt for both of us.

'And my questions?'

I regarded him a moment longer before speaking softly so that his wife would not hear.

'For hundreds of years, I've honed my skills to the point where I do not question the difficulty of what I attempt within the realm of magic. But I do consider what effect my magic may have on innocent persons. My personal sense of right and wrong has also evolved accordingly.'

Dr Perideaux watched me over the top of his glass as he downed the rest of his whiskey. He didn't even blink when I mentioned that I haven't just lived for this time, in this century. His assessment was mirrored in his eyes: scientific speculation, not the wide-eyed terror some men expressed on the rare occasions when I have told them tidbits of my history.

'How I interpret my ideals, or morals if you will, are as personal as every man's are.' I continued, 'But for now, let us say that I had no compunction in killing my guard, but I will go to great lengths to save your family.'

The doctor swallowed nothing several times but kept his gaze neutral. Thinking.

After a moment he managed, 'Exactly what did you do?'

The rain beat on the roof of the salon so loudly we could hear nothing else. The wind howled, furious at the ship. I told him, 'I'd been arguing with a priest at the cathedral in Madagascar. To make a point, I appeared during the church service and levitated myself onto the altar. Then I made myself comfortable to enjoy the services. When the ushers would have laid hands on me, I simply disintegrated within their fingers. Like ice that has melted or water that evaporates.' I elbowed the doctor. 'A miracle, would you not say?'

If he'd had any morsel of humor left from his stern upbringing, he'd allow a small smile to escape. But no.

'Later, when the authorities tried to arrest me, a few of the officers were injured.' I had dispatched them with mercy and alacrity. 'My temper can only be maintained so long when provoked.'

The doctor slammed his glass down. 'But what did you do to make them so afraid? There must be more.'

For a moment I contemplated him. When he finally met my gaze, I locked the contact and said, 'I have the ability to climb inside another man's mind, Doctor. Once there, I can wander anywhere and learn a man's darkest secrets and enjoy his most pleasant memories.' I flipped a hand. 'While there, I sometimes plant new thoughts. Of all sorts.'

After pouring more whisky, I wrapped his limp fingers around his glass. 'Thoughts are powerful, are they not, Doctor?' I asked him without speaking.

The storm intensified as the day bled into the night. It appeared so dark and turbulent outside it seemed hard to tell when the night actually became complete. As I looked out the porthole, a pirate fell against the rail near us. A hungry wave tried to pry his hands from the rail, but he held on tightly. The wave crested and receded, leaving behind another pirate rolled into a ball. The pirate that the wave delivered lay against the bulkhead. When he didn't move, the first pirate kicked him. Another wave broke over the rail, sweeping them both to the stern.

From behind me, the wails of childbirth filled the salon. For the last hour, Mrs Perideaux's cries had been growing more frequent and prolonged. The hurricane seemed to strengthen with each of her screams. The doctor had given Felicity a weak sedative to calm her, and she slept on the other settee. After our talk, he hadn't said much but appeared deep in thought, until his wife's condition changed and he devoted his attention to her.

As dawn broke, the baby's first cry could be heard, stark and sweet against the ugliness of the world. The *Sibylline* rocked in an exaggerated motion in the aftermath of the hurricane, but the wind no longer howled, and the rain fell in a gentle veil.

The wood across the salon door fell away as I walked outside, stepping over the pieces of debris, including dead pirates. A glassy sea of blue stretched to the horizon.

The pirates addressed me as Captain, most courteously, as they went about their duties, unfurling new canvases and getting the ship under way. I swept a hand, and all of the debris disappeared. The broken main mast stood whole once again. Midships, I stopped and admired myself in a polished brass dial, adjusting the buccaneer's hat that sat upon my head at a most jaunty angle. My waistcoat had given way to a silken shirt of crimson. The shoes I wore had become boots of the finest and softest leather.

My crew was freshly bathed and shaven. The ship shone from top to bottom and appeared to be in pristine condition. It would be most appropriate to honor the late Captain Falkenburg in some manner. I tapped my fingers on the rail and thought. Perhaps I shall rechristen the ship the *Flying Dutchman*. I imagined that he did go flying out with the wind, whirling far away into the sea. Yes, a most excellent idea. I called back inside the salon.

'Doctor, we shall arrive in Seville on schedule.'

The newborn's plaintive cries could be heard: life has been renewed. The game renewed also.

Is it possible they'll name the baby after me? I must wait and see.

Some gestures should be natural, gifts of gratitude.

Or memory.

THE BLOODFLOWER

Martin Meyers

I

*H*e was waiting to cross the street to the subway.
The truck rounded the corner.

It was a glazier's truck with slanted racks on the outside to carry glass. This one carried a mirror on the side facing him.

Rusty saw Hope and a man in the mirror. They were both naked and bloody. It was an obscene tableau framed on one side by a black wolf and on the other by a behemoth, three-headed silver dog.

Rusty thought he recognized the man writhing on the ground. The animals, eager to pounce on the dying man, lapped at the dark, wet ground. Hope knelt beside him, licking the blood that dripped from her lips.

The man's blood.

In the mirror Rusty saw the head of a snake-haired crone floating in midair.

Medusa was smiling.

Rusty Harper bolted up in his bed, gasping for breath. Next to him, Hope Brady slept peacefully, a half smile on her lips.

I absolutely light up for her, he thought as he relaxed and his breathing grew easier. His next thought was an immediate negation of the first. He didn't love Hope; love was pure crap, and he had no time for it. He did like her a lot, though.

Regretting that he wasn't up to the kind of go-round she would expect, he didn't wake her. Tonight would be better. Food and a few drinks and he'd be in just the mood to take care of her.

She stirred.

He left the bed, feeling guilty about deserting her.

His mind pushed on to other things. Like how good coffee and a cigarette would taste. And what the new job held in store. The realization that Hope was important to him lay in the background. It didn't advance, but it didn't retreat. It simply stayed there, waiting for him to get back to it.

Rusty blew his nose. His sinuses were killing him. He filled the bathroom sink with cold water and lowered his face into the basin.

When he raised his head, drops of blood bounced on the water, dying it a pale pink. Rusty peered in the mirror. His nose was bleeding. Christ, that hadn't happened since he was canned at the brokerage house and quit doing coke, 'Damn.' He grabbed several tissues.

At last the bleeding stopped. He washed his face again and brushed his teeth. When he spat, the toothpaste foam was also pink. Now his gums were bleeding. 'Rusty my boy, you are falling apart.'

He shaved while under the shower and pondered the brief time they'd been together. Less than two weeks. She was now such an integral part of his life that he felt he'd known her for a long time.

Yeah. Things were looking up. 'Admit it, Rusty, you never had it so good.' Donna had done him a big favor locking him out. Now he had a new girl, a new place to stay, and a new job. Who could ask for more?

After he got the coffee started, he poured two orange juices, drank one in a gulp, and carried the other in to Hope.

The clock radio went on as he entered the room. Hope turned it off and opened her eyes. She was smiling. 'Let's make love.'

Rusty handed her the juice. 'Great idea, but won't we be late?'

'Not if we make it a quickie.' She pulled him down on top of her. 'Come on.'

This woman excited him more than anyone he'd ever known. She engulfed him. Within seconds he was ready.

No.

She wouldn't be satisfied. And he couldn't disappoint her. It had to be good for her. But he couldn't hold off any longer.

Medusa's fearful head appeared in his mind. Horrible as the vision was, he welcomed the distraction and concentrated on it.

Hope bit him on the shoulder. The charm she wore dug into his chest. She clawed at him, grunting again and again, each grunt going higher in tone. When she reached the top of her lust song, she whined the final note and pulled him closer. He was done, dispelling Medusa, fear, everything.

This strange escapade they were all on had started on that particular Friday only two weeks before, when Hope found a new apartment.

'Pandora's Jar. This is Pandora,' the husky Greek-accented voice said. Pandora was really Asterodeia Alexander, the proprietor of the herb and spice shop on Eleventh Street, where Greenwich Avenue and Seventh Avenue converged. She was also Hope's new landlady.

The Greek woman owned a building across the street from the shop. She lived in the building and rented out apartments. Hope was in the process of moving into one of those apartments, a find if there ever was one.

Rent for her new place was so low Hope couldn't believe

her luck. She wouldn't even have to scour the earth for a roommate. The apartment would be all hers, her very own. Well, it was about time. Her luck hadn't been good since the day she was born.

Asterodeia spoke again. 'Pandora here.'

'This is Hope Brady.'

'Yes.'

'Your new tenant. Third floor, front.'

'I know who you are, Hope.'

'Thanks, Pandora.' As she always did when she was flustered, Hope touched the scarlet birthmark that encircled her left eye.

No matter how much makeup she used, she couldn't hide the port-wine stain.

She was also a pimply faced, fat girl with stringy brown hair, who worked in the mail room of UBS, a small cable company.

'My name is Asterodeia,' the woman said, pronouncing all the syllables. Slow and distinct. 'Pandora is just for the shop. All my friends call me Aster; anyone who lives in my house is my friend.'

'Thanks, Aster.'

'You are welcome, Hope.'

There was a silence.

'Yes, Hope?'

'Oh,' the girl blurted. 'I forgot. No, I didn't. Did the telephone man come today?'

'Yes, he did. And the locksmith, to change the locks. If you stop by the store or my apartment, I will give you the keys.'

'I didn't call a locksmith.'

'I did. I do that for every new tenant. Something extra. No charge. It is a shame to say, but nowadays, in the city of New York, one cannot be too careful.'

'Thank you, Aster.' Hope closed her eyes in embarrassment. Why was she constantly thanking the woman? She sounded like a half-wit. Grow up, she told herself. 'I really appreciate it.'

'That's quite all right. When are you moving in?'

'Tonight. I brought my suitcases to work this morning, so I only have a few more things at my old place, and I can put them in a couple of shopping bags.'

'Very well, then. Until tonight, good-bye.'

'Good-bye.' Hope cradled the phone.

'Who was that?'

Startled, Hope looked up. Her heart was pounding. She raised her hand to her birthmark. Mr Kesselring was leaning over her, his face close to hers. So close she could see his contact lenses floating in his eyes. Plastic boats in dirty water.

'Who was that, Brady?' he asked in a quiet voice filled with menace. 'Were you stealing phone calls again?'

'No,' was all she could manage as she looked about the room, wishing desperately for an interruption.

'Who was it, then?' he demanded, triumphant.

'Mr Porge in Personnel,' she answered just as triumphantly. 'He was wondering if a certain letter arrived.'

'Well, did it?' Kesselring squinted.

'Yes, it did.' She reached into the Personnel Department's basket. After a few anxious moments, she found the envelope and thrust it at her boss. 'Here.'

Kesselring was disappointed. He'd thought he had her. 'Don't just sit there, take it to him. If it was important enough for him to call, it shouldn't wait until the next delivery.'

She was halfway out the door when Kesselring said, 'Wait a minute, he didn't call. I didn't hear the phone ring.'

'That's right, he didn't. Yesterday. He asked me yesterday to be on the lookout for it. I called him.' Running to the front of the mail room she yelled, 'I'll be right back,' and dove through the closing doors of the elevator, exhilarated.

George Porge, Kesselring, Hope Brady, and quite a few

other people worked for the Universal Broadcasting System. It was a vainglorious title.

Despite the money and the location, just uptown of Rockefeller Center, and an entire midtown office building, albeit only a fifteen-story one, UBS was just another cable company.

But it owned the finest modern communications equipment and was home to the wheelingest and dealingest management ever to come down the pike.

George Porge and Personnel were on the tenth floor. Hope rode up to twelve to visit her friend Jessica Selby, who worked the reception desk in the combined Talent and Billing Department. Jessica had shiny ultra-black hair that just covered her ears. It was dead straight and cut Dutch-boy style with a precise part. Hope shook her head in despair. If only she had hair like that. 'Hi, Jess,' she said, inspecting the faces of the people waiting to go in on appointments. 'Any stars today?'

Jess's practiced smile never left her face. 'Christ, Hope, do you have to be such a dweeb all the time? In this place there are no stars. Only a lot of people who wish they were.'

A tall man wearing a charcoal jacket and a camel turtle-neck that matched his hair strode by the reception desk and toward the inner offices. Jess sat straighter in her chair. 'Good morning, Mr Lancaster.'

'Morning, sweets. Are they in there?'

'Yes, sir. They're waiting for you.'

'Good. Give 'em character. See you, sweets.'

Hope gazed after him. 'That was Vic Lancaster. He's a star. He called you *sweets*.'

'He calls everybody that. It's an act. And he's not a star; he's a used-to-be. Worse, an almost-was.'

'He's thirty-six, an Aquarius, and an avid sailor. I read that in *People*.'

'Give me a break. You better leave before you get me in trouble. Hey, you want to go to a Halloween party tonight?'

'I don't know. I've got all those boxes to unpack. What time?'

'Seven thirty.'

Hope scrunched up her face and chewed on her lower lip. 'Okay. Why don't you come see my new apartment?'

'Doesn't make any sense. The party's on the Upper West Side, not five blocks from me. Why should I go downtown and uptown again on that lousy subway when I can just walk to the party? I'll see your digs another time. Come home with me, and we'll go together.'

'I've still got some stuff in the old place I have to get.'

'All right, how about this? Do you have a lot to move?'

'No, it shouldn't take me long.'

'Good.' The phone on the reception desk rang. Jess answered it and told two women waiting that they could go in. 'Mr Wilson's office is the third door on the right.' Her practiced smile shone brightly. When the women were gone, she said to Hope, 'You do what you have to do, then come to my place.'

'What should I wear?'

Jess raised her right eyebrow, another practiced accomplishment. 'The gold lamé you wore to Madonna's birthday. Whatever you want to wear. It's not a costume party. Be comfortable. Don't wear jeans; your butt is too big.'

'Oh, Jess.' Hope tugged at her jeans and her bulky yellow sweater and wished she could be more like her friend, who looked great even in her plain white shirt, black pants, and vest.

'Don't oh-Jess me. Out of here before we both get fired. I'll see you later.'

Hope delivered George Porge's letter to the tenth floor.

'Hey, Kathy, guess who I saw on twelve? Vic Lancaster.'

'So?' George Porge's pretty Chinese assistant sneered. 'He was here twenty minutes ago. Screaming and yelling for all he was worth. I thought Georgie Porgie was going to go ballistic. Vic Lancaster just fired most of his staff, and here it is Friday, and he wants Georgie Porgie to set up a bunch of appointments by Monday. I don't see why they put up with his crap around here. It's just a lousy local cable show, and it sucks. Poor Georgie is tearing his hair out. And I don't blame him. Where's he going to find people to work for that maniac? I wouldn't for anything.'

Hope envisioned the blond god she'd seen upstairs. The thought made her sweat. 'I would,' she said, more to herself than to Kathy.

When Hope reached her new apartment, she dropped her stuff and collapsed in a purple armchair that had been left by the previous tenant.

She fell into a deep sleep and dreamed of a black wolf and a three-headed silver dog.

In the midst of sleep Hope said, 'What a strange dream,' as if it were a TV show and not a dream. She awoke with a big smile and a great feeling of contentment.

'Party time,' she yelled. But when she saw the daylight outside and stared at her watch, she realized that she had slept the night through.

Thoroughly panicked, she rushed out without changing her outfit or washing her face or using the John.

First she had to stop at Pandora's Jar and thank Aster again. No. She didn't have time. She would see Aster later when she came home.

Except Aster was out on the street in front of her store and calling to her. 'Good morning, Hope. I'm so glad you dropped by. I have a present for you.'

'I can't now . . .' The Greek woman was strange but sweet. In spite of her leathery skin, thick lips, and jowls, it was obvious that Aster had once been a beauty. She also had the oddest eyes – one green, the other black – they seemed to reflect dark light.

'Come inside. It's a charm against any evil spirits that may be following you.'

What were a few more minutes? Hope walked into Pandora's Jar. Her forehead wrinkled when Aster said something she didn't quite get.

'I'm so sorry,' the old woman apologized in her guttural voice. 'Sometimes I forget and speak Greek.' She pursed her thick lips, nodding wisely. 'I'll just have to teach you, that's all.'

Aster walked Hope to a cheval glass mirror on an oak stand. 'Sit.' The old woman stood behind Hope and slipped the chain over the girl's head. 'This is the Goddess Hecate. Keep her with you day and night, and you will always be protected.'

Hope gazed into the mirror at the charm, which was a small carving of a face. The face was deep green and flecked with red spots like drops of blood. It was enchanting.

Aster smiled and tilted the mirror so Hope's face was the main focus. 'Have a good look.'

More mesmerizing than the carving was Hope's reflection. Not only had most of her pimples cleared up, but her port-wine stain seemed to have faded.

She touched her face in awe, grinned at her mirror image, and told herself that her imagination was working overtime.

Her hair was so lustrous. She was prettier. And thinner.

Utterly confused, she turned to Aster, who said, 'You look very nice, my dear.'

'I know.' Laughing, Hope ran outside, caught a passing cab to the UBS building, danced like a madwoman as the express elevator took her up, up, up, and barged into Vic's office.

She was changed. More than her appearance. Her transformation had been as abrupt as an incantation and a puff of smoke. There had been no puff of smoke. Just a black wolf and a three-headed silver dog.

Marching up to Vic's desk, Hope suggested that he put on a show based on people's sexual revelations.

'Pretty sure of yourself, are you?'

'You're damn right.'

'Okay. You're the producer. Produce it.'

Sexploits was born.

II

As she arrived home after work, she spotted him walking toward her. It was the day following the party she'd missed.

He was absolutely beautiful. She wanted him. Surprising herself so much she nearly swooned, Hope said, 'Hi.'

He stopped. 'Hi, yourself. My name's Rusty. What's yours?'

'Hope.'

'And what can I hope for, Hope?'

In an even more spectacular surprise that made her head spin, she said. 'Why don't you come upstairs and find out?'

Rusty was wonderful. And though she was not up to his usual standards, he felt the same way about her.

Hope shanghaied Jess to be her assistant and hired Rusty as the office gofer. After the first day, during which he cracked her up with silly jokes, she decided he had served a long enough apprenticeship and promoted him to chief writer.

A year of madness followed. The *Sexploits* ratings went through the stratosphere.

Each day Hope's port-wine stain faded to almost a memory. She lost weight, and her complexion turned peaches and cream.

Until one day she realized that she was prettier than Jess.

Hope turned out to be a born producer, learning every aspect of the job quickly and efficiently. She never seemed to falter or grow weary, and she continued to find new and interesting people with alluring stories about their sex lives that the audience never tired of hearing.

Next, Hope came up with the idea *of Celebrity Sexploits*. The celebrities were eager to appear and tell all, admitting to outrageous events. Some actionable. One was even questioned by the DA's office after the show.

Of course, Hope happened to have a camera crew there to capture the arrest. Pop musicians were a glut on the market, and there was no shortage of exhibitionist actors or athletes.

Politicians clamored to be guests on the show after reports came in from pollsters that a *Sexploits* appearance would enhance their numbers and help them get elected.

Impatient with her talent coordinator, Hope took over the final interview of each guest before Vic met them. And, Rusty supposed, had sex with as many as she could. Male and female.

It wasn't long before they were making the big move. Full network and live. The only talk show of its sort. The gimmick had worked: *Sexploits* – or as some people were sarcastically calling it – 'Safe Sex' – was a great big monster of a hit.

Vic always claimed credit for the original idea. The man was a walking contradiction; he kept giving Hope more responsibility but at the same time continued to bad-mouth her, saying she was only there to implement his concepts, just another pushy bitch with no new ideas of her own.

The people at the top paid no attention to Vic's dissing Hope. They were high on the show and high on her.

This strange phenom called Hope Brady grew more and more beautiful, and more and more powerful.

Things hadn't been too bad for Rusty, either. He slept in Hope's bed. And much of the time she was there with him. He was also getting his own action on the side. Sauce for the gander was sauce for the goose. It was a brave new world, and he was all for it.

The dreams were horrible. But his new life was wonderful.

Hell, when he first met Hope, his prospects were lower than a snake's belly. Now he had a future with *Sexploits*, the greatest thing on TV since the tube itself. And he was getting sex that was better than his wildest fantasies.

That certainly was worth a few bad dreams.

Rusty shivered and began sweating; he pushed away the thought that nothing was worth those damn dreams.

Sexploits had gone through miraculous transitions. It had become the leading prime-time show on UBS.

After Lunar Broadcasting acquired UBS, the show became the bright star of Lunar-TV.

One of the first things Lunar did was rip out two floors of the Superior Broadcasting building and construct a new auditorium to seat five hundred people.

Sports, music, comedy, original movies for television, talk shows, all these and more were to be found on Lunar-TV. Plus, and most important, everybody's new favorite: *Sexploits*, live, Monday, Wednesday, and Friday.

As *Sexploits* grew bolder in using gutter language and becoming more explicit, religious leaders railed against it. Still, Lunar-TV's popularity and revenue soared.

Sexploits was described by the religionists as pornographic proselytizing. Nonetheless, in a quick turnabout, their power in the country seemed to be diminishing.

Applications to deal with the matter traveled quickly through the judiciary system to the Supreme Court, but the Court refused to get involved, declaring that the pornography issue was a matter for the lower courts.

Happily for Vic and company, an erstwhile conservative judge came down on the side of free speech. *Sexploits* had a clear and smooth path, and all systems were go.

The network was shifting to a weekly schedule. *Sexploits* was going to five nights a week, eight thirty to ten p.m., EST, toe-to-toe with the established networks at the start of the new fall season.

No doubt about it, Lunar-TV was the new network, an integral fact of life of the broadcasting industry, with highly rated programs and phenomenal billings.

Sexploits, their innovative live show, was a vital part of that fact of life. And Vic Lancaster was *Sexploits*.

He dreamed he was on that street corner again watching Hope and Vic in the bloody scene in the mirror. He heard the chanting voices. 'Hecate, Goddess of Darkness. Hecate, Goddess of the Moon. Hecate, Goddess of Blood.'

The bright part of the dull party was spotting Jess. Rusty lit a joint. Marijuana helped his headache lose its shape. After a while it would be just a dull, bearable throb.

'Hi,' he said, aiming a kiss at her cheek. She moved her face around quickly so that their lips touched. He pulled back and up, she followed, and her spiky black hair whisked his chin.

'What am I, poison or something?' she asked.

'Well, you know.'

'When we first met, you came on pretty strong.'

He didn't know why, but Jess was one line he didn't want to cross. Or maybe it was Hope he didn't want to cross. 'That was before Hope and I . . .'

'Before Hope and you what?'

'You know.'

'No, I don't know. It doesn't stop her. Why should it stop you? She used to think you could get AIDS out of thin air; now she goes after everything that moves.'

He clenched his right fist and relaxed it. What was the use? Jess was right. Except it hurt too much to hear it out loud. 'Ease off, will you? I thought we were friends.'

'Okay, friend,' she said without cheer.

He grabbed two cold brews from the tub of ice on the table and quickly took a swig of his.

Challenging him, Jess chugged her beer straight down.

He matched her, ending with a noisy burp.

'Charming,' she said.

He patted his jeans for his cigarettes.

'In your shirt pocket,' Jess said, pointing with the knife she was using to cut cheese.

'Careful with that thing.' He pulled out the pack of Luckies and another prerolled joint. 'You're liable to hurt someone.'

'Not me, Rusty, I'm not the one around here who hurts people.'

He lit up and took a deep drag. He did like Jess. A lot. He moved closer to her. 'Don't get so serious. Life's too short for that sort of crap.' When he kissed her, she kissed him back.

Hard. Demanding.

And he was afraid.

It was a struggle to admit it to himself, but it was true.

He was afraid of Hope.

'I don't get it,' Jess said later in Hope's apartment, which had become command central. 'She was changing all along, and I didn't realize it. Ugly duckling becomes super swan. That pimply faced, flat-chested, fat-assed thing now has skin like silk. She has spectacular tits, and the rest of her is great, too. How did it happen? Is she taking hormones or something?'

He dragged deep and handed Jess the joint. 'Give yourself a break. Leave it alone. You're only driving yourself crazy.'

'Damn bitch.' She took a deep toke, let the smoke drift lazily out of her nostrils. 'You know where she is now?'

'Don't say it.'

'She's shacked up with Vic this very minute.'

Hurt flooded Rusty's eyes.

'What the hell are you acting so injured about?' she demanded, grabbing him, kissing him.

Lightning flashed at the window, and the crack of thunder was right on top of it. The room seemed to vibrate from the force. Again. The sky flashed and snapped. Moaning with pleasure, he looked up. The ceiling was bordered with a continuing spiral circle.

How did they mold the plaster? No one did that kind of work anymore, that was for sure. The spiral ring began to move. His mind drifted, leaving Jess behind.

'No, don't go away,' Jess cried.

The room went black. In a glare of lightning, two figures, naked and hideous. During the next flash he watched as they took on new forms. The female now had three heads, and the male had become a snarling black wolf.

Rusty could barely breathe. He stared at the three heads. The middle face, eyes closed, was Hope.

Something grabbed at his legs. Jess. He dropped down beside her, held her tight. The wolf circled, snapping and growling. The three-headed horror came closer and closer.

Flying crones screeched and dove at Rusty and Jess, their whips flailing. 'Hecate, Goddess of Darkness. Hecate, Goddess of the Moon. Hecate, Goddess of Blood.'

'What was that crazy dope you gave me to smoke?' Jess asked.

He shrugged. 'Just pot.'

They were sitting in the kitchen.

'Hi, kiddies,' Hope said, charging in. 'Nice of you to wait up.' She sailed into the bedroom.

Rusty cast a worried glance at Jess and chased after Hope.

'How're you feeling, sweetheart?' Hope asked, shedding clothing, dropping it on the floor.

'Nothing happened. I swear.'

'I believe you, baby,' she said, planting a juicy kiss on his mouth. He pulled away. 'But I won't believe you if you won't let me touch you.'

'Sorry, I'm kind of wired.'

'Well, you better get your crap together. We have an important day coming up. Come on to bed. I've got the perfect medicine for what's wrong with you.'

Sex was the last thing Rusty wanted. He considered begging off, saying he wasn't feeling well, but he knew how she'd react and how miserable she could make him. He said nothing.

'Come on. Don't keep me waiting.'

'Uh . . . Jess.'

'Hey, Jess,' Hope shouted. 'Better grab some z's on the couch. We've got a big day ahead of us. It's the day Vic Lancaster becomes a superstar.' She fast-flapped the fingers of both hands, over and over, beckoning impatiently for Rusty.

Rusty was in a wood with Hope and the black wolf and the three-headed silver dog. He and Hope were having sex. Just as they had been before falling asleep.

Seconds before orgasm, the animals pushed in between them, destroying their coupling.

The three-headed silver dog went after Hope. The black dog attacked Rusty.

Rusty's scream merged with Hope's.

He snapped awake with all-too-lucid memories. He would not, could not, look at Hope.

Hope was smiling. Singing a happy song, she stepped into the shower and shrieked her delight at the ice-cold water.

Rusty glared in her direction and made himself instant

coffee. He turned on the TV. Half-asleep, slurping coffee, he flicked from news channel to news channel.

'A man was killed during last night's storm when he was struck by lightning in his own living room.'

'Charles Hamilton, forty-three . . .'

'. . . bolt of lightning came through the open skylight of his sixth-floor apartment . . .'

'The room was soaked by the rain.'

'In fact,' a man identified as Emmett Nichols, the building superintendent, was saying, 'I was under the impression the skylight was painted shut. I don't remember Mr Hamilton ever having it open in the ten years he lived here.'

'Wait a minute,' Hope said, coming out of the bathroom, pulling a brush through her tangled hair. 'What the hell are they saying about Charlie Hamilton?'

'Who?' Rusty rubbed his bleary eyes, as Jess wandered into the living room.

'What happened to Charlie?' Jess asked. Charles Hamilton was Vic's second banana.

The newscaster answered all their questions.

'The police said Hamilton appeared to have been killed instantly. His clothes were scorched shreds, and his body burned and bruised by the charge of electricity that surged through him.'

Jess screamed, 'Ohmygod!'

The newswoman kept talking. 'One officer is quoted as saying, "This is weird. There were blood stains in a circle around the corpse. It was as if the electricity boiled the blood out of his body."'

Ignoring Vic's protests, Hope appointed herself Charlie's replacement.

Rusty, already her slave, was blown away. She was beautiful, magnetic. From her confidence and ease you'd think she'd been working on TV for years. For Christ's sake, she even did the warm-up.

'Hello, America. Welcome to *Sexploits*, the program that lets it all hang out.'

'Ha!' The sound exploded from Rusty's mouth. Even with the memory of a snarling black dog haunting him, he couldn't stop laughing. Neither could anyone else in the control booth. Or the audience. It wasn't that funny, but it was.

The audience laughter was accompanied by deafening applause and foot stomping.

Hope's beautiful face lit up. 'Now, live and in New York, here's the star of our show, Vic Lancaster.'

Vic appeared, blond and handsome. 'Thanks, Hope, I trust you'll tell the world that I'm an equal opportunity employer.' His punch line was an overstated leer.

He hadn't let the audience down; they didn't let him down. The laughter continued and built with each line of Vic's very ordinary monologue.

Hope knelt at Vic's feet. After a moment, she thrust out her hands.

The crone placed the silver bowl and sickle in her open hands. Hope plunged the sickle into Vic's groin, chanting, 'Hecate, Goddess of Darkness, Goddess of the Moon, Goddess of Blood, may you live forever.'

Vic's wound seemed to explode as a bloody torrent shot into the silver bowl. The blood flowed over the sides and spilled to the ground. The three-headed silver dog, Cerberus, lapped at the spill.

Suddenly, the three-headed silver dog was no longer the dog but the three-headed woman.

The three heads shimmered and became one. The new face was Hope's, and it was smiling. Her smile was rapturous.

III

Hope opened her eyes; she had fallen asleep sitting up. The first thing she saw was the spiral design on the ceiling above her. It was comforting. She checked her watch. Almost three. Collecting her work, she pulled aside the blanket.

'Hi, sweets,' Rusty said sleepily.

'Hi,' she answered. 'Pew. One of us stinks, and I think it's me. I'm going to take a shower and get some sleep.' She yawned. 'I've put in one tough day.'

But when the phone rang, Hope fell on the bed and grabbed it. 'Hello.'

'Hope Brady?'

'Yes.'

'Harold Garment here.'

'Yes?' Harold Garment was Vic's doctor. 'What's wrong?'

'It grieves me to tell you, Ms Brady, Mr Lancaster died early this morning.'

Her body went numb. She felt sorrow and elation. Poor Vic. But now the show was hers alone.

The physician seemed to be in shock. His speech was disjointed, his voice strident. '. . . incomprehensible. I couldn't control the hemorrhaging. Spontaneous hemophilia. I don't understand. I don't . . .'

Monday night, an exquisitely gowned Hope hosted *Sexploits*. She was a triumph. The tabloids dubbed her 'the Queen Slut of Smut.'

Hope had found a home. From e-mail and telephone reaction during and afterward, predictions were that the Slut's audience share would break all records. The president, in a speech to the American Civil Liberties Union, was quoted as saying he thought *Sexploits* was a wonderful program.

*

Rusty understood something very important.

Hope was protecting him. She was his shield. From here on, everything was going to be all right. He had to believe. That's what this was all about. Hope had everything. And he had Hope, who was the servant of 'Hecate, Goddess of Darkness. Hecate, Goddess of the Moon. Hecate, Goddess of Blood.'

Was Hecate satisfied? Sure, why not? Hope would serve Hecate. And he would serve Hope. If that's the way it had to be, that's the way it would be. He was a survivor. Yes, he was.

Rusty turned. He thought he saw Jess standing in a corner. He wished he could tell her. But that was stupid. Jess was gone.

One day she walked out of the office and never came back.

Hope's blue eyes had changed. One was icy green, the other shiny black. With awe and fear, Rusty approached her. She was speaking a foreign language to the chauffeur as he helped her into the long, silver gray Cadillac limousine.

Her green and black eyes gleamed as she stared at Rusty. She couldn't abandon him now. Not after he'd come so far with her. He didn't care what she was. It didn't matter. As long as she didn't leave him behind.

The back door of the Caddy opened. Hope's lovely blonde head appeared. 'Come on, Rusty, move it.'

She wasn't going to leave him. Rusty jumped into the car. 'Thanks,' he said, all out of breath. Desperate for her to know how devoted he would be, he grabbed her hands and kissed them. 'We'll be great together, I swear.'

She pulled her hands from his and lifted her right forefinger to her lips.

He sat back and adjusted his tie. This wasn't going to be bad. In fact, this was going to be incredible.

*

He saw the truck when they stopped for a red light. It was a glazier's truck with slanted racks on the outside to carry glass.

Like the one he remembered, this truck also carried a mirror on the side facing them.

Rusty saw Hope and a man in the mirror. They were both naked and bloody. It was an obscene tableau framed on one side by a black wolf, and on the other by a behemoth, three-headed silver dog.

He thought he recognized the man writhing in agony on the gory ground as the blood spouted from his body. The animals, eager to pounce on the dying man, lapped at the dark, wet ground.

Hope knelt beside him, licking the blood that dripped from her lips.

The man's blood.

In the mirror Rusty saw the head of a snake-haired crone floating in midair.

Medusa's ancient and jowled leather face glowed. She was smiling.

The man lifted his head, and Rusty saw the agonized face.

It was his.

THE AWARENESS

Terrie Farley Moran

The awareness came on a Tuesday afternoon.

I was editing an article for a genealogy newsletter when I felt a disturbance in my soul and knew with calm certainty that, before this sun cycle was complete, my banshee keening would join the howl of the wind or disturb the silence of an unruffled atmosphere. In this time-honored way I would announce the passing.

Every American descended from Rory Dev O'Conor was in my charge. No death would go unrecognized. It had been ever so.

I boiled a cup of tea and waited, sitting on a footstool covered with a needlepoint so faded, its image of a rural Irish cottage was barely visible. My emerald eyes, a sure sign I'd inherited my father's mortal blood, closed of their own accord. All who come from the land of the sidhe have eyes the gray-blue of the ocean slapping at the base of the Cliffs of Moher. Among the banshee, we of mixed heritage will always be recognized by our eyes.

I sat motionless until the time came.

I stood and touched my right fingertips to my left shoulder and my left fingertips to my right shoulder. Time and space became one and the same. I was floating thirty yards or so above a rooftop garden. An old woman, kneeling on a pillow, was weeding with careful concern. She would not require my voice this day. I hovered patiently and reveled in the fragrance of the clematis vines and the sight of a few late-blooming sunflowers, faces turned west to their namesake as it ambled its way across the sky.

The roof door opened. The shimmering glow of looming death preceded the hulking man who slumped through the door. His tousled hair was a darker red than my own and deeply flecked with gray. I felt his name invade my heart with great urgency. It would not be long. A hum started in the back of my throat, easing into a low moan. The keen rose, octave by octave, until my voice was one with the angels in heaven, and sadness covered the immediate earth. My tears sprinkled from the sky like bold drops from an unexpected sun shower.

Then the urgency retreated, and I was back on my footstool, the tea at my elbow barely cooled. I took my mother's Galway shawl down from the top shelf of the bedroom closet and ran my fingers over the soft lambs' wool, woven centuries ago in an intricate Celtic knot pattern. I placed the shawl on the bed and unfolded its protective wings, revealing my O'Conor scroll. How do the names and dates get written? I know only that they are there. A name. A birth date. And after the awareness, a death date. I opened to the name of the hulking redhead. Casey Rheingold was seven generations down, through Rory's daughter Jane. His birth date was written some fifty-odd years before, with today's date newly added in the ancient, ornate script. His final line had been written, but I was not at ease with the reason for it. Something about Casey. Rheingold's death felt wrong, lighting the spark of my human curiosity. Banshees have no such attribute.

I wrapped the shawl around my shoulders, grabbed my bulky canvas tote filled with the odds and ends of a freelance writer's trade, and ran down to the cabstand on Second Avenue. The cabdriver, an African wearing a Yankees baseball cap, had pasted a sign on the glass partition boasting that his family village was only twenty kilometers from the village where President Obama's father was born.

I asked him to take Seventy-second Street through Central Park to the west side of Manhattan.

Then we rode north along Broadway. I peered toward the Hudson River at each intersection, looking for a sign. At Eighty-third Street, I could see the swirling lights of a half-dozen vehicles scattered in mid-street. After paying the cabbie, I walked to the splendid art deco building at the core of all the excitement.

I stuck my freelance press pass under the nose of the uniformed cop guarding access to the building entrance, which was cordoned with yellow tape. He waved me off, a movement that seriously jeopardized the seams of his dark blue shirt.

'DCPI briefing in a few. No info until then.' And he turned his expansive back, stifling any further word from me.

Reporters who regularly work the crime beat milled around complaining loudly that the deputy commissioner of public information's office was notoriously late to any and all on-scene interviews.

I was looking for a way to sneak past the yellow tape when I saw the old woman from the roof, sitting in a folding chair next to the latticework facade of the building. A policewoman was leaning against the wall but stood straight when she saw me walk over. I bent over the old woman, pulled a bottle of water out of my tote, and gushed, 'Have they given you anything to eat or drink? We can't have you dehydrating. Please take this.'

The old lady's rheumy eyes widened, then blinked. My heart nearly stopped beating, that's how taken aback I was by my own impudence, but then she handed me the ragged gardening gloves she'd been holding, took the bottle, and twisted the cap.

'Thank you, my dear. As you can imagine, it's been quite

a time.' She turned to the policewoman. 'This thoughtful young lady is one of our newer neighbors. Some people I've known for forty years have brushed right past me, without a word.'

The policewoman made a clucking noise at such a lack of manners and then relaxed against the building once again. I squatted next to the gardener while she took tiny sips from the Dasani bottle.

She recapped the bottle and leaned back in her chair.

'Did you ever meet Mr Rheingold? Top floor, full terrace? He was a blustery, winter kind of man. In all the years he lived here, the few times he broke his silence, it was with a snarl or a roar. Not the nicest of neighbors, but at least he didn't come home stumbling drunk like 5D or beat his wife like 3F. All the same, now he's dead.'

'He had a wife? How terrible for her.'

'A wife of sorts. She flits in and out of the building, covered in jewelry and wearing one flashy outfit after the other. Where does she go, in her revolving-door life? Clara from the sixth floor said she once saw Linda Rheingold get into a snazzy yellow car waiting at the hydrant around the corner. The driver was a young man. A very young man.'

She gave me a knowing nod. Abruptly, the events on the roof overtook her.

'I heard the shot. Big, loud bang. I thought it was the maintenance crew. You know how noisy they are when they clean or fix things.'

I nodded vigorously.

'I tell you, when I saw Mr Rheingold push through the roof door, clutching his chest, blood everywhere, my first though was that the missus and her young man decided to hurry him along his path to heaven. Not that it's likely he'll wind up there.'

She reopened the water bottle and took a quick nip.

'Fell right at my feet. It was too late to help him. He said something, sounded like Cladder, you know, ladder with a

C in front. Like that. Then his eyes glazed, just like my second husband's eyes, down at the veterans' hospital on Twenty-fourth Street.'

I watched as her whole being rolled back to her second husband's death, be it last week or decades ago.

She shook off the memory.

'I told the police to look for the young man Linda foot-sied around with. I bet his name is Cladder or something like it.'

Not Cladder. Claddagh! The old Claddagh village in Galway City. Casey Rheingold's dying word was connected to our heritage, if only I knew why.

I leaned on the back of the old lady's chair, hoisted myself up, and offered to go to the corner store to buy her something to eat.

'You're a good girl, but I'm too excited to be hungry. When the excitement dies down, stop by to see me.' She stretched out her right hand. 'Mildred Stresky, apartment 2D.'

I shook her hand with a warm two-handed clasp designed to cover my evasive answer. 'I'm Rynne Bannon. I promise to visit soon.'

A police siren was coming ever closer. I saw the print reporters and film crews gathering. Perhaps DCPI had finally sent a spokesman. I stepped away from Mrs Stresky and, morphing from caring neighbor to freelance journalist, I joined the crowd bunched around a makeshift podium. A dark-haired, middle-aged man, wearing black horn-rimmed eyeglasses, stood at the podium and held out his hands to quiet us. He clearly announced his title as captain, mumbled his name, and then droned on about the day's events.

'Responding to a 911 call at 18:20 hours, that's 6:20 p.m., two patrol officers assigned to the Twentieth Precinct found the body of Casey Rheingold, aged fifty-two. Mr Rheingold was a senior partner in the law firm of Stoddard and Weiss. He expired on the roof of the building where he lived.'

Captain Mumbles pointed in the general direction of the address plate above the entry way.

'FDNY emergency medical technicians pronounced him dead at the scene, probably from a gunshot wound to the chest. Mr Rheingold's body has been removed to the office of the medical examiner.'

A voice from the crowd intruded.

'So, it's murder, right, Captain? Oh, yeah, and could you spell your last name for us?'

'We expect the medical examiner to declare this death a homicide and are investigating accordingly. My name is Morales. M-O-R-A-L-E-S.'

For nearly three centuries on two continents, I keened for thousands of O'Conor deaths caused by old age or illness. The Famine, accidents, and some wild and bloody fights took their toll as well. This war or that war piled the numbers higher. Still, I always knew the reason.

Many's the time my mother, Roisin, Banshee Queen of Connaught, would argue with me. 'It doesn't matter why they die. Dead is dead.'

But I'm my father's child as well. After each awareness, I would savor the intimation, be it hospital bed or battlefield, which helped me to let the O'Conor rest in peace.

Not once in thousands of deaths over hundreds of years, have I suspected murder. How can I close the banshee scroll, knowing that Casey Rheingold's death was not a result of the natural order of things?

The press conference ended, and people were starting to drift away, when a buxom woman, in an ultralight leopard print sweater, stepped from a cab, drawing every eye. She moved toward the building door. Sitting on the edge of the rear seat of the cab, a sweaty young man ran one hand over his retreating hairline and then recounted a fistful of currency.

The doorman hurried forward, touched his cap, and offered the woman his arm. He addressed her by name, causing the reporters to regroup and circle her like vultures waiting for the last gasp of breath.

'Mrs Rheingold?'

'Hey, Linda, anything to say about your late husband?'

'How does it feel to be widowed by a murderer?'

Linda Rheingold spun on the tips of her open-toed, three-inch high-heeled shoes. Her white-blonde hair whipped from side to side as she spat the words like sour milk. 'How the hell do you think it feels?'

She looked past the crowd. 'Jeremy, let's get inside.'

The young man threw another bill at the cabbie and reached Linda Rheingold at the same moment as Captain Morales. Together, they swept her inside.

I didn't believe the new widow would bring her secret lover home, but I had to be sure. I pushed my way through the press crowd to Mrs Stresky, who was standing with both hands resting on the folding chair.

'I'm free to go upstairs. They're even taking down the yellow tape. Things will look normal again in a few minutes. I could use a small sherry. Would you care to join me?'

Of course I would. A perfect opportunity for a chat.

'Rynne, dear, would you carry the folding chair to Ivan, please?'

It was a long, blank moment before I realized that Ivan was likely the doorman. With the chair in one hand and Mrs Stresky leaning heavily on my other arm, I passed unquestioned through the crowd of police, reporters, neighbors, and spectators.

The doilies and antimacassars covering everything in sight gave an inkling of what Queen Victoria's sitting room must have been like. It would be generous to describe the old furniture as antiques, but even so, every piece was buffed to a high shine.

I settled in a high-backed velvet wing chair. Mrs Stresky

stood at a lace covered sideboard pouring sherry into microscopic stemware resting on a silver tray.

She served me elegantly, set the tray on the coffee table, and took her own glass in hand, raising it in a silent salute.

I touched my glass to hers, brought it to my lips, and then nearly choked when Mrs Stresky asked, 'Who are you really? Not a reporter, I hope. I know you don't live in the building. Why did you stop to talk to me?'

I took a deep breath. 'I came here to keep an appointment. Then I saw all the fuss and noticed you, looking exhausted and with a police guard and all. I just wanted to see if you were all right.'

That sounded lame, even to me, but Mrs Stresky seemed to accept it.

'I knew you were a kind person.' She nodded, satisfied her assessment was correct. 'Who were you meeting? Did you call and cancel?'

I plunged more deeply into the tangled web.

'Once I spoke to you, I knew someone had canceled the meeting for me. My appointment was with Mr Rheingold.'

'No.' Mrs Stresky gasped. 'I can't believe it. Whatever for?'

I edged closer to the truth.

'I'm a genealogist. We were supposed to discuss his O'Conor line.'

'What kind of line?'

'His O'Conor family lineage. Just after the American Civil War, Rory Dev O'Conor, his brother John, and sister Kate bundled their families aboard the steamship *Colorado* and came to America, leaving all they knew behind in the tiny village of Crosskil, County Galway. Mr Rheingold is descended from one of Rory Dev's children.'

'Fascinating. Do you create genealogy charts for many families?'

No reason to mention that my mother's royal banshee line had been tied to the O'Conors for a thousand years or more, or that she'd sent me along so that Rory Dev's family would never endure a death without a proper send away.

'I can do any number of families, but my specialty is the Galway O'Conors.'

I weaved the question on my mind into the conversation.

'Is that man, Jeremy, who arrived with Mrs Rheingold, a member of the family?'

'No. He works with Mr Rheingold. He's here so much, the Rheingolds pay for an extra parking spot in the garage for his use. Always trundling in stuffed briefcases and file boxes so full, they have to be tied with thick elastic bands.'

A short time later I took my leave, having no idea how any of what I learned would help me decipher the puzzle of Casey Rheingold's murder.

Once home, I spent hours creating a fancy genealogy chart of the links from Rory Dev's grandfather to Casey Rheingold. The tranquillity of copying the names and dates in a round cursive hand left my mind free to plan. And plan I did.

The next morning, my energy renewed, I was ready to track a murderer. Where better to start than with the widow Rheingold?

When a banshee decides to reveal herself to humans, she uses one of three guises: the young woman, the middle-aged matron, or the old crone. As one of what the pure banshees like to call 'the half-breed lot,' I'd decided centuries ago to function in the mortal world. I rotate through the three guises over any number of years and then begin again. I briefly considered a transformation, thinking Linda Rheingold might respond better to someone her own age or older. But provisional guise changes are chancy without time to invent a history for myself.

After making the decision to stay as I am, I called Mrs Rheingold, and she surprised me with an invitation to stop by at noon.

Linda Rheingold was standing in her open doorway when I got off the elevator. I thought she'd be surrounded by family and friends, rushing to take mundane tasks off her hands. But here she was, quite alone.

Her widow's weeds, a black silk tunic and slacks, were relieved only by the tawny stripes in her tiger print ballet slippers. She led me to a finely decorated living room, with high, wide windows covered in cream shantung. As we took our seats, I noticed she wore an Irish Claddagh ring. The hands, heart, and crown of the ring's design stand for friendship, love, and loyalty. Mrs Rheingold's ring was made distinctive by the large diamond centered in the heart.

I tried to express my condolences, but she was all business.

'Ms Bannon, you mentioned a genealogy chart you were working on with my husband. I suppose you want to be paid. Please send any outstanding bills to our accountant.' She handed me a business card and was clearly set to send me on my way.

In hopes I could rescue the moment, I pulled the O'Conor genealogy chart from my tote. 'Please, Mrs Rheingold.'

I opened the chart, handwritten with dark gray ink on pale gray paper, for her inspection.

'Please,' I said again, although the role of supplicant rarely suits me. 'You misunderstand. No payment is wanted. I'd only completed the chart yesterday. Then, when I heard the terrible news, I thought this would be a grand display for the wake. Poor Mr Rheingold never got a chance to see the final version, but I'm sure his friends and family would take pleasure in it.' I put my finger squarely on Rory Dev's name.

'Here is where the family crossed to America.'

Mrs Rheingold examined the chart for a long while, asking about this or that ancestor.

'This is extraordinary. It must have taken months to put together. My husband was proud of his Irish roots. His

German roots as well. Did he commission you to do a chart on the Rheingold family?'

'We didn't have a chance to get that far. Lately, he wasn't returning my calls, and if he did, he was gruff and hustled me right off the phone.'

'Gruff and in a hurry. That was Casey all right.'

Linda smiled, and for a moment I could see she held a strong connection to her husband, be there a younger lover or no. Then she tightened her eyes.

'That damned law firm. If he'd kept a mistress like any normal man, he'd have had to hide it and fawn over me at home. Out of guilt, if nothing else. But I couldn't compete with his job, his clients, his business entanglements.'

'Entanglements?'

'Entanglements like this jewelry problem, whatever that was about. Constant phone calls. Constant research. You'd think Casey was a first-year associate rather than a senior partner. Jeremy should have been handling that. Casey and I should've been having dinner uninterrupted.'

'Jeremy?'

'Jeremy Lycroft, Casey's toady. Well, I'm sure the firm gave him some important title, but that's how I see him. Casey and Jeremy were so attached that when the police notified the firm about my husband, the partners told Jeremy to find me and escort me home. You'd think a senior partner would have been more seemly.'

She harrumphed.

'You should talk to Jeremy. He'll know why Casey wanted the genealogy chart and whether or not he wanted one for his German ancestors. If so, I would commission you to do it. I could hang both charts in the den. Don't you think that would be fitting?'

Afraid to break her train of thought, I simply nodded.

'Call and tell him I said to talk to you. Being married to Casey gives me "toady by proxy" rights with Jeremy.'

'I will definitely speak with Mr Lycroft.' I could sense

Linda was done with me, so I switched to the touchiest subject. 'It must have been difficult being married to a man who was so intense about his work.' I sat quietly, leaving a gaping void.

Her face softened for a second or two and then rehardened.

'When we were younger, it was easier to accept Casey's unending hours. We were building a life together. Casey was determined that it be a well-cushioned life. He made partner, and then senior partner, but the work obsession never stopped. I once asked Millie Cranepool, the managing partner's wife, if it would always be like this. She seemed genuinely surprised. Her husband has been home for dinner nearly every night since he made partner twenty-two years ago. I decided there was something lacking in me. And I accepted my lot.'

'You must have been very lonely. No one would blame you for seeking companionship.'

'Whatever you're implying is none of your business.' Linda stood and began a diatribe about nosy people as she rushed me out the door.

I'd overplayed my hand. I'd have to abandon the search for any extracurricular partner of Linda's for now, but she'd given me a legitimate reason to visit Stoddard and Weiss. And who knows what I might find once I got there?

On the subway ride downtown, I rehearsed a number of ways I could introduce questions about the mysterious jewelry that had Casey so upset.

Three fifty Park Avenue turned out to be one of those multitiered glass buildings. According to the directory on the lobby wall, Stoddard and Weiss occupied the twenty-sixth, twenty-seventh, and twenty-eighth floors. I mentioned Linda Rheingold's name and handed my business card to the receptionist on the Administration floor. She pushed a few buttons on her telephone console and spoke into her headset. In a flash the elevator door opened, and Jeremy was trotting toward me with an outstretched hand, saying how nice it was to meet a friend of Linda's. He continued nonstop with consoling words about Casey's tragic death. Once I pushed 'hello' into the conversation, I never had the opportunity to say another word until we were in his mahogany and leather office on the twenty-seventh floor.

Jeremy was far more poised than when he'd gotten out of the cab with Linda the day before. Perhaps he could exude confidence as long as there wasn't a Rheingold in sight. He ushered me into a comfortable guest chair.

'Now, what can I do for you?'

I went through my genealogy spiel, not varying far from what I had told Mrs Rheingold.

Jeremy tilted back his swivel chair and steepled his fingers, a look of total concentration plastered on his face. When I finished talking, he dropped his chair forward and rested his elbows on the desktop.

'I never heard Casey mention his family, much less a genealogy chart. If you are looking for family records, I doubt they're in his office files, but I'll have someone look and let Linda know.'

'Actually, if you would let me know directly, I could relieve Linda of the burden and pick up the files. She's still so stressed about the work issues that took up so much of Mr Rheingold's time recently.'

'Why on earth . . . ? Oh, who's to say what will strike a bereaved spouse as important? I shouldn't be telling you this, but if it will comfort Linda . . . Casey was concerned about survivor rights, trying to make sure Linda would be well provided for in case, well, you know. As if she isn't well provided for now.'

I raised an inquiring eyebrow.

'No partner's surviving spouse will ever have to seek food stamps, that's for sure. Linda will never have to worry about money. Casey saw to that, but he persistently tried to make her future more secure. Just last week, he had, shall we say, "words" with the managing partner over the partner shares. Nothing serious. Just a small conversation.'

Linda had mentioned Mrs Managing Partner, so I knew that Mr Managing Partner's name was Cranepool. If he and Casey crossed swords, he was another potential suspect. I filed that away and continued on the one authentic lead I had.

'It's a relief to know that Linda won't have to worry. However, she is under the impression that her husband was deeply concerned about some problem involving expensive jewelry, and she's wondering if it was resolved.'

His eyes darted from side to side as if looking for the truth.

'Doesn't ring a bell. Besides, if it has to do with a client . . . confidentiality and all that.'

He stood and offered to give my card to someone named Naomi, who would check for family records in Mr Rheingold's files and be in touch. Then he escorted me to the elevator bank as if to make certain I got on an elevator heading straight down. Whether I landed in the lobby or hell was of no concern to Jeremy Lycroft. Of that I was sure.

I was crossing the lobby when I heard the security guard say, 'Hey, Mr Cranepool, how was the trip? Rope in any new clients?'

A dapper dresser in a well-cut charcoal gray suit set off by a bright red and yellow striped tie answered. 'Just shoring up some old ones. Changing planes at O'Hare is usually a nightmare, but not this time, so it was a good trip.'

When I spoke his name, Cranepool turned automatically. As soon as he saw a young woman, albeit one with wild red curls, his eyes awarded me a completely inappropriate up-and-down body survey. Then he offered his hand.

'Yes, Miss . . .'

'Bannon.' I supplied. 'I'm Casey Rheingold's genealogist.'

I could practically see his mind speculating whether genealogist was the new code word for mistress.

'Mrs Rheingold sent me here to check for family records.'

'Of course,' He took my arm and started steering me toward the elevator.

Last place I wanted to be. In an elevator. With him. I stood firm and surrounded myself with a confused air.

'Mr Lycroft is helping me with all that, but there is one other thing . . .'

He squeezed my arm while pledging he would do anything, anything at all, to assist me. I had no doubt that, although Mr Cranepool hardly ever missed dinner at home, he surely had reserved some playtime during the workday.

I widened the physical space between us by a few more inches and pulled a hint of Irish lilt into my voice.

'It's the relatives, you see. The Galway relatives. Within this very week, Mr Rheingold was on the telephone with cousins who live in the old Claddagh, in Galway City. Mr Rheingold was most upset about some business venture. The cousins are all hoping the issue was settled and that Casey Rheingold died with peace in his heart. They don't want to disturb poor Mrs Rheingold by asking. So can you tell me, have Mr Rheingold's recent business problems been settled?'

Cranepool looked surprised. 'Galway? He has family in Galway, Ireland? That explains so much. Recently, Casey was stressed to an extraordinary degree over a trivial matter. He was brokering a contract for a client to loan some jewelry to the Galway Museum. He worked on it constantly, to the detriment of business that was more important to the firm. We actually argued. It was such an inconsequential transaction, but now I understand. He wanted to be sure everything was perfect so he could shine in front of his family. Please assure the relatives. Casey was overanxious. Nothing more.'

Then the gleam of lechery slid back into his eye. 'Perhaps

I could check more thoroughly. If we have lunch later in the week, I could let you know what I discover.' He definitely oozed that last sentence.

'Thank you kindly, but no.'

I dipped a half curtsey, effectively slipping my arm from the old fool's grasp.

I walked over to Madison Avenue and boarded the M1 bus home. All the while, I was wondering. Linda knew Casey was stressed about a work project that had something to do with jewelry. Cranepool didn't understand why Casey was so beleaguered about the jewelry. Yet his assistant Jeremy had feigned complete ignorance about the matter. How could that be?

My tried-and-true recipe of a drop of Yahoo, a dash of Google, with a soupçon of Ask.com, produced Casey Rheingold's client in no time at all. Mrs Anna Curry was a world-famous collector of Claddagh rings. Not the kind you buy in an Irish import shop, but the heavy, hand-crafted rings made in Claddagh village centuries ago. In one picture, Mrs Curry is holding a velvet-lined jeweler's tray filled with hefty gold Claddagh rings crafted by Richard Joyce, who, it's been said, originated the design in the late-seventeenth century. I'd seen many such rings when I was a child in Galway.

The article alongside told of the other rings in Mrs Curry's collection. Some bore the jeweler marks of both George and Andrew Robinson, and any number were crafted by all three Dillons. Her entire collection was in the trusting care of her longtime attorney, Casey Rheingold, who stood smiling with his arm around Mrs Curry in a series of snapshots from her ninetieth birthday celebration. In one of the pictures I caught sight of both Linda and Jeremy in the background. Neither seemed to be having as fine a time as Mrs Curry.

I leaned back in my chair. This was a job for the crone.

She could easily pass for Anna Curry. I typed up a cheat sheet of information and attached some pictures that would help.

I called anyone who might be looking for me over the next day or so and said I'd be out of town on family business. Then I took a shower and went to bed.

I ate my yogurt and granola, while an egg boiled on the stove. The crone values high-quality protein as a start to the day. When the egg was done, I looked around, and satisfied that all was ready, I summoned her.

Fingertips poised on the opposite shoulders, I called for the wise auld one, and in an instant, the crone was sitting in my chair, and the young maid was gone. My wild, curly hair was still long, but the red had turned to gray.

I cracked the soft-boiled egg and went over the plan for the day while I ate.

I studied the pictures. I'd have to do something to hide all my hair. Finally I put on a blue serge dress, white knit jacket, sturdy walking shoes, and I was ready to make the telephone call.

The young lady who answered the phone put me through immediately.

'Mrs Curry, so nice to hear from you. So sad about Mr Rheingold. Naturally, I'm assisting Mrs Rheingold. Do you need to know the arrangements? We haven't . . .'

If I let him, he'd go on forever.

'Mr Lycroft, Mr Rheingold called and left a message for me just yesterday. He said it was urgent we speak about my collection. Is there a problem? Are my rings safe?'

Jeremy squeaked as if his tie were a thick rope tightening around his neck.

'Safe? Of course they're safe. The vault here at Stoddard and Weiss is impenetrable.'

'Fine. I'll just come down there and see them for myself.'

'I'd be glad to show them to you, but I have meetings outside the office all day. We'll get to it as soon as possible.'

I tightened the thumbscrews. 'Tomorrow, then. We must meet tomorrow. I won't stand for further delay. I want you to send my Claddagh collection to the Galway City Museum immediately.'

Jeremy tried to postpone, but I was adamant.

'Mr Lycroft, let's not argue. It's time for my exercise. The doctor says if I spend half an hour a day walking by the Pond in Central Park, I'll live well past one hundred. And I intend to do just that. I'll see you tomorrow. Your office. Ten o'clock.'

I twisted my long gray hair into a bun, topped it with a hat that matched my jacket, slipped on a pair of overlarge sunglasses, and left the house.

I leaned heavily on my father's blackthorn shillelagh as I climbed down from the M1 bus on Fifth Avenue near Central Park South.

I avoided the crowded park entrance near the statue of General Sherman, and shuffled along to Sixtieth Street, where I followed the descending path to the comma-shaped Pond that was tucked well below street level.

Two joggers, pushing oddly shaped baby strollers, waved as they sped past me.

I'd just reached the monstrous boulder that sits at a bend in the pathway and was eyeing the empty side lane to my left, when Jeremy Lycroft materialized before me.

I stopped walking and planted my shillelagh in front of me, resting both hands on the solid, knobby top.

'Mrs Curry, how nice to see you.'

He grabbed my arm and propelled me off the path.

'You sounded so eager to learn about your rings, I decided to meet you here. Let's move closer to the Pond, so we can speak without interruption.'

His forceful grip was impossible to shake off. He dragged me behind the boulder, in the direction of the Pond.

'Really, Mr Lycroft, this conversation would serve us both far better in your office. And I could review my collection.'

He kept advancing us to the Pond's edge. When we were inches from the water, he spoke.

'I'm afraid, Mrs Curry, that reviewing your collection is exactly what you cannot do. There have been some changes. Many of your rings are not what they were.'

And with a sudden push, he thrust me into the water, which lapped at my shins. My shoes were sinking into the muddy Pond floor. Only my father's shillelagh kept me from falling.

I raised the shillelagh and smacked Jeremy smartly across his hip. He pulled a gun from his pocket and held it a few inches from my face. Then he ordered me to move deeper into the Pond.

'I planned to drown you. I love the headline. "Decrepit old lady, walks by the Pond every day, finally falls in." But I'll shoot you if I must.'

I moved my forehead until it rested against the gun barrel and said, 'If that's the same gun that killed Casey Rheingold, then go right ahead, sonny.'

'It's the same gun, for all that matters. Casey left me no choice. He kept arguing that you had the right to send the collection to Ireland. I kept stalling. Casey got suspicious. When he insisted on having the collection authenticated, he signed his death warrant and yours, too, since you continue to insist on sending rings you no longer own to Ireland.'

'You stole the ancient Claddagh rings.'

'I borrowed a half dozen and replaced them with excellent copies. I gambled on your dying before anyone looked at the rings again, and then who would know what you really had in the collection. But the thought of an examination by a curator from the Galway City Museum made me nervous. Don't resist. Walk into the Pond. The end will come quickly.'

He wanted the end. So be it.

'You'll have to shoot me, sonny.'

And I rapped his chest with the knob of my shillelagh.

His knee-jerk reaction was to pull the trigger twice. The sound of the shots bounced through the bushes and trees. The bullets went right through my skull.

Jeremy froze, unbelieving.

Then he asked, 'Why aren't you dead?' and shot me in the head three more times.

Behind Jeremy, two mounted police officers were galloping past the boulder, riding toward the sound of gunfire.

Fingertips to shoulders, I vanished, leaving Jeremy to explain how he came to be shooting at ducks in the Central Park Pond with the gun that killed Casey Rheingold.

TADESVILLE

Jack Fredrickson

If you're reading this, you found my shiny box. If it was lying on the ground, the hanging twine all rotted, it might mean that it's over.

But if you found it hanging in the tree, the twine tight like I checked it recent, best you run.

If you can.

Of all the things I'd done, the thing bit me to hell was being a musician. I'd marvel at that, if I had the stomach.

Thing is, most folks didn't even consider the five-string banjo an instrument of music. It's not the tenor banjo strummed fast by fancies sporting striped vests and straw hats, doo-dah, doo-dah. The five-wire is redneck, Appalachian crude, favored by working folks in honest denim and sweat-stained caps. Back when I could get about, the five-string banjo was like a wart on a lady's hand – it wasn't much seen in society, except in television nonsense like *The Beverly Hillbillies* or on the lap of that smoky-eyed inbred in the movie *Deliverance*.

In road bands, when they suffered a five-string at all, it was the banjo man who drove the car and changed the oil. Onstage, he was to stand in the back and bounce the rhythm. And be joked at. Know how you tell the stage is level? The banjo player is drooling out of both sides of his mouth.

In April of 1954, I was twenty-two and had been knocking about with three other Korea vets. We was playing jug band music – an unusual-enough occupation for white guys – hauling around in a chalky blue '37 Plymouth with bad springs, pulling a flatbed trailer with red spoke wheels that we used for a stage. We split five ways, with Arnie, the guitar player, getting two shares because it was his car.

We'd made our way west from the Catskills, playing in towns too small to hear better. The way it worked was this: We'd pull into some jerkwater in the middle of an afternoon, four slicks in prewar suits and noticeable neckwear. First off, we'd strut around a bit, tipping our hats to the ladies, smiling at the kiddies, building interest. At 4:30, we'd throw the duffels off the trailer and climb up. Me and Arnie would start tuning, playing runs, but it was the washboard man and the jug blower that drew the people. Most folks had never heard washboard and jug, and they'd gather like bears to a dump. Up on the trailer, we'd be whooping and joking like we was having the absolute time of our lives, letting the crowd build.

At five we started singing: 'If the river was whiskey, and I was a divin' duck. I would dive to the bottom; I never would come up.'

That always got them laughing. Then Arnie would begin with the banjo jokes, and I'd shuffle forward, looking stupid, which truth be known, wasn't a stretch. They'd laugh louder, and we'd slide into 'Pig Ankle Strut.' By tune three, 'Rooster Crowing Blues,' the folks was usually ripe, and that was when Billy, the jug blower, would jump down from the trailer and start scatting through the crowd. Billy blew a small jug so he could hold it one-handed, and with his other, he'd whip off his hat and start collecting. Billy wasn't bashful; he'd shake that hat right in your chest until you was embarrassed enough to drop something in. And if it wasn't enough – say all you'd loosed was some pennies or a nickel, he'd keep shaking that hat, all the while blowing his brown jug right under your ear, until he tapped a quarter out of you. Up on the trailer, playing, the rest of us watched his hat like hunters tracking dinner, which we were.

If it was a good-time crowd, Billy would be down off the trailer a half-dozen times. Even in Christian towns, we almost always got enough for a sandwich dinner and a quart of the local ferment, if they was selling any, and gas enough to get us to the next burg.

But Tadesville was like nothing we'd ever seen.

The previous town, fifty miles west of Detroit, had been a four-tuner, our name for any place with two churches visible from the main square. Their police chief had hawk's eyes, and he'd kept them on us closer than stink on skunk. 'Divin Duck' was a thud, so we went right to singing down the gospel. That didn't work either; those folks was saving their money for the next life, and Billy only shook out two dimes. We were packed and rolling by 5:30, hoping it was still early enough to hit a new town.

After an hour, though, all we'd seen was trees, lining the road so thick they choked the daylight from the sky.

'We don't want to be running out of gas on these roads after dark,' Arnie said. Like me, he'd been watching the gas needle burrow toward the *E.*

I pulled over. Though we hadn't eaten since lunch, and had only the two quarts of homemade that Whiffer, the washboard man, pinched off the back shelf in a dry goods store in Detroit – nobody groused. It wasn't natural that there'd been no towns along the dark road, and the prospect of calming ourselves with a sip or two, even unfed, sounded fine enough for that particular moment. We stayed up late, drinking rot and telling lies, then slept as best we could, being hungry.

Late the next morning, when Arnie's eyes cleared well enough to drive, we got going again. From the get-go, nobody spoke, and I supposed the nervousness to be testament that we was still driving through dark trees, I had no firsthand knowledge of the conditions along the road, of course, slumped as I was in the backseat, cradling my pickled head in my balled-up suit jacket, wanting only smoother roads.

After a time, Arnie slowed the car as Billy laughed with what was surely relief. I opened one eye to the white fire of the midday sun.

Tadesville looked like any other one-block bump in the road: a dinky grocery, a feed store, and a long building without a sign, all of it squatting parched on brown dirt. It didn't have a gas station. Hell, it didn't have cars. I closed my eye.

'Amish, Arnie,' Billy opined from the front seat. 'Everybody else has cars.'

'Amish in the middle of Michigan?'

'Four-tuner,' Whiffer said from beside me.

'Better not be,' Arnie said, pulling to a stop. 'We need gas.'

I turned on the seat, trying to burrow my head into the mohair upholstery.

'Look,' Whiffer said beside me, the smell of sour mash coming out of his mouth hot, like bus exhaust. 'Jimcrack's heart started up again.'

Henry Olton is my name, but with the banjo, given names get flushed quicker than beer-joint toilets. I've been Huskweed, Bobby Barn, Twangin' Tom, and too many others. Jimcrack, as in Jimmy Crack Corn, was just the latest.

Arnie cut the engine. The pounding in my head pulsed louder in the quiet.

'There's no people,' Whiffer said, after a bit.

'Amish,' Billy said from up front.

'Just working people, too busy to be laying about on an afternoon,' Arnie said. Getting out, he sent my side of the car up a hundred feet. Then he slammed the damned door, firing a red thunderbolt into my skull.

I kept my eyes shut tight and swore I'd never touch another drop.

'For sure there must be people here,' Billy whispered quick to Whiffer and me in the back, but he sounded more like he was wishing than saying. 'It isn't right, not seeing towns for miles, then coming to one that's deserted.'

Arnie's shoes padded around slow in the dust outside the car. He was checking things out. His shoes came closer. 'Got to be people here,' his voice said through the open window. 'Best we just relax in the car until four thirty.'

Whiffer exhaled slowly beside me. Arnie opened the driver's door and got back in. Mercifully, he latched it gentle.

We dozed in the afternoon heat. I been to some dead places, but Tadesville had them beat to hell. No cars, no horses pulling wagons, no people walking by. Not even the air moved.

Ordinarily, that kind of quiet made me itchy. Not that afternoon. Trying to muffle the oil derrick slamming in my head, I was appreciative.

'Four thirty,' Arnie shouted. He probably did no such thing, probably hadn't even raised his voice, but I had not as yet healed.

The three of them scrambled out, rocking the Plymouth like a row-boat in a squall. I hugged the seat and held on.

'Jimcrack!' Arnie yelled through the window. 'Show-time!'

My door got yanked open. They was going to make me die standing up.

There was no choice. Ever so gentle, I eased onto my knees and backed out of the car, presenting myself ass-first to the bright of the world. After some confusion, my feet found the dirt, and I hugged the side of the Plymouth until it, the ground, and I were all moving in concordance.

Someone set my banjo case against my leg. 'Strap on, Jimcrack,' Arnie said. 'Time to yodel.'

Steadying myself with the door handle, I opened my eyes just enough to ease down vertical and hoist out the banjo. Banjos have lots of metal to make them ring loud, and even in sure hands, they weigh like lead. That afternoon, I was strapping on a battleship anchor, and it took both Billy and Whiffer to pull me up onto the trailer. With my eyes again blessedly shut, I began tightening the tuners, riffing into a few simple rolls I could do in my sleep.

'If the river was whiskey, and I was a divin' duck,' they started singing, with me croaking the base harmony, 'I would dive to the bottom; I never would come up.'

Like I said, in most towns those lines were surefire to bring folks nodding and laughing. But not that afternoon. Not in Tadesville.

I opened my least painful eye to the quiet. There was nobody there but us.

'This could be a one-tune town,' Whiffet's brushing hand fell from his washboard. 'First ever.'

'Can't happen.' Arnie eyed the empty street. 'We need gas.'

He started picking 'Swing Low, Sweet Chariot,' on his guitar and we picked it up. Plenty of towns, gospel was all that worked. We played 'Go Tell It on the Mountain,' then 'Amazing Grace' with a ripping banjo break by yours truly, especially considering each of my fingers was trembling at a different speed. Bedrock religious stuff, we played it loud enough to raise corpses. Billy even did his jig, jumping down and shaking around like he was summoning rain onto a drought, but we might as well have been playing in a cave. Nobody came.

Arnie set down his guitar, 'We'll have to browse.'

'Maybe everybody's at a funeral,' I said quick, and started riffing into 'Will the Circle Be Unbroken?' Whiffer joined in right away, rasping the rhythm hard across his washboard. He knew I hated the browsing. Arnie sighed, picked up his guitar, and strummed along, and Billy started his jumping, but it was no use. The street stayed empty.

We quit the song and looked at Arnie. He was scanning the grocery and the General Feed. Not even the white curtains in the window above the grocery fluttered.

'Easy for browsing,' Arnie said.

Browsing was stealing, and it shamed me. Truth be, we was thieves more than musicians, hunting most every town we played for small stuff – watches, jewelry, silverware – that we could slip into our pockets and hock when we got to a city.

We'd done it so much, the browsing was as smooth as our act, Arnie would wait behind the wheel of the Plymouth, key in the ignition, foot above the accelerator, while Billy, Whiffer, and I fanned out, carrying our instruments like we was trying to drum up attendance for a show. But we was looking for unwatched store counters and unlatched houses. Forty-five minutes later – timed exact, no matter what we had or hadn't got – we'd be back to the Plymouth, Arnie would hit the gas, and we'd be gone.

Being deserted, Tadesville looked ripe, for sure.

'Jimcrack, also be checking garages for a can of gas.' Arnie looked direct into my eyeballs. He was telling me I'd better not come back empty-handed this time, even if I was only toting gasoline.

I nodded a quarter-inch and shrugged my arm through my case strap.

Billy headed for the grocery, Whiffer toward the General Feed, though what he was expecting there I didn't bother to wonder. I walked the other way and turned the corner.

The side street was twenty degrees cooler and dark, another tunnel of trees. My liquored head was pulsing in march time from my fury and my shame, I'd honored myself fighting in Korea, yet here I was, skulking in a raggedy town, expected to steal a can of gas, a string of dime-store pearls, or a dollar watch from people too poor and too

233

trusting to lock their doors. I stepped down the center of the road, looking neither right nor left, Arnie be damned.

'Are you greedy, banjer man?' a woman's voice whispered, cool against my ear. My heart double-thudded as I did a quick one-eighty turn. The road stretched empty in both directions.

'Greedy like your friends?' her voice came again, a caress of silk with just a hint of the South softening her words.

I squinted into the woods. The shape of a woman, white and lacy, moved filmy in front of the dark outline of a cottage almost completely hidden in the trees.

'I don't guess I am, ma'am,' I answered back, having the queasy certainty she knew exactly what our little jug band was up to.

She moved a couple steps closer. Her hair was black in the shadows, her lips full and dusty red. At that distance, she could have been twenty, she could have been fifty. She was beautiful.

'Then play me a tune, banjer man.'

I could have sworn her breath touched my cheek.

Without hesitating at the foolishness of standing in the road, playing to someone half-hidden in the trees, I had the five-string out and cut into 'Soldiers'Joy,' an Appalachian standard from the Revolutionary War. She laughed and started swaying with the music, a shimmer of white in the black trees. I slid into 'Turkey in the Straw,' 'John Brown's Dream,' 'Ducks on the Mill Pond,' and a dozen more, one right after the other. She seemed to know them all, and danced in the woods while I played from the middle of the road.

After the last note of 'Eighth of January,' she stopped sudden, put a hand on her hip, and tilted her head, pouty-like. 'Sure you ain't greedy like the others, banjer man?' she called.

'I guess I'm not.' I wanted to look away, shamed by her knowing eyes.

'Greedy people is welcome for always in Tadesville,' she teased from the woods.

I shook my head. 'No, ma'am.'

She paused for a minute. Then suddenly, her hand flew up, and something small arched through the trees and landed next to me on the road. 'We'll see,' she called.

I bent down and picked it up. It was a small, blue felt jewelry box. Inside was a man's ring, green with cheap silvery plating, a gaudy chunk of cut glass set in its center.

I looked up. She was gone.

More than anything, I wanted to walk in those trees. To thank her, I told myself. To see her beauty is more the truth.

As I turned the little felt box in my hand, I caught sight of my watch. I'd been gone over an hour. Anyone back later than forty-five minutes got left behind, Arnie always said. Too risky for the rest to wait.

They'd be gone.

I dropped the little felt box into the open case, set in the banjo, and latched everything up. My head still hurt, and I felt dirtier than ever from the browsing and traveling with the likes of Arnie and the rest. But something new was trying to squeeze in between the pounding whiskey and the shame.

Relief.

A man don't get many chances to redeem himself, the little wise part of my brain said. That voice never had spoken up much, but that evening, on that road, I heard it clear and loud.

The woods was all black now, the trees melted into each other. I picked up my banjo and walked down the road, away from the strange, deserted town, trying not to think about liquor and browsing and the wise eye of the lady in the woods.

After a couple of miles, the dirt road came to one of gravel, and a farmer in an old Ford truck with shreds of hay clinging to the flatbed picked me up in his headlights.

'Where you coming from, lugging that banjo?' he asked through the side window.

'Tadesville,' I said, looking up.

'Tadesville?' He pushed open the door. 'Never heard of it.'

'Strange town,' I said, climbing up. 'Nobody there, except a lady that lives off in the woods.'

The driver didn't need to talk more, and we drove in silence through the dark until he dropped me just east of Kalamazoo.

I left the banjo at my sister's and went to sea as an oiler, thinking to put an ocean between me and liquor and any other temptations on the road to hell. But after three years of smelling bilge on one of the foulest buckets ever to bob between New York and Liverpool, all I'd done was grow a stronger thirst for drink and a bigger taste for easy. I quit the ship and thumbed through the South, stupored on woods-stilled mash, looking to work at anything that wouldn't raise a sweat. They wasn't hiring drunks much at the time, and mostly I did road repairs for small jails in Alabama and Georgia. Breaking and entering, public intoxication, and bad luck was what got me those road jobs, until one incident of accomplice auto theft put me inside a prison laundry for three years.

I got out at thirty years of age, vowing to get smarter. I went to my sister's. Though she'd been the one keeping the banjo all those years, I believe now that it was waiting of its own life force.

To save me, or to be my doom, depending.

The world I reentered was full of amazements. Astronaut men was routinely riding rockets, cars had air-conditioning, and music was coming out of radios no bigger than a pack of smokes. Most incredible to me, though, was that the five-string banjo had become stylish. Beard-and-sandal

Greenwich Village nuts had brought it up North and were treating it respectful. Suddenly, every street festival, county fair, and folk-damn hootenanny had to have a banjo player, and everybody took him serious. No banjo jokes.

I wasn't good enough for a big act, but I didn't need to be. There was plenty of easy work playing car dealerships and warming up county fair crowds, and I traveled with pickup groups all over the Midwest. The pay was miserable, but the hours was excellent – lots of time for sour mash and cards – and there was no need to risk thieving.

I took to wearing the ring I discovered lying in my banjo case because of the sparkle it gave off. Playing under a summer sun or on a bright-lit stage, I could sweep the glint off that ring like a beacon, starting and stopping, making the crowd laugh. It pleased every act I traveled with.

Never, though, did I wonder on the ring's origin. Any remembrance of Tadesville and the lady in the woods had long fallen out of my mind, gone like so many of my other gin-triggered hallucinations.

Until St Louis, June of 1964.

The mandolin player and I were in a hotel room playing stud poker with some of the locals. I'd dropped my last twenty, my flask was empty, and I was getting up to leave when one of them, a short guy in a black suit who'd been winning all night, asked me if he could see the ring. I slipped it off and handed it across the table.

Quicker than a pelican diving for lunch, he snagged a jeweler's loupe out of his vest, popped it into his eye, and leaned back under the floor lamp. 'I'll give you a thousand bucks for it,' he said after no time at all.

I'm sure my mouth fell open. In my entire misapplied life, I'd never once been packing a thousand dollars.

'A thousand bucks. Right here, right now.' The little man leaned forward. His eyes were tiny and wet, like a ferret's.

The table went quiet.

'Family heirloom,' I said, hoping he wouldn't notice my

hand shaking as I reached across the table for the ring, slow, giving him time to up the offer.

'Fifteen hundred.' He closed his fist around the ring.

'Not for five thousand,' I heard my voice say.

No one breathed. The mandolin player was looking at me like I'd just landed from Mars. Night after night, he'd seen me drop the ring like junk into my banjo case, giving it no thought. That night, I'd just forgotten to take it off, was all. Now he was watching me kiss off fifteen hundred solid for it.

The little man in the black suit hesitated for a long minute, then opened his hand and pushed the ring toward the center of the table. 'Not worth five grand,' he said.

The wind went out of my chest. My brain screamed to say I'd been kidding; fifteen hundred was fine. But my gut said pocket the ring, get up easy, and vamoose.

And that is what I did, not at all sure what had just happened.

That one time, my gut was right. The next day, I got thirty-two hundred for the ring from a pawnbroker. I'd started downtown first, in a fancy jewelry store just off the main drag.

'Where'd you get this?' the jeweler asked, setting the ring down on the black felt counter pad.

'Family heirloom.' It still sounded reasonable to me.

'It's four carat, clear quality, well-faceted,' he said. He eyed my greasy suit. 'If you can prove ownership, I'll give you six thousand for it.'

'For this ring?'

'For the diamond. The setting is junk.'

But he wouldn't spring a nickel without papers, nor would the next half-dozen jewelry stores I tried. So I went to the hockshops, and got the thirty-two hundred. Not as much as the fancy stores, but it was better than a poke in the eye.

I bought a used Pontiac ragtop, white on black with red

vinyl indoors, spinner hubcaps on the wheels. With the money left over, I embarked on a grand spree of black label whiskey and high stakes cards. The band, understandable, moved on, but that was no concern. I was living the high life.

I blew through the money in days. Most of it got left on card tables, and the last three hundred was beat out of me by two guys in knit hats outside a bar, I'd been shooting off my mouth, buying drinks for the room.

Stranded, broke, without prospect of a banjo job anytime soon, I started sleeping in my car.

And I started browsing.

At first I aimed for department store jewelry counters when they was at their busiest, taking care to nip only at vodka beforehand so the only thing on my breath would be the smell of Lifesaver peppermint. I acted the confused husband, torn between so many choices spread before me on the counter, figuring the clerks, mostly teenage girls, would be too eye-rollingly bored to notice a bauble missing when I told them I needed to think and turned to leave.

But whiskey had prickled my nerves. I started sprouting tremors, and that got me beady eyes from the counter clerks. And twice, serious-looking gentlemen followed me out. Both times I slipped them, but high-tone stores had lost their potential.

I aimed lower, started browsing hardware stores and bead shops. That was slow work, usually needing a whole day to boost enough to trade for a lone pint, and green goods at that.

The last day of July was inhospitable, sixty degrees and pouring gray rain. I was huddling under the eave of the train station to catch my breath after tapping the costume jewelry store across the street for a pocketful of junk. The owner had been on to me right off, but a half-dozen teenie girls had followed me in. Chattering and giggling, they swarmed the counters like bees, giving me enough cover for a quick sweep and a fast vamoose. Still, I'd been stupid, risking a grab when I knew the owner was watching, and the episode had left me shaking.

That year, black raincoats was the fashion. And in the downpour, the folks scuttling into the station looked like morticians racing to a train wreck. Except for one woman, hugging at the collar of a white coat that stood out bright against all the black ones. Dark hair, lush red mouth, she set my spine to tingling like I was leaning against needles. Brushing past, she whispered, 'Greedy now, banjer man?'

It wasn't just her mouth talking. It was the red of her lips and the white of her coat. It had been a long time since I'd remembered anything for sure, but that rainy afternoon, one memory came back sharp as the Devil's own pitchfork.

Tadesville, 1954.

'I believe I almost am,' I thought to yell at the back of her, as she disappeared into the terminal. 'I believe I almost am,' I said again, this time to myself.

People was looking at me. I hustled down to the viaduct to get away from the crowd and think.

A hallucination, I told myself. From the mash.

A vision, my other self said.

It's been ten years, my first self said.

She could have been only twenty then, or thirty, my other self said. She's still there, living in the woods, in a cottage full of diamonds.

That ring was the only one, my first self said. For sure, she didn't know it was valuable, else she wouldn't have tossed it to me for playing a few tunes. It was a fluke.

I shut down the voices. When you're dead broke, stealing for half-pints to quell tremors, flukes take on new importance. They become likelihoods.

I came out of the viaduct into bright sunshine. The darkness and the rain were gone. I took that to be an omen, a portent, of a better day coming.

Tadesville.

The drugstore map for Michigan showed no Tadesville, not west of Detroit or anywhere else. That made sense, being as there'd been no people there, save the woman. I pocketed the map for future use and went outside to ponder.

Problem was, I'd never known the route, because I'd been cradling my head in the backseat, caring only about the bumps Arnie wasn't dodging.

Arnie. Arnie Norris, of Randall's Corners, Illinois.

Approached like he was being called just for old times' sake, he might remember the route to Tadesville.

There was a phone booth at the corner. The operator said there was a Norris listed in Randall's Corners. I pulled my hand off the phone, having a better thought. Nudging his mind in person might be better, especially if he'd enjoyed enough good fortune since our jug band days to spot his old banjo man a twenty – money I could use for traveling. I went back to the drugstore to consult an Illinois map. Randall's Corners was in the middle of the state, right on the way to Michigan. I made a show of putting the map back and left.

I hocked what I could, excepting the banjo, sold the spinner hubcaps at a junkyard, and headed north with the top down, serenading the telephone poles, cars, and trucks with songs of whiskey, rivers, and diving ducks.

And cottages full of diamonds.

Randall's Corners looked to be suffering no prosperity. Two live souls stood jawing in front of a gas station.

'I'm looking for Arnie Norris,' I said to the one who shuffled over to the pump.

He gave me a careful look-over. 'You a friend of his?'

'Korea.'

'Arnie never came back here.'

The warmth of the gin in my gullet faded away. 'How about the Norris in the phone book?'

'His brother's son.'

I bought eighty cents worth of gas and followed his directions to Arnie's nephew's house. The nephew didn't warm much to the idea that I'd served in the army with his uncle.

'You have no idea where he might be?' I asked through the screen door, clutching my hands together behind my back so as to not betray any agitation.

'He never came back here after Korea.'

I drove back to the pay phone at the gas station, trying not to panic. I'd been counting on that tap for a twenty.

I couldn't recall where Whiffer was from, but Billy Dabbert hailed from Cedar Rapids. The operator had a number.

'Billy?' I almost shouted, much relieved, when someone answered.

'Is that you, Billy?' an ancient voice croaked back.

'I'm looking for Billy.'

'Where the hell you been all these years, Billy?' the confused voice asked.

The old gentleman was out of gray cells. I was out of dimes. I hung up. I'd have to detect the route myself.

I continued north, straining to remember what I could. We'd played a four-tuner outside of Detroit, then headed west. Low on gas, spooked by not encountering any towns, we'd stopped at sunset, drank, slept in the car. Next day, suffering the effects of the mash, I'd kept my head shrouded the whole way to Tadesville. Afterward, I'd hitched a ride from a guy driving a truck to Kalamazoo. Tadesville had to be in a line between Detroit and Kalamazoo.

It took four days to get to Ann Arbor, west of Detroit, being as I had to find gas stations crowded enough to allow a fast-exiting, nonpaying patron. Ann Arbor's courthouse had no record of a Tadesville, but they did have a big map showing county roads. I studied it for the route we'd likely taken, then set off westbound on skinny blacktop that wandered through towns named Bridgewater, Norvell, and Napoleon. I spent the night in the car outside Joppa. And then I came to Rasden. It had two church spires visible from the town square.

It could damned well have been that last four-tuner we'd played.

The sun climbed higher as I continued west through spindly, second-growth woods and long-abandoned farms. Then the trees got taller and thicker, until at last they twined together so thick I lost sight of the sun and the fields beyond the road.

I drove on, mindful of the drooping gas gauge and the growing thought that I could have made up the whole business about Tadesville and the lady in the woods. I'd been stupored that day, and in that condition, my mind had never been a stranger to inventing things. Maybe Tadesville was one such episode; maybe I'd browsed the ring someplace else, and my shredded brain had invented the woman so as to not remember the actual thieving.

I began to shiver. It had been hours since I'd swallowed the last of my provisions. I put the top up and turned up the heater full blast. Still I shook. Best to get out of this forsaken country, quit chasing a remembrance that never happened. I sped up, squinting ahead for a road I could take south to the interstate and, if fortune smiled, potentially a poorly tended package liquor store.

Suddenly, the cracked blacktop fell away, and I was driving on dirt, kicking back brown dust like I was fogging crops. There was a curve. The thick trees ended. And it was there, fifty yards up, baking under a full sun.

Tadesville.

And more.

I straight-armed the steering wheel and slammed on the brakes, crunching the tires deep into the dirt.

Arnie's '37 Plymouth was still parked at the side of the road.

The chalky blue paint was almost all weathered off, exposing huge blotches of gray primer and brown rust, and the tires had shriveled to thin black circles, but there was no doubt. It was Arnie's car. And behind, still hitched to the bumper, was our stage trailer, piled with the tattered, rotted remains of our army-drab duffel bags.

Long needles prickle-danced up my back. I shut my eyes and squeezed the steering wheel hard. Crazy; I'd gone crazy from the mash, crazy from the gin. I wanted to giggle, but I didn't have the courage. I begged God, to whom I had not spoken in decades: let it be a hallucination.

I opened my eyes, slow.

Arnie's car. The trailer. Both the same.

I killed the motor.

Nothing moved in the hot, sudden silence. No cars, no people, no damned, droning flies. The air was dead, like when we'd first pulled into Tadesville.

I got out, shutting the car door easy, but still the sound boomed off the storefronts like three beats from a marching drum: the grocery, the General Feed, the long building with no name. More paint was gone from each of them, weathered away like skin flaked from a corpse too long in the desert. Above the grocery, yellow strings – remains of curtains – hung limp in the window, like entrails dangling from something dead.

My feet kicked up dirty puffs, dry as brown talcum, as I crossed the street.

The Plymouth's windows were down. I leaned in. Arnie's keys and dog tags hung on a chain from the ignition. The cloth upholstery was shredded off the driver's seat, the tops of the exposed seat springs shiny. Someone had been sitting on them recent, keeping away the rust.

My old suit jacket lay crumpled on the mildewed mohair in back, still balled up from when I'd used it as a pillow. I reached in, pulled it out. The rotted fabric came apart in my hands.

I let it fall as I went back to the trailer. My duffel was on the bottom of the pile, the stenciled 'Olton' faded against the bleached army green. I undid the brass hook and pulled the putrid canvas open. My white shirts with their long, pointy collars rested on top, green-yellow now. I felt down, pulled out a pair of black gabardine slacks, a tie with a garden full of flowers, and my other suit. Everything was thick with black mold. At the bottom was a pint of Jack with two swallows left. Jesus.

I pushed it all back in the duffel, tried to wipe the black from my hands.

Run to the car. Turn the key. Get away from this place.

Once, I had the strength. Not now. Now I needed.

It was a perfect day for browsing.

I went back across the street, each step muffled by the dust, inevitable. I opened the Pontiac's trunk, took out the banjo case, dimly heard as the falling lid sent more drumbeats off the storefronts. At the intersection, I turned the corner. Like before, it was cooler under the thick, dark canopy of leaves. Almost cold.

I walked down the half mile.

There's no meat on Arnie, Billy, and Whiffer. Their skin hangs loose and yellow, like rotting shrouds. They look like the people that came out of Auschwitz – haunted, like they've seen hell. My skin's a little tighter. I haven't had to browse as long.

We come every day about four thirty, drag what's left of the duffels to the ground, and pull ourselves up on the trailer. We start tuning. Arnie's only got two rusty strings left on his guitar, but it doesn't matter. Always, we counted on Billy and Whiffer. Most folks have never seen jug and washboard.

We lead with 'Divin' Duck.' Surefire stuff, used to be. But nobody comes. Across the street, my Pontiac, white on black with red vinyl interior, sits low on rusted wheels.

The tires went flat years ago, and the top is tattered from sun rot. I sleep there. I don't know where the others sleep.

Arnie starts a banjo joke. I shuffle forward, make like I'm drooling. Nobody laughs. There's nobody there.

We try singing down the gospel: 'Swing Low,' 'Go Tell It,' 'Amazing Grace.' Used to draw them out, but that was in Christian towns. There's no God in Tadesville.

Arnie sets down his guitar, makes like he's squinting at the buildings. 'Well have to browse.'

I start picking 'Will the Circle?' but it's for show, like before. We have to browse.

Arnie eases off the trailer, slow because there's nothing left in his hip sockets. Clutching at the door handles, he pulls himself to the driver's door, drops onto the seat coils. He sighs through what's left of his teeth. He'll wait for us behind the wheel.

Billy levers himself down with his good leg. His right leg broke years ago and healed crooked. He keeps it strapped with his belt. He hobbles for the grocery.

Whiffer goes toward the General Feed, though what he's expecting there I don't begin to wonder.

I latch my case, walk to the intersection, and turn down the side road. It's always cooler there, under the leaves.

I walk down the half mile. The trees, thick and twisted, caress each other like vipers.

I know the spot. I set down the banjo.

'Are you greedy, banjer man?' The soft Southern voice brushes my skin like cold silk. It smells of mold. I cannot see her. Only the wind, moving the leaves.

I squeeze between trunks grown so thick they'll soon touch. One hundred, two hundred yards in, I look everywhere. There is no cottage, no ruins of a foundation. Still, I move through the trees. It is my need.

The specks of yellow sun on the leaves turn orange, then gray, embers snuffing in a dying fire. I push through the bramble as fast as the arthritis and my tea bag lungs allow, screaming as the thorns rip at my scabs to get at the soft, unhealed pink underneath. There is no cottage. There never was, except as a shadow the germ beginnings of my greed needed to see.

'Greedy, banjer man?' she whispers, through the wind, through the leaves.

'You know I am, you bitch,' I yell, hell's own supplicant. I push on.

When the last of the gray between the trees goes black, when the wind kicks up and chills the wet of my sweat and the new blood oozing out of my skin, when the shakes come so bad I can't go on, I start to feel through the darkness for a way out. It's almost over for another day.

Sometimes I see her then, in that last thin light. Faint, a mist, back in the woods. Laughing and swaying in the trees, mocking the weakness she has claimed at last.

I stand on the road, waiting for my raggedy breathing to regulate. I check my watch. It doesn't work, but I know it's been more than an hour. Arnie, Billy, and Whiffer will have gone to wherever they go. Arnie is real firm about not waiting more than forty-five minutes. I bend down, find the rope tied to the banjo case. For dragging. After the woods, I have no strength left for carrying.

I start back to town. There's no going the other way, no finding a road to Kalamazoo. That parts over. I'm greedy now, welcomed in Tadesville.

I always stop at the big oak where the shiny box hangs. I put it in plain view, back when I had hope that someone would come along. Back before it hit that this place was for us alone – Arnie and Whiffer and Billy and me.

And her. Especially, her.

I feel inside for the paper – this paper – and know again the little death as my fingers close around it. Nobody will come.

I give the twine a tug to make sure the string is still taut and then head back to the Pontiac, dragging my banjo, taking what comfort I can summon from the spongy, dark places on my skin and the lump the size of a walnut that's growing on my forehead.

I tell myself it will end soon, when the spongy places and the walnut ripen. That nothing will come after, except peace.

It can't last forever, I say to the dark.

Sure as hell.

LIMBO

Steve Brewer

I snapped awake on a cold autopsy table. A white-haired man with rimless eyeglasses stood over me, a scalpel in his hand, poised to slice my bare chest. I grabbed his wrist before he could break the skin.

The surprise was too much for the old man. The color drained from his face until he was as white as the smock he wore. His wide blue eyes rolled back in his head and he collapsed, his arm tearing free from my grasp as he crumpled to the floor.

I sat up and looked around. The room was chilly and close, lit only by one bright lamp that dangled above my aching head. The shiny steel table had a drain built into it. Shudder.

I was naked and, except for the headache, seemed uninjured. The usual chunky, hairy body. 'Semper Fi' tattoo on my forearm. Football scar on my knee.

I dropped my legs off the side of the table and my feet reached the cold concrete floor. I bent and checked the old guy's neck for a pulse, but I could tell at a glance that he was gone. Served him right, the son of bitch. Trying to cut me open—

As I straightened up, a glimmer of light caught my eye, off to the left. I looked over my shoulder, but found nothing. Feeling unsteady, I turned all the way around, searching for the source of the light, but it stayed just past my field of vision.

A washing-up sink stood in the corner. Above it hung a round mirror, and I stepped over the dead guy to reach it. My face looked the same, flat-nosed and square-jawed and dinged from a lifetime of fist-fights, I needed a shave.

A shaft of yellow light beamed from my head, just above my left ear. What the hell? I reached up and let the light play on the palm of my hand. Where was it coming from? Gingerly, I pressed my hand against my scalp, covering the beam, feeling for its source.

That's when I found the bullet hole.

I nearly joined the dead man on the floor. What the fuck was happening here? No blood, not much pain, but there was no doubt about the hole in my skull. I dipped a fingertip into it. A neat round hole, felt like a .38. When I pulled my finger away, yellow light poured out.

I didn't like that. Made me feel dizzy, weak. I covered the hole with my hand. Looked in the mirror. Lifted my hand away. Light beamed from the gunshot wound. I covered it again.

'I'm light-headed,' I said to my reflection in the mirror. Neither of us laughed.

Good to hear that my voice still worked. Clearly, I had survived getting shot in the head. The light must be a hallucination or brain damage.

Maybe I was simply dreaming. With my free hand, I slapped my own cheek. I felt the impact, but it didn't sting, didn't burn the way it should. I did it again. Nothing changed.

I leaned toward the mirror. I seemed pale, like maybe I'd lost a lot of blood when I got shot in the head.

It dawned on me to check my own pulse. I felt my throat, then my chest. No heartbeat, no familiar thump-thump. Frantic, I took my hand away from my scalp long enough to feel my wrist. Still no pulse.

Jesus Christ. I was dead. Up walking around, feeling okay except for a headache and the weird light beaming out of my skull. But dead.

That explained the autopsy room. I looked at the coroner sprawled on the floor. He'd just been doing his job. No wonder he keeled over when the corpse's eyes popped open. I wished he were still alive. Maybe he could explain the sunbeam pouring from my head.

I went to a white metal cabinet in the corner and opened the doors. Medical supplies. I pawed through stuff, locating gauze and adhesive tape. Light streamed out of my head while I used both hands to put together a bandage. I slapped the bandage over the hole and pressed the white tape against my bristly hair. The bandage glowed from inside. I stuck more strips of tape over it until no light seeped through. I didn't know what that internal light was all about, but it seemed important that I not lose it all.

The windowless room was small, old, clearly not part of a hospital. Must be in a little town or a rural area, someplace where the local doc acted as coroner. But how did I get here? Had there been an ambulance? Cops? I couldn't remember.

One thing was certain: I needed to get the hell out of here. Somebody would come looking for the coroner eventually, and I might get blamed for—

Wait a minute. What could they do to me? I was already dead. A ghost, a zombie, an angel, something. Okay, probably not an angel, not with the life I'd led. But whatever the explanation, nothing worse could happen to me. Right?

Still, I didn't want to get caught. I didn't know how long this situation would last. I had things to do.

I searched the room, but couldn't find my clothes. The cops must've taken them as evidence, along with my wallet and my keys and whatever gun I'd been packing. Christ, I was starting from scratch.

A hat and overcoat hung on pegs next to the door. I

reached for them, then stopped. It was a knee-length coat, but I couldn't go around without pants or shoes. It was winter, I remembered that much.

The dead coroner and I were about the same size. He was a little taller, a little leaner, but close enough.

I checked the mirror to make sure my bandage wasn't leaking light, then went to work, stripping the doctor of his clothes. The checked shirt he wore under his smock fit pretty well. The gray slacks were only a little long. Best of all, the wingtip shoes were my size. His wallet contained forty-seven dollars and a couple of credit cards, I took it – hell, he didn't need it anymore – and I pocketed his keys. Finally, I lifted the overcoat off the peg. It was an expensive coat, dark brown wool with a nice drape. The felt hat was brown, too, what they used to call a porkpie. I faced the mirror and gave the hat brim a rakish tilt to hide the bandage above my ear. I looked like a gangster in an old movie.

I picked up the scalpel from the floor and put it in my coat pocket. I always feel a little naked without a gun on me, but a blade was better than nothing.

Then I slipped out of the clinic, into the frigid night, with one mission in mind: to find the son of a bitch who killed me.

The coroner's keys fit a late-model Buick. After a few blocks, I reached the main road and recognized where I was: a little upstate burg called LaPorte. Picture postcard of a place, with evergreens and little cottages and an icy river snaking through the middle. Patches of snow glowed under the streetlamps.

Gino D'Ambrozio had a clapboard cabin near here, overlooking a small lake. Never could understand why a Brooklyn boy like Gino would love a place as rustic as a summer camp. He and his pals often spent weekends there, playing cards and drinking beer without their wives ragging them.

I must've come up here to meet with Gino. No other reason for me to be in LaPorte. I still couldn't recall what had happened to me, but I remembered the way to Gino's house. I pointed the Buick north and zoomed out of town.

I was never one of Gino's boys, though I'd dealt with him off and on over the years. Always freelance, always for decent money. I was never going to be on the inside, not with a name like Mercer. The Guidos only embrace guys whose names end in vowels. But sometimes they need a go-between.

You can't put competing gangs in the same room without the tension getting to somebody and guns being pulled. The Guidos hate the Ivans and the Jamaicans hate the Puerto Ricans and the fucking Colombians hate everybody. But they need to do business occasionally or discuss territorial issues. Then they need a guy like me – tough, practical, un-affiliated, expendable – to occupy the middle ground and sort shit out.

Nobody owns me, but they all know they can trust me. I never talk to the cops. I keep their secrets. I'm a pro.

I'd been doing some work lately for this fat-ass vodka slurper named Dmitri Godunov. Everybody called him Good-Enough, which was a pretty apt description of his business practices, but his money was green. Had Dmitri sent me up here to see Gino? About what? I intended to find out.

A mile outside of town, I passed the Shady Rest Motor Inn. The concrete-block building formed an L around a potholed parking lot, with the office at the end nearest the road. The green VACANCY sign reflected on the office windows, but inside I could see a doe-eyed woman with dark, wavy hair.

I slowed at a twinge of memory. The woman's face in close-up. I'd met her before. She'd moved here from the city. Dmitri bought the motel so he and his boys would have a place to stay during summit meetings, thumbing his nose at Gino, and he made her the manager.

She was connected to Dmitri's gang in some way. Somebody's sister. I couldn't remember exactly. I drove on.

I didn't have any trouble finding the turnoff to Gino's hideaway. My headlights sliced through the frosted evergreens that grew close to the paved road. The beams reminded me of my gunshot wound. I checked the rearview, but the bandage and the hat were doing the job. No sign of my strange internal light.

Halfway to the lake, the usual black SUV was parked on the shoulder. The driver's door opened as I approached, and one of Gino's sentries, a muscle boy named Chuck Graziano, climbed out from behind the wheel. He held up a gloved hand to shield his eyes from my headlights. The other hand was inside his leather coat, going for a shoulder holster.

What the hell, I had a deadly weapon of my own. I was driving it.

I gunned the engine, and the Buick lunged forward. Chuck tried to jump out of the way, but he was too slow. The heavy car knocked him down, and the tires went *ka-thump*, like I'd gone over a speed bump. I braked and, for good measure, backed over him. *Bump-thump*. When I could see his flattened form in the headlights, I put the car in park and got out.

The tires had squashed his head, and it wasn't pretty. No open-casket service for Chuckle. I dipped a hand in his jacket and came out with a heavy Colt .45 with a chrome finish. I checked the magazine, then stuck the flashy gun in my belt. I immediately felt better.

I dragged Chuck into some weeds at the side of the road, then got back in the Buick and drove to the cabin. I killed the headlights as I reached the clearing. A round moon was rising, and its liquid light rippled on the lake.

I sat in the car a few minutes, watching the house. Lights

glowed in several windows, but I couldn't see anybody moving around inside. I got out of the Buick and gently closed the door.

A thick bed of pine needles cushioned my steps. Pistol in hand, I circled the cabin, peeking in windows.

In the living room, four of Gino's boys sat wreathed in cigar smoke, deep in concentration over their poker hands. Gino wasn't among them. I figured I'd find him in his 'study', a small bedroom where he went to be alone. He liked to sit behind his secondhand desk, poring over his papers and counting his money.

I checked all the other windows first, then poked my head up outside of the study's single window. Gino's back was to me, but there was no mistaking the meaty neck or the black pompadour. Gino had the tall, thick mane of a televangelist, hair of biblical proportions.

The back door was locked, but I used the blade of the scalpel to slip the latch. I crossed the kitchen to the central hallway. The boys in the poker game roared with laughter, and I used the noise as cover as I tiptoed past their open door. I froze, listening, but they kept laughing over their cards. Idiots.

I stepped inside Gino's study and shut the door behind me. He looked up, annoyed at the interruption, but when he saw it was me, his fleshy face went slack and his mouth gaped.

'What's the matter, Gino? You act like you've seen a ghost.'

'You, you—'

'I'm what? Dead?'

He looked past my shoulder, like he'd remembered the boys in the other room. Before he could shout, I showed him the shiny gun.

'The cops said you were DOA—'

'Somebody got it wrong, Gino. I'm still kicking. And I want to know who shot me.'

'You don't know?'

'Was it you?'

Gino arched a thick eyebrow. 'You think I had you shot?'

I shrugged.

'If we'd bumped you, Mercer, you wouldn't be walking around. My guys might fuck up some things, but they're good at that.'

'I was in LaPorte to see you—'

'Our business was done. Nobody was more surprised than me when I got a call from Dmitri's motel, telling me you'd bought the farm.'

'I was shot at the motel?'

Gino looked me over again, hunting for bullet holes. I still wore the doctor's hat, so he couldn't see the bandage.

'You don't remember?'

I waggled the gun at him impatiently.

'Yeah, yeah, it was at the motel. That right there oughta prove I had nothing to do with it. If I wanted to get rid of you, I woulda put you at the bottom of that lake.'

What he said made sense. The Guidos don't leave bodies for autopsies. They dump them in lakes or bury them in concrete. They've had lots of practice.

'Dmitri sent me to see you,' I said.

'That's right. Some of our boys had gotten crosswise. He sent you to smooth things over.'

'And we made them smooth?'

'Far as I was concerned. You were supposed to talk to Dmitri, make sure we had a deal.'

A flash of memory: Dmitri leaning toward me across a table, sputtering about one of his boys who'd been killed in a fight. What was the name? Alexei. Just a kid.

'What about Alexei?' I asked Gino.

'What about him? He was a punk. He messed with Chuck at that nightclub Dmitri owns on Coney Island. Chuck was within his rights—'

'We covered all this.'

'That's right. You getting your memory back?'

'I remember enough.'

Gino's eyes settled on the .45 in my hand.

'Speaking of Chuck,' he said, 'isn't that his gun?'

'That's right.'

'So where is he?'

'He had a traffic accident. Unless you want to join him, you'd better sit quiet until I'm gone.'

'Thought you knew better than to make threats.'

'I got nothing to lose.'

I reached behind me for the doorknob. Soon as the door cracked open, I could hear the boys arguing over their cards. Clueless.

I met Gino's eyes. 'Don't tell anyone you saw me.'

'Who would believe me?'

I eased into the hallway and closed the door behind me. Then I slipped out of the house, quiet as a ghost.

When I pulled into the parking lot of the Shady Rest Motor Inn, the office looked empty. A few rooms down, one door was blocked by an X of yellow crime-scene tape. I parked in front and sat in the Buick, staring at the door. I didn't remember staying in the room, but this was bound to be the place.

I got out of the car, ripped the tape away, and tried the doorknob. The door swung open. I felt uneasy as I reached inside and flicked on the lights.

The bed was mussed, and every surface was dusted with fingerprint powder. But what captured my attention was the large red-brown stain on the tan carpet, near the foot of the bed. Blood. My blood.

There'd been a lot of it. I carefully circled the stain, measuring it with my eyes. I must've bled out right here, before the ambulance arrived, before anyone tried to save me.

The wavy-haired manager appeared at the open door. She

wore jeans and a lumberjack shirt, and she spoke with a strong Russian accent: 'What do you think you're doing?'

I looked up at her from under the brim of my hat. When our eyes met, she went pale. She whispered, '*Nyet*.' Then she fainted dead away.

Shit. I kept having that effect on people.

Careful not to step on the bloodstain, I went to the door and checked the parking lot. No sign of anyone except for the young Russian woman who lay in a heap at my feet. I got my arms under her and lifted her up.

She felt light and loose, as if she had no bones. I carried her to the bed and gently set her down. I brushed her hair away from her face. She had creamy skin, high Slavic cheekbones, and full lips. I felt drawn to her. I wanted to kiss those lips.

Her eyelids fluttered, and I backed away. Gave her a chance to look at me without going into another swoon. I closed the door in case she started screaming.

She stared at the ceiling for a second, then stiffened all over as she realized where she was. Her eyes narrowed when she saw me.

'You,' she said.

A memory sparked. Her in this same bed, naked under the sheets, smiling up at me. A name flashed in my mind. Irina. Her name was Irina.

How had we ended up in bed together? What had we meant to each other? Did she know why I was in LaPorte, what I did for a living? Did she know who the hell killed me?

I didn't get to ask her. Cars roared up outside, screeching to a stop on the asphalt. Doors slammed. Aw, hell.

I went to the window and peeked between the heavy curtains. Gino was out there with four of his boys, crouching behind a Cadillac and the hood of a black SUV. The neon light made their faces a sickly green. Two were standard-issue goombahs, but I recognized the other two:

Gino's lifelong chum Frankie and a steroid case named Vinnie, brother of the late Chuck Graziano. Guess they found Chuck's body and came hunting for me. That would explain all the guns.

'Get in the bathtub,' I told Irina as I pulled the .45 from my belt.

Once she was out of sight, I threw open the door and stepped into the cold night air.

'What's up, Gino?'

'Thought we'd find you here, Mercer,' Gino shouted from behind the SUV. 'This time, you'll stay dead.'

I didn't wait for them to start shooting. I lifted Chuck's .45 and blasted away. One bullet clipped Gino's shoulder and sent him spinning. Another caught Frankie in the forehead, and his skull exploded.

Bullets whined past me. Vinnie had some kind of automatic rifle, sounded like applause as it stitched a line of holes across the front of the building. A couple of bullets hit me in the chest and slammed me against the doorjamb, but it didn't hurt at all.

I shot Vinnie in the throat, and he forgot all about his machine gun, too busy grabbing at his collar and hunting for air. One of the goombahs shrieked as he fell backward, blood spurting from his chest.

The last guy shot me again, a punch in the gut, but then he stopped, gaping at me. Bright pencils of light jutted from the bullet holes in my shirt.

The shooter freaked. He tried to run away, but I took careful aim and nailed him between the shoulder blades. He pitched forward onto the pavement.

My ears rang. Gun smoke stank up the air. As I turned to go back inside, I heard a groan from the other side of the cars.

I stalked around the vehicles and found Gino on the pavement, squirming and whimpering. I stopped right in front of him, the coroner's wingtips an inch from his nose. Gino rolled over and looked up at my bright quills of light.

'What the fu—'

I shot him in the eye.

It was the last bullet in the .45, and I tossed the gun aside as I hurried to the motel room. I needed to plug these holes. I felt weaker by the second.

Irina stood framed in the bathroom doorway, shaking with fear.

'It's over,' I said. 'They're all dead.'

She stared at the light streaming from my chest.

'What *is* that?'

'No time to explain,' I wheezed. 'I need bandages—'

Dizziness overwhelmed me, and I dropped to my knees rather than fall on my face. No pain, but light poured out of the holes in my torso. I covered two of them with my hands, but it still felt as if I were slipping away. I looked up at Irina, who hadn't moved.

'Help me.'

Her face twisted into a scowl, and she spat on the floor.

'Like you helped my brother?'

She pronounced it 'brudder,' and for a second I didn't know what she meant. Her brother?

'They left Alexei bleeding on the sidewalk,' she said. 'His life draining away. But did you care? No, to you it was just business.'

Alexei. The kid Chuck killed at Coney Island.

I remembered now, her telling me her brothers sad story. She'd wanted vengeance against the Italians. She wanted Dmitri to declare war. But I hadn't come here for that—

'Now,' she said, '*you've* made them pay.'

I wilted. Why hadn't I seen it sooner? Someone had been in my motel room when I was shot. Someone I trusted. I'd turned my back on her, which I never would've done with the Guidos or the Ivans, and she popped me behind the ear with a .38. Probably my own damn gun. Then she coolly watched me bleed to death before calling the cops. Just like she was doing now.

I kneeled next to the bloodstain, trying to hold my light inside, but it spilled everywhere. The yellow light filled the motel room, blinding me.

I fell forward onto the same spot where I'd died once before. Right at her feet. But all I could see was light.

THE INSIDER

Mike Wiecek

It was nice to have my office back.

Not strictly an office, mind you, and not strictly mine. In our profession, nobody would dream of paying for a hundred square feet behind pebbled glass. But the Tasty-Time Coffeehouse had not long ago been completely overrun by the New Unemployed. You know who I mean – laid-off bankers, mostly – hogging the chairs, frowning at their laptops, stretching a single caramel mint latte straight through lunch. The Tasty-Time's manager tried switching off the Wi-Fi, but it wasn't until he bolted plates over every power outlet that the freeloaders finally got the idea.

Today even the best table in the house was open, up front by a plate glass window. I steered my client over – we'd arrived at the same time – and got two stale donuts and coffee.

'Ernest Eppleworth,' he said. He didn't look much like an Ernest, with his movie-star jaw and short, fashionably graying hair. 'Thanks for seeing me, Mr Clark.'

Ernest ran a little hedge fund, and he knew a guy whose sister had a friend I'd helped out last year. It wasn't much of a case – the ghost had already been fading away, and the friend held on to his marriage – but everyone seemed happy at the end. A recommendation apparently traveled along, as they do.

Anyway, I was glad for the business.

'So how can I help you?' I asked.

'Well.' Ernest hesitated. 'The thing is . . . I'm making too much money.'

'Ah.' An obvious solution presented itself, but – 'Why don't you tell me about that?'

'Since November, we've earned a 13,000 percent return.'

'Holy—' I choked on my donut. 'A little over half a year – you've been doubling your money every *month*?'

'Yes.'

'How?'

'Short-term forex trading.'

'No way.' And I meant it.

See, I used to be a banker myself. Lehman Brothers, maybe you heard of them. After my own layoff, I drifted into private security. Crime is just about the only growth industry going nowadays. The ghost specialization thing – all that came later.

But anyway, that's how I knew my way around the markets. Day-trading foreign exchange? – most folks would do better piling up their money and putting a match to it. Ernest wasn't telling the whole story.

'Well,' I said. 'What currencies?'

'A range. Nairas, lately, and good action in hryvnias, kyats, and Qatari riyals.'

'There's a *market* in this stuff?' Nairas were Nigerian, and I was pretty sure hryvnias were Belorussian or Ukrainian or something, but I'd never heard of kyats.

'We get better leverage in the unregulated venues.' He noticed my skepticism and added, 'It's fully documented. We use a London-based clearinghouse, report every trade, pay our taxes. Entirely above-board.'

I started to get a glimmer of the problem. 'So you're just very good traders, is that it? Never wrong-footed by the market, ice-cool under pressure, all that?'

Ernest had the grace to look embarrassed. 'More or less.'

'Someone's feeding you trades.' I didn't make it a question.

'No.'

'No?'

'Not someone,' he said. 'Some*thing*.'

Considering how much sheer energy and intellect has gone into analyzing the markets, it's surprising that no one saw the correlation decades before. Hemlines, sunspots, AFC vs. NFC in the Super Bowl – every other conceivable, spurious relationship has been studied to death. But only recently did someone notice that market volatility marched neatly in step with parapsychological phenomena.

In other words, the more ghosts showing up, the wackier the Dow.

Ouija boards and séances? Had their peak in the late 1920s and early '30s, and you know what was happening then. The Age of Aquarius? Maybe it was all the dope those kids were smoking, but paranormal visitations skyrocketed right when the economy tanked in the early 1970s. Which led directly to all that New Age out-of-body crap and the first Reagan recession – and by the time the bubble economy crashed, everyone and their dog seemed to have a personal angel.

Potted history, to be sure, but now that we're in the Great Depression Two, the ectoplasm's been flying like mud. Basically, economic distress translates into a lot of unhappy deaths, with hauntings following right behind.

'I don't know who he is,' said Ernest. 'I've never seen . . . one before.'

'What's he look like?'

'You know – like a ghost.' Ernest frowned impatiently. 'His shirt's all torn up, blood everywhere on his head and chest, and he kind of shimmers, and you can see outlines of the furniture behind him.'

'So he didn't die in his sleep.'

Here's how it works – or the best current understanding, maybe not worth much. Most people, they die, and they go somewhere else straightaway. Nobody knows what's beyond that long tunnel with the warm light at the end of it. But sometimes, if someone is really upset, if they feel they have vital, unfinished business – basically, if they're incredibly resentful about being dead – they can hang around for a while, pestering the living.

It's almost always revenge, of course. Once in a blue moon some star-crossed Romeo can't believe he died before his beloved, and he comes back, blubbering and fading in and out, until Juliet gets fed up and tells him to just get *going*, already. But usually shades are angry, vindictive losers who are happy to take a rain check on heaven if they can get just one more chance to screw with their enemies still on earth.

I'd never heard of a ghost who stayed behind simply to help out.

'Why you?' I asked.

'I have no idea.' Ernest hesitated. 'And, well, I haven't tried to press, you know? I mean, the guy's making me a fortune, no reason to rock the applecart.'

Nice. The hedge fund mentality in a nutshell, if anyone still doesn't understand why Wall Street cratered the world economy recently. But we could let that go for now.

'He appears in my office,' said Ernest. 'Always late at night, when I'm the only one there.'

'How often?'

'Every week or two at first. Then more frequently. This week on Monday and Thursday.'

'And he—'

'Gives me a recommendation. This or that currency, up or down, for the first thing the next morning.'

Forex, especially in the bizarro currencies Ernest had mentioned, was more than volatile. It would be like putting your entire stack on red or black, every time. And with leverage – he could probably multiply his bets by ten or twenty, on margin, with a cooperative broker – he was gambling the car, the mortgage, and the girlfriend, too.

'Wait a minute,' I said. 'How does he communicate the details?'

'He must have died with a pen in his hand.' Ernest shrugged. 'He writes on his shirttail and shows it to me.'

That's another of the rules: the ghost shows up with whatever he happened to be wearing or holding at the instant of death. For most people, of course, that means a hospital johnny and the nurse-call button. Or if you have a massive heart attack shoveling snow, you get to keep your parka and the shovel.

Ernest's ghost was apparently killed in the office.

'How long does he stay?'

'The first time, maybe half an hour. It took me a while to get the idea, you can imagine. After that, hardly more than a minute, just long enough to show me the tip.'

'He sounds efficient, this shade.'

'The last few times it's been longer, like five or ten minutes. I don't know why.'

'And every tip is good?'

'Every single one. He's never missed, even once.'

I chewed some donut. 'Is your fund still taking investors?'

'What?'

'Never mind.' I probably couldn't make the minimum. 'You know, most of my clients in situations like this, they want help getting *rid* of a shade. The golden-goose thing, I'm not sure what the problem is.'

'I saw a lawyer,' Ernest frowned. 'He says the situation might be construed as insider trading, depending on who the . . . who he is. Was.'

'Really?' I couldn't see how, exactly – had the SEC started going after psychics and palm readers? But paranormal litigation was a brand-new specialty, and case law was scant. 'I think I see why you're talking to me, though.'

'That's right – everyone says you're the best.' Ernest looked at me, well . . . earnestly. 'I need to know who this ghost is.'

It's always scams or revenge.

Maybe not words to live by, but true for most of my cases.

Except now. I just couldn't see the angle. *Any* angle. Some dead guy – murdered, from the description – takes an indefinite stopover from the Paradise Express, simply to help make Ernest very, very rich.

At least I didn't feel guilty tripling my usual rates.

It was Monday, and Ernest expected the ghost that evening, so I went over to his office after dinner. Twentieth floor, Midtown, a block off Fifth Avenue. The ground-floor security desk had three guards, all of whom seemed to be moonlighting from their day jobs as counter-terrorist paramilitaries – boots, machine guns, armored vests. Good thing Ernest had told them I was coming.

Out of the elevator it was all teak and marble and hand-woven Kashmiri rugs. Ernest had the corner office, a single desk lamp lit, so we could see the skyline glitter and twinkle all the way downtown.

Oh, and a surprise.

'This is Jake Tims,' said Ernest, as a man stepped from the shadows.

Mid-thirties, a little younger than Ernest, dressed in hedge fund casual: gray pants, open-collar shirt, John Lobb loafers, and a Breguet wristwatch.

'Nice to meet you.'

'Jake is making an investment,' said Ernest. 'A *major* investment in the fund.'

'Six hundred million,' said Jake.

I nodded like this was the sort of pocket change I could lose at the dry cleaners, too. 'Let me guess – you're here for the due diligence?'

'Damn right.' Jake smiled tightly at Ernest. 'If I'm shifting 90 percent of current assets, I need to see the genie at work.'

'Of course.' Ernest turned to me. 'You don't mind?'

'Not at all.'

We settled into some incredibly soft leather armchairs near the windows. I tried to figure Ernest's game – was he using me for protection? To evaluate Jake? To bolster the ghost's legitimacy somehow?

No obvious answers, so I just sat quiet, listening to them talk about real estate. You'd think, a couple of guys this wealthy, they'd be living on a whole different plane, but no, it was just the usual complaints about parking and brokers and the other co-op owners.

More square feet, of course.

After a half hour Ernest looked at his watch – a Patek Philippe maybe, I couldn't be sure in the dim light, but definitely more gauche than Jake's – and said, 'Should be just a few minutes now.'

And sure enough.

The ghost materialized over by the bookcase, three or four seconds to become mostly opaque. Bloody wounds over shirt and tie, as Ernest had said. It looked like he'd taken a bullet in his chest and another right in the nose. His face was unrecognizable carnage, one good eye peering out above a mess of bone and bloody tissue.

He looked around, saw us, and startled. For a moment he shimmered and began to fade.

'It's okay!' said Ernest, jumping up. 'They're investors. More money for the fund. That's good, right?'

The shade hesitated, then resolidified. It seemed to stare at me, then Jake, and then kind of shrugged.

'No problem.' Ernest gestured behind his back, at us – *stay quiet*. 'Okay?'

Pause, then another slight shrug.

'Good. So, ah, what do you have to recommend today?'

After one more hard look at us, the ghost pulled up his

shirt. One side had been shredded by the gunshot, but the other was more or less whole. With a pen or pencil in one hand, he scribbled on the fabric, then held it out.

Ernest walked up and bent down to squint at the shirttail.

'Forints?' he said. 'Appreciating?'

The ghost nodded.

'Excellent.'

And that was that.

The next morning, I couldn't help myself – I turned on the computer as soon as I woke up and checked the foreign exchange ticker. The European markets had been open for two hours.

	Bid	Ask	Change	High	Low	Time
USD/HUF	244.10	244.60	+13.28	275.11	239.57	11:39:04

So there. Hungarian forints were up more than 5 percent. Good call, ghost.

And I have to admit I felt a chill. Even after everything Ernest had told me, I still hadn't quite believed.

After a shower I had a choice to make. I could chase down the shade's identity – basically a database search, checking morgue records and police reports and so forth. The problem was, a lot of people die every day, and even the gruesomely violent means of death wouldn't narrow it down that much. We live in a murderous age.

Or I could follow up on Jake Tims.

He'd been remarkably cool last night. I don't care how many thousands of zombies you've killed in shoot-'em-up video games, real corpses freak most people out. Plus, Ernest said Jake had approached him out of the blue. Sure, the hedge fund's remarkable returns were generating all kinds of industry buzz, but it seemed remarkably keen timing on Jake's part.

No contest.

And next to no effort, either, A single phone call reminded me of why Jake's name was familiar.

'You don't remember?' Detective Gatling yawned at the other end of the line. I heard bullpen noises behind him – a cell phone ringing, muffled complaints, the clatter of chairs. 'Jake Tims used to have a partner, Randall. They ran a boutique investment firm, but last year Randall disappeared, along with the entire sweep account.'

'Oh, yeah.' Active traders keep their operating cash in a separate account, carrying a slightly better interest rate. 'How much did he abscond with?'

'Three million, plus or minus.'

'Now I remember.' Once Randall's pilfering would have been big news, but after Madoff and Stanford and Lewis, a mere seven figures was chump change, hardly worth a B-section headline. 'You never found him?'

'Naw.' Gatling didn't have to say, *And we didn't look that hard, either*. In the nihilist landscape of post-collapse Wall Street, there were plenty of bigger fish to fry.

'Jake's about to move most of his assets over to Ernest Eppleworth,' I said.

'Really.' His tone was flat, but I could hear Gatling's interest perk up.

'What do you know about Eppleworth?'

'Nothing,' Gatling said, but he was a lousy liar, especially for a cop.

'Uh-oh.' I closed my eyes. 'There's an investigation open, isn't there?'

'Not for me to say. What's your interest?'

I hesitated, then explained the ghost. Concealing evidence is not my style.

'Huh.' Gatling was silent for a moment. 'The returns are too good to be true. We were thinking Eppleworth had a mole in one of the black pools.' Where large transactions could be conducted directly, between large entities, free of the oversight from regulated exchanges – in other words, an ideal spot to front-run the big dogs. Totally illegal, but that never stops the sharpies. 'A ghost – I'm not sure that's even against the law.'

'Exactly.'

By the time I hung up, I knew the clock was ticking. Gatling was annoyed about losing the mole idea, and I was certain he'd be talking to the DA in about five seconds, to see what they might do with Ernest's unorthodox tipster.

Now, not only did I have to solve the case before the fraud squad hauled Ernest away, but I was going to have to insist on cash-and-carry. Ernest's credit rating had just fallen into the basement.

'*Recognize* him?' Jake's voice rose. 'His face was blown off!'

'I noticed that.' We were in Jake's office, mid-morning. I'd hung around the street entrance – also Midtown, only a few blocks from Ernest, but with more casual security – and buttonholed Jake when the armored limo dropped him off out front. Jake brought me upstairs mostly to avoid a scene in public.

'Thing is, you didn't seem surprised,' I continued. 'Which got me wondering.'

He put up some resistance, but when I mentioned Gatling's interest, we both knew it was only a matter of time. The police would be far more tenacious than me.

'The ghost is Randall, of course,' he said finally. 'My former partner.'

'Aha.' I'd suspected – people rarely disappear *and* keep living – but it was nice to hear Jake agree. On the other hand, the ghost's face really was nothing but gore. 'How can you be sure?'

'Because he visited me, too.'

Okay, *that* was a surprise. 'When?'

'Two days ago. Middle of the night.' He made a peevish frown. 'Don't they ever show up during business hours?'

'Not usually. So . . . he didn't hare off with the petty cash after all.'

Jake snorted. The ghost – might as well call him Randall, now – explained that he'd been kidnapped and tortured into revealing the bank password, then shot and dumped into a Hudson River garbage scow.

'Randall's really angry,' said Jake. 'But the kidnappers wore masks the whole time, so he has no idea who they are.'

'Which means he can't go haunting them. I get it.'

'He can't stand the idea that everyone thinks he's a thief, living the high life in Fiji or whatever. So he's making it up to me, with this guaranteed-return trading scheme.'

'Randall directed you to Ernest?'

'Yes. Of course, I did a thorough check on the Epple-worth funds. The returns are honest – the forex streak is real, just like Randall said.'

'Hmm. How did Randall tell you all that?'

'Writing on his shirt, like you saw last night. It took forever.'

'I bet.' I considered. 'There are a couple of really obvious questions—'

'Yeah, I know.' Jake leaned back in his ergonomic, sleek-leather, post-Aeron chair. 'Like, why not give *me* the tips, instead of going through Ernest?'

'That's one.'

'He doesn't want to bring too much suspicion on the firm here. You said the cops are already sniffing around – he figured, let Ernest take the heat. I can still keep the earnings.'

'Okay.' That sort of made sense. 'But how does he *know*? How can he read tomorrow's box scores today?'

'It's an afterlife thing. Short-term time dilation, quantum tunneling effects.' Jake shrugged. 'I didn't understand his explanation, but so what? The point is, it works.'

'Uh-huh.' I looked out Jake's window, where a pigeon

was waddling around on the ledge. 'So did you double your money on those forints?'

'No.' Jake looked annoyed again. 'I wasn't quite convinced. Stupid, huh? But Ernest expects Randall back tonight, and I'm going all in then.'

I hit the Rolodex again.

Jake got the two questions, all right, but there was one more he seemed not to have thought of: If it was so easy, why hadn't it happened already?

Like I said, with the economy hitting lows in the Mariana Trench, plenty of Wall Streeters were moving to the Great Beyond. Between stress-related cardiacs, Provigil overdoses, and wiped-out investors bursting in with semiautomatic weapons, it was a wonder the big firms still had to resort to redundancies. Anyhow, that meant a steady flow of financially savvy type A's into the afterlife. If they really could game the day traders, you'd think some of them would have tried it before now.

Many more phone calls, and I discovered that, in fact, they had. But no one wanted to talk about it.

'It's like this,' said one of my ex-colleagues from Lehman. 'I have some friends, they'll tell me stories over drinks, but they'll never admit anything publicly.'

'Why not? Even if it's a ghost doing the legwork, positive returns are positive returns. The Street'll take its alpha from anywhere – shades, vampires, flesh-eating zombies, who cares?'

'Because it never lasts long,' my former desk mate said. 'Three people told me they had, uh, *visitations*, I guess, but every one flamed out after just a few tips. And then what – you're going to send a shareholder letter explaining you lost a bundle by taking advice from the Ghost of Christmas Yet to Come? No way. So they keep quiet.'

'Ah. So nobody actually made money on the advice.'

'Nope. It was all currency trades, too, in the last few months. But the shade always screwed up after a while.'

'One last question. Was it the same ghost each time?'

'I didn't ask. But everyone said he'd been murdered, so messily they couldn't possibly identify who he'd been in real life.'

I was too late.

I waited until the morning to talk to Ernest. Hey, the Knicks were in the playoffs – talk about an unexplainable phenomenon – and I didn't want to miss the game.

Ernest, I'm sorry. Really.

When I got to his office, there were police cars, two TV trucks, and a herd of pedestrians clicking cell phone photos as a covered gurney was lifted into the coroner's van. I couldn't talk my way through the uniforms standing guard behind the yellow tape, so I waited until Detective Gatling came out. When I waved, he frowned and hustled me out of the crowd.

We stood inside the lobby, out of the way as a pair of forensic technicians in Tyvek bunny suits lugged their kits to the elevator.

'Security cameras caught the whole thing,' said Gatling. 'Video'll probably be on the Internet by lunchtime . . . Jake Tims walked into Ernest's office, started screaming, and pulled out a Glock. Eleven rounds, eight through the torso.'

'What were they doing?' I pointed to the armored security guards across the lobby, apparently under interrogation by another detective. Gatling shrugged. 'There's no metal detector here. They caught him quick enough after the shooting stopped.'

I shook my head. 'Jake lost some money this morning, I take it.'

'Just about every penny. He went the wrong way on, uh . . . just a minute.' Gatling flipped through his notebook.

'Ringgit. Some kind of Asian money? I don't know the details, but he blew his entire packet on the trade.'

'Randall.' I muttered some profanities. 'The ghost.' And I explained how Jake had thought his former partner was steering him to riches.

Gatling started to catch on. 'Don't tell me.'

'Yup. Randall seems to have been recommending up/down currency positions to traders all over the city. But none of them were talking to each other.'

'A tip-sheet scam!'

'I think so.'

Gatling's grin spread wide. 'I haven't seen one of those in decades.'

In ancient times, long before the Internet, a grifter would mail out a newsletter to, say, a hundred sports bettors, predicting who'd win the big game on Sunday. The trick was, half the tip sheets would say one team – and half, the other. Next week, the newsletter would go out again, but only to the fifty recipients who'd gotten the correct prediction the first time – and so on down the line, half the marks falling away each week. See how it works? At the end, three gamblers would have gotten seven examples of a tip sheet with a *perfect* record.

And then the grifter would send one more mailing, asking if the marks would like to subscribe. Sure, it was costly, but now that he'd proven himself . . .

The beauty was, it was even halfway legal. Oh, the good old days.

Gatling shook his head. 'Randall set Eppleworth up to fail, spectacularly. But why?'

'Not Eppleworth. He just happened to be the last mark still making money. The target was Jake.'

'Why?'

'Because Jake killed Randall.'

A pause while Gatling thought it over. 'Gunshots, yeah, same as Eppleworth upstairs this morning, I could see that.

But if that was true, why would Randall come back to Jake – and why in the world would Jake believe anything from the guy he'd just murdered?'

'Because Jake must have hired the thugs who kidnapped Randall. It really happened the way he said – fingernail pulling, the bank password, the garbage scow. Only when he was on the other side did Randall have time to figure it out. He set this whole elaborate scheme up simply to ruin Jake – and Jake went along with it, because he assumed Randall didn't know what actually happened.'

We stood in silence for a moment. Outside, the coroner's van finally drove away.

'You'll find the motive if you look,' I said. 'My guess is Jake wanted the whole pie for himself – and the three mil from the sweep account was just a lagniappe.'

'You're probably right.' Gatling put his notebook away. 'Let's do the formal interview later, after I check into it.'

'Sure.'

We walked toward the door. Sunshine spilled across the lobby's polished floor.

'Good thing New York doesn't have the death penalty,' Gatling said. 'I'm sure your new pal Jake wants a word with you, but he'll have to wait, oh, about forty years.'

'Yeah.' I sighed.

'What?'

'Ernest,' I said. 'He'll probably be visiting me tonight.'

SWING SHIFT

Dana Cameron

Jake Steuben knew it would be easy to find Harry amid the crowd at North Station. All he had to do was find the highest density of pretty girls; his friend would be within fifteen feet.

Sure enough, there he was, ten feet away from a group of secretaries by the newsstand, watching as they chattered about the stars on the cover of *Life*. Jake picked up his valise and edged his way through the crowd. He leaned over and whispered into Harry's ear.

'If you get into trouble and you can't get out, it'll be because of a girl.'

'There are worse reasons.' Harry startled, his morose stare gone, and stood up to shake Jake's hand. 'Train was on time. Any trouble?'

'What trouble would there be? It was crowded but quiet; I stood in the vestibule most of the way.'

Harry looked askance. 'No doubt the conductor made you stand out there – that's the ugliest hat I've seen in quite some time, my friend.'

Jake took off his hat to look at it fondly. It was a little shiny, stretched, and the brim needed reblocking. 'It's just getting broken in.'

They walked out of the train station, past drunken sailors

staggering to Scollay Square, then a few blocks to the Boston Common.

Harry said, 'How's the wife?'

'Sophia is fine, thanks. How's the war effort in Washingt—?'

'And the baby's doing well?'

Jake couldn't help smiling. 'Cutting his first tooth, so he's a handful. Say, Harry, what is it you—?'

'Good, glad to hear it. And everyone in Salem?'

Jake looked around. There was no one to overhear their conversation, so why did Harry keep interrupting? Politeness was all well and good, but he had come to Boston on the double. 'Real good,' he said slowly. 'Thanks for asking.'

They settled on a bench on the Common. The leaves on the trees were starting to turn and would soon fall, but for now, the sun was warm and high.

Harry looked around carefully, then sighed. He shoved his hat back, mopped his forehead with his handkerchief. He sat forward, clapped his hands together, but didn't say anything.

Jake had had enough of waiting. 'So, what's the problem you couldn't wire me about?'

Harry shifted uneasily. 'I got a case I can't crack. It's a doozy. You've got a knack for getting into the tough ones, seeing angles I don't.'

'Tell me.' They'd worked occasionally as deputies for the Essex County sheriff until Harry started with the Bureau, and Jake inherited his family's farm near Salem.

Harry hesitated. 'It's not easy. You know I deal with . . . government secrets.'

'Are you sure you should tell me, then?' Jake enjoyed the sun on his face. His feet ached inside his shoes. The grass of the Common looked inviting.

'It's okay,' Harry said, a little impatiently. 'I cleared it upstairs. And got you clearance, too.' He took a deep breath. 'It's one of the research facilities, over in Cambridge. There's a bad leak. I can't pin it down.'

'And what do you think I can do that the FBI can't?'

'I . . . I think I'm too close to it. You're outside.' Harry looked up. 'Like I said, you see angles no one else would. Remember the Beverly Slasher, how you knew he was the guy who found the first body? I wouldn't ask, but we got two strikes, two outs, bottom of the ninth. I don't find a DiMaggio soon, it's gonna be my fat in the fire.'

'Sure, Harry. You know, I'll do whatever I can.'

'Thanks, Jake.' Harry smiled for the first time since Jake had gotten off the train, but it didn't reach his eyes. 'The security is tight enough, I've been watching for weeks. I just don't know how the information is getting out.'

'What do you think's going on? They've somehow learned to walk through walls? Use *magic* to whisk the secrets away?'

'Stop razzin' me, Jake.' Harry shook his head, dead serious. 'You know the Krauts are involved with some pretty unsavory investigations into the paranormal and mystical. The trips to Tibet, the archaeology, their obsession with skulls . . . don't even joke about it. My boss, Mr Roundtree, has stories that would curl your hair.' Harry shuddered. 'Nope, I'm hoping like heck it's good old human sneakiness and greed. I want you to get in there, see what I'm not seeing.'

Harry pulled an envelope out of his jacket and handed it to Jake. 'Your credentials, the location of a boardinghouse, description of your job. And a new name; we're not going to suddenly introduce a new guy with a German name. No offense.'

Jake nodded. 'Where will I be, and what will I be doing?'

'Janitor at a computational research lab. We want someone who will blend in, who no one will take too seriously. It's all in the file.' He stood up, began to pace. 'I should get going.'

Jake was surprised. He wondered when his friend last slept through the night, ate a square meal, or bathed: his aftershave was faintly, nauseatingly sweet. 'Hey, wait a minute! What do you think will happen, someone will go "Psst, hey bud, want some government secrets?" You're gonna have to give me a few more—'

'Look, it's all in the file!' Harry said. 'Wise up! I called you in because I need help. I can't sit around babysitting you; I got a job to do, an important job. There's a war on.'

He mopped his face again. 'Sorry, Jake. The pressure's killing me. I'll stop by your room in a couple of days. We can talk then. Okay?' Harry stood and held out his hand. Jake stared at his friend, nodded slowly, and shook. He was genuinely worried now. His friend wasn't telling him the entire truth. 'Yeah, sure. Don't take any wooden nickels, Harry.'

Later that night, Jake sat on the quilt-covered bed in his rented room, reading the file. Harry was right. He'd covered all the bases – waste disposal, deliveries, repairs – and checked some less obvious ways. Harry was a good agent for the same reason he'd been a good deputy: he had a mind like a criminal, and though he went to extremes, he was thorough. Harry had already followed several of the potential suspects: The secretary who'd been complaining about the rationing complained about everything else. The technician who seemed to have an unlimited supply of gasoline for a car with an A sticker was found to be siphoning fuel from his brother's trucking business. No one was obtaining the information any way he could see.

It was time to call in reinforcements, Jake decided. He went down to the drugstore and called his cousin Vic, arranging to meet him at the boardinghouse in two hours.

When Vic arrived, the cousins set out for a walk along the Charles River. Jake explained everything, not sparing the details. 'I want you to follow up on what Harry started.

You and Rosalie tail the employees, sniff around, see what you turn up. It can't be magic that's getting those secrets out.'

'Hey, there could be vampires,' Vic said. He waggled his fingers, widened his eyes. 'Turning into mist and going under the doors.'

Jake shot his cousin a dirty look. 'Stop clowning.' Then he began to worry that Vic might not be too far off the mark.

Vic nodded. 'Okay, you want Rosie's sister – you remember Olivia? – to cuddle up to anyone? She's got a real knack for making men want to please her.'

Jake thought about it. Olivia might get Harry to reveal what he hadn't told Jake. As badly as he wanted to know, he shook his head. 'No, thanks. Best not to raise our profile, now of all times, if we can avoid it.'

After confirming their plans, Vic left for downtown, and Jake went about assuming his new identity.

Every day for two weeks, Jake – wearing Coke-bottle-bottom glasses and coveralls – swept, emptied the trash, and did odd jobs at the research facility. Even though he had access to almost everyone and everything, he still couldn't figure out how the information was leaving the lab. Rosalie and Vic had no better luck.

After two weeks working the day shift, Jake switched to the swing shift. The second night, he was mopping up in the office area when he heard a hiss from the doorway to Section Sixteen.

'Psst! Hey, buddy!'

Half convinced Harry was playing a joke on him, he looked up from the bucket to see a stacked redhead in a white lab coat beckoning to him. He recognized her as one of the computers, the women who operated the large, impossibly complicated analytical machines that were behind the locked door.

He made a point of looking over his shoulder, turned back, and raised his eyebrows – surely *she* couldn't mean *him*? She nodded vigorously, waved at him to hurry. He could barely believe his luck at this break. Supposedly, all the computers, mostly women, had the highest clearance, but maybe—

'Hey, I'm not trying to borrow money,' she whispered. 'I just need someone with good, strong hands.'

Jake knew what she meant, but stayed in character. He backed away a step or two, holding his hands up. 'Sister, I may be on the dumb end of the mop, but you move too fast for me.'

The redhead blushed six different shades of mortified. 'I . . . I didn't . . . I never . . . Oh, golly, I just need you to help me fix something, and quick!'

'I'm not supposed to go in there,' Jake said. No sense appearing too eager. 'I don't have clearance.'

'I've hidden all the sensitive material,' she said, bouncing a little with impatience. 'Unless you think a bearing that's come out of a rotor is top secret. And you're cleared to be *here*, right? I need to finish this set of calculations tonight, mister! Please?'

Jake shrugged. 'You're the boss.'

When he entered the long, wide room, the racket almost floored him. On one side of the room were rows of shelves of electronics, bulbs and dials like 10,000 radios. The other side, a spaghetti mess of wires, all the way down the wall. The heat from the analytical machines was oppressive; a few curls stuck limply to the redhead's cheek.

'It's over here,' she said and handed him a screwdriver. 'If you could get that bearing back on track, I'd owe you.'

Jake saw the problem right away. He grimaced; his hand was too big to fit comfortably, but she was right. All it took was brute strength to get the bearing reset. When it snapped into place, the woman's face lit up.

'Oh, thanks a million! I'd just gotten the – well, I can't

really say. But if you hadn't been there, a lot of hard preparation would have gone down the drain, and some of our boys would have been in a real jam.' Satisfied the machine was in order, she ushered Jake back to the administrative area.

The door safely shut behind her, she exhaled. 'Phew! Thank goodness you were there. Those machines are so twitchy! Anyway, thanks.'

'My pleasure.' An idea blossomed. 'Say, how do you manage when I'm not here?'

'Oh, I'm usually on the day shift. There's a supervisor to help out then. And funny, they don't think they need one after five o'clock. Sometimes the fireman on duty – you saw how hot it gets? Sometimes he helps me.' She stuck out her hand. 'I'm Ginny.'

Jake shook her hand, being careful not to crush her delicate fingers. 'Stuart.' He grinned. 'Call me Stu.'

'Well, Stu, I'd be happy to buy you a cup of coffee. I've got a ten-minute break coming up.'

Good thing he'd hidden his wedding band under the lining of his bag at the boardinghouse. 'Why, thanks, Ginny. That sounds fine.'

They drank the coffee, didn't even miss the sugar. Ginny unwrapped a piece of newspaper, offered Jake a molasses cookie.

Sighing deeply, Jake said, 'I sure am glad we met! What a treat.'

Suddenly shy, Ginny said, 'I'm covering for my friend Ida. Her boyfriend got the night off. They went to see Duke Ellington at the Roseland. And tomorrow, they'll see Sabby Lewis at Le Club Martinique.'

Jake perked up; he was a fan of jazz and the local bands. 'The boyfriend's either missing a leg, an eye, or is about a hundred and forty-seven.'

Ginny laughed. 'It's not that bad. He tried to sign up – three different recruitment stations – but they all caught on to his gimpy leg and marked him 4-F. But we can use every pair of hands we get. This place is always humming, always something new. Eddie – that's the boyfriend – he's the head of grounds services, here.' She smiled, compressing her lips hard together. 'So many boys gone . . . if a gal gets the chance to go on a date, you help her out.'

There was such a wistfulness in her voice, Jake asked, 'And your young man?'

'It shows, huh?' She nodded. 'Italy. Or last I heard, two months ago.'

'That's tough. War won't last forever, though.' Jake thought a minute. 'Ida and Eddie must get to take lunches, breaks, together, though. He helps her out with the, er, machinery in there?'

'Oh.' Ginny looked around, nervously. 'That's how they met, actually. And that's why they keep it quiet. We're supposed to be really strict about access.'

'Mum's the word,' Jake said. He mimed turning a key in front of his lips, then throwing it away.

'But you and he couldn't even be in this building if you didn't check out, right?' she said, now obviously wondering whether she'd made a mistake. 'And I'm usually pretty good at telling the good eggs from the bad.'

Jake believed her; he was good at reading people, too. He laughed. 'I got more papers than a show dog, and to do what? Push a broom, wash windows. Even with these cheaters, I can barely see three feet in front of me. Nah, just be careful with everyone else.' He stood up. 'Thanks for the coffee, Ginny.'

'Thanks for the company,' she replied. Then she winked. 'And the help.'

Jake finished his shift, then went back to the boarding-house. He had warmed-over dinner – meatloaf and green beans – for breakfast, went up to his room, took off his shoes, and stared at the peeling paint on the tin ceiling.

After about an hour, he thought he had it pretty well figured out.

It was all just a little too easy, like it had all been laid out for him. And that made him nervous. He decided he needed to go to Le Club Martinique that evening.

Jake crossed the bridge over the Charles River to Boston and walked down Massachusetts Avenue. The neighborhood was still bustling six hours after the close of regular business. The clubs and bars on this end of town drew whites and Negroes, all dressed in their finest. Music seemed to create places where Jim Crow occasionally blinked. Jake appreciated that; he knew something about not fitting in.

Down toward Columbus Avenue, past the Savoy and the Hi-Hat, was the place Jake was looking for. Le Club Martinique might not have had the size or the garish splendor of the Roseland Ballroom, but it was hopping. Every time the door opened, a blast of swinging trumpet music threatened to knock passing pedestrians off their feet. Jake put it on his list to visit, after this job – maybe he'd even be able to talk the tin-eared Harry into coming with him. It was the kind of place where famous musicians would come after their sets to jam until morning.

A uniformed doorman tipped his braided hat as Jake entered. A big band was playing on the stage; they were good, not cluttering up the music with an unnecessary vocalist. The dancing couples got more and more daring with flips and twirls, putting aside care for a few hours, banishing worry with the joy and audacity of the music. They'd pay for it in the morning, but for now, it was worth every sore foot and hangover-to-be.

Inside the club, Jake saw a number of extravagantly long and baggy zoot suits. He wondered whether the uniformed soldiers there would call out the wearers as unpatriotic and wasteful as the beer flowed and the evening grew more raucous—

Jake's attention was drawn suddenly to a couple sitting alone. They matched Ginny's description of Ida and her boyfriend, Eddie.

The band tore into a version of 'Cotton Tail' that would have done Ellington proud. Drinks were set aside, and the dance floor was mobbed.

The couple sat still, though Ida looked like she wanted to dance, too. Eddie, a weasely-looking fellow, said something to her. She pouted; he refilled her coupe with champagne – Jake could see the French label – and patted her hand. Ida smiled, and Eddie limped over to another table.

Jake thought about Eddie the groundskeeper pouring French champagne.

Unless the dolly sitting at the table was Eddie's sister, Jake thought Ida was right to pout. The other girl was all done up in blue satin and had on more rouge than was smart. Jake couldn't really tell – the smell of beer and chicken mingled with cigarettes and liquor sweat – but he would have bet she was wearing too much perfume, too. Eddie was leaning in a little too close; she let him. When their hands disappeared under the table simultaneously and stayed there for too long, Jake began to understand.

The drum solo ended, the horns jumped in, and a burst of energy surged through the club. Eddie stuck something into his pocket. The girl put an envelope into a satin clutch with rhinestones bigger than a Packard's headlights. Everyone's eyes were on the dancers or the band; Jake was the only one who'd seen the transaction.

The couple, Eddie and Ida, left then; she was protesting, but he was having none of it. Jake thought about following them, but realized there were bigger fish to fry. He had to keep his eyes on the glamour puss in blue satin. He waited about twenty minutes.

When Harry came into the club, Jake cussed and ducked behind a pillar.

If things had been so plain to him – how Eddie was working and why – why hadn't they been plain to Harry? And what was he doing here now? He *hated jazz*.

Afraid he'd queer his friend's plans, Jake stayed hidden, watched his friend go through a similar routine with Glamour Puss, hands under the table, swapping envelopes. Only this time, the girl wasn't so pleased. She and Harry exchanged heated words, to judge by their expressions. They were lucky the band had started in on a rowdy version of 'Bugle Blues,' drowning them out. Finally, Harry left, the girl looking more irked than ever.

Jake knew he could come back any night and find the girl sitting in her evening gown at that same table; he'd only have this one chance to find out what was up with Harry. He decided to follow Harry, intending to straighten this out, once and for all.

Two toughs grabbed Harry as soon as he reached the front door. As they dragged him outside, the song ended, and the dancers mobbed the bar. Jake struggled to get through the packed ballroom.

When he reached the street, Jake paused. It had rained briefly while he was indoors, but that wasn't what stopped him. What was a guy supposed to do? Let his best friend get roughed up – maybe even killed – or blow his cover? Jake knew a thing or two about discretion and knew it was just as important to Harry the G-man.

If it took blowing his cover to save a friend, Jake would do it. The risk came with the job.

But he was going to pick his moment, if he could. No sense in undue haste.

Jake spat out his gum and followed the two goons who had Harry – they were professionals, no doubt about it, keeping things quiet while they were among the crowds on the street. Had Harry done something so stupid he'd gotten

287

on the wrong side of a mobster? Jake recalled the glamour puss in the club. Harry should have known better, doing the work he did. Dames like that didn't sit alone for no reason.

If you get into trouble and can't get out, it'll be because of a girl.

Jake picked up speed; the trio was heading into a shady-looking neighbourhood, even darker than normal because of the enforced blackouts. Things would happen quickly.

They were in an alleyway, now, and it wasn't to talk. At first, Harry played it smart and got in a few good punches; Jake hoped he could keep himself out of it. But two against one was too much, and Harry faltered, went down. The darkness made it the perfect place for trouble; there'd be no rescue from anyone on the street.

Jake couldn't wait any longer. He had to get in there.

Jake took a deep breath and concentrated, Changing only halfway. Tissue rippled, and bone stretched; the slack of his suit was filled with new muscles and thick, rough fur. The wolf-self, contained too long by the city, by the cheap shoes, by Jake's cover, was let loose. The joy of the Change ran through his body, from lengthening teeth and pointing ears to sharpening nails. Jake couldn't resist chuckling, a guttural, inhuman noise. The stink of evil was strong on the two goons.

He felt traces of power crawling through his system as he sized up the men. One, a guy the size of a moose, had a shiv that looked a mile long, sharp as sharp could be. The shorter one – Jake thought of him as 'Cagney' – had just laid a cosh upside Harry's head. Harry looked like he was down for the count.

Good, Jake thought. *That will make this easier.*

Jake growled. The goons ignored him. Guys like that don't scare easy, and they were busy.

He hurled himself on them. They couldn't ignore that.

Jake landed on the back of Moose; best to lose the knife first, especially if the thug was any good with it. Moose kept his head, even as he found himself slammed into the brick wall, slimy with rain and God knows what else. He twisted fast, ignoring the blood pouring from the side of his forehead. He held on to the knife, tore it along Jake's arm. Jake pressed his face close, so the other man could see the teeth that didn't belong in a human mouth, feel the heat of a lupine mouth as it tore his ear.

Moose yowled and clutched his head, as Jake took the steel blade and snapped it like a cheap toy. It fell to the ground with a tinny clink. Moose turned and ran, screaming bloody murder and bleeding like a stuck pig.

No time to waste; even in this crummy a neighborhood their racket would bring unwanted attention. His hat went flying as Jake bounded to the end of the alley and tackled Moose. Jake tore out his vocal cords with another slash. There was only a wet gargling noise, now.

Jake turned to Cagney, who was going through Harry's pockets. The guy must have feared whoever he was working for more than he feared what was happening to Moose, because he had worked all through the fight—

Cagney suddenly looked up. His eyes were wide and unfocused, and his face slack. At first Jake thought he might be drunk or a little soft in the head, but then the sweetish smell worked its way past the filth of the alley. Jake knew Cagney was high on opium.

Jake recognized another smell now. This was a stronger version of Harry's sickly aftershave.

Jake knocked the cosh out of Cagney's hand with one paw while raking claws down his cheek with the other. Cagney screamed, his hands flying up to his face as much to block as to hide from the Anubis-like monster before him. Jake's face had lost nearly all trace of humanity: elongated snout, fangs and a row of jagged teeth, ears sharply extended above his head. The fur wasn't the worst, or the whiskers, Jake had been told. It was his eyes. Somehow it was wrong that such human eyes should be set into the face of a slavering animal.

But Moose's screams had brought interest; Jake heard automobile engines and police sirens moving closer. He couldn't just leave Harry in the alley; one way or another, he was responsible for getting him out of the trouble he was now in.

Jake leaned over, grabbed his hat, and picked Harry up effortlessly. He slung him over his shoulder and turned to leave when a car pulled across his path, blocking his exit. He loped to the other end of the alley, but a Cadillac screeched to a stop there. The headlights from both cars lit the narrow lane; Jake was trapped in the middle near a couple of rank-smelling ash cans. The five men who spilled out of the cars brandished revolvers, aiming them at Jake and the unconscious Harry. Crazy shadows made many-armed monsters on the walls.

The three toughs at one end stumbled over the bodies Jake had left behind. There were exclamations, and one of the men retched at the sight and smell.

'That's the guy, Mr MacLaren.' At the other end of the alley, Eddie limped behind a large man in a flashy, double-breasted suit. He gestured to where Jake was trying to melt back into the shadows. 'I'd recognize that cheap suit anywhere. I watched him eyeballing Sadie at the club while she was dealing. Then I followed him here, when I saw *him* trailing Sid and Joey as they hauled off that deadbeat Harry Gray.'

Then Eddie got a look at what was left of Sid and Joey at the far end of the alley. He moved farther behind Mac-Laren.

'Wait a minute,' MacLaren said. 'Gray is the junkie? He's a Fed – he was at the big bust two years ago! The new boss is going to be *very* interested in what Gray knows about us!'

Jake was in a bind. He could run for his life, but leaving Harry behind with these goons would be tantamount to killing him. Jake could Change back to his human form, maintain his cover, and although he'd be able to fight, the chances of Harry *and* him surviving the armed gang were slight.

Jake adjusted Harry over his shoulder and pulled his hat lower. He'd try to make a break, hoping that in the mayhem, no one would notice a werewolf too much.

Fat chance.

He tensed himself, ready to spring, when he heard the clatter of ladies' shoes on the pavement at the top of the alley.

He froze. It was Rosalie and her sister Olivia.

It wasn't until the ladies called out that the gunmen noticed the two women had passed the cars and were right smack in the middle of things.

'Jake? You there, Cousin Jake?' Their voices couldn't have been more out of place in that dirty alley.

MacLaren didn't lower his pistol. 'Ladies, this is a private party. Best you turn right around and get yourselves home.'

'I think not,' Rosalie said. 'Not without Jake and his friend.' She and Olivia were dressed for an evening out. They stood primly, in their best coats and hats, between the two groups of gangsters. Their arms were linked, their gloved hands folded over their handbags. They might have been strolling to church.

The other gunmen didn't bother stifling their laughter. Even MacLaren grinned at the ridiculousness of the situation. He snapped his fingers. 'Walt, Jonesy, Studs.'

The men moved forward quickly. Walt stepped behind Rosalie and shoved her hard to the ground. She didn't raise her head, and she was shaking.

At the same time, Jonesy grabbed Olivia by the arm.

'Take your hands off me!' Olivia demanded.

Jonesy laughed again but did as he was told.

'Jonesy! What are you doing!' MacLaren said.

When Jonesy realized what had happened, he looked at

his hand and shook his head. 'I don't know! It was like . . . I didn't have any choice!'

'Well, get them out of here,' MacLaren said. 'Or shoot 'em. We ain't got time for this.'

Jonesy grabbed Olivia again and yanked her into him.

'C'mon, you! You'd better scram – argh!'

Olivia had turned in to Jonesy and latched onto his neck with her mouth. As he screamed, perhaps Jake was the only one of the men capable of seeing her skin change, becoming violet snake scales. Her eyes enlarged, her nose diminished, and her teeth became . . . vampiric.

Studs and Walt tried to pull Olivia off Jonesy; she lashed out at them with razorlike claws. With a growl, Rosalie hurled herself from the ground and landed on top of the men attacking her cousin. Rosalie's face was like Jake's, now: furred, fanged, furious. Her little hat fell to the mud as she and Olivia shredded the gangsters. Bones crunched, blood ran.

As surreptitiously as he could, Jake deposited Harry behind the ash cans.

MacLaren was smarter than his men. He stared for only a moment, then aimed his pistol at Jake.

Jake rose up and threw an ash can at MacLaren, bowling him over. Jake turned to Eddie, who had the sense to run. Jake hesitated: Eddie now knew Harry was a government officer with an opium problem. Jake couldn't let him get away. But MacLaren was already scrambling up, his pistol cocked and ready—

A flash of fur. Something bounded over the Cadillac, knocking Eddie over. A large wolf, wearing a red union suit, grabbed the dope dealer by the back of the head and shook.

Jake dove for MacLaren, who managed to fire a shot. Jake clutched his shoulder but landed on top of MacLaren. The mobster screamed, the fear widening his eyes as Jake lowered his wolfy head toward him and snarled . . .

'Jake, no!' Olivia placed her hand on his back. 'Don't kill him!'

Jake growled, thinking about what MacLaren was: he would have killed Harry, he was a poison to his community, he was betraying his country by stealing secrets. 'Since when are you squeamish?' Jake said, his voice made harsh by his elongated jaw.

'We need him for the FBI to quethtion. So Harry can wrap up his cathe.' She, too, spoke awkwardly around a mouthful of sharpened teeth and two long fangs.

MacLaren, unable to see past Jake's head, still had it in him to be offended by mercy from a lady. 'What makes you think I'll talk, sister?'

Olivia leaned down so MacLaren could see her. Her black eyes narrowed, and her head swayed slightly, fixing MacLaren with her gaze. He almost screamed, but stiffened, stared as if in a trance.

'You'll thing like a canary, when I get done with you,' she said. No one hearing her would, have doubted her, even with her hissing lisp.

A thrill of power rushed through the air. Vic had Changed back to human form, shivering in the night air wearing only his union suit. 'Hey, Jake, we got to finish up quick. I left the car a few blocks back after I dropped off the girls and tried to make sure the coast was clear for us to join you. But we won't stay alone forever.'

'Right,' Jake said. He got up and Changed back to his skin-self, handed the shivering Vic his jacket. 'You and Rosalie move the bodies so it looks like they were fighting each other. The big guy down the end was a knife man; use that to cover up the worst of the claw and bite wounds.'

He turned to Olivia. 'And how about you lay one of your Lament Cranston-Shadow whammies on MacLaren? Suggest he remember this was a fight among his own men, and we were never here. And that he's dying to confess to the FBI, starting with who the "new boss" is. I'm willing to bet he's a Nazi or linked to them, if he's dealing in top secret calculations.'

'Right, Jake.' She pulled MacLaren up by the lapels and slammed him against the wall. 'I know what evil lurks in the hearts of men.' She sank her fangs into his neck; MacLaren went limp, his eyes wide.

'Jake?' There was a weak voice from the sidelines; Harry struggled to pull himself upright. 'Jake, what the heck—?'

'Harry, it's all right!' Jake tried to reassure him, but Vic was standing in his long underwear and a borrowed suit coat, and Rosalie was Changing back from her wolf-self, mourning a run in her last whole pair of stockings. Olivia, still a purple vampiress in a muddied coat, was whispering to MacLaren, who nodded eagerly.

Harry rubbed his head woozily. 'Jake, there was a wolf-man. And he was wearing your ugly hat . . .'

'Harry,' Jake said, 'We're Fangborn. And we're here to help. Give us a hand, Olivia?'

She turned from MacLaren, delicately licking the blood from her fangs.

'We need to clean up my friend. And please give him a good story about how he followed Eddie from the club just in time to see the fight among MacLaren's men. How he flagged down the local cops and brought them here.'

Olivia cocked her head. 'It'll be tricky. It's harder to alter the blood chemistry of an opium addict. And he's con-cussed.' It sounded like 'concuthhhed.'

'Do your best. We'll alert the Family down in Virginia to keep an eye on him. They'll give him more forget-me juice, if he shows signs of remembering us too well.'

After they rearranged the bodies to suit their story, they loaded the still-dazed Harry in the back of MacLaren's Cadillac, his head cradled in Olivia's lap.

Jake handed Rosalie into the front seat and, after she smoothed her skirt around her knees, got in beside her and shut the door. He leaned around to the backseat. 'Hey, Harry? How'd you like a kiss from my cousin Olivia?'

Harry's head ached from the beating, and the need for a fix was almost crippling. He looked up woozily at the lady who was stroking his hair in the dark. He couldn't see her well, but he knew, somehow, she was pretty.

He did like a pretty girl.

'Okay,' Harry said. Was it his imagination, or was the pain that consumed him lessening?

Olivia leaned down to him, her lips slightly parted. Harry imagined a glint of white teeth. She brushed right past his lips and went for his neck.

By the time her fangs had pierced his skin and his blood was flowing into her mouth, Harry was so overwhelmed by a sense of well-being and comfort, the pain and the call of the opium needle was as remote as Shangri-La. There was room for only one thought:

That's some A1 kissing . . .

In the front seat, Vic peered into the night, navigating their way back to his car. 'So the girl, the computer – Ida? She was letting her boyfriend, Eddie there, into the lab?'

'She thought Eddie was just helping her out,' Jake said. 'But he was helping himself to the calculations *and* the information about who they were for. We were looking for some criminal mastermind, not Eddie trying to keep his junk supplier happy. MacLaren's men, well, let's say they didn't just deal drugs. I'll be surprised if they weren't being encouraged to expand their businesses by the Nazis. The Bureau will track down the rest, shut them down, as soon as they find MacLaren's "new boss".'

Jake continued. 'Harry couldn't afford to reveal himself as a Fed to MacLaren's men. He couldn't admit to his boss that he was taking opium. So he brought me in to get the evidence, while he kept himself out of the picture.'

A voice came from the backseat, as if from a great distance. 'Wow,' Harry said.

'How you doing, Harry?' Jake asked. Vic and Rosalie exchanged tense glances.

'Well, I don't mind telling you, Jakey, I'm feeling pretty fine. But, tonight I saw a wolf-man wearing your darned hat. I saw a giant dog kill that cut-rate hood Eddie. And Olivia, well, apparently, she's a vampire – but nothing like what you see in the movies, let me tell you! At first, I thought I was high – who knows what that lovely, wicked Sadie has been giving me? – but I hadn't fixed. And it all seems so clear now. Like that time, up in Salem, when you—'

Time for Jake to step in. 'Yes, Harry, my Family is full of werewolves and vampires, but not like in the movies. We're the good guys.'

'Gee.' Harry sighed. 'That's swell.'

'Olivia?' Vic said quietly. 'You got the mix a little off. A little rich on the truth-telling serums and light on the memory blockers.'

'Hey, it's a complicated case,' she said, weaving a little. She was drained and giddy from the night's work. 'But I'll take another crack at it.' She smiled blearily and regarded Harry. 'C'mere, lover boy.'

A week later, Harry was back in Washington, whistling his way down Pennsylvania Avenue, his second-best suit cleaned and spruced up, a brand-new fedora cocked jauntily on the back of his head. There was a spring in his step that would have been out of place during wartime, save that everyone who saw him was suddenly filled with encouragement. Everything about his attitude shouted: *We can do it!*

Something had changed him in Boston. Maybe it was solving the case, maybe it was seeing his old friend, maybe it was getting hit on the head in that filthy alley, but Harry hadn't had the urge to use since then. It was days before he even noticed. Before Boston, he would have described himself as possessed by opium.

No more of that, now. Never again.

He'd already convinced his boss, Mr Roundtree, to keep him on the job. In a month or two, Harry'd be back on track to run his own projects. Heck, he'd win the war from this side of the Atlantic!

He was still whistling as he entered the Department of Justice. He'd be hunting and pecking his way through another night at the old Smith Corona, and his fingers would be sore and stiff from jabbing the heavy keys. But his work – with Jake's help – had been a significant break, uncovering a major conduit for drugs and industrial-military espionage in the Northeast.

Something stopped him in his tracks. It took one minute to realize he wasn't ill, another to wonder what the problem was. But there was no problem. It was the image of the family sitting at the cloth-covered table, joined in company, sharing food, giving praise. On the left-hand side was a large, scruffy, shepherdlike dog, his head happily uptilted to the woman serving coffee.

He had passed the murals every day, had never really taken the time to examine them. Too tied up with work and then the pursuit of the needle, he'd barely bothered to look up. He did now. Amazing.

It was the dog that caught his attention. He wasn't much for dogs, didn't like the way they slobbered and jumped all over you—

In the alley. In Boston. Something had attacked MacLaren's men, Harry had been rattled, his head half-caved in, but he hadn't been high, and he knew what he saw. A wolf, standing on two legs, wearing a suit and one damned ugly hat—

The hat had been Jake Steuben's. He'd have recognized it anywhere.

As Harry stared at the mural, he remembered it all.

Jake had pulled a Lon Chaney in the alley, turned into a wolf-man. And Jake's friend Olivia had bitten him in the neck, just like Dracula. Only Harry was in better shape than he had been in years, and clean, to boot.

The first thing he thought was: Oh, *no. I don't want to want to have to get high again . . .*

And when he realized the idea left him with distaste, rather than that burning desire, he took a deep breath and considered. He'd done shady things to feed his addiction, seen horrors on the job. And now he realized Jake and his family were something out of a Saturday matinee.

But he'd trusted Jake with his life on more than one occasion. And Jake had always come through. Olivia had taken the most terrible burden from him, given him his life back.

Jake and his family *were* the good guys. They were patriotic and discreet, too. Had to be.

Harry decided that there was nothing monstrous about them. He was eternally grateful to them.

It took him a while to find out the name of the mural – *Society Freed Through Justice*, by George Biddle. It stuck him as particularly appropriate. He wondered why the artist had included the dog. Wondered how many more – Fangborn? – there might be out there.

Harry thought long and hard. If Jake and his family could defeat MacLaren, and save a lost cause like Harry, imagine what they could do with a little help from the Federal Bureau of Investigation . . .

He made an appointment to discuss the matter with Mr Roundtree. He had a feeling that after hearing what they could do, these Fangborn would suit his boss down to the ground.

RIDING HIGH

Carolyn Hart

I hovered above my beloved hometown of Adelaide, Oklahoma, enjoying a late summer evening and the sparkle of lights on the terrace of the country club. Women in summer frocks and men in dressy sportswear mingled at a party. I wished I could plunge down and have a glass of wine and some Brie and crackers, and chat up that good-looking young man illustrating his golf swing.

Hovering? It's easy for me. No, I don't have a personalized jet pack. The reality is both less and more startling.

I'm Bailey Ruth Raeburn, late of Adelaide, a green-eyed, freckle-faced redhead, who loves laughter, good times, gorgeous clothes, and adventure.

You did note the modifying *late*? In short, I am a ghost.

Shh. That's just between us. My supervisor at the Department of Good Intentions refuses to describe those temporarily on Earth as ghosts. Wiggins is vehement that we are Heavenly agents assisting those in trouble. In his view, ghosts have quite a shady reputation on Earth. You know, clanking chains, pulsating protoplasm, dank drafts even when all the windows are closed.

Ghost or emissary, I loved coming back to Earth to be of help. I should perhaps be frank – I'm known for frankness, too – and admit I'd had a few challenges attempting to become one of Wiggins's regulars. Wiggins is a dear fellow but set in his ways. On Earth, he'd been a stationmaster. Since his idea of Heaven was a well-run train station, the Department of Good Intentions resided in just such a station, and emissaries were dispatched to earth on the glorious coal-burning Rescue Express, charged with providing a helping hand but – great emphasis here – circumspectly. Wiggins impressed upon all emissaries the necessity of observing the Department's Precepts for Earthly Visitation:

1. Avoid public notice.
2. No consorting with other departed spirits.
3. Work behind the scenes without making your presence known.
4. Become visible only when absolutely essential.
5. Do not succumb to the temptation to confound those who appear to oppose you.
6. Make every effort not to alarm earthly creatures.
7. Information about Heaven is not yours to impart. Simply smile and say, 'Time will tell.'
8. Remember always that you are *on* the Earth, not *of* the Earth.

I suppose that all seems simple to you. Certainly the strictures are straightforward. I cannot say emphatically enough how great an effort I have always made to observe these rules.

However, I am chagrined to reveal that on previous earthly visits I careened from one contravention of the Precepts to another.

Not this time.

I would put that in capital letters (NOT THIS TIME!) except I don't want to appear proud. Pride is not becoming to a Heavenly emissary. Boasting would indicate that I was too much *of* the Earth. Please don't take umbrage. We all know that earthly creatures exhibit pride, greed, avarice, anger, and all manner of unworthy behavior.

So, of course, I am not proud.

I FOLLOWED THE RULES THIS TIME.

Oh. Quickly. Make that lower case.

However, I feel I am entitled to admit to pleasure. This time I didn't break a single Precept. Not one. I came to Earth, assisted my charge, and was now awaiting the arrival of the Rescue Express for my return to Heaven. Admittedly, my path had been smoothed by Ogden, a rail-thin seventeen-year-old with a shock of black hair, thick glasses, and an affinity for electronic gadgets. We'd saved his father from a false accusation of embezzlement, and I hadn't had to appear once. Ogden, with assistance from me, had traced the peculations to a squinty-eyed accountant with a penchant for ponies. Of course, Ogden was unaware of my participation. His electronic sophistication made it easy to use a false identity to send him txt msgs that exposed the thief.

I'd learned more than I ever wanted to know about the new electronic world from Ogden, all about a computer pen that turned handwriting into a computer file, a card that wirelessly downloaded photos from his digital camera, and even a robotic pet – Willie – who talked and responded to Ogden's mood. In the trap I helped him set, he'd filmed the entire matter on a small video camera with sound. That had been my suggestion, txtd of course. I'd first become familiar with the cameras through my association with the Adelaide Police Department. I quite missed not having appeared this time as Officer M. Loy (a tribute to famed film star Myrna Loy, the better of half of Nick and Nora with William Powell). All uniformed officers carried such cameras. A picture with words is worth its weight in gold in a courtroom. All in all, my mission had been a resounding success.

Thanks to Ogden, my good behavior should convince Wiggins to remove me from probationary status.

'Yee-hah.'

Upturned faces from the revelers on the terrace brought

home to me that I had shouted aloud. Oh dear, a clear violation of Precept One.

However, libations were flowing and, after that short, startled pause, voices lifted again in intense conversation, punctuated by occasional guffaws.

No harm done.

The Rescue Express would be here soon, and I would report my outstanding conduct to Wiggins. Yet I felt restless and vaguely dissatisfied. I'd succeeded with my mission, but I'd never really felt I'd been here, hands on.

Because, of course, I hadn't.

I'd not appeared in person. I hadn't swirled into being, donning lovely clothes simply for the sheer delight of them. I hadn't talked to anyone. I'd never had a chance to pop here and there. No car chases. No confrontations. No challenges.

To be quite honest (always a desirable intent for emissaries), this perfect mission had been bor-ing.

BOR-ing.

Without volition – I assure you I didn't deliberately flaunt Precept One again – I groaned aloud. 'I'd been BOOMS.'

Fortunately the sound of my voice was lost in a rattle of castanets. Still, what I had spoken aloud appalled me. Was I succumbing to the assault of txt msgs on the English language?

What a dreadful prospect for a former English teacher. Obviously, the solution was to clear out the electronic cobwebs, immerse myself in the real world as opposed to the virtual reality that reminded me of Plato's shadows on the wall.

Truth to tell, I'm a gregarious sort. I like for things to be lively. My husband Bobby Mac (the late Robert McNeil Raeburn) said I added more fizz than champagne to any occasion. Believe me, Bobby Mac and I on Earth had fizzed as brightly as July Fourth sparklers. In Heaven . . . Oh yes.

Precept Seven. I will only say you have much to look forward to.

I swooped nearer the terrace. The party was bright with a Latin theme, serapes for tablecloths, the terrace bordered by luminarias, colorful maracas for party favors, and, of course, the best in Latin music. What harm would it do if I joined the revelers? I deserved a little recreation.

I landed behind a potted palm and swirled into being in a floral tunic and skirt, red plumeria vibrant against a black background. I chose slingback sandals until I spotted a cunning pair of black crocheted shoes and switched.

In no time at all, I was dancing a samba with the attractive fellow whose pink nose indicated too much golf under a July Oklahoma sun. '. . . and my lie was right at the edge of the sand trap . . .'

I made admiring murmurs and thrilled to the music. I soon realized many of the guests were from out of town, present for a members-guest golf tournament. That eased my concern about a hostess wondering who in the world I might be. I was soon in demand as a partner. I will confess that I dance rather well. (Stating an accurate observation in no way indicates pride.) I sambaed, rhumbaed, tangoed, and cha-chaed.

It was such a joy to once again be with people. I knew my time was almost up. The Express was scheduled for midnight, and I intended to be high in the sky, ready to swing aboard. I still had an hour to play.

Would it be safe to say that Fate intervened? Was it written in the stars that I should drop into this evening's party? Or had Wiggins considered possibilities and felt no need to dispatch another agent in the expectation that when en route to the Express and with time on my hands, I couldn't possibly resist the temptation of a party? Was Wiggins that crafty?

I pictured Wiggins, stiff dark cap riding high on brown hair, broad, open face still youthful despite a walrus mustache and muttonchop whiskers, white shirt high-collared, gray flannel trousers sturdily upheld by broad suspenders. Yes, he had a turn-of-the-century formality about him (the early twentieth century), but Wiggins often surprised me with a glint of humor.

Certainly I was on the most innocent of errands when I strolled to the ladies' lounge to check on my hair. Red hair is distinctive, and I was afraid that last vigorous tango had left me looking as if I'd stepped out into an Oklahoma wind. (It isn't vain to want to appear at your best.)

Moreover, a quick glance in the mirror would remind me to be thankful that I always appeared as I had been at twenty-seven, even though I'd been considerably older when I departed the earth. It is one of Heaven's thoughtful aspects that we are seen as we were at our best. I found twenty-seven splendid. There are many other cheerful surprises in Heaven, such as the way that joy can be seen in colors. For example, imagine an incandescent violet with . . . Oh. Sorry. Precept Seven again. One of these days you will see for yourself.

As I crossed the hallway, a dark-haired woman in her thirties bolted toward the door of the ladies' lounge. She gave a hunted look over her shoulder. Her eyes were wide and strained. The hand reaching for the knob trembled. She yanked open the door and entered the lounge.

Quick footsteps sounded behind me.

I paused to admire a tapestry, one of those dun-colored, pretentious representations of an English hunting scene.

A plump blonde in a pink palazzo jumpsuit, her face creased in concern, opened the door. I saw the convulsive start of the dark-haired woman. As she turned, her low-cut beige blouse slipped from one shoulder, revealing a purplish-red bruise on her upper arm. She gasped and yanked the blouse up, hiding the mark. The door closed.

I disappeared. In an instant, I was in the mirrored ante-room with its comfortable tufted-satin hassocks. I still get a thrill when I move through a solid wall. It gives me such a sense of freedom.

One hand still clasped to her blouse, the brunette sank onto a hassock and gave a travesty of a smile. 'Hi, Joan. I haven't seen you in a long time.' Her voice was brittle. 'I heard you and Jack went to Alaska. Did you have a good time?'

'What happened to your arm, Eleanor?'

'My arm? Oh.' A strained laugh. 'Just one of those odd accidents. I'm fine.'

The blonde frowned. 'You and Brad didn't look like you were having fun tonight.'

It might have been a non sequitur. It wasn't. She stared at the younger woman with anxious, worried eyes.

Eleanor fumbled with the clasp of her purse, lifted out a lipstick. Her hand shook. She stared at the tube, abruptly thrust it back into her purse. Did she fear that her hand was shaking too badly to be able even to dab color to her lips? She came to her feet, stared at Joan with hollow eyes. 'Brad? Oh, it's nothing to do with him. I'm afraid I'm getting a migraine. I'll ask him to take me home.' She moved toward the door.

Joan stepped in front of her. 'Are you sure? Look' – her tone was awkward – 'if there's anything we can do. If you'd like to come home with us—'

Eleanor gave a trill of ragged laughter. 'I'm all right. I promise. It's just . . .' She gripped Joan's arm. 'Please, don't say anything to anyone. It would be dreadful for me. Please. You've got to promise me.'

'Don't go with Brad. Come home with us. Or let me call the police.'

Eleanor dropped Joan's arm. 'The police? Oh, my God. Never. You don't understand. Everything's okay. I swear it is. I just can't think straight when I have a headache. You've misunderstood. Brad would never . . . No. It isn't like that at all.' She whirled away.

Joan took a step after her, but as the door closed, she stopped with a frown and shook her head. She'd tried to help, and her help had been refused. She had no real option. If she called the police, they would need more than her assumptions.

However, there might be another way to forestall abuse.

In an instant, I was walking alongside Eleanor. She moved steadily, managing strained smiles to acquaintances. I wondered if she realized that her distress was obvious.

Her steps grew slower as she approached the terrace, then, with a quick-drawn breath, chin held high, she curved around a cluster of tables.

An athletic young man stood near a splashing fountain. I was reminded of a young Van Johnson, a broad, freckled, all-American face topped by reddish gold hair. Instead of disingenuous charm and good humor, however, this face was set and hard, blue eyes burning with anger.

She stopped a few feet away. 'I need to go home, I have a headache.'

'Is that what you've been telling everyone?'

She folded her arms, looked frightened.

'Dammit, stop that. If anyone sees you like that—'

Shoes clicked on the terrace. Joan strode up to them. She stopped and gave Brad an uncompromising look. 'I'm sorry Eleanor isn't feeling well. Perhaps it would be a good night for her to come home with us. I've had migraines. They're hellish.'

Brad flushed. 'She'll be all right.'

The chunky blonde stared at him. 'I'll call tomorrow. I'm sure everything will be all right. Now.'

I had underestimated Joan. Her commanding stare warned him.

Brad flashed a black look at Eleanor. 'If you're ready.' His tone was clipped.

Eleanor avoided looking at Joan as they walked past.

*

306

My first surprise was when they reached a Mercedes coupe and she clicked to unlock the car and slid into the driver's seat.

He slid into the passenger seat and stared glumly forward as she expertly maneuvered the small car and whipped out of the parking lot.

She drove with the sunroof open, the warm summer air ruffling her hair. He turned his face away, stared out at the moonlit night.

They spoke not a single word.

In only a few minutes (Adelaide is a small town), she pulled into a circular drive in front of a big house with a bloated appearance and a plethora of superfluous spires on the steep roof.

When the car stopped, he threw open the door and walked toward the front steps, ignoring his wife.

She followed him into the marbled entry way and dropped her evening bag on a side table. Her reflection in a huge beveled mirror was at odds with her appearance at the party. She looked cool, amused, and confident.

A double staircase embraced a fountain and clumps of greenery. He was halfway up the left stairs, shoulders hunched, fists clenched.

'You haven't asked,' she lifted her voice to be heard over the splash of the fountain, 'if I had a good time at the party.'

He stopped, his back rigid. Slowly, he turned and looked down at her. 'You're a bitch.'

She continued to smile. 'Sticks and stones . . . Come down. We're going to talk.'

He remained midway up the stairs. 'I want out.'

'Not in this lifetime.' Her tone was relaxed.

'I've got proof about you and Roger.' The muscles ridged in his face.

She shrugged. 'A private detective? I've always wondered if they get a kick out of wondering what goes on behind the closed doors. I don't care if you have a picture of us in bed;

it isn't going to do you any good. And here's my hole card: you're running for reelection next year. Do you think anybody will vote for a judge who beats on his wife? Shall I tell you what good work I managed at the party this evening?'

He gripped the handrail as if forcing himself to remain there. 'I'm surprised someone hasn't killed you, Eleanor.'

Her peal of laughter was derisive. 'You're too good a boy to commit murder, Brad.'

She stood with her head uplifted, quite beautiful and arrogant and terrible. I didn't know what had brought their marriage to this stage, but there was no mistaking her intent. She had publicly played the part of a fearful woman trying to hide spousal abuse. He could proclaim his innocence, but whispers and sidelong looks and disbelief would dog him forever.

'I'll tell everyone you're lying.'

She waved a hand in dismissal. 'Be my guest. No one will believe you. I've already made a good start on that. You'd better come down. I will explain' – and now her face was formidable, her voice cold – 'exactly what I want and why you will be happy to cooperate.'

She didn't wait to see if he complied. She turned to her left, flicked on a light, and walked into a comfortable den.

He started down the stairs, and I felt a pang of sorrow. He had a lost, bewildered look, a man facing ruin with no way out.

I dismissed thoughts of Precept Three. Though I would be happy to work behind the scenes, this time I had to make my presence known. There was only one chance to outwit Brad's unscrupulous adversary.

I popped next to him on the stairs, gripped his arm, and whispered, 'Keep her talking. I'll video everything she says.'

He froze.

The clink of ice sounded from the den.

Brad stood rigid.

'You'd better get down here.' Her raised voice had a

308

metallic edge. 'I might have to call a friend for help. Big, bad old Brad. I don't think you want me to do that.'

I tugged at his arm. 'Do what I say.'

His head jerked from side to side.

Honestly, some men are so difficult to lead. With a little huff of exasperation, I swirled into being, admiring, as I did so, the crisp French blue of the Adelaide police uniform. Very flattering to a redhead. (A simple factual comment.)

He leaned back against the banister.

I jerked a thumb. 'I'm here to help. Get down there and talk to her.' I tapped the small video camera anchored to my belt. 'Every word will be recorded. Don't give me a thought.' I disappeared.

The click of shoes on parquet flooring announced her impatient arrival in the doorway. 'What's keeping you?'

He rubbed his head as if it hurt, then made an odd, helpless gesture. 'I'm coming,' He started down the stairs, but he darted several quick glances behind him.

Of course, there was no one there.

She waited, arms folded. 'Who are you looking for?' She, too, gazed up the stairs, her face uneasy.

'I don't know.' His voice was thin. 'I thought I heard something.'

'Maybe you wish you did. You'd like an audience, wouldn't you? Sorry not to oblige.'

Slowly, his expression befuddled, he followed her into the den.

She finished making her drink. 'What's your pleasure?' she asked.

I moved behind her, dropped down behind a brown leather sofa, and appeared. I unhooked the video cam from my belt and turned it on. I placed it on the floor, moved several feet away, and disappeared. The camera remained where I had placed it. Wiggins had never fully explained the physics of appearing along with whatever accessories I might need. I had learned that an accessory separated from my person remained in existence. Voilà, I now had the instrument for Eleanor's undoing.

I lifted the video cam and propped it near a vase, the lens aimed toward Eleanor.

Brad ignored her question. He stood stiffly near a potted palm, arms folded. 'I'll tell everyone you're lying. You know I've never struck you.'

She bent forward a little, pulled down the edge of her blouse, revealing a reddish purple splotch. 'How do you like it?'

He strode forward, face incredulous.

I nodded in unseen approval. Now he, too, was within camera range.

He lifted a shaking hand. 'Where did that come from?'

She tore off a length of paper toweling from the minibar, held it beneath a gushing faucet. 'Now you see it.' She lifted the damp toweling, swiped at the splotch. 'Now you don't. The wonders of makeup, Brad. Of course' – and her tone was careless as she pulled her blouse up to cover the now unblemished skin – 'what matters is that Joan Grainger got a very good look at my awful bruise in the ladies' lounge at the club this evening. She was quite sympathetic. Of course I told her, my voice shaking, that I was perfectly all right when she offered to put me up tonight.'

'She thinks I hit you?' His shock was obvious.

'Afraid so.' She swirled the ice cubes in an amber drink, took a sip.

'You can't do this to me.'

'Yes, I can. Tonight I laid the groundwork for some very ugly gossip that I'm an abused wife. Joan saw the bruise. Now, here's the deal. Joan keeps her mouth shut. That's why I picked her. Joan never says anything bad about anyone. Your secret is safe with her. She will check in with me, make sure I'm all right. If you play up, I'll convince her the bruise was from a fall and I appeared distraught tonight because, poor little me, I had the onset of one of my dreadful migraines.'

'Play up? What do you mean?'

'No divorce. You've got evidence on me, but you will never use it. I like being the judge's wife. I like the fact that you are rich enough that I can do what I like, travel, shop, entertain. You will strive to be the gentleman you are, pleasant in public, out of my way in private.'

'If I refuse?' His voice was grim.

'That would be a grave mistake. You see, most of the women I know are not as reticent as Joan. Tomorrow night I'm playing bridge with some ladies whose mouths never shut, and gossip is their life-blood. I can create quite a spectacular bruise for them. So' – she took another drink – 'it's up to you, Brad. If you file for a divorce, I'll convince everyone who matters in Adelaide that you use me for a punching bag.'

'That's extortion.' His voice was harsh.

'How lovely to have a lawyer in the family. Extortion has an ugly sound. Let's say it's quid pro quo. You do as I say, or I set you up as a wife beater.' She lifted the glass in a toast. 'Here's to us, Brad.'

In the faraway distance, I heard the unmistakable wail of the Rescue Express. Within minutes, I must be done.

I eased the camera below the side table and moved behind her to French doors that likely opened onto a terrace. The camera appeared to be floating in the air. I waggled it, catching Brad's attention. The evident shock in his face appeared to her to be the result of her taunt.

I swirled into being, camera held high.

He appeared frozen.

I reached behind me, opened the French door.

She heard the creak of the opening door and jerked about. Her eyes widened in shock.

I suppose a police officer approaching with a stern expression was unnerving.

Brad shook his head in disbelief, but there was a sudden aching hope in his blue eyes.

I held up the video camera. 'Extortion is an offense punishable by a sentence of up to four years in prison and a substantial fine.'

'You have no right to be here.' She was struggling to breathe. 'You can't come into someone's home and tape them—'

I interrupted, 'I have a full videotape and recording of your attempt at extortion.'

'—without their permission.'

'I am here at the invitation of your husband' – I looked warningly at Brad – 'who had reason to believe he might be subject to threats. Therefore' – my smile was bright – 'I am lawfully present and' – I tapped the video cam – 'the evidence contained here is admissible in court.' Again I looked at Brad. 'As any judge would explain.'

The train whistle sounded again. Of course, only I could hear. Would the Express leave without me?

'Isn't that correct, Judge?' My tone was sharp. I was desperate to depart.

His sandy lashes blinked, then he responded firmly, 'That's right.' He looked at his wife. 'There is no doubt this evidence would be presented and accepted at the hearing where you would be arraigned.'

I nodded approval. 'In that event, I will proceed to file my report, and a summons will be issued.' I had no idea as to police procedure at this level. Certainly Brad, as a judge, would know, but I was counting on him to remember that I wasn't here. Was he clever enough to understand?

Did I smell coal smoke?

'Officer, I might be willing to drop the matter.'

I frowned. 'Your Honor, a crime has been committed. Extortion, as I don't need to remind you, is a felony.'

'However' – he spoke quietly – 'it is my prerogative to

settle the matter without the filing of charges.' He turned toward his wife. 'Eleanor, it's up to you.'

I folded my arms and looked as menacing as a five-foot-five-inch redhead can manage.

'You got me, didn't you? I never expected you to be clever, Brad.' She stared at him as if he were a stranger. 'What do you want?'

'First, call Joan. You are to sound cheerful and upbeat. Here's what I want you to tell her . . .'

The Rescue Express wailed, the high, wavering cry much nearer.

In a moment, Eleanor was on the telephone. 'Joan,' she sounded at ease, 'I'm afraid I gave you a wrong impression tonight . . . That bruise had nothing to do with Brad. I got whacked by that automatic door at the grocery. You know the one I mean. You take your life in your hands when you go through that door. Tonight I was upset because I knew I was going to ask Brad for a divorce . . . Actually, it isn't because of him. I've met a guy, and I was worried about how Brad would take it, but he's being the perfect gentlemen.' Her eyes burned as she looked toward him.

Brad gave a thumbs-up.

The whistle sounded overhead.

'Anyway, it always helps to talk things out. I'm off to Dallas tonight. Everything's working out . . . Right . . . I'll keep in touch.' She clicked off the phone. 'Satisfied?'

'Yes. In exchange, I'll make a fair settlement with you. Now. Pack a suitcase and go.'

She flicked a furious look at the video cam in my hand. 'What will happen to the video?'

'It is police property. It will be in my custody.'

She looked sick. Obviously, if the camera was at the police station, there was no way she could ever hope to be free of the threat of exposure.

She whirled and ran to the hall and pounded up the stairs. Quick as a flash, I darted to Brad, thrust the camera at him. 'She can't be trusted. Put this in a vault. Sorry, I have to go.'

With that, I disappeared and zoomed out of the house and up into the sky and there, almost beyond my grasp, was the rail to the caboose.

Oh. And oh. I couldn't quite reach it!

What would happen to a missing emissary? Would I be adrift, become one of those ghosts aimlessly walking about in their haunts of old?

'Here we go.' Wiggins's shout was robust, and there he was, reaching out from the red caboose, his strong hand grabbing mine and pulling me aboard.

When I stood beside him, breathing in gasps, he turned to me and folded his arms in mock disapproval, but his eyes were twinkling almost as bright as the stars we passed.

'That was a near thing, Bailey Ruth. You cut it rather fine. However, your mission was flawlessly executed.' He smiled in approval. 'As for your delay in coming aboard' – his tone was casual – 'that's neither here nor there. Sometimes, as far as official reports go and your status as an emissary, least said, soonest mended.'

'Oh, that's wonderful.'

'However—'

I should have known I wasn't quite home free.

'I have a question.'

I steeled myself.

His ruddy face folded in puzzlement. 'BOOMS?'

I laughed in relief. 'Things have changed on earth, Wiggins. Young people send each other text messages on their cell phones, and they use a great many abbreviations. BOOMS means bored out of my skull.'

'BOOMS,' he repeated with delight. 'I'll remember that. BOOMS! Not' – and his tone was kindly – 'a state you were long willing to endure. Bully for you, Bailey Ruth.'

Bully for me. Ah, every age has its style.

'Thank you, Wiggins.' I almost told him what a fine

fellow he was, then decided that might be presumptuous. But I was too ebullient not to celebrate. 'Wiggins, we have a bit of time before we get to Heaven.' I reached out and took his hand. 'Have you ever cha-chaed?'

GRAVE MATTER

A MIKE HAMMER STORY

Max Allan Collins and *Mickey Spillane*

AUTHOR'S NOTE: In the early 1990s, Mickey Spillane and I created a science-fiction variation on his Mike Danger character for comic books. (The Danger character had been developed for comics by Mickey just before World War Two, and he attempted to market it after the war, as well, without success. In 1947, he decided to change 'Danger' to 'Hammer' and *I, the Jury* was the result.) At some point, the comic book company asked Mickey and me to develop a prose short story for a market that fell through. Mickey approved this story and gave me notes but did not do any of the writing, which explains the unusual byline above (with me getting top billing). Later, I recycled this idea for a third-person short story that used a different lead character, but this represents the first appearance of the story in its original, intended form . . . although for various reasons, I have changed 'Danger' back to 'Hammer.' The tale takes place in the early 1950s.

If I hadn't been angry, I wouldn't have been driving so damn fast, and if I hadn't been driving so damn fast, in a lashing rain, on a night so dark closing your eyes made no difference, my high beams a pitiful pair of flashlights trying to guide the way in the vast cavern of the night, illuminating only slashes of storm, I would have had time to brake properly when I came down over the hill and saw, in a sudden white strobe of electricity, that the bridge was gone, or anyway out of sight, somewhere down there under the rush of rain-raised river. When the brakes didn't take, I yanked the wheel around, and my heap was sideways in a flooded ditch, wheels spinning. Like my head.

I got out on the driver's side, because otherwise I would have had to swim underwater. From my sideways-tipped car, I leapt to the slick highway as rain pelted me mercilessly, and did a fancy slip-slide dance, keeping my footing. Then I snugged the wings of the trench coat collar up around my face and began to walk back the way I'd come. If rain was God's tears, the Old Boy sure was bawling about something tonight.

I knew how he felt. I'd spent the afternoon in the upstate burg of Hopeful, only there was nothing hopeful about the sorry little hamlet. All I'd wanted was a few answers to a few questions. Like how a guy who won a Silver Star charging up a beachhead could wind up a crushed corpse in a public park, a crumpled piece of discarded human refuse.

Bill Reynolds had had his problems. Before the war he'd been an auto mechanic in Hopeful. A good-looking, dark-haired bruiser who'd have landed a football scholarship if the war hadn't gotten in the way, Bill married his high school sweetheart before he shipped out, only when he came back missing an arm and a leg, he found his girl wasn't interested in what was left of him. Even though he was good with his prosthetic arm and leg, he couldn't get his job back at the garage, either.

But the last time I'd spoken to Bill, when he came in to New York to catch Marciano and Jersey Joe at Madison Square Garden, he'd said things were looking up. He said he had a handyman job lined up, and that it was going to pay better than his old job at the garage.

'Besides which,' he said, between rounds, 'you oughta see my boss. You'd do overtime yourself.'

'You mean you're working for a woman?'

'And what a woman. She's got more curves than the Mohonk Mountain road.'

'Easy you don't drive off a cliff.'

That's all we'd said about the subject, because Marciano had come out swinging at that point, and the next I heard from Bill – well not from him, *about* him – he was dead.

The only family he had left in Hopeful was a maiden aunt; she called me collect and told me tearfully that Bill's body had been found in the city park. His spine had been snapped.

'How does a thing like that happen, Chief?'

Chief Thadeous Dolbert was one of Hopeful's four full-time cops. Despite his high office, he wore a blue uniform indistinguishable from his underlings, and his desk was out in the open of the little bullpen in Hopeful City Hall. A two-cell lockup was against one wall, and spring sunshine streaming in the windows through the bars sent slanting stripes of shadow across his desk and his fat, florid face. He was leaning back in his swivel chair, eyes hooded; he looked like a fat iguana – I expected his tongue to flick out and capture a fly any second now.

Dolbert said, 'We figure he got hit by a car.'

'Body was found in the city park, wasn't it?'

'Way he was banged up, figure he must've got whopped a good one, really sent him flyin'.'

'Was that the finding at the inquest?'

Dolbert fished a pack of cigarettes out of his breast pocket, right behind his tarnished badge, lighted himself up a smoke. Soon it was dangling from a thick, slobber-flecked lower lip. 'We don't stand much on ceremony around here, mister. County coroner called it accidental death at the scene.'

'That's all the investigation Bill's death got?'

Dolbert shrugged, blew a smoke circle. 'All that was warranted.'

I sat forward. 'All that was warranted. A local boy, who gave an arm and a leg to his country, wins a damn Silver Star doin' it, and you figure him getting his spine snapped like a twig and damn near every bone in his body broken, well, that's just pretty much business as usual here in Hopeful.'

Under the heavy lids, fire flared in the fat chief's eyes. 'You think you knew Bill Reynolds? You knew the old Bill. You didn't know the drunken stumblebum he turned into. Prime candidate for stepping out in front of a car.'

'I never knew Bill to drink to excess—'

'How much time did you spend with him lately?'

A hot rush of shame crawled up my neck. I'd seen Bill from time to time, in the city, when he came in to see me, but I'd never come up to Hopeful. Never really gone out of my way for him, since the war . . .

Till now.

'You make any effort to find the hit-and-run driver that did this?'

The chief shrugged. 'Nobody saw it happen.'

'You don't even know for sure a car did it.'

'How the hell else could it have happened?'

I stood up, pushed back, the legs of my wooden chair scraping the hard floor like fingernails on a blackboard. 'That's what I'm going to find out.'

A finger as thick as a pool cue waggled at me. 'You got no business stickin' your damn nose in around here, Hammer—'

'I'm a licensed investigator in the state of New York, pops. And I'm working for Bill Reynolds's aunt.'

He snorted a laugh. 'Working for that senile old biddy? She's out at the county hospital. She's broke! Couldn't even afford a damn funeral . . . we had to bury the boy in potter's field . . .'

That was one of Hopeful's claims to fame: the state buried its unknown, unclaimed, impoverished dead in the potter's field here.

'Why didn't you tell Uncle Sam?' I demanded. 'Bill was a war hero – they'd've put him in Arlington . . .'

Dolbert shrugged. 'Not my job.'

'What the hell *is* your job?'

'Watch your mouth, city boy.' He nodded toward the holding cells, and the cigarette quivered as the fat mouth sneered. 'Don't forget you're in *my* world . . .'

Maybe Bill Reynolds didn't get a funeral or a gravestone, but he was going to get a memorial by way of an investigation.

Only nobody in Hopeful wanted to talk to me. The supposed 'accident' had occurred in the middle of the night, and my only chance for a possible witness was in the all-night diner across from the Civil War cannon in the park.

The diner's manager, a skinny character with a horsey face darkened by perpetual five o'clock shadow, wore a grease-stained apron over his grease-stained T-shirt. Like the chief, he had a cigarette drooping from slack lips. The ash narrowly missed falling into the cup of coffee he'd served me as I sat at the counter with half a dozen locals.

'We got a jukebox, mister,' the manager said. 'Lots of kids end up here, tail end of a Saturday night. That was a Saturday night, when Bill got it, ya know? That loud music, joint jumpin', there coulda been a train wreck out there, and nobody'da heard it.'

'Nobody would have seen an accident out your windows?'

The manager shrugged. 'Maybe ol' Bill got hit on the other side of the park.'

But it was just a little square of grass and benches and such; the 'other side of the park' was easily visible from the windows lining the diner booths – even factoring in the grease and lettering.

I talked to a couple of waitresses who claimed not to have been working that night. One of them, Gladys her name tag said, a heavyset bleached blonde who must have been pretty cute twenty years ago, served me a slice of apple pie and cheese and a piece of information.

'Bill said he was going to work as a handyman,' I said, 'for some good-lookin' gal. You know who that would've been?'

'Sure,' Gladys said. She had sky-blue eyes and nicotine-yellow teeth. 'He was working out at the mansion.'

'The what?'

'The mansion. The old Riddle place. You must've passed it on the highway, comin' into town.'

'I saw a gate and a drive, and got a glimpse of a big old gothic brick barn . . .'

She nodded, refilled my coffee. 'That's the one. The Riddles, they owned this town forever. Ain't a building downtown that the Riddles ain't owned since the dawn of time. But Mr Riddle, he was the last of the line, and he and his wife died in that plane crash, oh, ten years ago. The only one left now is the daughter, Victoria.'

'What was Bill doing out at the Riddle place?'

She shrugged. 'Who knows? Who cares? Maybe Miz Riddle just wanted some company. Bill was still a hand-some so-and-so, even minus a limb or two. He coulda put his shoe under my bed anytime.'

'Victoria Riddle isn't married? She lives alone?'

'Alone except for that hairless ape.'

'What?'

'She's got a sort of butler, you know, a servant? He was her father's chauffeur. Big guy. Mute. Comes into town, does the grocery shopping and such. We hardly ever see Miz Riddle, less she's meeting with her lawyer, or going to the bank to visit all her money.'

'What does she do out there?'

'Who knows? She's not interested in business. Her daddy, he had his finger in every pie around here. Miz Riddle, she lets her lawyer run things, and I guess the family money, uh, under-what's-it? Underwrites, is that the word?'

'I guess.'

'Underwrites her research.'

'Research?'

'Oh, yeah, Miz Riddle's a doctor.'

'Medical doctor.'

'Yes, but not the kind that hangs out a shingle. She's some kind of scientific genius.'

'So she's doing medical research out there?'

'I guess.' She shook her head. 'Pity about Bill. Such a nice fella.'

'Had he been drinking heavy?'

'Bill? Naw. Oh, he liked a drink. I suppose he shut his share of bars down on a Saturday night, but he wasn't no alcoholic. Not like that other guy.'

'What other guy?'

Her expression turned distant. 'Funny.'

'What's funny? *What* other guy?'

'Not funny ha-ha. Funny weird. That other guy, don't remember his name, just some tramp who come through, he was a crip, too.'

'A crip?'

'Yeah. He had one arm. Guess he lost his in the war, too. He was working out at the Riddle mansion as a handyman – one-handed handyman. That guy, he really was a drunk.'

'What became of him?'

'That's what's funny weird. Three, four months ago, he wound up like Bill. They found him in the gutter on Main Street, all banged up, deader than a bad battery. Hit-and-run victim – just like Bill.'

The wrought-iron gate in the gray-brick wall stood open, and I tooled the heap up a winding red-brick drive across a gentle, treeless slope where the sprawling gabled tan-brick gothic mansion crouched like a lion about to pounce. The golf course of a lawn had its own rough behind the house, a virtual forest preserve that seemed at once to shelter and encroach upon the stark lines of the house.

Steps led to an open cement pedestal of a porch with a massive slab of a wooden door where I had a choice between an ornate iron knocker and a simple doorbell. I rang the bell.

I stood there, listening to birds chirping and enjoying the cool breeze that seemed to whisper rain was on its way, despite the golden sunshine reflecting off the lawn. I rang the bell again.

I was about to go around back, to see if there was another door I could try, when that massive slab of wood creaked open like the start of the *Inner Sanctum* radio program; the 350-pound apparition who stood suddenly before me would have been at home on a spook show himself.

He was six four, easy, towering over my six one; he wore the black uniform of a chauffeur, but no cap, his tie a loose black string thing. He looked like an upended Buick with a person painted on it. His head was the shape of a grape and just as hairless though considerably larger; he had no eyebrows, either; wide, bugling eyes; a lump of a nose; and an open mouth.

'Unnggh,' he said.

'I'd like to see Miss Riddle,' I said.

'Unnggh,' he said.

'It's about Bill Reynolds. I represent his family. I'm here to ask some questions.'

His brow furrowed in something approaching thought.

Then he slammed the door in my face.

Normally, I don't put up with crap like that. I'd been polite. He'd been rude. Kicking the door in, and his teeth, seemed called for. Only this boy was a walking side of beef that gave even Mike Hammer pause.

And I was, in fact, pausing, wondering whether to ring the bell again, go around back, or just climb in my heap and drive the hell away, when the door opened again, and the human Buick was replaced by a human goddess.

She was tall, standing eye-to-eye with me, and though she wore a loose-fitting white lab jacket that hung low over a simple black skirt, nylons, and flat shoes, those mountain-road curves Bill had mentioned were not easily hidden. Her dark blonde hair was tied back, and severe black-framed glasses rode the perfect little nose; she wore almost no makeup, perhaps just a hint of lipstick, or was that the natural color of those full lips? Whatever effort she'd made to conceal her beauty behind a mask of scientific ster-ility was futile; the big green eyes, the long lashes, the high cheekbones, the creamy complexion, that full, high-breasted, wasp-waisted, long-limbed figure, all conspired to make her as stunning a female creature as God had ever created.

'I'm sorry,' she said, in a silky contralto. 'This is a private residence and a research center. We see no one without an appointment.'

'The gate was open.'

'We're expecting the delivery of certain supplies this evening,' she said, 'and I leave the gate standing open on such occasions. You see, I'm shorthanded. But why am I boring you with this? Good afternoon . . .'

And the door began to close.

I held it open with the flat of my hand. 'My name is Michael Hammer.'

The green eyes narrowed. 'The detective?'

I grinned. 'You must get the New York papers up here.'

'We do. Hopeful isn't the end of the world.'

'It was for Bill Reynolds.'

Her expression softened, and she cracked the door open, wider. 'Poor Bill. Were you a friend?'

'Yes.'

'So you've come to ask about his death.'

'That's right.' I shrugged. 'I'm a detective.'

'Of course,' she said, opening the door. 'And you're looking into the circumstances. A natural way for you to deal with such a loss . . .'

She gestured for me to enter, and I followed her through a high-ceilinged entryway. The hairless ape appeared like an apparition and took my trench coat; I kept my porkpie hat but took it off in deference to my hostess.

In front of me, a staircase led to a landing, then to a second floor; gilt-framed family portraits lined the way. On one side was a library with more leather in bindings and chairs than your average cattle herd; on the other was a formal sitting room where elegant furnishings that had been around long enough to become antiques were overseen by a glittering chandelier.

She led me to a rear room and it was as if, statlingly, we'd entered a penthouse apartment – the paintings on the wall were abstract and modern, and the furnishings were, too, with a television/hi-fi console set-up and a zebra wet bar with matching stools; but the room was original with the house, or at least the fireplace and mantel indicated as much. Over the fireplace was the only artwork in the room that wasn't abstract: a full-length portrait of my hostess in a low-cut evening gown, a painting that was impossibly lovely with no exaggeration by the artist.

She slipped out of her lab coat, tossing it on a boomerang of a canvas chair, revealing a short-sleeved white blouse providing an understated envelope for an overstated bosom. Undoing her hair, she allowed its length to shimmer to her shoulders. The severe black-framed glasses, however, she left in place.

Her walk was as liquid as mercury in a vial as she got behind the bar and poured herself a martini. 'Fix you a drink?'

'Got any beer back there?'

'Light or dark?'

'Dark.'

We sat on a metal-legged couch that shouldn't have been comfortable but was; she sipped her martini, her dark nyloned legs crossed, displaying well-developed calves. For a scientist, she made a hell of a specimen.

I sipped my beer – it was a bottle of German imported stuff, a little bitter for my taste, but very cold.

'That's an interesting butler you got,' I said.

'I have to apologize for Bolo,' she said, stirring the cocktail with her speared olive. 'His tongue was cut out by natives in the Amazon. My father was on an exploratory trip, somehow incurred the wrath of the natives, and Bolo interceded on his behalf. By offering himself, in the native custom, Bolo bought my father's life – but paid with his tongue.'

With a kisslike bite, she plucked the olive from its spear and chewed.

'He doesn't look much like a South American native,' I said.

'He isn't. He was a Swedish missionary. My father never told me Bolo's real name . . . but that was what the natives called him.'

'And I don't suppose Bolo's told you, either.'

'No. But he can communicate. He can write. In English. His mental capacity seems somewhat diminished, but he understands what's said to him.'

'Very kind of you to keep somebody like that around.'

'Like what?'

I shrugged. 'Handicapped.'

'Mr Hammer . . .'

'Make it Mike – and I'll call you Victoria. Or do you prefer Vicki?'

'How do you know I don't prefer "Doctor"?'

'Hey, it's okay with me. I've played doctor before.'

'Are you flirting with me, Mike?'

'I might be.'

'Or you might be trying to get me to let my guard down.'

'Why – is it up?'

She glanced at my lap. 'You tell me.'

Now I crossed *my* legs. 'Where's your research lab?'

'In back.'

'Sorry if I'm interrupting . . .'

'No. I'm due for a break. I'd like to help you. You see, I thought a lot of Bill. He worked hard. He may not have been the brightest guy around, but he made up for it with enthusiasm and energy. Some people let physical limitations get in their way. Not Bill.'

'You must have a thing for taking in strays.'

'What do you mean?'

'Well . . . like Bolo. Like Bill. I understand you took in another handicapped veteran, not so long ago.'

'That's right. George Wilson.' She shook her head sadly. 'Such a shame. He was a hard worker, too—'

'He died the same way as Bill.'

'I know.'

'Doesn't that strike you as . . . a little odd? Overly coincidental?'

'Mike, George was a heavy drinker, and Bill was known to tie one on himself. It may be coincidental, but I'm sure they aren't the first barroom patrons to wobble into the street after closing and get hit by a car.'

'Nobody saw either one of them get hit by a car.'

'Middle of the night. These things happen.'

'Not twice.'

The green eyes narrowed with interest and concern. 'What do *you* think happened, Mike?'

'I have no idea – yet. But I'll say this – everybody seemed to like Bill. I talked to a lot of people today, and nobody, except maybe the police chief, had an unkind word to say about him. So I'm inclined to think the common factors between Bill and this George Wilson hold the answer. You're one of those common factors.'

'But surely not the only one.'

'Hardly. They were both war veterans, down on their luck.'

'No shortage of those.'

'And they were both handicapped.'

She nodded, apparently considering these facts, scientist that she was. 'Are you staying in Hopeful tonight?'

'No. I got a court appearance in the city tomorrow. I'll be back on the weekend. Poke around some more.'

She put a hand on my thigh. 'If I think of anything, how can I find you?'

I patted the hand, removed it, stood. 'Keep your gate open,' I said, putting on my porkpie, 'and I'll find you.'

She licked her lips; they glistened. 'I'll make sure I leave my gate wide open on Saturday.'

I'd gone back into Hopeful to talk to the night shift at the diner, got nowhere, and headed home in the downpour, pissed off at how little I'd learned. Now, with my car in the ditch and rain lashing down relentlessly, I found myself back at the Riddle mansion well before Saturday. The gate was still open, though – she must not have received that delivery she'd talked about, yet.

Splashing through puddles on the winding drive, I kept my trench coat collar snugged around me as I headed toward the towering brick house. In the daytime, the mansion had seemed striking, a bit unusual; on this black night, illuminated momentarily in occasional flashes of lightning, its gothic angles were eerily abstract, the planes of the building a stark, ghostly white.

This time I used the knocker, hammering with it. It wasn't all that late – maybe nine o'clock or a little after. But it felt like midnight, and instinctively I felt the need to wake the dead.

Bolo answered the door. The lights in the entry way were out, and he was just a big black blot, distinguishable only by that upended Buick shape of his; then the world turned white, him along with it, and when the thunder caught up with the lightning, I damn near jumped.

'Tell your mistress Mr Hammer's back,' I said. 'My car's in a ditch and I need—'

That's when the SOB slammed the door in my face. Second time today. A red heat of anger started to rise up around my collar, but it wasn't drying me off, even if the shelter of the awning over the slab of porch was keeping me from getting wetter. Only I wasn't sure a human being could be any wetter than this.

When the door opened again, it was Victoria. She wore a red silk robe, belted tight around her tiny waist. The sheen of the robe and the folds of the silk conspired with her curves to create a dizzying display of pulchritude.

'Mr Hammer . . . Mike! Come in, come in.'

I did. The light in the entryway was on now, and Bolo was there again, taking my drenched hat and coat. I quickly explained to her what had happened.

'With this storm,' she said, 'and the bridge out, you'll need to stay the night.'

'Love to,' I said. Mother Hammer didn't raise any fools.

'But you'll have to get out of those wet things,' she said. 'I think I have an old nightshirt of my father's . . .'

She took me back to that modern sitting room, and I was soon in her pop's nightshirt, swathed in blankets as I sat before the fireplace's glow, its magical flickering soothingly restful, and making her portrait above the fire seem alive, smiling seductively, the bosom in the low-cut gown heaving with passion. Shaking my head, wondering if I'd completely lost my sanity, I tucked my .45 in its speed rig behind a pillow – hardware like that can be distressing to the gentle sensibilities of some females.

When she cracked the door to ask if I was decent, I said, 'That's one thing I've never been accused of, but come on in.'

Then she was sitting next to me, the red silk gown playing delightful reflective games with the firelight.

'Can I tell you something terrible?' she asked, like a child with an awful secret.

'I hope you will.'

'I'm glad your car went in the ditch.'

'And here I thought you liked me.'

'I do,' she said, and she edged closer. 'That's why I'm glad.'

She seemed to want me to kiss her, so I did, and it was a long, deep kiss, hotter than the fire, wetter than the night, and then my hands were on top of the smoothness of the silk gown. And then they were on the smoothness underneath it . . .

Later, when she offered me a guest bedroom upstairs, I declined.

'This is fine,' I said, as she made herself a drink behind the bar, and got me another German beer. 'I'll just couch it. Anyway, I like the fire.'

She handed me the bottle of beer, its cold wetness in my palm contrasting with the warmth of the room and the moment. Sitting next to me, close to me, she sipped her drink.

'First thing tomorrow,' she said, 'we'll call in to town for a tow truck and get your car pulled out of that ditch.'

'No hurry.'

'Don't you have a court appearance tomorrow?'

'Acts of God are a good excuse,' I said and rested the beer on an amoeba-shaped coffee table nearby, then leaned in and kissed her again. Just a friendly peck.

'Aren't you thirsty?' she asked, nodding toward the beer.

Why was she so eager for me to drink that brew?

I said, 'Dry as a bone,' and reached for the bottle, lifted it to my lips, and seemed to take a drink.

Seemed to.

330

Now she gave me a friendly kiss, said, 'See you at breakfast,' and rose, sashaying out as she cinched the silk robe back up. If you could bottle that walk, you'd really have something worth researching.

Alone, I sniffed the beer. My unscientific brain couldn't detect anything, but I knew damn well it contained a mickey. She wanted me to sleep through this night. I didn't know why, but something was going to happen here that a houseguest like me – even one who'd been lulled into a false sense of security by a very giving hostess – shouldn't see.

So I poured the beer down the drain and quickly went to the couch, got myself under the blankets, and pretended to be asleep.

But I couldn't have been more alert if I'd been in a foxhole on the front line. My eyes only seemed shut; they were slitted open and saw her when she peeked in to see if I was sleeping. I even saw her mouth and eyes tighten in smug satisfaction before the door closed, followed by the click of me being locked in . . .

The rain was still sheeting down when, wearing only her daddy's nightshirt, I went out a window and, .45 in hand, found my way to the back of the building where a new section had been added, institutional-looking brick with no windows at all. The thin cotton cloth of the nightshirt was a transparent second skin by the time I found my way around the building and discovered an open double garage, also back behind, following an extension of the original driveway. The garage doors stood open and a single vehicle – a panel truck bearing the Hopeful Police Department insignia – was within, dripping with water, as if it were sweating.

Cautiously, I slipped inside, grateful to be out of the rain. Along the walls of the garage were various boxes and crates with medical-supply-house markings. I heard approaching footsteps and ducked behind a stack of crates.

Peeking out, I could see Chief Dolbert in a rain slicker and matching hat, leading the way for Bolo, still in his chauffeur-type uniform. Dolbert opened up the side of the van, and Bolo leaned in.

And when Bolo leaned back out, he had his arms filled with a person, a woman in fact, a naked one; then Bolo walked away from the panel truck, toward the door back into the building, held open for him by the thoughtful police chief. It was as if Bolo were carrying a bride across the threshold.

Only this bride was dead.

For ten minutes I watched as Bolo made trips from the building to the panel truck where, with the chief's assistance, he conveyed naked dead bodies into the house. My mind was reeling with the unadorned horror of it. I was shivering, and not just from my water-soaked nightshirt. Somehow, being in that nightshirt, naked under it, made me feel a kinship to those poor dead bastards, many of them desiccated-looking souls, with unkempt hair and bony, ill-fed bodies, and finally it came to me.

I knew who these poor dead wretches were. And I knew why, at least roughly why, Chief Dolbert was delivering them.

When at last the doors on the panel truck were shut, the chief and Bolo headed back into the building. That pleased me – I was afraid the chief would take off into the rainy, thunderous night, and I didn't want him to.

I wanted him around.

Not long after they had disappeared into the building, I went in after them.

And into hell.

It was a blindingly well-illuminated hell, a white and silver hell, resembling a hospital operating room but much larger, a hell dominated by the silver of surgical instruments, a hell where the walls were lined with knobs and dials and meters and gizmos, a hell dominated by naked corpses on metal autopsy-type tables, their empty eyes staring at the bright overhead lighting.

And the sensual satan who ruled over this hell, Victoria Riddle, who was back in her lab coat now, hair tucked in a bun, was filling Chief Colbert's open palm with greenbacks.

But where was Bolo?

I glanced behind me, and there he was, tucked behind the door, standing like a cigar-store Indian awaiting his mistress's next command, only she didn't have to give this command: Bolo knew enough to reach out for this intruder, his hands clawed, his eyes bulging to where the whites showed all around, his mouth open in a soundless snarl.

'Stop!' I told the looming figure, as he threw his shadow over me like a blue blanket.

But he didn't stop.

And when I blew the top of his bald head off, splashing the white wall behind him with the colors of the inside of his head, red and gray and white, making another abstract painting only without a frame, that didn't stop him, either, didn't stop him from falling on top of me, and by the time I had pushed his massive dead weight off of me, his fat corpse emptying ooze out the top of his bald, blown-off skull, I had another fat bastard to deal with, a *live* one: the chief of the Hopeful Police Department, his revolver pointed down at me.

'Drop it,' he said.

He should have just shot me, because I took advantage of his taking time to say that and shot him in the head, and the gun in his hand was useless now, since his brain could no longer send it signals, and he toppled back on top of one of the corpses, sharing its silver tray, staring up at the ceiling, the red hole in his forehead like an extra expressionless eye.

'You fool,' she said, the lovely face lengthening into a contorted, ugly mask, green eyes wild behind the glasses.

'I decided I wasn't thirsty after all,' I said, as I weaved my way between the corpses on their metal slabs.

'You don't understand! This is serious research! This will benefit *humanity* . . .'

'I understand you were paying the chief for fresh cadavers,' I said. 'With him in charge of the state's potter's field, you had no shortage of dead guinea pigs. But what I *don't* understand is, why kill Bill and George Wilson, when you had access to all these riches?'

And I gestured to the deceased indigents around us.

Her face eased back into beauty; her scientific mind had told her, apparently, that her best bet now was to try to reason with me. Calmly. Coolly.

I was close enough to her to kiss her, only I didn't feel much like kissing her and, anyway, the .45 I was aiming at her belly would have been in the way of an embrace.

'George Wilson tried to blackmail me,' she said. 'Bill . . . Bill just wouldn't cooperate. He said he was going to the authorities.'

'About your ghoulish arrangement with the chief, you mean?'

She nodded. Then earnestness coated her voice: 'Mike, I was only trying to *help* Bill and George – *and* mankind. Don't you see? I wanted to make them *whole* again!'

'Oh my God,' I said, getting it. 'Bill was a *live* guinea pig, wasn't he? Wilson, too . . .'

'That's not how I'd express it, exactly, but yes . . .'

'You wanted to make them living Frankenstein monsters . . . you wanted to sew the limbs of the dead on 'em . . .'

Her eyes lit up with enthusiasm and hope. And madness. 'Yes! *Yes!* I learned in South America of voodoo techniques that reanimated the dead into so-called "zombies". The scientific community was sure to reject such mumbo jumbo and deny the world this wonder, and I have been forced to seek the truth with my mixture of the so-called supernatural and renegade science. With the correct tissue matches and my own research into electrochemical transplant techniques—'

That was when the lights went out.

God's electricity had killed man's electricity, and the

cannon roar aftermath of the thunderbolt wasn't enough to hide the sound of her scurrying in the dark among the trays of the dead, trying to escape, heading for that door onto the garage.

I went after her, but she had knowledge of the layout of the place, and I didn't, I kept bumping into bodies, and then she screamed.

Just for a split second.

A hard *whump* had interrupted the scream, and before I even had time to wonder what the hell had happened, the lights came back on, and there she was.

On her back, on the floor, her head resting against the metal under-bar of one of the dead-body trays, only resting wasn't really the word, since she'd hit hard enough to crack open her skull and a widening puddle of red was forming below her head as she, too, stared up at the ceiling with wide-open eyes, just another corpse in a roomful of corpses. Bolo's dead body, where I'd pushed his dead weight off of me, was – as was fitting – at his mistress's feet.

I had to smile.

Bolo may not have had many brains in that chrome dome of his, but he'd had enough to slip her up.

DEATH OF A VAMPIRE

Parnell Hall

Sergeant MacAullif was less than pleased. That wasn't surprising. Less than pleased was his default position, the attitude he usually affected whenever I walked into his office. Which was hardly fair. I'd done him a favor once, and he'd gotten me out of a tight jam now and then, and when you added it all up, it wasn't like we'd hurt each other much. Except the time he threw me up against my car, or the time he tried to push me through a wall. If the truth be known, I think his ritual expression of disgust was no more than that, a ritual expression, full of sound and fury, signifying nothing, except that everything was fine, everything was normal, everything was par for the course. If MacAullif ever seemed glad to see me, I'd be worried.

Only this time he had cause.

'A vampire?' MacAullif said.

There is no way I can do justice to the skepticism, sarcasm, and mistrust with which MacAullif managed to imbue the word.

'That's right.'

'You want me to find a vampire?'

'I'd be relieved if you could. I'm afraid he might be dead.'

'Aren't vampires already dead?'

'Good point. I see you're up on vampires. That will help.'

'I'm not up on vampires,' MacAullif said through clenched teeth. 'I was ridiculing the notion.'

'I noticed.'

'What are you really here for?'

'I'm a private investigator. I don't have the resources of the police department.'

MacAullif sighed. 'Oh, hell.'

'Can you trace a guy for me?'

'Is he a vampire?'

'I refuse to answer on the grounds that it might subject me to ridicule.'

'Who is this vampire?'

'Morris Feldman.'

'Not Valmont? Or Count Gootsagoo? Or whatever?'

'Sorry.'

'Who is he? Aside from the obvious.'

'That's what I'd like to determine.'

'What makes you think he's dead?'

'His girlfriend hasn't heard from him.'

'You think someone killed him?'

'That's a possibility.'

'How do you kill a vampire? Silver bullets?'

'That's werewolves.'

'Cloves of garlic?'

'That's French bread.'

'Come on. How do you kill a vampire?'

'Stake through the heart.'

'Of course.'

MacAullif opened his desk drawer and took out a cigar. His doctor made him give up cigars; still, he liked to play with them in times of stress. I'd seen him play with them a lot. 'Who hired you?'

'The girlfriend.'

'Who's she?'

'Debbie Dwyer.'

'Why does that name sound familiar?'

'She runs an escort service. You've probably patronized it.'

He leveled the cigar. 'You want me to do this or not?'

'She's a college student at Columbia University.'

'What's she studying?'

'Pre-law.'

'Are you kidding me?'

'Not at all.'

'How'd she get involved with a vampire?' MacAullif made a face. 'Geez, I can't believe I asked that question.'

'She's a goth.'

'What?'

'You know. She wears that white and black makeup, looks like death warmed over.'

'From that you conclude she's a goth?'

'Not a rough deduction.'

'It is with your track record. I think it's safe to assume she's something else entirely, and you misdiagnosed it. How'd you get mixed up with her?'

I flashed back to my first meeting. Which seemed somewhat appropriate when dealing with a vampire, not to be fettered with normal time constraints. Not that vampires can time travel. At least as far as I know. Even so.

It was almost a week since she had walked into my office. I was surprised to see her. First, because she looked like she did. Second, because I don't get a lot of walk-in clients. The Stanley Hastings Detective Agency primarily services the law firm of Rosenberg and Stone. Richard Rosenberg is one of New York City's premier negligence lawyers. I'm his top investigator, which isn't saying much. His cases are mostly trip-and-falls, someone suing the city of New York for having broken their leg on a pothole or a crack in the sidewalk. I stop by every morning to check my messages and pick up my mail, but most of the time my office is closed. So walk-in clients have a rather small window of opportunity.

Debbie Dwyer made it.

She knocked rather faintly, like the scratching of a cat, so I wasn't sure there was someone there. I opened the door, expecting to see the corridor empty. Instead, I found a young woman with coal black, spiky hair and white makeup accentuated by black shadow around the eyes and black liner around the mouth.

'Yes?' I said. It was the wittiest private eye remark I was able to come up with on the occasion.

'Mr Hastings?' she said.

I hate that. Granted, she was college-age, and I am not. Still, it is the sort of thing I dislike having flung in my face, being addressed as *sir* or *mister*, knowing the worst is yet to come in the form of a devastating *young fella*.

'What can I do for you?'

'I may want to hire you.'

The word *may* was disappointing. I liked the word *hire*, however. I needed money.

'Come in.'

I sat her in the client's chair, then went and sat behind my desk, as if interviewing prospective clients were a daily routine.

'What's your problem?' I asked.

'It's my boyfriend.'

'Yes?'

'Promise you won't laugh.'

'Why?'

'He's a vampire.'

'I didn't promise.'

She made a face. 'Don't be like that.'

'Like what?'

'Closed-minded. Think of the movies.'

'Movies?'

'You know, in all the movies when someone is trying to

339

warn everyone or looking for help or whatever, and the police won't believe her because her story is a little out of the normal. Say she has premonitions.' She scrunched up her nose. I could tell she was getting close to dangerous ground. 'Sometimes it's supernatural. Ghosts, the undead, or something, and everyone in the movie theater knows what she's saying is absolutely true, and they're really pissed off at the cops for not paying attention to her. You ever watch a movie like that, and you're thinking, "How can the cops be so stupid?" You know what I'm saying?'

I knew *exactly* what she was saying. I also knew the difference between a movie and real life.

Still, there was that possibility of money in the offing.

'Go on,' I said.

'So. Morris is a vampire.'

'Okay.'

'Yes, I know,' she said. 'I don't expect you to believe me. I don't expect anyone to believe me.'

'What do you want?'

'I want to know if he's for real.'

'What do you mean?'

'I want to know if he's a vampire.'

'Are you kidding me?'

'Do I look like I'm kidding you? I want to hire you. Do you want the job?'

'What do you want me to do?'

'I have a date tonight. When he drops me off at my dorm, I want you to follow him and see where he goes.'

'Why can't you do it yourself?'

She made a face.

'Oh, I see. You tried.'

'He's on guard against me following him. It's gotta be someone else.'

'You mean you don't know where he lives?'

'No.'

340

'You got his name. Haven't you Googled him? Or some sort of Internet search?'

'I came up empty.'

'Isn't that interesting in itself?'

'Fascinating,' she said dryly. 'Look, you want the job or not?'

I wanted the job.

There was only one problem.

Alice was amused. I expected her to be amused. I just wasn't sure what form her amusement might take. On the one hand my wife has a good sense of humor. On the other, she is perfectly capable of ridiculing me within an inch of my life. 'You're involved with a vampire?'

'In a way.'

'And what way might that be?'

'I'm involved with his girlfriend.'

'What a surprise.'

'I'm not *involved* with her. I've been hired.'

'How old is this girlfriend?'

'Oh.'

Alice smiled. 'Okay, we've established young. Are we talking thirty-something?'

'I don't see how the exact age makes any difference.'

'Good God, is she a teenager?'

'I don't think so.'

'You don't *think* so?'

'She's a college student. At Columbia University. Pre-law.'

'Ah. And what does she look like, this college student?'

'Oh.'

I tiptoed Alice through the whole goth bit. Needless to say, her commentary was withering.

When I was done, as usual, she put the whole thing in perspective.

'Well,' she said. 'We need the money.'

'That's what I thought.'

Alice cocked her head. 'She pay in advance?'

'Oh.'

That night I was at Columbia University outside Miss Pre-law, goth-dressing, vampire-dating's dorm. I had changed from a suit and tie, my standard PI gear, to a leather jacket and jeans, my standard vampire-tailing gear. I was trying to look inconspicuous, which wasn't all that easy. The problem with Columbia University is it's full of college students, and they tend to be young. I get older every year. Coeds were looking at me strangely. After a while, it dawned on me in my current outfit I must have looked like a pervert trying to pick up young girls. I should have worn a tweed jacket, passed for a professor. The problem is, I don't see myself as old enough to be a professor. Whereas, in truth, I'm probably old enough to be the *father* of a professor.

They were back at eleven thirty. I spotted him first. Remarkable, since I knew her. But then he was a vampire. Not that he wore a cloak or a cape or a hood. Or had fangs. Or any of your standard cliché vampire gear. He was actually wearing a leather jacket, not unlike mine, though mine was brown, and his, of course, was black. Granted, his collar was up, but that didn't have to be vampire, it could easily have been motorcycle tough. He also wore a black T-shirt and black jeans. All in all, his vampire was no wilder than Debbie's goth. No, what caught your eye was the lean face, light blue eyes, and thin lips.

It was the lips, in particular, that merited attention. Unusually thin, as if he'd deliberately sucked them in, covering up his teeth.

He kissed her good night at the door. Then, in a flash, he ducked down a side alley next to the dorm.

Damn! There I was, waiting for him to go back out the main gate of the quad the way he came, and the son of a bitch takes a shortcut to the side street. I fell all over myself trying to follow, but by the time I got there, he was gone.

You ever ask anyone which way the vampire went?

Debbie was pissed. 'You lost him?'

'I never had him.'

'What?'

' "*You lost him*" implies I was following him, and he got away. That didn't happen. He was gone before I even started.'

She made a face at me. Trust me, it's no fun to have a goth make a face at you. 'Oh, isn't that clever? What are you, a moron? Didn't you see us come back to the dorm?'

'Yes.'

'Then you saw Morris. If you saw him, you had him. You had him, and you lost him, end of story.'

'I take it I'm fired.'

'Fired? Fired from what? You haven't *done* anything yet.'

'I staked out a dorm.'

'You expect me to pay you for *that*?'

I hadn't expected her to pay me at all. But she was pissing me off. 'In this business there are no guarantees.'

Her eyes blazed. 'What the hell are you talking about, guarantees? It's not like you tried and failed. It's like you didn't do anything.'

'I'm sorry you feel that way.'

'How much do you think I owe you?'

'You don't owe me a thing. Good luck with your vampire. I hope the next private eye you hire does better.'

She immediately began to backtrack. 'Don't be an old grouse,' she said. I wasn't thrilled by the adjective. 'It didn't work last night. Now you know better. Now you'll do better. I'm seeing Morris again tonight. Be there when he brings me home.'

Having graciously relented and allowed me another shot

at vampire surveillance, the goth proceeded to launch into a lecture on how this time I shouldn't fail.

There were a lot of things I could have said right then, but I'd have had to interrupt her. And nothing was going to help. I shut up and let her rant.

The vampire was wearing a sports jacket. The fact that it threw me was rather unsettling. It meant I'd accepted the premise. That I was thinking it funny for a vampire to wear a sports jacket.

I was dressed differently, too, in a polo shirt and khaki pants. I had my hair parted on the other side and felt sheepish about it. It was as if I were wearing a disguise so the vampire wouldn't recognize me. Leaving out the word *vampire*, it still seemed strange. In my line of detective work, a disguise is about the last thing I'd ever use. I tried to tell myself it's not a wig or a mustache, just running a comb though my hair in the wrong direction, but I wasn't buying it. Nothing was going to keep me from feeling like a fool.

I was positioned at the mouth of the alley, as opposed to the night before, when I'd been on the other side of the quad. If he went down the alley, he was mine. If he went anywhere else, I'd have time to follow.

After a lingering kiss, (no, his mouth did not venture anywhere near her neck), he turned and walked off as if he hadn't a care in the world.

I followed him out of the quad at 116th Street, where he ignored the bus stop and subway station on the corner, instead crossing Broadway and looking uptown as if to hail a cab.

That was a problem. If I wanted to follow him, I'd have to hail a cab, too. If I crossed Broadway to get one, he'd see me. Which is why I didn't do that. I stayed right where I was. I'd grab a cab going uptown, make him make a U-turn at 116th. I walked a few car lengths downtown, so when I

344

hailed a cab he'd have room to get left and make the turn. There was nothing coming uptown at the moment, which concerned me. I looked to see how the vampire was doing.

That's when I saw the other guy. He was crossing Broadway, just the way I said I shouldn't, jaywalking to reach the north side of 116th, right in position to hail a cab.

Only he wasn't looking for a cab. He was spying on the vampire, while pretending he wasn't, looking to all intents and purposes exactly like I was afraid I'd look, and probably would have. He was an older man, older than the vampire, anyway, though probably not older than me. Nobody's older than me these days. He had heavy beard stubble, like he hadn't shaved that morning. If he *had* shaved that morning, he had *very* heavy beard stubble. He wore a gray suit and white shirt, open at the neck.

Cabs were coming, which was good news for them, bad news for me, as none were coming uptown. Which, put me in the position of having to sprint across Broadway, hoping to finish a poor third.

The vampire hailed a cab. Now there's a phrase I never expected to say. But he did, and as it pulled away from the curb, the heavy-bearded, fearless vampire tailer stepped out and hailed another.

I was about to make the mad dash across Broadway when a cab pulled out of a side street, and I hopped in. I was tempted to say, 'Follow that vampire.' It was bad enough saying, 'Follow that cab.'

'Make a U-turn right here, follow that guy getting into the cab across the street.'

The cabby was a stocky Hispanic in no mood for trouble. 'Hey, buddy, what is this?'

I flashed my license. I felt foolish, as usual, which is why I seldom do it. 'I'm a PI, it's a boy-girl thing, no one's getting hurt.'

The cabby wasn't sold. 'What's your interest in this guy?'

'None. I'm interested in the guy *he's* following.'

The cabby nearly twisted his head off turning to look at me. 'What the hell?!'

'You want the fare or not?'

That settled it. The cabby started the meter, pulled out from the curb. He hung a U-turn at 116th Street, and away we went.

It didn't take long to catch up. The vampire was tooling down Broadway, and his shadow was right on his tail. The guy was following way too close. If I'd been in the cab, I'd have made the cabby drop back. I made my cabby drop back and was a good half a block behind when the vampire's cab signaled for a left turn.

'He's turning, don't lose him!' I told the cabby.

His grunt was eloquent. I tell him to drop back, then I'm afraid he won't make the light.

It's important to make the light on Broadway. It's a two-way, divided street. If you're in the intersection when the light changes, you can turn left. If you're *not* in the inter-section, you have to wait for the light to change twice. Once to green on Broadway to let you go, then to green on the cross street to let you complete the turn. Miss a turn like that on a tailing job, and you're dead.

We made it, but just. My cab broke the plain of the crosswalk somewhere between the last split second of the yellow and the first split second of the red.

The vampire didn't turn left onto 108th Street. Instead, his cab made a U-turn heading back up Broadway. That was okay, because the light at 109th and Broadway was red, so he couldn't get away, and there was time to catch up.

But the maneuver meant he'd probably spotted his tail.

He had.

The vampire hopped out of his cab, darted across Broad-way, and hailed *another* cab that had just turned downtown off 109th. When the light changed, he was gone, leaving his two tails caught at the light, snarled in uptown traffic, without a prayer of ever catching up.

Debbie couldn't believe it. 'You lost him again!'

'Yes, I did. But it wasn't my fault.'

'Oh, come on.'

'I'm serious. I don't think he ever spotted me. I think he spotted the other guy.'

'What other guy?'

'The other guy tailing him.'

'Oh, come on.'

'I know how you feel. I couldn't believe it, either. I feel like a PI caught in a shaggy vampire story. Morris hailed a cab. The guy hailed a cab and followed him. Morris spotted him and ditched him. Since I was in the third cab, there wasn't much I could do.'

'You're not making this up?'

'If I were making it up, it would sound much better. It's the truth, so it sounds like hell.'

'This other guy. What was he like?'

'Medium height. Stocky. Maybe forty-five to fifty. Thick black hair, a little gray. Heavy beard stubble.'

She exhaled sharply. 'Dad!'

'The gentleman is your father?'

'Damn it!'

'I take it he doesn't approve of your vampire.'

'He doesn't know he's a vampire.'

'What does he think he is?'

'A boy.'

I nodded knowingly. 'I see.'

'Hey, don't get chummy with me. You're not my pal.'

'I understand. I'm your employee. Tell me, how does it work? I know when *I* lose the vampire, I don't get paid. What happens when *your father* loses him?'

She said nothing, just glared.

347

'Anyway, the job is off. There's no way to do it with Daddy involved.'

'I'll take care of him. We'll have a little talk.'

'And if that doesn't work?'

'It will.'

'I'd like to believe that.'

'Hey, I'll do my job. You just do yours.'

I cocked an eye ironically. 'You mean you're giving me another chance.'

'You say it's Daddy's fault. I guess I have to give you the benefit of the doubt.'

'I'm thrilled. What's the deal this time?'

'Same thing. I've got a date with Morris.'

'At the end of which he'll be dropping you off at your dorm?'

'That's right.'

'But he won't be going up to your room.'

'No.'

'And you've never been to his.'

'What's your point?'

'I'm just trying to define the relationship.'

'What's the matter? I'm not promiscuous enough for you?'

'Don't be dumb. I've never known anyone who was dating a vampire before. Naturally, I'm a little curious. If you don't go to each other's rooms, what do you do? Just hang out in the park and suck each other's blood?'

'You wanna check my neck?' she said sarcastically.

'Not necessarily.'

'Go on. Take a look.'

She was wearing a black turtleneck. She pulled it over her head, which gave me a clear view of her neck. Among other things. She was wearing a pushup bra, and it was doing its work. All in all, she was one attractive goth.

The door flew open, and a blur of heavy stubble rushed in.

Talk about bad timing! You could count on the fingers of no hands how often young girls show up at my office and take their shirts *off*. It no sooner happens than her father bursts in to kill me.

It occurred to me maybe they were pulling a badger game. Right before it occurred to me my paranoia had reached absurd limits. Right before I bounced off the file cabinet and slammed into the floor.

'Daddy!' Debbie screamed.

I couldn't see her, but I hoped like hell she was pulling on her shirt. I sprang to my feet, grabbed a folding chair, did my best impression of a lion tamer.

'Don't be a jerk,' I said. 'She's just trying to prove he didn't bite her.'

That caught him up short. His mouth fell open. He turned to his daughter. 'What's he talking about?'

She shot me a look. 'Blabbermouth!'

Daddy had forgotten I was there. 'Debbie, sweetie, what's this all about?'

She told him. More or less. He showed all the skepticism you would expect, peppered with a dose of overprotective dad, though what could be considered overprotective under the circumstances, I'm not sure.

The remarkable thing is, she got him out of there. Her powers of persuasion were considerable. She'd make a fine lawyer if she ever got a chance. The way she showed Daddy the door was impressive indeed.

The minute he was out, however, she broke just like a little girl. 'Oh, my God! This is awful! This is just awful!'

I figured her next segue would be how it was all my fault. I wasn't up for that again.

'No, it isn't,' I said. 'It's great.'

She gave me the classic goth-dealing-with-a-moron look. If you haven't had it, trust me, you don't want it. It'll stay with you. 'In what way is this great?'

'I wasn't getting anywhere, and I wasn't about to. The

whole problem was, my hands were tied because you didn't want the vampire to know you were investigating him.'

'So?'

'You're *not* investigating him.' I smiled, spread my hands. '*Daddy* is.'

I caught up with the vampire that night as he was hailing his cab. The goth must have worked her magic, because Daddy was nowhere around.

I sidled up to the vampire, said, 'Wanna share a cab?'

He didn't sink his teeth into my throat. I took that as a good sign. On the other hand, he didn't seem pleased to see me. And not in the ritual Sergeant MacAullif way. The guy was pissed. 'Who the hell are you?' he said.

He had a Brooklyn accent. The goth hadn't mentioned that. Of course, I hadn't asked. My interrogation techniques are a little suspect. Just ask Alice.

'I don't wanna give you a hard time. Believe it or not, I was young once, too. You're dating the guy's daughter, and he's less than thrilled. He wants to know the score. I could tell him myself, but that's not what he wants. So why don't you cut me a break?'

'Her father hired you?'

'Did I say that? I don't recall saying that. I would certainly be in a position to deny saying that if you ever made the claim. But the gentleman is concerned with whether or not you're a vampire.'

'Oh,' he said with disgust. 'Debbie ratted me out.'

'*You* ratted *yourself* out. You look like a vampire. You act like a vampire. Granted, you don't dress like a vampire. But you walk around like the Prince of Darkness. It's a little hard to miss. What's your story?'

'You wouldn't understand.'

'Try me.'

'Fine,' he said. 'Let's make a deal. I'll tell you what you wanna know. When I'm done, you go about your business,

350

I'll get in a cab and go about mine. You won't try to follow me, find out where I live, stake out my apartment, tap my phone.'

'Done.'

'Okay, what do you want to know?'

'Are you a vampire?'

He grimaced. 'That's not the point.'

'It may not be the point, but it's what I wanna know.'

'The point is not whether I'm a vampire; the point is whether you *believe*. I am. Debbie does. That's enough for her, and it's enough for me. If it's not enough for her father, that's tough. That's the way it is.'

'Our deal was you'd answer my questions.'

'I'm answering your questions. You may not like the answers, but that's not our deal.'

'Do you have an apartment, or do you sleep all day in the ground covered with a layer of dirt?'

'That's just the type of ridicule I could expect.'

'From a mere mortal?' I asked impishly.

He smiled. 'You're not helping yourself.'

'Maybe not. I'd like just one denial I can take to the bank.'

'Fine,' he said. 'Ask me if I mean Debbie any harm.'

'That isn't what I meant.'

'Yeah, but isn't that what this is all about? Does her old man really give a damn who or what I am, or is he concerned for his daughter's safety? If it's the first thing, he's an idiot, and I can't help him. If it's the second thing, he should be reassured.'

'What do you do?'

'I'm a student.'

'At Columbia?'

'Yeah.' He cocked his head at me. 'What do *you* do?'

That question always throws me. Despite all evidence to the contrary, I always think of myself as an aspiring actor/

writer. At my age, that's tough to claim. 'I'm a private investigator,' I said.

'Uh-huh,' he said. 'Are you a *real* private investigator, or are you just pretending to be one?'

My mouth fell open. He nailed me. Put his finger right on the inner conflict that's haunted me most of my adult life.

He smiled at my confusion. 'There you are. That's just it. Am I a vampire, or do I just pretend to be? I am what you want me to be. To Debbie I am. To you, maybe I'm not. But who gets hurt?'

I frowned.

He reached into his jacket pocket, pulled out a stick of wood. One end was fashioned to a point.

'You know what this is? This is death. I keep it close to my heart, to remind me death is near.' He grinned. 'You wanna tell that to her father? He won't be pleased. And who does it threaten? Debbie or me?'

He stuck the wooden stake back in his pocket. 'Life's an illusion. Yours, mine, Debbie's. Even her old man. Believe what you want to believe. I can't help what you think.'

The light changed. Traffic streamed by.

'Ah, here's a cab.' He raised his arm, flagged it down. 'Remember our deal,' he said.

He hopped in the cab and drove off.

I remembered our deal.

I let him go.

Needless to say, Debbie felt I'd failed.

'You didn't find out where he lives. You didn't find out where he goes during the daytime. Which is the whole point. If he's a vampire, he can't exist in sunlight. If he can, he's not a vampire. It's that simple. Don't you get it?'

'Can I tell you something?'

'You're gonna give me advice?'

'I suppose.'

'You gonna charge me for it?'

'You're going to make a good lawyer.'

'That's your advice?'

'That's an observation.'

'I don't need your approval.'

'Yeah, I know. Look. There's no such thing as vampires. But if you wanna play the game, this is not a bad guy to play with. Is he a vampire? No, he's not. I can't prove it, but I'll bet the ranch on it. It doesn't matter. You're young. This is a passing fancy.'

'Just a phase I'm going through,' she said sarcastically.

'I didn't say that. But, frankly, I don't see you in a courtroom in your Kabuki face.'

She pouted, then switched gears. 'All right, look. He's taking me out again tonight.'

I put up my hand, shook my head. 'No. I'm done. That's it. You don't owe me anything. We're all square. Let's leave it at that.'

She looked betrayed. 'But . . .'

'Sorry,' I said. 'I've done all I can. Probably more than I should. Anyway, I got work to do.'

I snapped my briefcase shut and went out the door.

I wasn't worried about leaving her alone in my office. If she could find anything there worth stealing, she was welcome to it.

She was back the next morning. I almost didn't recognize her without her makeup. It was a vast improvement. She looked like any other college girl.

Except for the fact she was hysterical.

I tried to calm her down, find out what was the matter.

Turned out it was simple.

'He didn't show up!'

Ah, youth.

I smiled reassuringly. 'You're not the first girl in the world ever got stood up.'

She shook her head. Practically stamped her foot. 'No!

He's not *like* that. He wouldn't *do* that. If he didn't show up, something is wrong!'

'Did you check up on him?'

'How could I check up on him? You didn't give me his address. You just assured me everything was all right. Well, guess what. Turns out you were wrong.'

'I understand. You're upset. You feel helpless. But I'm sure it's not that bad.'

'*You're* sure? Like you were sure everything was okay. Why won't anyone pay attention to me? Why won't anyone listen?'

And there she was, the girl in the horror movie, pleading for help. Which is what brought me to MacAullif's office. That and a sense of obligation and a desire to pass the buck. In the movies, the people pleading for help are the good guys, and the people not listening are the jerks. Not that I wished the role of jerk on MacAullif. I just didn't want it on me. I talked MacAullif into running a trace on the guy and went out on my rounds.

He got back to me later that afternoon. I was in Queens interviewing a woman who'd fallen on a city bus when the office beeped me, told me MacAullif wanted me to call. That couldn't be good.

It wasn't.

'A corpse matching your description turned up yesterday morning.'

'Yesterday? How come you're just getting to me now?'

'You gave me Morris Feldman. This guy's Michael Fletcher. Same initials, so I ran it down. You gonna be grateful for that, or you gonna be pissed off I didn't pick up on it sooner, seeing as how I have no workload for the NYPD.'

'Yesterday morning?'

'Yeah.'

'Where was the body?'

'Riverside Park at 114th. Just off the upper path, buried in a shallow grave.'

'What do you mean by shallow grave?'

'That's the way it was described to me. I didn't happen to see it. The guy was at the morgue by the time I got the lead.'

'How'd he die?'

'Multiple stab wounds. From a sharp object, most likely a butcher knife.'

'What about the time of death?'

'About twelve hours before he was found.'

I sucked in my breath. 'Right after I saw him.'

'You saw him?'

'Yeah.'

'You were the last person to see him alive?'

'Aside from the killer.'

MacAullif let that lie there just long enough for the silence to become uncomfortable. 'Wanna run down to the morgue and see if it's him?'

It was.

The guy on the marble slab looked exactly like the vampire I'd met. With perhaps a few pints less blood.

The medical examiner was cutting up some woman. He stopped long enough to check us out.

'You did the autopsy on this one?' MacAullif asked.

'Yeah.'

'Can you give me the cause of death?'

'You want me to talk in front of him?'

'Relax. He's on our side. What killed him?'

'Multiple stab wounds to the torso. Some sharp object, probably a butcher knife.'

'Which one killed him?'

'The one in the heart,' he shrugged. 'He might have died from the one in the lung. But the one in the heart wasn't postmortem, because it was still pumping blood. Was it the last wound? I don't know. Was it a mortal wound? Yes, it was. What "killed him"' – he made quotation marks around the word with his fingers – 'is splitting hairs. You sure this guy's not a lawyer?'

'Any contributing cause of death?' I said.

'Funny you should ask.'

'Why? Was he drugged?'

He shook his head. 'Tox screen was clean. But when you mention contributing cause of death . . .'

'Yeah?'

'He was also stabbed with a sharp piece of wood. I didn't see it at first. Found it in his clothes. It was in the wound and had fallen out.'

'The wound?'

'The wound in his heart.'

'Are you saying a wooden stake caused his death?'

'No. He was stabbed in the heart with a butcher knife, just like all the other wounds. The killer stuck the stake in his heart afterward.'

'You mean he was dead?'

'He was probably still alive. There was a lot of blood on the wood. But he died shortly thereafter. I figure the heart pumping blood pushed the wood out of the wound. Just before he died. We're not talking a long time here. A few seconds, maybe.'

I walked out as if in a fog. MacAullif had to take my arm, guide me to the car.

'Are you all right?'

'Yeah.'

'It's a shock, seeing 'em cut up like that.'

'I've been in a morgue before.'

'Don't get hung up on the stake. There's more important things here. Like who killed him, for instance.'

'I know who killed him.'

'Oh?'

356

'It was her father. He couldn't stand him messing around with his little girl.'

'You sure?'

'Pretty sure. If I was her father, I might have killed him myself.'

'He was that bad?'

'Actually, I kind of liked him.'

'You really think it's the father?'

'Yeah.'

It was Daddy all right. MacAullif picked him up, shook him down, he caved right in. That's how it is with some tough guys. They put up a good front until their luck turns. Daddy spilled his guts. Admitted it all.

'Except for the stake,' MacAullif said. 'He won't admit to the stake.'

'What?'

'Claims he never saw the stake. Didn't mention it till we brought it up. Then he denied it.'

'Really?'

MacAullif waved it away. 'Not that it matters. He admits to the knife. Between his confession and the testimony of the medical examiner, we got him dead to rights.'

I nodded as if I agreed. But that wooden stake would haunt me long after the event. As would the image of the goth girl, her boyfriend dead, her daddy convicted of the crime. A hell of a legacy to carry with her. I had visions of her getting a law degree, finding a loophole, getting Daddy out. A pipe dream, of course. But sometimes pipe dreams keep you going.

Yeah, MacAullif was satisfied. But I couldn't help thinking of that wooden stake.

The way I saw it, there were only two ways that could have happened.

I only met the vampire once, but as I told MacAullif, I liked him. I don't know if he was crazy or playacting or what, but within his own separate universe, he seemed to have his own set of rules. There was a certain gallant nobility about him. I could imagine him, realizing he was dying, wanting to go out with a bang. Or not wanting to disappoint the goth. Or wanting to keep up the mystique, for to him image was everything.

I could imagine him pulling the wooden stake out of his pocket and sticking it in the knife wound in his heart.

Either that, or Daddy was lying. Not unusual in a perpetrator, though somewhat unlikely in one confessing all. Still, I could imagine the guy being embarrassed about it, withholding it because he figured it didn't matter.

And because he couldn't face it.

Because, according to the medical report, Daddy killed the vampire right after I left him that night. Which meant that, despite Debbie's warning, and in spite of the fact I never spotted him, Daddy was there when I spoke to the vampire. Daddy saw the vampire show me the stake and put it back in his pocket. So Daddy knew it was there.

I could envision Daddy stabbing the kid again and again and again with the butcher knife, and he still won't die. Until, in spite of himself, Daddy takes the wooden stake out of the vampire's pocket, and plunges it into his heart. He drags the body into the bushes, throws dirt over him. And refuses to admit, even to himself, that the stake was what killed him.

It had to be one or the other.

Either way, it freaks me out.

TAKING THE LONG VIEW

Toni L. P. Kelner

'Do we have to go?' Mark asked, trying to make it a question instead of a whine.

'Yes.' Stella finished brushing her hair. 'Ramon throws lovely parties.'

'With dribble glasses and whoopee cushions on every chair?' It was Ramon who'd told Mark that vampires had to sleep in the dirt of their native land, who'd talked him into drinking canine blood so he could tell everybody that Mark was sick as a dog. He'd nearly convinced Mark to cut off a finger by swearing on his own grave that it was painless and would grow back, but Stella had stopped him before he found out how much the regrowing process would hurt.

'Even Ramon wouldn't make a mockery of his own sire's anniversary celebration,' Stella said. 'And Vilmos would be extremely offended if we didn't attend.'

'God forbid we should offend Vilmos,' Mark muttered. 'Should I call him Grandfather or Granddaddy?' Since Stella was Mark's dam, surely her sire deserved a title.

'I wouldn't advise it.'

'Gramps? Grandpa?'

'Just Vilmos. He isn't known for his sense of humor.'

'There's a surprise.'

She cocked her head to look at him. 'Are you jealous?'

359

'Just because we're spending the weekend honoring the vampire with whom you spent decades traveling from one exotic hot spot to another? Why would I be jealous?'

'I have no interest in Vilmos.' She kissed him so thoroughly that he was forced to admit her sincerity.

'What about his interest in you?'

'He has none.'

He took in her curvaceous figure, currently enhanced by a perfectly fitted strapless red gown; the chestnut brown hair that just brushed her bare shoulders; and the lovely face that always seemed to have a secretive smile. 'Why the hell not?'

She kissed him again, even more sincerely. 'Please come to the gala with me?'

'Since you put it that way.' They took a moment to wipe off and reapply lipstick respectively, and he said, 'What about Pop-Pop?'

She squeezed his arm affectionately, but hard enough to bruise a human.

'Vilmos it is,' he said as he opened the door.

Despite Ramon's questionable taste in humor, Mark had to admit that he had superb taste in mansion decorating. Stella's and his suite was as luxurious as the finest hotel, and some of the others made theirs look like a Motel 6. Vilmos had the best accommodations, but he was the birthday boy as well as one of the oldest vampires there.

A crowd of vampires was mingling in the ballroom when Mark and Stella made their appearance, plus a scattering of humans. Mark was surprised. He wasn't used to humans socializing with vampires, but before he could ask Stella about them, Ramon bounded over.

With a name like that, he should have been swarthy and sleek, but like everything to do with Ramon, it was a joke. He was a bearded teddy bear with strawberry blond hair and deceptively innocent blue eyes. Mark had it on good authority that he'd been freckled before spending so many years out of the sun.

'Stella, you look fabulous,' Ramon said, kissing her hand. 'And Marcus, you're perfectly adequate.'

'That's one of us,' Mark said. He knew he looked damned good in his new tuxedo. With his dark hair and swimmer's build, he was made for evening wear. Ramon, on the other hand, looked like a waiter. Maybe it was the cummerbund. Mark had never seen one decorated with happy faces before.

Ramon just grinned before going to greet more guests.

'Excited much?' Mark asked.

'It's his first time hosting Vilmos's gala. He wants everything to be perfect.'

'Then he should lose the cummerbund.'

A gaunt but elegant vampire waved them over to the couch where she lounged. 'Stella, dearest!'

'Alexis,' Stella said as she went toward her. 'How have you been?'

'Eternally bored,' she said, and gave Mark the once-over. 'This must be your new protégé.'

'Alexis, this is Mark. Mark, Alexis.'

'It's so brave of you to add to your line in these uncertain times, Stella.'

'I simply couldn't resist him.'

'Has Vilmos seen him yet?'

'I haven't had the pleasure,' Mark said for himself, 'but if he's as warm and welcoming as you, I can hardly wait.'

Alexis's eyes narrowed for an instant, then she smiled. 'I can see where you might be amusing. Come visit me in a few years, and we'll talk.'

'I'll count the days.'

'Well done,' Stella said as she and Mark moved away. 'I haven't seen Alexis smile in decades.'

'Really? I thought she was a hoot. What was that about your bravery?'

'Very few of us are offering the Choice these days, what with the economic downturn.'

The tradition was for a vampire sire or dam to settle a chunk of change on their undead offspring, which Stella had done for Mark, even though as a successful financial planner, he already had a solid nest egg. The two of them met when he took over her investment portfolio and had only known each other a few months when she offered him the Choice.

'Does that mean that all the other vamps here tonight are older than I am?'

'Probably.'

'Great. I love being the low vampire on the totem pole.'

'No one cares about that.'

'Please. Every meeting between vampires is a pissing contest, and you know it.'

'Don't be silly.'

Just then the guest of honor arrived. Mark had seen a portrait of Stella's sire, but even without it he'd have known Vilmos the second he strode in. There was something about the way he chose which people to acknowledge, and how the other vampires almost wriggled in their eagerness to be noticed. It wasn't his looks, though he was devastatingly distinguished – it was sheer force of charisma. Vilmos dominated the room.

'Don't look now,' Mark whispered to Stella, 'but I think he's about to start marking his territory.'

Stella elbowed him, but was watching Vilmos as intently as everybody else. That initially included Mark, but when he made himself look away, he noticed another person who wasn't watching. A gorgeous human woman with flaming red hair was pointedly looking at a statue in the corner of the room and, when Mark glanced back at Vilmos, he saw that the vampire was staring at her, as if he could make her look his way. Slowly, all the other people in the room, vampire and human, followed the direction of Vilmos's eyes, and soon everyone was watching the sublimely oblivious woman.

It was Ramon who broke the spell by clapping his hands, and a moment later a crew of waiters began to circulate with toothsome morsels to tempt the palates of vampires who no longer needed anything but blood. Since Mark still had to eat at least one full meal a day, it was most welcome – he'd been afraid there'd be no solid food.

Unfortunately, that meant that his mouth was full when Vilmos sauntered in their direction, and he suspected that the older vampire had planned it that way. Vilmos embraced Stella at length before turning to regard Mark appraisingly.

'So,' he said, 'this is the new member of our line. Tell me, Stella, is it true? What I've heard about his talents?'

Stella raised a delicate eyebrow in polite inquiry.

Vilmos laughed heartily. 'I refer only to his financial acumen.'

'Mark is a genius,' she said simply.

Deciding that modesty wasn't called for, Mark didn't argue the point.

'Then perhaps I have work for him,' Vilmos said. 'My own financial adviser has sadly passed away.'

Stella gave Mark a prompting look, so he said, 'I would be happy to make some recommendations.'

'Splendid!' Vilmos said. 'We shall talk later.' He embraced them both before moving on.

'Did I pass inspection?' Mark asked.

'Tentatively,' Stella said. 'Just be warned that I heard that Vilmos's previous adviser didn't die of natural causes.'

'Message received.'

Mark knew that, objectively, it was quite a celebration. Food and beverages were served in abundance, there were plenty of willing blood donors available, and the band was excellent. Admittedly, Mark wasn't expecting bluegrass, but Stella explained that Vilmos was currently fascinated with the form. Had anybody treated Mark as something other than Stella's arm candy, he would have had a terrific time. As it was, he would rather have been watching wrestling, and he hated wrestling.

Even the humans seemed aware that he was just a pup, relatively speaking. When he approached the lovely redhead who'd resisted Vilmos's charm, she said, 'Sorry, I'm taken.' Before he could protest that he was just looking for conversation, she retreated to the side of a trim-looking specimen who could have stepped out of any boardroom in corporate America if he'd still had a pulse.

Interestingly, Vilmos was watching her, too, and for an instant the civilized veneer slipped away to show avarice.

After that, Mark stayed with Stella, pulling her onto the dance floor as often as possible to keep from having to listen while he was assessed as though he weren't even in the room.

As dawn approached, the guests began to leave for their beds, Mark heard the redhead complaining that her feet were sore, and her vampire companion whisked her up the stairs in his arms. Several vampires laughed at the display, but Vilmos wasn't among them.

Clearly there was a story there, but Mark couldn't get it out of Stella that night. They barely had time to strip off their finery and wash up before snuggling in bed as the sun rose. Then they slipped into death together.

Mark was still able to move around during the day, and woke a little after noon. He'd intended to catch up on some paperwork while Stella lay in bed, but a note had been slipped under the door to tell Mark that there was a package waiting for him in the hall. When he opened the door, he found that Vilmos had arranged for a fat stack of financial data to be left for him. It was presumptuous as hell, but for Stella's sake, Mark was willing to see if he could help.

After checking in vain for a CD or spreadsheet printout, he sighed and got out his laptop to create a data file. Entering and analyzing it took the rest of the day, and he began to think that whatever had happened to Vilmos's previous adviser, it wasn't enough.

Mark still had an hour to go before he could expect Stella to rise when he finally stood and stretched. Hungry for actual food, not just blood, he wandered downstairs to see what was available. Since there were humans around, there had to be something. The ballroom was empty, but in an adjoining dining room a handsome array of meats, cheeses, fruits, and vegetables was waiting. As Mark helped himself, a servant came to offer him something to drink.

At first, he was the only one at the table, but halfway through his meal, the redhead came in and filled a plate. Considering how she'd acted the night before, Mark wouldn't have been surprised if she'd gone elsewhere to eat, but instead she joined him.

'I don't believe we've met formally. I'm Mark.' He didn't give a last name. Vampires usually didn't.

'I'm Reinette.'

'Pleased to meet you, Reinette. That was some party last night, wasn't it?'

'Not bad,' she said, 'but just wait until Geoff's – it'll be much nicer.' She watched him for a moment. 'You're still a baby, aren't you?'

'I bet I'm older than you are.'

'I mean a baby vampire. Geoff never eats food.'

Mark couldn't think of an appropriate response, so he kept on eating.

'Who's your sire?' Reinette asked.

'My dam is Stella.'

'Stella . . . Oh, one of Vilmos's line. He bid for me, you know.'

'I beg your pardon?'

'Vilmos really wanted me, but Geoff outbid him.' She held her hand out. 'Geoff even gave me this ring as a signing bonus.'

'Very nice,' Mark said, which was a massive understatement. It was a wondrous confection of diamonds and emeralds.

'Geoff is so generous. I could never be a concubine to somebody who wasn't generous.'

'Naturally not.'

'He gives me new jewelry every month on our anniversary. Of course, it's in our contract, so he has to, but he has such wonderful taste.' She sighed happily. 'Tomorrow is our anniversary, and I can't wait to see what he got me. He has something in a velvet bag that he wouldn't let me look at. Maybe it's a necklace or a bracelet.'

'I'm sure it'll be lovely.'

'I want something really special to show Vilmos how much Geoff appreciates me.' She lowered her voice. 'Vilmos only got Ramon to invite us because he wanted Geoff to send me to him for a birthday present.' She wrinkled her nose. 'Geoff would never do that, and besides, it's in my contract that he can't lend me out. So don't bother asking.'

Deciding that he didn't want dessert enough to put up with Reinette any longer, Mark said, 'Lovely to meet you,' and left.

By the time he got back to the room, Stella was stirring, and he climbed into bed with her to speed the process. Ironically, this resulted in their remaining in bed somewhat longer.

Once they were both up and dressed, Mark told her about his progress with Vilmos's finances.

'Can you help him?'

'Of course. I'm a genius. But why are vampires such wimps with their money?'

'We're just cautious.'

'Cautious investors don't pull their money out the second the market drops half a point, which is what most of them were talking about doing last night. Cautious investors know how to ride out the tough times, to take the long

366

view. If anybody should know how to take the long view, vampires should.'

'Vilmos isn't broke, is he?'

'Not even close. In a year's time, he'll be able to buy and sell women at will.'

'Excuse me?'

'I met a woman named Reinette downstairs who said Vilmos couldn't afford her, though I hadn't realized that slavery was part of the vampire lifestyle. You do realize that I come from an old New England family. We were abolitionists long before it was cool.'

'It's not slavery.' She rolled her eyes. 'Foolish humans have trophy wives and boy toys. Foolish vampires have concubines. They actually contract with humans to act as regular blood donors.'

'Are you serious?'

'Reinette's family has served vampires for generations. She offered herself for auction last year and signed a contract with Geoff.'

'What if she changes her mind?'

'Don't ask. Besides, Reinette was quite willing. Ramon found the whole process amusing, and told me that a dozen vampires put in bids, but it came down to Geoff and Vilmos. They kept upping their offers until Vilmos ran out of money. As it was, Geoff had to pay twice the usual stipend, plus expenses and monthly gifts of jewelry. When the term is up, she gets a house and pension.'

'That's a lot of bucks just to win a pissing contest.'

'Geoff is an idiot. And now he's got to put up with Reinette for the next five years.'

They were about to head downstairs when a scream ripped through the mansion. With a place that large, few humans would have heard the screams unless they were nearby, but vampires came from every corner with blinding speed. Mark, of course, was the last to arrive and pushed his way into the spacious suite, mindless of protocol.

At first, it didn't register that the heavy draperies were open, exposing the room to the nighttime sky. Then he realized how wrong that was. He'd never seen any of the house's drapes open, for obvious reasons. As far as he knew, he was the only vampire young enough to endure the sun.

Reinette was staring at the bed, no longer screaming, but as pale as the oldest vampire. The blankets were pulled back, and the sheets rumpled as if someone had slept there, but the bed was covered in a fine coating of steel-gray dust.

Mark wasn't sure what he was seeing. Stella knelt by the side of the bed farthest from the window, then stood holding something. Mark's mind rebelled when he realized it was an arm, a man's arm.

'He always slept with one arm hanging over the edge of the bed,' Alexis said, 'ever since I gave him the Choice.'

'Who?' Mark asked.

'Geoff,' Stella answered. 'This is all that's left of him.'

Reinette swayed, and Ramon moved to catch her as she fainted.

'How did this happen?' Alexis demanded, eyes flashing. Her languor of the night before was gone – Mark hadn't realized that she was Geoff's dam.

'I don't know,' Ramon stammered. 'My servants are trained to perfection. They would never do such a thing.'

'They must be questioned.'

'I'll see to it immediately.' Realizing that he was still holding Reinette, he looked around, as if for a convenient shelf on which to place her.

'Take her to my room,' Vilmos said. Mark hadn't even seen him – for once, he wasn't the center of attention.

'Gods above, Vilmos!' Alexis said. 'Control your appetites!'

'How dare you imply—'

'Give her to Mark,' Stella said calmly. 'He can watch over her.'

Mark wasn't sure if it was because he was trusted or because he was too low in the pecking order to be a threat, but both Alexis and Vilmos nodded in agreement, and Ramon passed the unconscious woman to him almost tenderly. The other vampires stepped aside, and Mark carried Reinette to his and Stella's room. Fortunately, they'd left the door open. He hesitated about whether or not to put her on the bed, and deciding to avoid giving the wrong impression, laid her on the sofa.

Reinette stayed out for over an hour, while Mark went back to work on Vilmos's finances. Though he kept hoping Stella would let him know what was happening, they were left alone. Finally Mark heard Reinette's breathing and heart rate change, and after a moment, she spoke.

'Is Geoff really dead?' she asked in a tiny voice.

Technically, Geoff had been dead for years, but Mark didn't think she was in the proper frame of mind for technicalities. 'I'm afraid so.'

Her eyes filled with tears, and he was touched by the depth of her emotion until she choked out, 'Then what happens to me?' and burst into the most annoying sobs he'd ever heard.

Mark found a box of tissues to give her, but felt helpless otherwise. Presumably he could have held her or patted her back, but he didn't want to touch her.

Suddenly she stopped. 'There was something about this in my contract! Think, Reinette, think!'

'Silly girl, nobody expects you to do that.'

Mark and Reinette looked up to see Ramon in the doorway.

'Ramon, do you know what my contract says about Geoff dying before the term is up?' she asked.

'Probably the usual provision for you to get everything you would have if he'd lived: the stipend, the pension, the house.'

'And the jewelry?'

'I suppose,' he said, 'but that's all moot.'

'What does that mean?'

369

'It means that the only provision of your contract that applies is one about punishment for killing your patron. Once you're found guilty by the tribunal, you'll be given to Geoff's sire, which means you'll be spending the rest of your life as Alexis's belonging. Did I mention that she's quite angry at you for killing Geoff?'

'But I didn't!'

'Every other human in the house has been bespelled and questioned, and none of them went into that room today. It had to have been you who opened the curtain.'

'It wasn't! Bespell me and ask me.'

'You know that's not possible.'

'Why not?' Mark asked.

'Reinette was rendered immune from bespelling,' Ramon explained. 'It's part of the bond between a concubine and a vampire. How else could it be a binding contract?'

Reinette said, 'You can't give me to Alexis! I told her she looked old, and she hates me because it's true.'

'That wasn't very diplomatic,' Ramon said, clicking his tongue.

She started crying again, even more loudly.

'Ramon, are you serious? Alexis is going to *own* Reinette?'

'Marcus, don't tell you me you're squeamish about the fate of a murderer.'

'What I'm squeamish about is slavery. How do we even know she's guilty?' Mark had eaten at the same table as Reinette no more than two hours before Geoff's remains were found. He couldn't believe she'd just killed her patron or intended to do so within the next few minutes. Nobody was that good an actress.

'Don't worry. The tribunal will prove that she's guilty first – it shouldn't take long.' He checked his watch. 'They've given Reinette an hour to prepare.'

'An hour?'

'Why waste time? I'm to stay with Reinette so she doesn't

cheat by killing herself – Alexis is hinting that she'll let us all sample her this evening.'

The concubine broke into fresh wails. As for Mark, he wished he hadn't eaten real food that evening, because he felt very close to losing it at the thought. 'But Reinette will have a chance to defend herself?'

'If she likes, or she can pick a spokesman. Maybe I'll volunteer. It might be fun.' Ramon snapped his fingers. 'Hold on! Didn't Stella tell me you're a lawyer?'

'I do financial planning, not courtroom work.'

'Close enough. You can give me some tips. Are there any appropriate Latin phrases? Habeas corpus?'

'Ramon, you can't make a joke out of Reinette's life. Get somebody who'll take it seriously.'

'Oh, nobody else dares face Alexis's wrath. I'm only willing to risk it for the amusement value.'

Mark looked at Reinette, who'd thrown herself on the couch sobbing, then remembered the stories his mother had told him about their ancestors who'd been part of the Underground Railroad. 'Tell me how the tribunal works, Ramon. I'll defend Reinette.'

Given the choice between Ramon's mocking and defending herself, Reinette leapt at Mark's offer, even if he was a baby vampire. Fortunately, Ramon restrained his sense of the absurd long enough to give Mark a brief but thorough description of vampiric legal procedures, which were fairly simple.

The vampires present would choose a judge to oversee the tribunal, usually the most senior vampire present. Both sides would present their cases, and the judge would make a ruling. Any punishment would be carried out immediately. Fairness was ensured by vampires' long memories – nobody wanted to be accused of favoritism by a vampire who might be in charge of his tribunal in a decade's time.

There were no formal rules of evidence or testimony, and of course, nobody swore on the Bible.

'Is there anything else I should know?' Mark asked.

'Like the part about your having to suffer the same punishment as the accused, should she be found guilty?'

Mark blinked.

Ramon broke into laughter. 'I'm kidding, Marcus. We're a tad more civilized than that.'

'Other than the part about letting Alexis torture Reinette.'

'I did say "a tad." '

'Fine.' With only a few minutes left, and knowing vampires' love for style, Mark dressed in his best suit while Reinette made what repairs she could to her face. She ran roughshod over Stella's makeup in the process, but that was the least of Mark's worries. At the last moment, he grabbed a pad and pen just because he thought he should have one.

Reinette clung to his arm the whole way to the ballroom, and Mark was afraid he was going to have to carry her the last few steps, but just before she reached the door, she straightened up and stepped inside proudly and defiantly.

'Very Joan of Arc,' Ramon said, but Mark was impressed. Maybe she wasn't a total waste of space after all.

The ballroom furnishings had been rearranged to mimic a modern-day courtroom, with a judge's bench, tables for the prosecution and defense, and a witness chair. The gallery was already filled with vampires and, at the very back, frightened-looking humans. Presumably they were there to witness the cost of treachery.

The judge's place was empty, but Alexis was already seated at the prosecutor's table. She watched Reinette menacingly as the girl stepped past her to sit in the defendant's seat, and the look she gave Mark was nearly as hostile.

He hadn't seen Stella as he came in, but didn't have a chance to look for her before Ramon went to stand in front of the room and said, 'By the traditions of our kind, this tribunal has been convened to determine the truth behind the death of Geoff, of the line of Alexis.' Everyone rose, and when the judge came in, Mark realized he didn't need to look for Stella after all.

Stella was the judge.

Mark could tell she was as shocked to see him defending Reinette as he was to see her as judge. He glared at Ramon, who must have known, but the trickster shrugged and tried to look surprised.

Reinette whispered, 'Isn't that your sire? That's going to make it easier, right?'

'You don't know Stella,' Mark said. She'd be fair, but she'd do her duty as she saw it, even if it meant ruling against him. He honestly didn't know if he could stay with her should she allow Reinette to be enslaved.

Stella sat, and everyone else followed suit.

'Who asks for judgment?' she asked formally.

Alexis said, 'As Geoff's sire, I call for judgment against the concubine Reinette for foully betraying her patron to the sun.'

'Is the accused present?'

'Yes,' Reinette responded meekly. 'I've asked Mark to speak in my place.'

'Mark, have you been made aware of our customs?'

'I have, Your Honor.'

'Then we shall proceed. Alexis, state your case.'

'It is brutally simple. This creature drew the curtains during daylight while Geoff slept helplessly. He burned to nothingness until his arm fell from his ravaged body.' She paused to let the horrific image sink in. 'Under our laws, she is mine to do with as I will.'

'Mark? What is your defense?'

'The defense is just as simple,' Mark said. 'Reinette is as much a victim as Geoff.'

There was hissing from the gallery until Stella quelled it with a look.

'I call Reinette to the stand,' Mark said.

Reinette went to the chair that had been set up, and Stella warned, 'Be aware that a lie – any lie – will cause me to rule against you.'

'Yes, Your Honor.' She saw the gallery of vampires watching her hungrily, and swallowed visibly.

'Reinette,' Mark said, 'tell us what happened from the time you left Vilmos's gala to the moment you discovered Geoff's remains.'

She could barely speak at first, but with Mark's coaxing, managed to give her account. Geoff had carried her to her room and enjoyed a nightcap of her blood before going to his own suite. 'I don't like being with him when he's, you know, not breathing, so I always have my own room.' She'd slept until after two, and after performing a remarkable amount of grooming, had gone to the dining room, where she'd found Mark, After he'd left – 'kind of suddenly' in her opinion – she'd finished eating and went back to her room to watch TV and primp still more. She would normally have waited for Geoff to come to her, but was hoping to convince him to present her monthly gift a day early, so used her key to get into his room. They all knew the rest.

Unfortunately, the only piece of the story that could be confirmed was her meal with Mark, and that wasn't nearly enough to prove her innocence.

Lastly Mark asked if she had any reason to want Geoff dead. 'Of course not! Geoff gave me everything I asked for, no matter how much it cost. I know he had to because of the contract, but he never fussed. And he was good in bed, too.'

Mark turned it over to Alexis, who asked a single, devastating question. Did Reinette know that if Geoff died before the end of the term of their contract, she would get everything she would have had he lived?

She did, meaning that she knew she stood to benefit substantially from Geoff's death.

Next Mark called Ramon, who explained that the only keys to the room had been in the possession of Geoff,

Reinette, and Ramon himself. Even if there had been a way for a servant to gain access, all the humans on the estate had been questioned, and none of them had gone into Geoff's room. Mark asked about other security measures, but while the perimeter of the estate was thoroughly protected with both high-tech and mystic measures, there was nothing comparable inside the house.

After Ramon stepped down, Alexis said, 'Reinette's guilt is clear. I demand that judgment be made immediately.'

'You are not in a position to demand anything,' Stella said. 'I will make my decision when I am ready, not one second before.'

The two vampires locked eyes, but it was Alexis who finally relented.

For once, Mark was grateful for the pissing contest.

Then Stella said, 'Mark, do you wish to call further witnesses?'

He flipped through the blank pages of his pad, trying to come up with something. He wasn't a trial lawyer, and this was like no trial he'd ever seen, anyway. Perhaps he could use that to his advantage, 'Your Honor, I would like to make an observation, if you will allow it.'

Stella raised one eyebrow, but nodded.

'Ramon's testimony suggests that no human could have entered Geoff's bedroom, but there are far more vampires in residence than humans.'

'Geoff, Ramon, and the girl were the only ones with keys,' Alexis pointed out.

Mark said, 'Locks can be picked. All that is required is a set of easily obtainable picks and a person with good hearing, a steady hand, and patience. I think that would apply to any of the vampires here.'

There was a great deal of murmuring until Stella said, 'We will have quiet.'

'Since any of the vampires could have picked the lock,'

Mark went on, 'any of them could have opened the curtains.'

'How?' Alexis wanted to know. 'None of us woke until dusk. The only vampire awake before then was you.' She bared her teeth. 'Are you confessing?'

Mark didn't dignify that with a reply. He was still trying to find some way to prove that somebody else had been in that room. Could he be wrong about Reinette? Could she have casually insulted him after killing Geoff? He looked at her again, but still didn't believe it. The only thing that had been on her mind was jewelry. Jewelry . . .

'Your Honor,' he said, 'Geoff gave Reinette a piece of jewelry each month on their anniversary, and she told me he had brought along this month's gift wrapped in a velvet bag. I request that a search be made to find that gift.'

Stella looked uncertain, but Alexis threw up her hands and said, 'If it will speed this charade, then find the creature's bauble.'

'I will allow it,' Stella said. 'Ramon?'

Ramon, grinning of course, picked two other vampires as witnesses and sped away. In just a few moments, they returned, with Ramon triumphantly holding a black bag. He handed it to Stella, who turned it upside down. Only a sprinkle of dust emerged.

Mark asked, 'Ramon, was there anything else in that room that could have been this month's gift?'

'Nothing,' Ramon said.

'So?' Alexis said. 'We have only Reinette's word that there was anything in that bag in the first place.'

'But we do know that tomorrow was their anniversary,' Mark countered, 'and that Geoff was meticulous about providing gifts.'

Alexis scoffed. 'Then Reinette took it. She probably has it on her now.'

'I do not,' Reinette said. 'You can strip me here if you want!'

Ramon leered. 'Anything to please a lady!'

'Ramon!' Stella admonished. 'Come here, child.' She wasn't overly rough with Reinette, but she was thorough. 'There is no jewelry on her.'

'She must have hidden it,' Alexis said.

'When?' Mark asked. 'She hasn't been alone since Geoff's remains were found.'

'She hid it before raising the alarm.'

'Then I request a search of the house to find it.'

Now there were sounds of anger from the gallery.

'That could take days!' Alexis sputtered. 'Your Honor, I object most strenuously.'

Stella looked at Mark. He knew she wanted to know if he was stalling, but he didn't move a muscle – if she could be a stickler for procedure, so could he.

Then she said, 'With the jewelry missing, you have adequately established the possibility that a vampire could have gotten into Geoff's room and taken it, but unless you can provide a viable suspect or suspects, I will have to make my decision.'

Mark wanted to kick something extremely hard, but he didn't dare show doubt, or Reinette was doomed. Maybe she already was. All he had was an empty bag that could have contained jewelry, and a dead vampire's arm. Alexis had means and opportunity on her side, and one of the best motives imaginable: greed. Mark had managed to cloud means and opportunity a little, but he had nothing for motive. Unless . . .

'Mark?' Stella asked.

'Your Honor, I call Vilmos to the stand.'

Mark heard gasps, and even Ramon looked appalled. But Stella said, 'Vilmos, will you take the stand?'

Mark had been expecting haughty indignation, but instead Vilmos was chuckling as he sat. 'Of course. Who am I to argue with genius?'

Mark took a deep breath. 'Vilmos, it is my understanding

that you made an offer for Reinette's services as a concubine.'

'I did. Under the circumstances, I count myself fortunate that I did not succeed.' He chuckled again.

'I also understand that the bids were unusually high.'

'We got caught up in the moment, I fear. No woman is worth that much money.' He twinkled at Stella. 'No human woman, that is.'

'In other words, you bid more than you could afford?'

'I would have honored any promises made,' Vilmos said stiffly, no longer affable.

'Presumably Geoff felt the same way.'

'Geoff would not have shamed me by failing to meet his obligations,' Alexis said.

Mark was sure that he had the answer now, but he needed one last thing to prove it. The question was, how far would Stella be willing to play along? 'Your Honor, I again request a search of the house.'

Alexis jumped up, furious, while Vilmos laughed out loud, and said, 'A genius!' But Mark looked only at Stella. He'd told Reinette that having Stella as judge would give them no advantage, but he was hoping he'd been wrong. It all came down to one question. Did she trust him enough to risk loss of face in front of her fellow vampires?

It didn't matter to him what anybody else did.

Finally she spoke. 'I will allow a one-hour recess for a search. No more. Ramon, you may choose assistance as needed.'

Mark said, 'May I make a private suggestion to Ramon?' He whispered his thoughts to Ramon, who looked at him as if he were making the joke for once, but nodded before enlisting a trio of vampires.

Stella left the room, but Mark and Reinette remained as the rest of the vampires and humans speculated wildly. It was all he could do to keep from pacing, but preventing Reinette from going into hysterics kept him distracted.

Stella came back into the room five minutes before the hour was up, and Mark could tell she was as anxious as he was. Half the people were watching the clock, while the others were watching the door. One minute before the time was up, Ramon came into the room, grinning widely. 'I believe we have the missing item,' he said. His assistants came behind him pushing Geoff into the room ahead of them, still alive, but with only one arm.

Mark turned to Stella, who was smiling at him, and neither of them noticed that Reinette had fainted again.

'It was the joke of a lifetime!' Ramon said admiringly.

'Perhaps not so funny to Reinette,' Stella said.

They had gotten the whole story out of Geoff. It was a classic case of buyer's remorse. After signing Reinette's contract for far more money than he should have spent, he'd had to meet the terms even as the economy drained his pocketbook. As Mark had verified with a quick audit, Geoff was fast approaching bankruptcy, and the monthly gifts of jewelry were the last straw.

So he'd staged his own death, spreading around the dust he'd brought in the velvet bag Reinette was so covetous of and cutting off his own arm to add the right touch of horror.

'Because he'd rather lose his arm than lose face,' Mark said.

Stella rolled her eyes. 'Aren't Ramon's jokes enough?'

'Sorry.'

After setting the stage, Geoff snuck out of the room and locked the door behind him before going to hide in the attic.

'I'm surprised it took so long to find him,' Mark said to Ramon. 'I told you to look up there first.'

'Oh, we found him in the first ten minutes. We only waited to make a better entrance.'

There was nothing Mark could say to that, and no point, anyway. Ramon was incorrigible.

Geoff had planned to escape from the mansion at the earliest opportunity and had already arranged a new identity to use for as long as necessary. He'd assumed that Reinette wouldn't survive long as Alexis's belonging, but that by the time he reemerged from hiding, nobody would care enough to bring a case against him. Reinette was not well-liked.

Once the plot was revealed, Reinette, with prompting from Mark, asked for judgment against Geoff for trying to skip out on their contract. Alexis, furious that he'd dishonored her line, had supported the concubine.

Stella's judgment was that Reinette be released from her contract but that she immediately receive everything promised to her, including the jewelry or its cash value, which would drive Geoff into poverty. Moreover, since Geoff had been willing to go without an arm, he could continue to do so. Each time it grew back, it would be cut off again. For a full five years. Knowing how much it hurt to regrow a finger, let alone an arm, even Vilmos winced at Stella's decision, while Alexis offered up another one of her rare smiles.

Reinette was so grateful that she offered to feed Mark right then and there, but he respectfully declined. He hadn't wanted her enslaved, but that didn't mean he liked her. He did accept her emerald ring as a thank-you gift and planned to give it to Stella at the first opportunity.

'I think Reinette has learned something from all this,' Ramon said. 'She's going to change her life around, perhaps attend college or go into charity work.'

Mark and Stella stared at him.

Ramon chortled. 'Just kidding. As far as I know, her only goal is to see how fast she can spend Geoff's money. When that gets old, she may sign another contract. Or perhaps I'll offer her the Choice.'

'Ramon, tell me you're joking,' Mark said, aghast.

'Oh, I know that she's vapid and vain and greedy, and honestly, not terribly bright.'

'Then why?'

'Because I'm in love with the little bitch!' Ramon snapped. Then he gathered himself enough to put the clown mask back up. 'It would give me somebody else to play jokes on instead of you, Marcus – won't that be a relief? Maybe after a decade or two or three, shell grow up.'

He sauntered off, leaving Mark and Stella to enjoy their first time alone in what seemed like days. They took advantage of it promptly.

Afterward, Mark said, 'I just realized that Ramon purposely maneuvered me into defending Reinette.'

'That's quite a compliment, to put the life of his beloved in your hands.'

'That kind of compliment I can do without. Setting me against you, then dragging out the search for Geoff to the last minute. Which reminds me. I never thanked you for giving me that hour.'

'You're welcome. Besides, I needed it, too.'

'Oh?'

She looked embarrassed. 'It took me most of that time to get in touch with a sorcerer I know. He was ready to teleport into the house on my signal, and teleport out with Reinette.'

'You mean you would have—?'

'I know you, Mark. You wouldn't have defended Reinette unless you thought she was innocent, and could never have accepted what would have happened to her if I had found her guilty. That helped me realize that I couldn't, either.'

There was no way he could say anything to match that, so he didn't try. Instead, he showed her how he felt even more enthusiastically than before.

By the time he'd exhausted his gratitude, dawn was nearly upon them.

'There's something I've been meaning to ask you,' Mark said. 'Why did you give me the Choice instead of making me your concubine?'

'I knew five years with you wouldn't be enough,' she said. 'I was taking the long view.'

About the Authors

Author and journalist Steve Brewer has published sixteen books, including the comic Bubba Mabry private eye series and the recent thriller *Cutthroat*. The first Bubba book, *Lonely Street*, was made into an independent Hollywood film starring Jay Mohr, Robert Patrick, and Joe Mantegna. Brewer's short fiction has appeared in the anthologies *Damn Near Dead* and *The Last Noel*. A longtime newspaperman and syndicated columnist, he now writes a column for www.anewscafe.com, an online magazine in Redding, California, where he's lived since 2003. Brewer has served on the national board of directors of Mystery Writers of America, and has twice been an Edgar® Award judge. More at www stevebrewerbooks.com.

In addition to her award-winning archaeology mysteries, Dana Cameron's Fangborn short story, 'The Night Things Changed' (in *Wolfsbane and Mistletoe*, edited by Charlaine Harris and Toni L. P. Kelner), won a 2008 Agatha and a 2009 Macavity and was nominated for a 2009 Anthony award. Her historical short story, 'Femme Sole', appears in *Boston Noir* (edited by Dennis Lehane). Dana lives in Massachusetts with her husband and is hard at work on a Fangborn novel. Learn more about her writing at www.danacameron.com.

Barbara D'Amato has won the Carl Sandburg Award for Fiction, the Agatha twice, the Anthony twice, the Macavity, the first Mary Higgins Clark Award, and several Lovies. She is a past president of Mystery Writers of America and of Sisters in Crime. She divides her time between Chicago and Michigan.

Brendan DuBois of New Hampshire is the award-winning author of eleven novels and more than one hundred short stories. His short fiction has appeared in *Playboy*, *Ellery Queen Mystery Magazine*, *Alfred Hitchcock's Mystery Magazine*, and numerous other magazines and anthologies including *The Best American Mystery Stories of the Century*, published in 2000 by Houghton Mifflin Harcourt. His short stories have twice won him the Shamus Award from the Private Eye Writers of America, and have also earned him three Edgar® Award nominations from the Mystery Writers of America. Visit his website at www.BrendanDuBois.com.

Jack Fredrickson's latest mystery, *Honestly Dearest, You're Dead*, is a selection of the Mystery Guild and received a starred review from *Library Journal*. His first novel, *A Safe Place for Dying*, received a starred review in *Publishers Weekly* and was nominated for a Shamus Award. His short fiction appears in *Ellery Queen Mystery Magazine* (most recently, 'For the Jingle', May 2009) and is anthologized in *Chicago Blues* and in Michael Connelly's *The Blue Religion*. His most recent essay appeared in the *Chicago Tribune Sunday Magazine*, His next novel, *Hunting Sweetie Rose*, came out from St Martin's in January 2011. Jack lives west of Chicago. Check him out at www.JackFredrickson.com.

Parnell Hall is the author of the Puzzle Lady crossword puzzle mysteries, the Stanley Hastings private eye novels, and the Steve Winslow courtroom dramas. Parnell is an actor, singer, songwriter, screenwriter, former private eye, and past president of the Private Eye Writers of America. His books have been nominated for Edgar®, Lefty, and Shamus awards.

Charlaine Harris, *New York Times* bestselling author, has been writing for twenty-seven years. Her body of work includes many novels, a few novellas, and a growing body of short stories in genres ranging from mystery to science fiction and romance. Married and the mother of three, Charlaine lives in Texas with her family, three dogs, and a Canada goose. She pretty much works all the time. The HBO series *True Blood* is based on Charlaine's Sookie Stackhouse novels.

Carolyn Hart is the author of forty-four mystery novels. New in 2010 is *Laughed 'Til He Died*, twentieth in the Death on Demand series. *Merry, Merry Ghost*, second in the series starring the late Bailey Ruth Raeburn, an impetuous, redheaded ghost, was published in autumn 2009. Hart has been nominated nine times for the Agatha Award for Best Novel and has won three times. She has twice appeared at the National Book Festival in Washington, DC. *Letter from Home*, a stand-alone World War II novel set in Oklahoma, was nominated for the Pulitzer Prize by the Oklahoma Center for Poets and Writers. She lives in Oklahoma City with her husband, Phil.

S. W. Hubbard is the author of three mysteries set in the High Peaks area of the Adirondack Mountains: *Take the Bait*, which earned an Agatha Award nomination for best first mystery, *Swallow the Hook*, and *Blood Knot*, all published by Pocket Books. She has also ghostwritten a thriller released by Knopf in 2009. Her short stories have appeared in *Alfred Hitchcock's Mystery Magazine* and in the anthology *Adirondack Mysteries*. She lives in Morristown, New

Jersey, where she teaches creative writing to enthusiastic teens and adults, and expository writing to reluctant college freshmen.

Toni L. P. Kelner figures that vampire mysteries are the same as other mysteries, except that the dead people are a lot more active. Kelner is the author of the 'Where Are They Now?' mysteries, featuring Boston-based entertainment reporter Tilda Harper, and the Laura Fleming series, which won a *Romantic Times* Career Achievement Award. She also coedits urban fantasy anthologies with Charlaine Harris and is a prolific writer of short stories, including the Agatha Award-winner 'Sleeping with the Plush' and 'How Stella Got Her Grave Back', which introduced the vampire pair from this story. Kelner lives north of Boston with author/husband Stephen Kelner, two daughters, and two guinea pigs.

Lou Kemp's writing has appeared in several anthologies, and she received an honorable mention from Ellen Datlow in 2005's *The Year's Best Fantasy and Horror* for one of her short stories. Her story, 'Sherlock's Opera', appeared in *Seattle Noir*, edited by Curt Colbert, Akashic Books (May 2009). She is actively seeking an agent for her novel *Farm Hall*. She recently retained the services of Spectrum Literary for her novel *The Sea of the Vanities*.

Harley Jane Kozak, a sometimes actress, lives in California with her three children, two dogs, a rabbit, and several half-dead fish. Her debut novel, *Dating Dead Men*, won the Agatha, Anthony, and Macavity awards. It's sequel was *Dating Is Murder*, followed by *Dead Ex* and *A Date You Can't Refuse*. Her short prose has appeared in *Ms.* magazine, *Soap Opera Digest*, the *Sun*, the *Santa Monica Review*, and the anthologies *Mystery Muses, This Is Chick Lit*, and *A Hell of a Woman*. She blogs regularly on the *Lipstick Chronicles*.

William Kent Krueger writes a mystery series set in the great North Woods of Minnesota. His protagonist is Cork O'Connor, the former sheriff of Tamarack County and a man of mixed heritage – part Irish and part Ojibwe. The series has received a number of awards, including the Anthony Award and Barry Award for best first novel, the Anthony Award for Best Novel in 2005 and 2006, the Loft-McKnight Fiction Award, the Friends of the American Writers Prize, and the Minnesota Book Award. He makes his home in St Paul, a city he dearly loves. He does all his creative writing in a coffee shop whose location he prefers to keep secret.

Margaret Maron is the author of twenty-six novels and two collections of short stories. Winner of several major American awards for mysteries (Edgar®, Agatha, Anthony, Macavity), her works are on the reading lists of various courses in contemporary Southern literature and have been translated into sixteen languages. She has served as president of Sisters in Crime, the American Crime Writers League, and Mystery Writers of America. A native Tar Heel, she still lives on her family's century-old farm a few miles southeast of Raleigh, the setting for *Bootlegger's Daughter*, which is numbered among the 100 Favorite Mysteries of the 20th Century as selected by the Independent Mystery Booksellers Association. In 2004, she received the Sir Walter Raleigh Award for best North Carolina novel of the year. In 2008, she was honored with the North Carolina Award for Literature, the state's highest civilian honor.

Martin Meyers is the author of five Patrick Hardy PI mysteries, beginning with *Kiss and Kill*. His short stories have appeared in anthologies and magazines. Using the pseudonym Maan Meyers, Martin and his wife Annette Meyers have written seven Dutchman historical mysteries and numerous short stories set in New York in the seventeenth, eighteenth, and nineteenth centuries. The seventh in the series, set in 1899, *The Organ Grinder*, was published in October 2008. Martin's latest short story, 'Nate Devlin's Money', was a Black Mask feature in *Ellery Queen Mystery Magazine* in 2009.

A lifelong New Yorker, Terrie Farley Moran dabbles in genealogy and is learning to play the Irish tin whistle, which she finds far more troublesome than babysitting for her ever-increasing number of grandchildren. Her short stories have been published in several venues, including the anthologies *Murder New York Style* and *Dying in a Winter Wonderland*, as well as in the final issue of the never-to-be-forgotten e-zine, *Hardluck Stories*. Terrie invites one and all to drop by the blog www.womenofmystery.net to enjoy the grand banter of nine talented New York mystery writers.

Jeff Somers strongly regrets the quote he chose for his high school yearbook, which was a lyric from an Iron Maiden song, and wishes he could devise time travel specifically to fix this gaffe. Since math makes him sleepy, however, he never gets further than writing 'Time Masheen' on a cardboard box before falling asleep in his jammies. As with most other folks who can't comprehend physics, he writes instead – most notably the Avery Gates series of science fiction noir novels, published by Orbit Books. He maintains a blog at www.jeffreysomers.com just in case.

Mickey Spillane (1918–2006) and Max Allan Collins collaborated on numerous projects, including twelve anthologies, two films, and the Mike Danger comic book series. Spillane was the best-selling American mystery writer of the twentieth century. He introduced Mike Hammer in *I, the Jury* (1947), which sold in the millions, as did the six tough mysteries that soon followed. The controversial PI has been the subject of a radio show, comic strip, and two television series; numerous gritty movies have been made from Spillane novels, notably director Robert Aldrich's seminal film noir, *Kiss Me Deadly* (1955). Collins has earned an unprecedented fifteen Private Eye Writers of America Shamus nominations, winning twice. His graphic novel *Road to Perdition* is the basis of the Academy Award-winning film starring Tom Hanks and Paul Newman, directed by Sam Mendes. An independent filmmaker in the Midwest, he has had half a dozen feature screenplays produced. His other credits include the *New York Times* bestsellers *Saving Private Ryan* and *American Gangster*. Both Spillane and Collins received the Private Eye Writers life achievement award, the Eye.

Elaine Viets writes two national bestselling mystery series. *Publishers Weekly* called her Dead-End Job series 'wry social commentary.' In book nine, *Half-Price Homicide*, Helen Hawthorne works at a designer consignment shop in south Florida. Her Josie Marcus, Mystery Shopper series is set in Elaine's hometown, St Louis. Elaine has won the Agatha Award and Anthony Award, as well as the Lefty for the funniest mystery novel in 2008. Her grandmother Frances Vierling believed she had second sight. Elaine is relieved she has no psychic gifts.

Mike Wiecek once traveled widely in Asia and worked many different jobs, mostly in finance. Now he lives outside Boston, at home with the kids. His short stories have received wide recognition, including a Shamus Award. His first novel, *Exit Strategy*, was short-listed for the ITW's Thriller Award. More at www.mwiecek.com.

About the Editor

Charlaine Harris, *New York Times* bestselling author, has been writing for twenty-seven years. Her body of work includes many novels, a few novellas, and a growing body of short stories in genres ranging from mystery to science fiction and romance. Married and the mother of three, Charlaine lives in Texas with her family, three dogs, and a Canada goose. She pretty much works all the time. The HBO series *True Blood* is based on Charlaine's Sookie Stackhouse novels.